The Calling

By
Michael Strickland
Copyright 2021
Mayport Publishing Company

Edited By
Gayle Blackstock

ALSO, BY MICHAEL STRICKLAND
THE RED COTTON FIELDS
FIELDS OF GOLD AND SORROW
ANGRY SKY

Prologue

June 5, 1968

The thunder roared in the near distance. Bishop
Shapiro watched in silence as a portion of the large crowd

gathered to take advantage of the overhead canopy against the onslaught of the afternoon thundershower, common during this time of year in Southern Louisiana. Shortly, only the low, roaring thunder sounded as the hard rain fell upon the overhead canvas. Bishop Shapiro's eyes fixed on the flower-draped coffin that lay before him. Slowly, his eyes scanned the substantial entourage of mourners who sat and stood around the dark oak casket. The burial box left no mark of the greatness of the man whose body it now held. The large spread of flowers only camouflaged its cold confines of death as they, too, would soon wither and die.

Only some of the more notables gathered under the small tent. Many others were among the thousands who'd squeezed into the tiny, ancient cemetery. Noticeably present under the small shelter was the President of the United States, William Banes Johnson. Next to him was the Prime Minister of England. Next to him sat the Foreign Minister of the Soviet Union. Other notables in attendance were six members of the Polish Executive Committee, representing the people of Poland for the man they had so deeply loved. There were many more representatives present from virtually every country in the world. Sitting across from these powerful political figures was another group as distinguished and powerful in their own special way as their counterparts. The colors of black and scarlet were prominent among these men. Over seventy cardinals and bishops had joined in this tiny graveyard to pay their last respects to their fallen comrade. Only in the confines of Vatican City had such a number of cardinals and bishops gathered before. The pope had wished to attend, but a terrible sickness had prevented such a trip. Also in this impressive group were men of other religions, great men in their own rights. The cardinal that they buried today knew no religious boundaries. He showed this with his miraculous deeds at the now famous Ostrow Station, where the cardinal had been credited with saving 2,500 Jews from the death camp of Auschwitz in Poland. Some would argue that these figures were much too low. Perhaps this man's most famous act was when he refused the papal seat itself. His refusal had shaken the church to its foundation and saddened the peoples of the world. For an American to even be considered for such a position in an Italian-dominated role was astounding enough in its own right. To reject it bordered on lunacy.

The great cardinal, however, had his reason, and only two people in the world knew what it was. They sat hand in hand today. Bishop Shapiro's eyes had already rested on one of them. Lori, the cardinal's loving sister, sat in silence. A black veil draped over her aging face concealed her grief. Next to her sat Richard's other love, Elisabeth. On this sad day, her green eyes that her Richard adored so much, did not sparkle. They had turned dull and lined with red streaks. Yes, they bled as badly as Elisabeth's heart for the only man she'd loved so dearly. Sitting next to her was Agatha, Elisabeth's beautiful, young daughter, looking so much like Lori when she was young, with her dark hair and golden complexion, her beauty accented by large, brown eyes that were the Carver trademark. Some who knew Richard in his younger days would say how much the ravishing girl favored the late cardinal without ever seeing Elisabeth's late husband, the cardinal's brother, Joe Carver. Yes, the beautiful girl favored them both, all right, but she definitely inherited the best of both their qualities.

It was a rather short service, which would've suited Richard. He'd always been a private and mostly lonely man, having never wished for the world notoriety that was destined him. He'd only wanted to serve his God and help the people who needed him. It was through these deeds that he was made the most popular and revered man of his time.

Nearly everyone had left the grounds. Lori and Elisabeth were still sitting alone next to one another, cherishing these last moments alone with their beloved Richard.

Bishop Shapiro came before them to express his last condolences. He bent down before the two women, taking each of their hands in his, "This was the greatest man I have ever known, and he loved you both."

Elisabeth wiped a tear from her cheek. "God had made him special."

The Power
By
Cardinal Richard Carver

I have flown amidst clouds with man-made wings
I have walked among kings
I have fought with soldiers and sat with a mother as she grieves
I have stolen with thieves

I have sailed upon the sea for months on end
I have forged mighty rivers with the stroke of a pen

I have built great structures out of mortar and steel
I have waged many battles and brought generals to
kneel

I have worked the land with great labor and pain
I have walked among murderers and watched as they
have slain
I have preached in great cathedrals in distant far off
lands
I have crossed the burning deserts with their ever
shifting sands

I have voyaged to distant worlds and returned to tell
I have prayed with noblemen and peasants as well
I have written many books and played many songs
I have seen many evils and righted many wrongs

I have been with my son when kings fell at his feet
I have been with the hungry when they had nothing to
eat
I have been with a child as he took his first step
I have been with brave men as they openly wept

I have been with you in greatness as well as in strife
I have been called the spirit of life
I have walked with you in victory and defeat as well
I have risen with you among angels and fallen with you
to the gates of hell

I have been with you always and in this hour of need
I have been waiting for you to plant this simple seed
I have not left you in these times of sadness and shame
I have been waiting for this moment, please, please call
my name

Part I
Chapter One
Fall, 1920

Red flames of death danced before the young boys' eyes.

"My God, Richard, it's your house," Billy screamed.

The boys ran down the dirt road toward the bellowing smoke rising in the gray Louisiana sky.

"Ma! Pa!" Richard watched his burning home atop a small hill that overlooked his family's homestead. The screams of his mother pierced his ears as he and his schoolmate ran towards the fire-engulfed house.

Billy grabbed Richard by his worn overalls, pulling him down onto the cold Louisiana ground. "No, you can't go in there. It's too late."

"No!" Richard screamed as the farmhouse gave way to the raging inferno, crashing to the ground.

Mr. McCumber and the rest of Richard's classmates caught up with him and Billy. They knelt side by side, embracing and crying as they stared at the smoldering fire.

"My family is gone." Richard folded to the ground, sobbing for his parents.

Mr. McCumber knelt beside him and cried. He bowed his head, whispering to the soil and the young man beside him. "Richard, your mother and father might be gone but your brother and sister live and you live. Life goes on . . . and your life will also."

Richard slowly lifted his head from the ground. Mr. McCumber gently wiped the soil from Richard's forehead. With tear-filled eyes, he asked, "Why has God killed my parents? They were good Catholics and God-fearing people. Why, Mr. McCumber, would they die this way?"

Mr. McCumber's eyes shifted to the smoldering remains of Richard's home. "Richard, you ask questions I can't answer. Only the Almighty has the answers to life and death."

Richard made the sign of the cross and lowered his head to the earth. "God," he whimpered, "why have you given me life as you have taken the purpose of life from me?"

A sudden clap of thunder rolled over the countryside, as if God, indeed, was sending his answer to young Richard Carver's question. The gray clouds opened up and a heavy, cold rain fell to the earth.

"Come, Richard, we must be getting back to the school and notify your next of kin." Mr. McCumber helped Richard to his feet. Richard's classmates followed in somber silence as Richard and Mr. McCumber began their wet journey back to the old wooden schoolhouse.

Lightning danced in the sky as claps of thunder roared like heavy locomotives across the land. Perhaps the sudden storm was but a forewarning of the heroic and tragic life that lay ahead of this young man from Louisiana. Richard would need the strength of his God to get him through the daunting task that lay ahead in the form of forbidden love and his ultimate destination: his heroics and heartaches in World War II. The curtain of life for Richard had opened now with the tragic deaths of his parents. There were many acts yet to follow, dramas played on the world

7

stage. These events, however, remained in the future. Richard and Mr. McCumber entered the schoolhouse, followed by his classmates.

***

It had been a week since the fire and Richard couldn't take his eyes off his beautiful sister, Lori, and older brother, Joe, so finely dressed in their funeral clothes.

Uncle Ed poked the steel rod into the burning logs, causing the hot flames to leap up the chimney of the brick fireplace. "Good, it's decided then. Your farmhouse is gone and there is no money to rebuild it. So, everyone has to get on with their lives. Uncle Ed leaned the steel rod against the fireplace. Ed's eyes settled on Joe. "It seems you already know what you want to do with your life and the university you're attending has assured us you will be afforded a scholarship for your remaining three years. Congratulations, Joe, you're a fine young man and we're all proud of you."

Joe smiled. "Thanks, Uncle Ed."

"Now we turn to beautiful Lori." Lori blushed with Uncle Ed's compliment.

"Lori, it's decided then. You'll come stay with me and your Aunt Ruby and take that job offer from Fred Thompson working at his drugstore. Fred says there a lot of good-looking young fellows that come into his store and bets it won't take long before one of them will want to do some serious courtin' with you."

"Uncle Ed, you're embarrassing me," Lori said, glancing over at Aunt Ruby sitting quietly on the couch.

"All right, I'll leave you alone." Ed turned to Richard. "And now we come to Richard."

Everyone's eyes fixed on Richard. He looked at

Uncle Ed. "Richard, we've spent many hours talking about you, and when I say we, I mean everybody you see in this room."

Richard looked about the room at the faces of his brother, sister, Uncle Ed, and Aunt Ruby. Mr. and Mrs. McCumber also sat with them, to show their respects and offer support.

"Richard, I've had a long discussion with Mr. McCumber," Uncle Ed continued, "and I've also talked to Joe and Lori."

Ed leaned over a little closer to Richard, looking him straight in the eyes. "Richard, Mr. McCumber says you are, without a doubt, the brightest student he's ever had since he's been at Lafayette High. Mr. McCumber has talked to Father O'Malley, head of St. Paul's Catholic School over in Acadia Parish, which ain't too far from where your Aunt Ruby and I live. Anyway, seeing as how you're baptized a Catholic, you're eligible to attend this Catholic boarding school."

Joe smiled and said, "I wish you would do as Uncle Ed says, Richard, not just because Lori and I think you should. We both feel Pa would've wanted you to, and I know Ma would have."

Richard looked at Lori. "Do you think this is best, Lori?"

"Oh yes, Richard. I do."

Richard smiled. "Okay, I'll go to Catholic school."

Lori reached over, putting both arms around his neck. "Richard, I love you."

***

Joe returned to college and Richard left with Aunt Ruby and Uncle Ed until after Christmas, at which time he reported to St. Paul's Parochial School in Acadia Parish. Lori got the job at Fred Thompson's drugstore where she met a young man named Jeff Roberts who won her heart. Jeff came from one of the wealthiest families in Southern Louisiana. His father was J.J Roberts, the founder of Norfolk Shipbuilding Company out of Norfolk, Virginia. Richard, on the other hand, settled down to the disciplined life of private school. It was a small school, nestled among the ancient oaks of northern Acadia Parish. The teachers were Catholic nuns, outstanding teachers, and strict disciplinarians.

Richard maintained straight A's. Father O'Malley grew very fond of Richard. Perhaps, even at this young age, he saw in Richard that certain something that elevated him a cut above everyone else. He spent many hours talking to the boy, telling him about God and all the wonderful things he could do for those who loved and believed in him. At first, Richard paid little attention to Father O'Malley and this God of which he spoke. Richard had known little about the teachings of God before coming to the school. When he was a small boy, his mother would tell him stories about the birth of Jesus and other children's stories about the miracles God performed. As he grew older, the stories stopped and, to Richard, so did God.

Now he became infatuated with this ancient man from Jerusalem. He spent most of his free time studying the Bible and other books that told the history of the Catholic Church and its many teachings. It seemed this quiet, young farm boy from Southern Louisiana had found something in which he could become absorbed. After only a short time with Richard, Father O'Malley knew God was the boy's calling. For in God, Richard had to share with no one else;

his thoughts and feelings were safe.

***

Six years passed. Lori had married Jeff four years earlier. They had a two-year-old son, Richard James Roberts, and lived in Virginia Beach. Jeff had been elected vice president to his father's company. Joe had graduated from college and was living in New York City, where he'd secured a job with Porter Investments, one of the largest brokerage houses on Wall Street. He was assured a great future with the Wall Street giant. Richard, on the other hand, had completed seminary school and was currently one of three residing priests of St. John's Parochial School in Lexington, Kentucky. He hadn't seen Lori or Joe since graduating high school. He'd been at St. John's a little over a year. It was the beginning of a hot summer, June 5, 1928. Richard had been transferred to Boston. He would visit with Lori and her family for a few days, then travel to New York to spend time with Joe before traveling on to Boston.

"Well, Father, we've arrived at your destination, Virginia Beach," the elderly Negro porter said as he helped Richard with his suitcases. Richard followed the porter to the exit. "Father, I know you're anxious to see that sister of yours."

Father Carver smiled. "It's been almost seven years. I hope she recognizes me."

The porter laughed. "Father, there's one thing for sure; she'd have to be blind not to recognize you when you step off this train. I don't see no overabundance of Catholic priests standing around."

Richard looked at his black coat and trousers. "I guess you're right."

The train door opened. "Good-bye, Father," the old

11

Negro said as Richard stepped off the train into the large terminal.

It was a hot, sultry morning. The steam from the large locomotive did little to help the situation, as white vapor spewed from the mass of steel like a giant teakettle. Richard searched for a familiar figure. A small group of people stood at the far end of the train. He strained his eyes, trying to see if she was among them.

"Richard," the soft, familiar voice said from behind him.

Richard turned. His dark eyes met Lori's. They stared at one another for what seemed an eternity.

Richard dropped his suitcases. "Lori."

"My dear, Richard," she whispered.

Richard placed his arms around Lori's tiny waist and lifted her off the ground. Again, they looked at one another as he slowly lowered her to the ground.

"Oh, how fine you look, Richard. My brother, the priest. I always knew you were special. How right I was."

"Lori, you look as beautiful as ever. The years have passed you by."

"Oh, you always did say the right things." Lori's brown eyes sparkled in the faint light of the dreary depot. "Richard, I'd like for you to meet my husband, Jeff." Richard's eyes shifted from Lori to the tall gentleman silently standing next to his sister.

Jeff smiled. "I've heard so much about you. I feel we've been friends for many years already."

Richard smiled as he shook Jeff's hand. "I can see why my sister fell for you, a man of your fine looks. The two of you make a fine-looking couple. God has blessed you."

Jeff blushed, proudly placing his arm around Lori's waist, and pulling her gently to him.

"Here's something else God's blessed us with." Lori and Jeff turned toward the young lady standing behind them, holding the hand of a small boy dressed in a light blue suit and high-topped shoes, his dark eyes staring cautiously at the tall stranger. Lori bent over and took the small boy in her arms. "Richard, I'd like you to meet your Uncle Richard. Or should I say, Father Richard."

Richard smiled at the boy. "Uncle Richard is just fine." He took the boy from Lori and held him in his arms. "What a fine son the two of you are blessed with," he said, looking into the boy's dark eyes, a Carver trademark.

Again, Jeff wrapped his arm around Lori, holding her tight and smiling. "Shall we go?" he said, taking Richard's suitcases.

Richard nuzzled the younger Richard in his arms. "Oh yes."

It was a long ride from the train station to Jeff and Lori's home. The large, chauffeured limousine turned off the two-lane road onto the long, narrow drive that would take them to the front of the "home." Lori had always refrained from calling it what it really was: a large mansion built on the side of a hill. The thirty-room home was nestled among 400 acres of Virginia countryside. The butler met the limousine at the front of the mansion.

Richard stood next to Jeff and Lori, staring at the two-story, columned mansion standing majestically before them. "I can honestly say, Lori, this place is a bit larger than our farmhouse back in Louisiana." Lori smiled as she took Richard's hand and led him into the house.

***

Richard spent five glorious days with Lori and Jeff, but it was about to end. Again, Richard sat in the backseat of the big limousine with the happy couple as it made its way back to the train station. Lori sat between Jeff and Richard, holding Richard's hand as the limousine moved steadily through the township of Virginia Beach toward the train depot. "You be sure and tell that brother of mine he'd better start answering my letters."

Richard smiled at his sister. "I'll be sure and tell Joe exactly what you said."

Jeff laughed.

"He does know you're coming to see him, doesn't he?" Lori asked.

"Yes, Lori, don't worry. He knows I'll be there day after tomorrow."

"You'll hate New York. Jeff and I spent three days there last fall. It's so big and dirty. Ugh." Lori shivered as she spoke about New York City.

"I'm sure I can tolerate it for three days."

"You'll probably like Boston. They say it's a pretty town. How long will you be there?"

"As long as the church says."

"Well, at least you won't have a school full of kids to look after."

Richard grunted. "Oh, I didn't mind the youngsters. The nuns made sure they were well behaved. I'm looking forward to having my own church, though, and especially St. Andrew's, which is one of the oldest churches in Boston. I've heard nothing but good things about Bishop O'Toole. Yes, I'm real fortunate to be going there."

Richard said his good-byes at the station and boarded his train for Boston.

Chapter Two

It was mid-morning when Richard stepped off the train. The train station in Virginia was a dwarf to the one in which Richard presently found himself lost. People were everywhere—hundreds of them. They all seemed to be in a great hurry to be going somewhere, shouting at one another, trying to be heard above the noise of passenger trains lined up, side by side. Richard walked slowly, toting a suitcase in each hand, keeping an eye peeled for Joe. It would take a miracle to pick him out among the hundreds of other people that shared this massive building. A miracle it would be, though. Richard spotted Joe some twenty-five yards away, walking slowly and searching for Richard in the mass of humanity. "Joe! Over here, Joe," he hollered.

Joe turned, scanning the crowd in the direction of Richard's voice. "Richard," Joe shouted, waving his hand in the air. Richard dropped his suitcases as Joe ran toward him. "Damn, I'm glad you're here." Joe slung his arms around him and patted his brother on the back. "Let me get a look at you, little brother," he said, taking Richard by each arm. Joe took a step back and looked Richard up and down. "God, none of my friends in this town really believe my only brother is a priest!"

"You can't be that bad a person."

Joe laughed. "Sometimes I wonder little brother— sometimes I wonder." Joe nodded surveying his younger brother with an air of pride etched in his dark eyes. "Richard, you're very handsome in that outfit you're wearing."

Richard smiled. "You, also, are very handsome in that outfit you're wearing." He nodded in approval of Joe's garb, which consisted of a loud, checkered sport coat, dark blue trousers, and matching bow tie.

Joe extended his hands. "Surely they've told you that this is the nineteen twenties. Even Kentucky has newspapers, don't they?"

Richard laughed. "Yes, Joe, even in Kentucky they have newspapers."

Joe looked around. "Come on let's get the hell out of this dirty, stinking place." Joe handed Richard one of the suitcases while he carried the other one.

Richard struggled to keep up with his brother as they made their way through the depot, toward Thirty-Seventh Street and fresh air. Joe had been in New York so long he even walked like a New Yorker. Richard wiped the perspiration from his forehead as the taxi driver placed the suitcases in the trunk of the car. This was Sunday, and little traffic clogged the streets as the taxi made good time through the city. Richard peered out the window, examining the rows of tall buildings that lined both sides of the street like giant soldiers standing in formation.

"Little bigger here than in Lafayette, isn't it?" Joe pulled out a pack of cigarettes.

Richard grunted and pulled his head back inside the car window. "You mean bigger than all of Louisiana combined, don't you?"

Joe offered a cigarette. "There ain't nothing in that religion of yours that says you can't take a drink, is there?"

Richard leaned his head out the window, gazing at the skyscrapers. Retracting his head, he said, "No, there's no rules against a person drinking, as long as he doesn't

16

overindulge."

"Well, I'm glad to hear you can have a drink because I got some friends, I want you to meet tonight, and every one of them believes in having a little drink every now and then."

Richard never heard Joe. He was too engrossed in all the magnificent sights that only New York City could offer.

Joe's apartment was in a well-heeled neighborhood. Many of the young and upcoming businessmen had apartments in this part of the city.

"I can tell you one thing," Richard said, having just finished touring Joe's apartment. "My brother and sister have done well for themselves. A mighty fine place you have here, Joe."

"Oh, it'll do for now, until I can find something a little more comfortable."

Richard shook his head. "Why you snob!"

Joe laughed. "I guess I've done all right for myself."

"You always said you knew what you wanted and would go after it. Well, it appears you're a man of your word."

"Little brother, I can tell you this much. No one is prouder of his brother than I am of you. Look at you, a man of the cloth. Lord, Mama would be proud of you."

Richard smiled. "She'd be proud of you and Lori."

Joe stared at Richard for a few moments as a picture of their mother flashed in his mind, then turned to fetch a bottle of bourbon. He poured a small amount into two glasses. "Here's to you little brother, a toast to you and your first trip to the Big Apple."

Richard raised his glass. "And to the finest brother a man could have." Joe smiled as they touched the two glasses and downed the bourbon.

Joe set his glass on the table. "Man, that's good stuff."

"That wouldn't be Kentucky bourbon there, would it, Joe?" Richard said, grinning.

Joe laughed. "So, they have good whisky. That still don't mean they have newspapers down there."

Richard laughed and set his empty glass down. "Case closed."

"Let's clean up. I have some friends I want you to meet."

Richard unpacked his suitcases, joining Joe in the living room. "I sure feel better after that bath and some fresh clothes." Richard walked to an open window next to the couch. He held the curtain back and looked out at the tall buildings that lined both sides the street. It was late afternoon and the shadows of the buildings darkened the street below. He'd never been up this high before and was fascinated. Automobiles moved silently up and down the street below as if ants instead of power-driven steel.

Joe fixed them another drink. "Now you know how a bird feels." Joe handed Richard his drink. "Here, drink this and we'll meet those friends I've been telling you about. Afterwards, we'll get some food in our bellies."

Richard took the drink. "I was beginning to wonder if you ever ate around here. Joe, you don't drink this much all the time, do you? I hope it's a celebration thing because we're here together again."

"Naw, I don't drink like this every day, little brother. I try to eat at least once a day . . . just to keep up appearances. Just kidding," Joe said, downing the rest of his drink. "Come on, drink up. We got places to go." Joe retrieved his coat from his easy chair and slipped it on while Richard didn't finish the last of his bourbon, feeling suddenly uncomfortable about Joe's drinking.

Outside, Joe waved for a taxi, parked halfway down the block. They nearly had the street to themselves as the '27 Ford moved briskly through the fading twilight of the city streets. Joe noted points of interest to Richard as they moved through the city. In a short time, the taxi came to a stop in front of the Plaza Hotel.

"Welcome to the Plaza, gentlemen," the doorman said, opening the back door to the taxi.

Joe exited the taxi. "How are you this evening, Ted?"

"Just fine, Mr. Joe—just fine, sir." The elderly Negro smiled brightly.

Joe handed the doorman a dollar bill.

"Thank you, sir."

Richard followed Joe as they walked toward the double glass doors of the Plaza, its name displayed in gold lettering across etched glass. Richard took one last look at the Negro doorman, clad in a dark green suit and black cap. "Yes sir, Joe, you're doing all right for yourself."

Joe held the door open. Richard had trouble keeping up as the brothers walked through the expansive lobby, bustling with some of the most prominent people in New York. The Plaza Hotel had been considered for years as the place to be seen, the gathering spot of the city's so-called who's who. The young and the old loitered about the lobby, most looking for someone they knew, or hoped to know, before the night was out.

Joe and Richard paused at the elevator. Joe turned and glanced back across the lobby, at the gathering of chatty idlers dressed in their fancy suits and expensive furs. "Classy joint, ain't it?"

"You certainly have expensive taste. There's no question about that," Richard said, stepping into the waiting elevator.

"Fifth floor, gentlemen." The young elevator operator slid the metal door back, exposing a long, carpeted hallway.

Richard walked silently beside Joe. They passed doors on either side of the hall, entrances to some of the swankiest rooms in the city. Joe stopped in front of room 542. "This is the place." He straightened his tie and looked nervously at Richard, who stood there staring at the wooden door that, at present, concealed the sources of the loud talk and boisterous laughter. "You'll love these people, Richard."

Something in his brother's voice made Richard think Joe wasn't certain of his impending affection for the hotel revelers.

Joe knocked on the door. The door cracked open, and the face of a young gentleman peered at them. "I'm Joe Carver, and this is my brother, Richard Carver," Joe said in a low voice. The young man stared at the two, then disappeared behind the cracked door. Joe looked at Richard and shrugged his shoulders. "Just the usual precautions."

Another face appeared from around the edge of the door. "Hell, come on in Joe," the man bellowed. He opened the door just wide enough for Joe and Richard to enter. The huge living room was crowded with young people around Richard and Joe's age, up-and-coming executives who'd formed their own social clique and met every Sunday afternoon in one of the finer hotel rooms about town.

Joe introduced Richard to his friends. Richard could feel the uneasiness of a few guests, having a Catholic priest in a room where drinking and partying went on. Joe must have also sensed this and hurriedly fixed himself and Richard a stiff drink. He was amazed at how the presence of a drink in his hand melted the iceberg surrounding him.

Time wore on. Richard listened while Joe and his friends talked nonstop about the stock market. He did his best to disguise his boredom. Young ladies, the wives or girlfriends of the young gentlemen who filled the room, flittered by. Richard wandered away from Joe and the four other men presently in a heated conversation over the political issues affecting the nation's economy. Richard helped himself to another drink and took a seat on one of the three large couches scattered about the room. He wiped the perspiration from his forehead. The room was humid and muggy and most of the men had removed their jackets, while the women stood around fanning themselves with anything that would stir the air.

Richard looked around the room, for the first time really taking notice of the folks. His eyes settled upon a young lady dressed in a short blue dress. The dress ended at her knees, exposing two of the finest looking legs Father Carver had ever seen. The woman stared at him with her sparkling green eyes. Richard became oblivious to his surroundings, captivated by the brunette. He forced his eyes away from her.

Richard felt the closeness of her eyes, even as he looked toward Joe and the four men, still embroiled in a hot debate over national issues.

"So, you're Joe's little brother?"

Richard's eyes moved slowly upward. The pair of legs was even more ravishing close up. Her skirt fit loosely about her slender hips. The white cloth belt lay loosely about her waist. She fondled a string of white pearls. Richard's eyes were frozen, her radiant smile captivating.

"My name is Elisabeth Downs."

Hesitantly, Richard reacted to the woman's outstretched hand. "Oh . . . yes, my name is Richard—I mean Father Carver." Richard stood quickly, spilling his drink attempting to shake her hand while holding a full glass of scotch. "I'm . . . I'm sorry," he stammered, setting the glass down.

She smiled. "You sure are a handsome thing. How come God couldn't have picked some old, ugly man to be his priest and leave the likes of you to some lucky girl like me?" Richard felt his face grow flush. Elisabeth sipped whisky from her glass. "Mind if I sit down next to you? My date—the man in the dark suit—" Elisabeth said, pointing at him as he stood talking to three other men across the room, "every Sunday it's the same thing. He brings me here to enjoy myself, and this is what happens. He forgets about me and starts talking about some damn oil wells down in Texas somewhere. Well, at least I can sit next to you, and he won't say a thing with you being a priest and all." Richard took a long swig of scotch. Elisabeth leaned in. "How long are you in New York, Father?"

"I'm leaving for Boston at the end of the week."

Elisabeth sighed. "I wish I were going somewhere. This town is getting on my nerves. The country . . . that's where I would go." She looked at Richard. "You're from the South. I can tell by the way you talk. Don't you miss

22

the peace and quiet of a small town?"

Richard grinned. "Yes, I miss it sometimes, but it gets awful lonesome at times."

"Do you get lonely—I mean being a priest and all?" She paused for a moment. "You know, missing women?"

Richard nodded his head yes. "I get lonesome but not for sexual reasons." For the first time in his life, he felt that might not be the case anymore. After a short pause, he said, "At times I grow lonely from lack of companionship, but when that happens, I turn myself over to God and he becomes my companion."

Elisabeth sighed. "You have to be a strong-willed person to give up all the fun things in life and do whatever it is you people do."

Richard laughed. "It isn't that bad."

"Tell me it isn't!" she countered.

Richard laughed again, but not with the confidence he would have had if it had been an hour earlier. Over the next two hours, Richard grew infatuated with the young beauty, telling him her life story, right up to the moment they met.

"Well, Elisabeth, what do you think of my little brother?"

Elisabeth and Richard looked up at Joe standing before them. Her emerald eyes flashed back at Richard. A warm smile crept upon her lips. "He's adorable . . . absolutely adorable." Richard stared into her eyes, feeling an inner passion for Elisabeth that, until now, he'd only felt for his God.

"Richard, aren't you getting hungry?" Neither Richard nor Elisabeth took notice of Joe's question. "Richard, old boy," Joe said again, tapping Richard gently on the shoulder, "we haven't eaten all day." Richard broke from his momentary trance, looking up. Joe held up an empty glass. "One more of these on an empty stomach and you'll have to carry me home." Richard looked up at Joe and then the nearly empty room.

After a short pause Richard said, "I have an idea, why don't you have dinner with Joe and me, and we'll see you home afterwards."

Elisabeth stammered. "I couldn't impose on the two of you."

Richard laughed. "Impose! We'd consider it an honor, wouldn't we, Joe?"

"Yeah, sure we would," Joe said.

"But what about my date?"

Richard drew his attention to the three men. "Oh, he won't mind. After all, I am a priest."

"Yes, I'd forgotten."

Richard stood. "I'll go tell him." In seconds, he'd crossed the room, headed for Elisabeth's drunken date.

Richard and the man joined Elisabeth and Joe. "Father Carver has asked if he could take you to dinner." The man lopped his arm around Richard. "Well, I can't see any harm in trusting you with a man of the church, can you?" The man pulled away and leaned over to Elisabeth.

Elisabeth turned aside. "No, Jerry, I see nothing wrong with my having dinner with Father Carver."

"Take care of my sweetie, Father," Jerry said, leaning over and kissing Elisabeth on the cheek. She flashed an empty smile as Richard kept Jerry from falling down.

"Nice meeting you, Jerry," Richard said.

Jerry patted Richard awkwardly on the shoulder,

then started back to his chums, laughing and clinking their tumblers together in some grandiose toast. "Same here, Father Carver," Jerry mumbled.

Joe cleared his throat and set his empty glass on a nearby coffee table. "Well, are the two of you ready?" Richard and Elisabeth followed Joe out the door.

***

"That was one fine meal, Joe. I don't know if I've ever eaten any better Chinese food," Richard proclaimed, leaning back in his chair.

Joe took a sip of his coffee. "Yes, I have to agree with you. Elisabeth and I've had lunch here together many times and it's always good. Isn't it, Elisabeth?"

"Yes, Joe, and like you said, it was really good tonight, but I was starving to death, also."

"I'll say one thing, Richard. I don't ever remember you having so much to say as you did here tonight. Grant you, much of it was between you and this ravishing young lady sitting here next to me. However, you're a man of the church, my brother, so I don't have any problem with that. I'm just glad you enjoyed yourself." Joe lifted his coffee cup in a toast. "Here's to the both of you for a wonderful evening together."

Richard noticed Elisabeth's embarrassment as he lifted his coffee cup in response to Joe. "I'm sorry, Joe. I didn't realize I was talking so much. I don't know what got into me."

Joe set his cup back onto the table. "Hell, I know what got into you. This beautiful, green-eyed lady here. You might be a priest, but you're still a man. However, don't worry about me introducing you to any more of my lady friends, little brother."

25

Richard and Joe laughed, but Elisabeth didn't. She sat quietly, head bowed, staring at the table. Finally, she looked up at Joe and said, "I'm sorry for ruining you and your brother's meal, Joe. I never meant to ignore you tonight. You know how fond I am of you." Elisabeth reached over and placed her right hand on Joe's hand.

Joe smiled. "That's what scares me. I was hoping for a stronger word, but I'll take 'fond' for now. Let's get the hell out of here before I kiss you in front of all these people, including my brother, the priest."

***

Joe waited in the cab as Richard walked Elisabeth to her door. Then, Richard got back in the cab and the cab driver headed for Joe's apartment.

"Nice girl, Elisabeth. Don't you agree, Joe?"

Joe nodded. "A very nice girl and very pretty also."

"Yes, she is," Richard said in a low voice. He stared at a scrap of paper in his hand, then held it up to Joe. "Where Elisabeth eats lunch every day during work." Suddenly Richard felt guilty. It had to be the way Joe looked at him that made him feel so ill at ease, or was it for his own benefit, to justify his sudden actions toward this young lady he'd just met?

"I think it's a wonderful idea to have lunch with her, Richard. Hell, at least you'll have some company during the day while I'm working."

Richard smiled. Joe had tried to hide it, but he could feel Joe's uneasiness.

"I know you're a priest, and I also know you're a man. I took you to that party to meet Elisabeth. I wanted her to go with us as my date, not yours."

Richard nodded. "I see. I'm sorry. I forgot. I'll

cancel our lunch date."

"No, for Christ's sake! I want you to go and have a good time. You're a priest as well as my brother. If I can't put trust in that combination, I've lost all faith in mankind."

Joe and Richard returned to Joe's apartment. After nightcaps, they retired for the evening.

***

Joe was up early the next morning. Richard heard him stirring in the kitchen. Soon, he too was up and about. Joe prepared them a large breakfast. Richard pitched in, doing the dishes. Joe got dressed for work while Richard read the morning paper. The noise from the open window grew louder as the morning wore on. Richard stared out the window at the morning traffic on the street below.

"Makes you wonder where all those people are going this early in the morning," Joe said, leaning out the window next to Richard.

Richard stared at the street below. "So many people in this town. It's hard to believe, especially where we come from."

"Yes, it is, little brother, but I love every one of them, especially the ones that invest in stocks."

Richard laughed. "I suppose you do."

They pulled back from the window. "I have to get to work." Joe placed his right hand on Richard's shoulder. "Hate to leave you by yourself, but I still have to work for a living."

"I understand, and, anyways, I'll have plenty to do sightseeing and all."

"Are you having lunch with Elisabeth today?"

Richard turned away. "Perhaps, if I get time."

Joe smiled. "Well, have a good time whatever you

do, and I'll see you after work."

"OK, Joe," Richard answered as Joe walked toward the door.

Richard got dressed. Though still mid-morning, it was already hot and muggy as he walked slowly down the bustling sidewalk, looking for the small gift shop Joe had told him about. Richard found the gift shop and the pamphlets on what to visit while in the city and spent the morning taking in some of these places with one thing on his mind: his luncheon date with Elisabeth. He glanced at his watch as he stepped from the cab and walked toward the small restaurant located in the center of the block. It was twelve thirty. The place bustled with people.

"Just one, Father?" the young waiter asked. Richard's dark eyes scanned the room, searching for the familiar figure that had drifted in and out his dreams the night before. The waiter looked about the room, trying to help Richard locate the person he seemed so determined to find. "Would the person you're looking for happen to be a very attractive young lady?"

"She has brown hair and beautiful green eyes."

The waiter smiled. "She spoke of meeting a young gentleman for lunch but didn't mention him being a priest."

"Where is she?"

"Follow me, Father." Richard followed the waiter through the dining room. "Is this the young lady, Father?" The waiter smiled slyly at Elisabeth.

"Yes," Richard whispered.

"Won't you join me, Father?"

"Yes, I'd love to." Richard took the seat across from her.

"I hope you like Italian food."

"I love Italian food." Richard smiled back at Elisabeth, then looked about the room, a quaint restaurant with tables and booths covered in checkered tablecloths. He returned to Elisabeth. "You might have to order for me."

Elisabeth leaned over the table. "They have great hamburgers here."

Richard was again captivated by Elisabeth's beauty. She gazed at him with brilliant green eyes that sparkled like fine crystal. Light from the noonday sun shone through the large glass window. Richard laughed. "Hamburgers!"

"Yes, hamburgers."

"OK, hamburger it is."

Richard ordered their hamburgers. After a few moments, Elisabeth turned to Richard and said, "I'm sorry about last night. I hope Joe isn't upset with you or me for obviously ignoring him during our dinner together."

Richard thought for a moment. "Oh, he's fine. He apologized to me for what he said, blaming it on having too much to drink."

Elisabeth sighed. "I'm concerned about Joe's drinking. He drinks a lot, you know."

Richard nodded. "Yes, I've noticed. He gets it honestly, I suppose. Our father had the same problem. Elisabeth, can I ask you a personal question?"

It was apparent by Elisabeth's expression that she was surprised by Richard's request. "I suppose," she replied as the waiter served their hamburgers.

The waiter left the table, and Richard turned to Elisabeth. "Are you in love with my brother? I have this strong feeling he's in love with you."

Elisabeth's hand shook as she sipped her iced tea, obviously unprepared for Richard's question. "You don't mince words, do you?"

Richard grunted. "I suppose I got that attribute from my mother. You don't have to answer my question if you don't want."

Elisabeth sat quietly, as if deep in thought, then said, "I have strong feelings for Joe, but I'm not sure that I'm in love with him. To be honest with you, Richard, I thought I was in love with him until you appeared. Please don't ask me if I'm in love with you because you might not like the answer. I'm not sure I would like my answer. You're a priests and women aren't supposed to be in love with priests, are they?"

Richard bowed his head and said, "I suppose not, unless the woman is his mother."

"I'm sorry I couldn't give you a better answer, Richard," Elisabeth said, taking his hand. The warmth of her hand sent a chill through Richard's soul. She removed her hand. "I've lost my appetite, and I must be getting back to work."

Richard could see the tears welling in Elisabeth's eyes as he said, "Yes, I seemed to have lost my appetite as well."

He walked Elisabeth back to her place of work. She was the secretary to one of the finest lawyers in New York. Outside the building, she pointed toward one of the many windows that fronted the skyscraper. "Well, this is it. I work on the twentieth floor."

Richard looked at her, and she at him. He hesitated, as if afraid to ask, but found the courage and said, "I'll be leaving in a few days. I have to report to Boston. I was thinking, if you have nothing planned, I'd like to have dinner with you the night before I leave." Elisabeth's gaze lingered across Richard's face a few moments before she turned and looked away. He fell silent, as he knew what she was feeling; he felt the same way. Finally, Richard reached over and took her hand. "Please, Elisabeth, have dinner with me before I leave."

She looked into his eyes and then stared at the white collar, snug around his neck.

Richard asked again, "Please have dinner with me. I don't know if I'll ever see you again."

Elisabeth hesitated. Finally, an answer formed on her lips. "I'd love to have dinner with you, Father Carver."

Richard smiled. "I'll pick you up at seven."

"Seven is fine," she answered. "I have to get to work now."

"Good-bye, Elisabeth," he said softly. Richard turned and walked down the sidewalk. Turning back, he waved good-bye as she stepped into the doorway.

He spent the rest of the afternoon taking in some sights, struggling to dispel Elisabeth from his mind—but to no avail.

By the time Joe arrived at the apartment at seven o'clock, Richard had been home for quite a while.

"How was your day, Joe?"

Joe stripped the tie from around his neck. "Hectic . . . very hectic. It's this damn infernal heat that's making everybody so irritable."

Richard fixed them drinks.

Joe took the drink and sank into the couch. "Thanks, Richard, I need this."

Richard made himself comfortable on the cushioned chair facing the couch.

"I'll tell you one thing," Joe said, downing a large

31

swallow of bourbon and water. "There's no shortage of investors in the market these days. Some analysts keep saying the market can't hold up much longer. Of course, those same analysts have been preaching doom and damnation for our country's economics for years now. I don't know why people even pay attention to them. I damn sure don't anymore."

Richard grinned. "It sure looks like people are prospering in this town to me."

Joe finished the last of his drink. "You got that right. There's a lot of people going to make a lot of money these next few months, and I plan on being one of them."

"I'm sure you will, Joe."

"Let me take a quick bath and we'll get supper." Joe strolled to the kitchen, set his empty glass in the sink, then turned and faced his brother. "By the way, did you have lunch with Elisabeth?"

He'd been anticipating Joe's question.

"Yes, we had lunch. Near her work."

Joe nodded his approval. "Good. Glad you had a chance to see her again before you left for Boston."

"Yes," Richard replied as Joe headed for the bedroom and a fresh bath. He wanted to tell Joe about his future dinner engagement with Elisabeth the last night he was in New York, but this seemed not to be the right time to talk about that.

The brothers had a quiet dinner together at Joe's favorite Chinese restaurant a few blocks from the apartment. Richard got a good night's sleep, exhausted from the prior day's sightseeing and the prior night's dreams of Elisabeth.

***

He spent the next two days touring the city. He and Joe spent the first evening together, talking about old times and looking to the future. It was evident none of Joe's ambition had waned through the years; if anything, it had only grown stronger. Richard admired his brother's accomplishments. He enjoyed his time with Joe, and was it not for his evening plans, he would have been more than satisfied to share another quiet evening discussing old memories and speculating on the future. The special night, however, had arrived, his engagement with Elisabeth on his last night in town . . . that night had come—finally.

Richard had never been this nervous. He knocked gently on the door, standing alone in the hallway that served as a corridor to the four plush apartments located on the second floor of the fashionable complex. Richard raised his fist to knock again when the door slowly opened. He stared in silence at Elisabeth, standing in the doorway, her brilliant green eyes sparkling. He was struck speechless. In her scarlet ruffled dress, Elisabeth had stolen his voice.

"Father, won't you come in?" Elisabeth finally asked, smiling. A few more moments passed. "Father?" she said again.

"Yes, Elisabeth, how lovely you look this evening," Richard finally said, snapping out of his trance. Elisabeth giggled. "I'll ask you one more time. Won't you come in?"

"Yes . . . oh yes indeed," he answered, as if hearing her ask for the first time. Richard walked into the room. "What a beautiful place you have here." He ambled about the large living room, admiring the fine paintings displayed proudly on the richly colored walls.

"Yes, it's a nice place. Of course, I could never afford a place like this on the salary I make."

Richard turned and stared at Elisabeth, busily pouring them a glass of wine. She crossed the room and handed Richard his glass. "Of course, I learned a long time ago not to argue with my father. He's spoiled me all of my life." She smiled and the color slowly returned to Richard's face. Elisabeth raised her wine glass. "To your last night in the big city."

Richard lifted his glass to hers. Softly, he said, "For my last night in this beautiful city, and the beautiful people who live in it." A low ping rang out as their glasses met. It was a lonely sound, a sound of good-bye. They stared at one another in silence, drinking their wine—their eyes locked, their breathing quickening. Elisabeth took in a staggered breath and dropped her glass. Richard dropped his wine glass to the floor. The beautiful woman in scarlet removed the white collar from around his neck.

"Forgive me, God," she whispered as she cast the collar across the room.

Richard reached out and tenderly pulled Elisabeth into his embrace. He'd never experienced true passion. His body and mind were aflame in the ecstasy of life. Their bodies joined as one as Elisabeth led Richard to her bedroom, disrobing him as they went. He fumbled with her dress, finally discarding it as they reached the edge of her bed. They fell upon the soft mattress, embracing one another, their bodies entangled in passionate lovemaking. Soon, too soon, the raging lust was soothed, and they held one another atop the rumpled sheets.

Richard ran his fingers slowly through Elisabeth's silky hair. She kissed him tenderly. "I love you, Richard," she said, rubbing her soft hand over his cheek. He started to speak but stopped. "Do you love me, Richard?" Tears welled in her eyes.

Once again, Richard tried to speak but failed. Finally, he rolled over on his back and stared in silence at the overhead ceiling. Tears streamed from Elisabeth's eyes. He imagined the reason for her despair. It lay on the floor outside the bedroom: stiff and white and choking.

After what seemed forever, he leaned toward her and reached over, gently wiping away her tears. "I've loved you from the moment I first set eyes on you, Elisabeth." His voice broke. "I've never loved anyone the way I love you, not even God." A lone teardrop fell from his eye, upon the blue pillowcase. His heart broke as he continued. "Elisabeth, I've taken a solemn vow to my church and to God. I've committed a grave sin this night, but I pray God will have pity on me, knowing the love I have for you." Tears streamed from her eyes as he continued. "I must return to my church and my God. I could never live with myself if I went back on my solemn oath. What would you think of me if I didn't live up to my word?"

"The hell with your church and your oath to God," she cried out. "I want you. I love you."

Richard pulled her to him. She buried her head into his chest. Tears streamed down his face as he lay there holding his love. Satan had stolen his body this night, and now God wanted it back.

They held one another silently for a long period. Words weren't necessary; they sensed one another's innermost thoughts during their final hours together. Time passed swiftly, and they had made love only once this night. Once was all they needed to remember the night for a lifetime. Richard dressed in silence. Elisabeth lay quiet in bed as she watched Richard slip on his black coat. Dressed, he came to the edge of the bed and looked down at her. She stared at him. Her beautiful green eyes were marred with red streaks, a sign of her enveloping sadness.

Richard bent on one knee next to the bed, reached over and ran his fingers through Elisabeth's brown hair. "I must be going now," he whispered, looking into her eyes. She showed no emotion as she stared back at him. He attempted to speak but the words wouldn't come. He leaned over and kissed her good-bye. A horrible sadness flashed across her face.

Richard rose to his feet. "Good-bye, my darling Elisabeth." He moved toward the door. Pausing just outside the bedroom door, he listened with great pain as the woman he loved cried her heart out for him. His heart was broken.

Chapter Three

It had been a brief and comfortable trip from New York to Boston, even though thoughts of Elisabeth played upon Richard's mind continually. The brief time he was not thinking of Elisabeth, his mind was on Boston and Bishop O'Toole, of whom he'd heard wonderful things. The cab pulled in front of the ancient stone building on the corner of Liberty Boulevard and Castile Street as the mid-afternoon sun shone brightly over the great church.

Richard put on his hat and stepped from the cab. The cab driver met him with his suitcases. Richard marveled at the wondrous house of God.

"She's a beauty," the cabbie said.

"Yes, she's something all right."

"I assume you're going to the rectory, Father?"

"Yes."

"Follow me, Father." The cabbie started for the stone pathway that ran along the north side of the church.

Richard followed him down the narrow path. His eyes settled on the stone structure at the pathway's end, the rectory, webbed in green ivory.

"This is it, Father." The cabbie set down the suitcases and knocked on the dark wooden door. He moved to knock again when the door opened.

Richard examined the elderly, white-haired woman standing inside the open doorway. He removed his hat. "My name is Father Carver."

The woman stepped aside. "The Bishop has been expecting you. Come in, Father."

Richard stepped into the large foyer, the cabbie following close behind with the suitcases. He turned to the driver. "That's fine. I'll take them from here." He reached into his pocket for a tip.

"No, Father. It's been my pleasure."

Richard patted the cabbie on the shoulder. "Thank you for your kindness."

The driver nodded. "Father, enjoy your stay in Boston. It's a fine old city . . . a fine old Catholic city, I should say."

Richard smiled. "Yes, I know."

"God bless you, Father," the driver said, then headed out the door and down the walkway.

The old woman closed the door. "Follow me, Father. I'll show you to your quarters."

Richard grabbed the suitcases and followed the woman down a long corridor.

"Here we are, Father."

Richard followed the old woman into the rather

spacious room that made up the main living area. He set the suitcases on the floor as he studied the room more closely. A small couch and two padded chairs were centered in the room. A wooden desk sat next to a large, open window where the afternoon sun presently shone through, lighting the room. The woman showed Richard his bedroom and neighboring bathroom. He set his suitcases on the bed.

"Bishop O'Toole will see you in his study after you've made yourself comfortable."

"Thank you very much for your hospitality," he said. "And, by the way, what's your name?"

"Sarah. I've been housekeeper here for forty-two years. Twelve years of those for Bishop O'Toole. He was only a priest like you when he first arrived."

Richard smiled at Sarah. He could tell she was a feisty little lady, and he liked that. "Thanks again, Sarah," he said as she left. Richard unpacked his suitcases and cleaned up a bit. Then he decided it was time to meet Bishop O'Toole. He walked slowly down the hallway toward the study, stopping along the way to peer into the other rectory rooms.

The sound of Richard's footsteps hadn't distracted Bishop O'Toole from his afternoon reading. Richard paused briefly in the open doorway of the bishop's study. Bishop O'Toole sat silently in a large, cushioned chair, absorbed in an American classic *Moby Dick*. Richard entered the room. Light from a cathedral-sized window shone over the bishop. Richard watched the man of God in silence, not speaking until the bishop looked up from Melville's tale of ambition and obsession. The bishop shifted back in his chair, obviously startled.

Richard dropped to one knee and took Bishop

O'Toole's right hand, kissing the bishop's ring. "I'm Father Carver."

"So, you're the man from the South." The bishop laid his book on a nearby end table.

Richard rose before the bishop. "Yes, Your Reverence, I am guilty of that."

Bishop O'Toole's deep blue eyes sparkled in the nearby window's bright light. "That makes us even, seeing that I'm also a stranger of a kind to this proud, old New England town, being just a wee bit Irish and all." He chuckled, his Dublin brogue little changed since leaving Ireland some twenty-four years earlier. "You're quite a handsome young man," the Bishop said, rising from his chair.

Richard felt the heat of his blushing face. "If I might say so myself, you're much younger looking than I expected."

Bishop O'Toole laughed. "I can tell right now we're going to get along well, Father Carver." The bishop crossed to a small wooden table on which sat a canister of red sherry and four empty glasses. "Would you share a glass of wine with me, Father?"

"Yes, Your Reverence, that sounds fine after such a long day."

Richard met the bishop across the room, gladly accepting the sherry.

The bishop touched Richard's glass with his own. "Here's to a good relationship." Bishop O'Toole poured himself a second glass. "You must tell me all about yourself."

The two servants of God moved to the deep cushioned couch and sat side by side, as Richard told

Bishop O'Toole a brief history of his life and what had led him to the priesthood. The uneasiness soon disappeared, and Richard quickly became comfortable in the company of the bishop. Of course, this was typical, for it was a fact that almost all who encountered Bishop O'Toole quickly found themselves at home with this friendly man with the beautiful Irish accent. Like Richard, most were surprised to find how young the Irishman was to be a bishop in one of the most prestigious churches in New England. It would take little time for Richard to understand why this jovial, middle-aged man held his present position in the church. He, like Richard when he was Richard's age, was gifted with a brilliant mind that far exceeded his surrounding colleagues. Unlike Richard, he knew what he wanted at an early age and threw his whole mind and body into the priesthood, never faltering from that goal. Now, he was the youngest Bishop in the United States.

The bishop leaned over and turned on a table lamp. The day's light had faded as their conversation passed. "You've had quite a life." The bishop stood. "Shall we have one more glass of wine before dinner? You'll enjoy Sarah's cooking, Father." Bishop O'Toole rubbed his slightly pudgy stomach. "You see what she's done to me."

"She seems nice." Richard joined the bishop as he refilled their wine glasses.

The bishop raised their glasses in a toast. "Here's to your happiness as you do God's work."

***

Summer faded into fall as a close friendship developed between Richard and Bishop O'Toole. Perhaps it had been fate that had drawn these two men together. In any case, it was to be a period of great learning for Richard.

Bishop O'Toole spent every moment of free time teaching Father Carver the many intricate workings of the church.

Over the next two years, under Bishop O'Toole's tutelage, Richard mastered three new languages, including Italian. Christmas of '28 passed, Richard missed Lori and Joe during the holidays, but he'd received Christmas gifts from each. Lori was pregnant with child again. Jeff was doing well in the shipping business. Joe was made a general partner in the New York firm and was still very much a bachelor, being too busy in the business world for any type of lasting relationship with any particular lady. For a while, Richard's thoughts of Elisabeth were limited; the bishop left little time for him to think of anything except his studies. He never questioned the bishop's drive to tutor him in such an extreme manner. In fact, no one besides Sarah knew why Bishop O'Toole had spent nearly every waking hour teaching the young man from the South his invaluable knowledge of the church's inner workings. A man of the bishop's position and high esteem, after all, might best spend his time elevating himself in the hierarchy of the church.

Only Sarah knew the beloved bishop was dying. Neither she nor the bishop had discussed the agonizing disease. Sarah lay awake at night crying, listening to the bishop's pitiful moans as he rested his pain-riddled body in the lonely confines of his room.

Another two months passed. It became evident to Richard that the bishop was indeed gravely ill, no longer able to hide the ever-present pain that had cruelly deteriorated his body to a weak shell.

By early summer, the bishop was bedridden. Cardinal Algado in Baltimore assigned Monsignor Kelly to the duties of running St. Andrew's. Cardinal Algado was also pleased that Father Kelly was, like Bishop O'Toole, Irish, though much older than the incapacitated bishop. Richard and the monsignor got along well, although the relationship would never come close to rivaling the closeness shared by Richard and Bishop O'Toole in their season together.

Sarah nursed the bishop as if he were her son, loving him as if he were her own flesh and blood. Richard spent countless hours reading to the bishop from his beloved classics. He imagined the stories were the bishop's escape to worlds he could never enter.

On a late July night, Richard had been reading aloud for some time from one of the bishop's favorite books. He paused mid-sentence and looked down at his friend, who lay in his bed wearing a broad but distant smile upon his face. Richard imagined that the bishop was in another place, that in his feeble consciousness his friend and teacher had become Sinbad, the fabled ancient sailor. Perhaps he was standing upon the bridge of a magnificent craft, grinning as his crew worked feverishly to raise massive white sails into a gale that had sprung suddenly from the east. The bishop smiled from ear to ear. Richard knew that he was witnessing the smile of death.

He laid the book by the bishop's side, took his cold hand in his own, and knelt beside the bed. He made the sign of the cross and lowered his head, praying aloud as his friend approached death. Bishop O'Toole smiled as his ship captured the strong wind, propelling it through the roughening sea and toward the peaceful island that lay over the horizon. Only the tearstained sheet told where Richard lay his head as he prayed. He looked at his friend as the smile faded from his lips. The whiteness of death crept over his face. The shallow breathing was no more. This man of God had gone to his maker, and Richard laid his head upon the bed and cried.

It was a large funeral and a beautiful service. The bishop had acquired many friends since his arrival fourteen years earlier. Cardinal Algado of Baltimore performed the mass.

Richard had spent little time with the cardinal since his early arrival that morning. Now that the service was over, however, he and the cardinal would have time to become well acquainted. The cardinal was scheduled to spend two more days at the rectory. Sarah fixed a fine supper for the visiting cardinal, after which he, Richard, and Monsignor Kelly retired to the study for a relaxing nightcap of fine sherry. This was Richard's first experience with a fellow clergyman that was neither American nor Irish. The cardinal had just turned sixty-nine. Small in stature, with dark skin and black pupils, accented by bright silver hair, the cardinal's appearance left little doubt as to his Italian heritage.

Richard finished pouring the three glasses of wine. Cardinal Algado took his seat in the cushioned chair in which Bishop O'Toole had passed thousands of hours reading. He watched as the cardinal sipped on his glass of wine. Cardinal Algado's dark eyes shifted his direction. Richard downed the remainder of his wine and squirmed uncomfortably under the cardinal's inquisitive stare.

"Bishop O'Toole was very fond of you, Richard, and wrote me often about your gifted qualities. The monsignor has also told me about your many abilities, knowledge of church affairs, and understanding of changing international situations, political and economic. That knowledge is an enormous attribute if one is to excel in this global church of ours."

Richard was taken aback by the cardinal's remarks. He sat silently as the cardinal and Monsignor Kelly peered at him. "You seem surprised that I know so much about you, Father."

Richard cleared his throat before answering. "I am surprised . . . I should say quite surprised, Your Reverence. I had no idea the bishop or the monsignor had ever discussed their opinion of me with anyone, much less the head of our dioceses."

The cardinal laughed. "My son, don't you understand it is my job to know as much about the church's servants in my dioceses as is humanly possible?"

"I guess that is as it should be, Your Reverence. I've just never given it much thought."

"Yes, I can understand that. It's a wonder that you had enough time to go to the bathroom the way Bishop O'Toole kept you busy every moment of the day."

"But—"

The cardinal interrupted Richard before he could reply. "No, I mean no animosity against the bishop. To the contrary, he and I have been friends for many years. He was probably the most brilliant man I've ever met." Richard nodded in agreement. The cardinal continued, "And for that same man to say that you were by far the most gifted person that he'd ever come in contact with definitely stirred my interest. The monsignor tells me that the bishop taught you three languages, one of these being Italian."

"Yes, Your Reverence, he did."

Cardinal Algado glanced at Monsignor Kelly, then focused again on Richard. "Are you a happy man?" he asked in Italian.

The personal question and change of language rattled Richard. His gaze cut to the monsignor, then to the cardinal, who sat quietly, awaiting a reply. "Yes, I'm happy," he replied in Italian.

The cardinal stared into Richard's eyes. Richard stared back. After a few moments, Cardinal Algado nodded and, speaking again in his native language, said, "Good, my son. If one is not happy with one's life, he is as dead as the man we buried this morning, and that would be a tragedy in your case. It's not difficult to see what the late bishop saw in you. I, too, feel as he did: a man with your God-given abilities will go far in this world. I only pray it will be in the Catholic Church."

Richard wondered if the cardinal had believed him when he'd said he was a happy man. Elisabeth flashed in his mind. One day I'll be happy, he promised himself. The memories of Elisabeth would fade with time. They had to, as he was now committed to serving the church and God. He would do this service for Bishop O'Toole, if for nothing else. From this day forward, he would rededicate himself to becoming a full servant to the Church of Rome and to its tributaries that would lead him there.

Chapter Four

Richard got little sleep that night. The loss of his

friend plagued him, as did recollections of his conversation with Cardinal Algado.

The next morning, Monsignor Kelly greeted him warmly. "Good morning, Richard, did you sleep well?"

"Very well, Your Reverence." Richard took a seat at the breakfast table.

The cardinal glanced up from the morning paper. "Good morning, Richard."

"Thank you, Sarah," Richard said as the faithful housekeeper finished pouring his first cup of coffee.

Cardinal Algado laid the newspaper on the table. "I don't like the looks of it."

"What is it you don't like, Your Reverence?" the monsignor asked, sipping his coffee.

"The economy of this country, as well as the economy of the whole civilized world for that matter." The cardinal furrowed his brow and stared at the paper, as if it might talk back. "The so-called economists are denying there's any danger to the nation's financial security. Believe me, they don't know what they're talking about. Just last week I received a letter from the Vatican warning there's real possibility of a severe economic recession to take place in the near future."

"Do you really think it could happen?" Richard asked.

Cardinal Algado's dark eyes fixed on him. "My son, I learned long ago that whether it is the voice of God speaking directly to His Holiness Pope Pius XI or not, one thing is for certain: His Holiness, and the ones I've known before him, have never been wrong when it comes to forecasting the world's monetary trends that change like the rising and falling of the tides."

Thoughts of Joe raced through Richard's mind.

"Enough about gloomy forecasts, Richard. I've asked your boss, the monsignor, if he could spare you for most of the day so that you may show me about this historic city of Boston."

Richard looked at the monsignor, then back at the smiling cardinal. "It would be an honor, Your Reverence."

"Good, I'll treat us to lunch," Cardinal Algado boasted. He slid his chair away from the table and stood, his raven eyes glancing at the large clock that hung on the west wall of the dining room. "It's now quarter after seven. Say we leave at nine o'clock?"

"Yes, Your Reverence. That will be fine."

"Good." With that, he left the room.

Richard finished his morning meditation and waited on the cardinal in the small courtyard between the church and rectory. It was another fine July morning. The sun shone brightly overhead. Songbirds filled the morning air with rhapsodies of sound that Richard thought could only be made in heaven. He was admiring a pair of robins as they searched the ground for specks of food when a deep voice interrupted. "What a magnificent day God has given us for sightseeing," the voice said.

Richard jumped slightly as thoughts of his home back in Louisiana, of the fire and the loss of his mother and father, took flight. Richard sighed. "Yes, it is a fine day, Your Reverence."

The cardinal put an arm around him. "Shall we go see the town, my son."

Richard forced a smile as they started down the walkway toward the waiting cab.

It turned out to be a magnificent day for the two

men. The powerful cardinal from Baltimore shared portions of his life with Richard—his dreams as well as his fears. He was somewhat astonished to discover this small man from Italy, with his awesome powers in the church, was no different a man than any other. He, too, possessed unanswered dreams, as well as fears, that would seem trivial to most men but were horribly real to this man from across the sea. Richard enjoyed the hours the two spent together and was amazed at the cardinal's ability to masquerade himself with the winking of an eye.

"I've enjoyed this day immensely, Richard, and I hope I haven't burdened you with being my tour guide."

The men strolled together down the church's side walkway.

"I, too, have enjoyed this day, Your Reverence. It's not often I have the opportunity to speak Italian."

Cardinal Algado sighed. "You've mastered the language well, my son."

"I had an excellent teacher."

The cardinal nodded. They neared the door to the rectory. The faint sunlight vanished quickly after the two men entered the doorway. Monsignor Kelly joined the two tourists for dinner, after which they retired to their rooms for the evening, the sightseeing having tired the elderly cardinal.

It was another warm morning as the three men gathered at the breakfast table.

"I've enjoyed my visit to Boston," the cardinal said. "I only wish I'd come for a more pleasant occasion."

Richard's thoughts turned to Bishop O'Toole. He raised his coffee cup for Sarah. Suddenly, he felt uneasy as his two peers fixed their gazes on him.

"I had a small chat with the monsignor before you came in for breakfast, Richard," the cardinal said.

Richard sipped from his coffee, certain he was the major topic of the small chat.

"It seems I have a sudden vacancy in my church for a priest. After my conversation with Monsignor Kelly, he and I believe we have a solution to this somewhat urgent problem. How would you like to come to Baltimore and serve in my church?"

Richard took another sip of his coffee.

"Well, Richard, what do you think of the idea?" the monsignor asked.

What did he think of the idea? He hesitated, then spoke in a low, soft voice. "It would be a great honor to serve under Cardinal Algado."

"Good, then it's settled," Cardinal Algado boasted. "After breakfast, you will pack and accompany me this afternoon on our trip back to Baltimore."

Richard hurriedly finished his breakfast, then excused himself to pack for Baltimore.

Sarah fixed tuna salad for lunch, Richard's favorite. It would be hard to say good-bye to the kindly woman who'd cared so well for him.

"Father, your cab is here," Sarah announced.

Richard said his good-byes to Monsignor Kelly. He liked the monsignor. They'd become good friends in the short time they'd known one another.

Then, his eyes settled on Sarah, who stood quietly by the front door. "My dear Sarah, I will miss you."

Richard crossed the hallway and took Sarah into his arms. "Take care of Monsignor Kelly and yourself. We will meet again in heaven. God bless you," Richard whispered.

It was a pleasant train ride back to Baltimore. The cardinal fascinated Richard with his stories of his rise in the church—from his humble beginnings as an orphan in a small monastery in Florence to the powerful cardinal he was now, in a country thousands of miles from his homeland.

Their train arrived in Baltimore in late afternoon the following day. It was cloudy and drizzling rain as the two men boarded the cardinal's waiting automobile for the thirty-minute ride to the church. Soon the rain stopped, and the sun peeked through the broken clouds, turning the sky red to the west.

Richard stepped from the cab and took in the massive Baltimore Cathedral. "Magnificent."

Cardinal Algado stood beside him. "If only we could age as beautifully as she has." Richard nodded in agreement. "Come, Richard, I want you to meet the bishop."

Richard followed Cardinal Algado toward the rector'y which sat a short distance behind the cathedral. Richard's thoughts turned to Bishop Flanagan, whom he was to meet and who was, like Bishop O'Toole, an Irishman whose reputation as a strict disciplinarian was well known throughout the dioceses.

"Welcome home, Your Reverence," the middle-aged nun said as she held the door open for the approaching cardinal with Richard following closely.

The cardinal paused at the doorway. "Glad to be home, Sister Carmen. I'd like you to meet my new aid, Father Richard Carver." Cardinal Algado leaned over and whispered in the sister's ear. "I stole him from Monsignor Kelly." The cardinal turned to Richard. "Richard, this is

Sister Carmen . . . my Sarah, you might say."

Richard removed his hat, surprised by the attractiveness of the woman dressed in her nun's habit.

"Welcome to our home," Sister Carmen said, smiling and reaching to shake Richard's hand.

"Thank you, Sister."

Richard followed the cardinal into the rectory. Inside a large study, two men sat quietly behind two of four desks situated in the room, one in each corner.

"Welcome home, Your Eminence," the man said, standing from behind his desk.

"Thank you, David," the cardinal replied.

The second priest stood at his desk. "Welcome home." He was much younger than the other man, who happened to be Bishop David Flanagan.

"Thank you, Juan," the cardinal said as he took a seat in a straight-backed New England rocker.

Richard's eyes focused on the young priest as he stepped from behind his desk.

The cardinal motioned toward the young priest. "Father Lopez, meet Father Carver, our new colleague."

Richard sensed the surprised reactions the two men showed with the cardinal's announcement.

The young priest extended his hand. "Welcome to our home," he said in somewhat broken English.

"Thank you, Father," Richard replied.

Richard felt the presence of Bishop Flanagan standing behind him.

"Richard, I'd like you to meet Bishop Flanagan."

Richard turned to face the bishop, his icy stare unnerving. "Your Reverence." Richard took the bishop's hand and knelt, then kissed the bishop's ring. Richard stood slowly, awaiting a response from the solemn-faced bishop.

"Welcome to Baltimore," the bishop said flatly.

The bishop's continued stare gave Richard a hollow feeling. "Thank you."

Bishop Flanagan's body was in great contrast to the cardinal's and the young Mexican priests. He was a large man, standing six feet three inches and weighing just over two hundred and fifty pounds. His once massive chest had settled in his midsection over the past few years, but he still had a humbling effect on most men. His light complexion and Irish brogue reminded Richard of his late friend Bishop O'Toole, but the reminders stopped there. A blind man could see the rumors of this man's disciplinarian temperament were true, plainly written on his stern face.

"Have the two of you eaten?" Cardinal Algado asked, looking up at the bishop.

"Yes, Your Eminence, we weren't certain what time you would return. Sister Carmen has kept supper waiting for you."

"Good, I'm about to starve to death. How about you, Richard?"

"Yes, I'm a little hungry come to think of it."

"Fine. I'll tell her to fix two plates while Juan shows you to your quarters. You'll have plenty of time to unpack after supper."

Richard looked at the smiling Father Lopez. "That sounds fine."

"If you care to follow me, Richard . . . you don't mind if I call you Richard, do you?"

"Not at all, as long as you don't mind if I call you Juan."

"You have a deal," Juan said and started toward the

door.

Richard followed Juan out the room. The rectory was almost twice as large as the one in Boston. There were three guest bedrooms, besides those of the four resident priests for visiting clergy.

Juan opened the door to Richard's room. "Here's your new home."

Richard and Juan entered the room. "Very nice." Richard walked about the large room. An antique desk sat in solitude next to a small window. "This is a very nice room."

"You will like working with the cardinal," Juan said. "He's a very kind man."

"Yes, he certainly seems to be. What about the bishop? Is he a kind man also?"

Juan's dark eyes peered into Richard's.

"The rumors are true," Richard continued, "aren't they? He isn't so nice?"

Juan paused, then said, "Let us say they are quite different in temperament."

Juan smiled as Richard laughed. "I've never heard anyone call a person a bastard in such kind words before."

"How long do you plan on making His Eminence wait on you before he can eat?"

The new friends' smiles vanished from their lips with the unexpected arrival of Bishop Flanagan at the open doorway.

"I'm sorry," Richard muttered. "I forgot about the time, Your Reverence."

"Yes, so I see," Bishop Flanagan said as he turned sharply and started back down the hallway.

Richard glanced nervously at Juan, whose fright

was written plainly on his face. Richard raised his right hand and pretended to wipe sweat from his forehead. "Close," he whispered, as once again a faint smile returned. "I'd better get to the dining room before Flanagan returns with the whip."

Juan laughed. "It's good to have you here," he said. "I haven't laughed like this since coming to Baltimore."

Richard liked the sound of Juan's laughter.

Chapter Five

The cardinal leaned back in his chair. "Another fine breakfast, Sister Carmen." The nun removed his empty plate from the table. Cardinal Algado turned to Juan. "Why don't you take Richard over to the church and show him around. You have plenty of time before mass. After mass, I'll take him to the main office and introduce him to the other hooded ladies we have here . . . of course, I am referring to the nuns," the cardinal joked.

"Shall I show you to the cathedral?" Juan smiled as he and Richard entered the hallway.

"Yes, I'm anxious to see this beautiful work of architecture."

The two walked outside. It was a beautiful, clear morning. The air was fresh and clean, as it always was the morning after a good rain.

"The cardinal seems very fond of you Richard and that is good. He is a very important man in the church and especially liked by the Vatican."

The men walked down the pathway toward the cathedral. "What about you, Juan? He must like you, too."

"Oh, I suppose, but I know I'm of little importance, except for being of use as the secretary to the bishop. I'm from a very poor country. Most of my people are strict and avid, but poor Catholics. The church looks upon my country as more of a hindrance than a benefit."

Richard stopped abruptly. "You mustn't think that way about yourself and your people. Our church doesn't care if a person is rich or poor. The church only asks that one believe in its teachings and God."

Juan shook his head. "You really believe what you just said, don't you?"

"Of course, I do. Only a small portion of Catholics are wealthy. It's a church founded by the poor."

"Yes, it is a church comprised mostly of the poor people of this earth, but it is ruled by the wealthy and powerful. It is called the universal church, but why is it that for a few exceptions it is ruled by the Italians? Tell me, Richard, how many Mexican American, English or Irish popes have there been?"

Richard stared at Juan, frantically searching his mind for some kind of rebuttal to his barrage of statements. Finally, in desperation, he said, "But these are young countries compared to Italy." Richard knew instantly the stupidity of his statement. What he'd said would only solidify Juan's beliefs about power in the church.

Juan placed his arm around Richard's shoulder. "The subject is forgotten, my newfound friend."

The friends once again started toward the church.

Richard walked silently, hanging his head as he thought of Juan's words and the power of the church. He looked up just as they stood inside the entrance to the cathedral. "Magnificent," he uttered. "Magnificent, to say the least."

The priests walked slowly down the center aisle of the massive church. Neither spoke as they made their way toward the main altar, passing a scattering of people who, like many others, would come throughout the day and night to worship and pray to their God. Richard went to his knees to pray at the foot of the altar. Juan watched from a short distance behind.

People were beginning to enter the church for eight o'clock mass when Richard left, having only fifteen minutes to ready himself. Only his second day and already he was to help Cardinal Algado serve the first of two masses of the day. Besides Sunday, this was the only day the cardinal would say mass, and already the church was close to capacity. There were only a few churches in the world in which a person had the opportunity to attend a mass given by a reigning cardinal.

***

The summer passed swiftly. Already it was October. Richard found his new job very satisfying. He and the cardinal soon became close friends. His mastery of certain languages helped him and the cardinal immensely when it came to written correspondence with other countries, especially Italy, where the greatest majority of correspondence was taking place. Richard was suddenly placed into a position of firsthand knowledge of global affairs, discovering quickly just how close the church was intertwined with many countries and their ever-changing political powers.

Richard had finished reading aloud the letter received that morning from the Vatican, signed by His Holiness. Alone in the cardinal's study, where even the bishop was shielded from the substance of the cardinal's transactions . . . especially information such as Richard had just read to Cardinal Algado, the men discussed certain turn of world events over a fine Italian wine.

"Richard, pour us a glass."

Richard stepped to the small table where two bottles of wine awaited. The cardinal stopped pacing and took a seat in his rocker. Richard poured them each a glass, then took a seat directly in front of the cardinal's rocker. He sipped his wine as he watched the cardinal slowly rock, every few moments taking a sip.

The cardinal looked at Richard, as if studying him. "What is to become of this world, Richard? What great plan has the master got in store for us?"

Richard shook his head slowly. "I don't know, Your Eminence. Perhaps he can't even keep up with the rapid chain of events that seem to be taking place in the world."

"Let's hope he can keep up with these changing times. God forbid if there ever becomes a time when man is in charge of his own destiny."

Richard looked at the cardinal. The strain of worry had etched deeply into the cardinal's aging face. A great uneasiness swept through Richard's body. For a man who'd seen the worst of times in his sixty-nine years to show this much concern, it had to be of the most serious nature.

Richard would discover just how serious in less than twenty-four hours.

Cardinal Algado spent most of the afternoon and evening in meditation. Richard struggled to conceal his anxiety from those around him, especially Juan who'd come to know Richard's moods.

The cardinal requested an early supper. It was

evident that the mental strain had taken its toll on his elderly body. Richard too was worn out. Little was said during dinner. The four men had a single glass of wine after dinner and retired to their rooms for the evening.

Richard lay on his bed after his bath. His body ached for rest, but his mind wouldn't cooperate. It seemed that whenever he found himself caught up in uncertainty about the future, his thoughts returned to the small farm in Louisiana. The peaceful time of his childhood drifted like ancient clouds through his mind, but the ending was always the same. The horrid flames roared through his brain like a raging beast sent by Satan. This night would be different, though just as cruel as the raging fire, as images of Elisabeth wrecked his mind. He believed he'd succeeded in blocking her from his thoughts—but he had not. There she was, as beautiful as yesterday, appearing in his mind's eye as he lay in the darkness of his room, reliving those beautiful days when he and Elisabeth were together. Tonight guilt wouldn't make an appearance . . . tomorrow, he'd do penance for the thoughts presently flowing through his tired mind like some great rhapsody slowly drifting him off into oblivion. Shortly, Richard was asleep.

***

"We missed you at breakfast."

"Yes, I wasn't hungry this morning. I thought I'd spend time alone."

"I can see you were granted your wish," Juan said as he looked about the empty cathedral. "You look tired, Richard. Do you feel well?"

"Yes, of course. I feel fine."

"Well, anyways, Sister Carmen is waiting breakfast for you."

Richard started for the church door. "Perhaps I can eat a little."

"I will see you after mass," Juan said as Richard walked out onto the church steps.

A brisk wind chilled the early morning fall air. It was only a few minutes past seven when Richard started toward the rectory. He'd spent most of the early morning asking God for his forgiveness for the lurid dreams of Elisabeth he'd experienced during the night. Even now, as he walked toward the rectory, images of Elisabeth flashed in his mind.

This was the morning of October 23, 1929.

"Good morning, Richard. So, you decided to have a little breakfast after all, I see."

"Yes, Your Eminence. I've gotten a little bit hungry."

"Good," Cardinal Algado said as Richard took his seat at the table.

"Any good news in the paper this morning, Your Eminence?" Richard watched the cardinal skim through the morning paper.

"Not much to speak of, good or bad, I'm glad to say."

Richard swallowed some juice. "That's good."

"It seems though that the Germans are having a difficult time making up their minds what kind of political party they want to run their country. It appears that this Hitler fellow might be emerging as somewhat of a strong political figure. Do we know anything about him, Richard?"

"Thank you, Carmen," Richard said as the sister set his plate in front of him. "I haven't received much information on him, Your Eminence, but we do know he recently joined the Nationalist Party, elevating his national status dramatically. It's also thought he's strongly anticommunist."

"Then he mustn't be too bad from the things I've heard about the Communist Party spreading like wildfire throughout the countries of Europe."

Richard nodded in agreement and finished off his sausage.

Cardinal Algado walked to Richard's side of the table. He placed his hand on Richard's shoulder. "Perhaps you'd better write Bishop Snyder in Berlin for what information he might have on this Adolf Hitler. Hopefully, he's Catholic."

Richard smiled at the cardinal. "Perhaps he is, Your Eminence."

"By the way, German is one of the languages you speak, isn't it?"

"Yes, Your Eminence, it is. Although I must confess, I'm probably a little rusty in my German, not having much opportunity to use it these last several months."

The cardinal scratched his head. "You know, I can understand how the late Bishop O'Toole could speak Italian, since his mother was born not too far from my village outside of Naples. But how would he be fluent in the German language?"

"His Father was born in Munich."

"Ha!" Cardinal Algado bellowed. "That answers my question. I don't think I will even ask you how he came about speaking French."

Richard grinned. "He studied French while he was

in college, Your Eminence."

Cardinal Algado bellowed again. "I'm now thoroughly confused. I should have let it be after Italian. I'll see you after mass in the study," the cardinal said, patting Richard on the shoulder.

***

Richard sat at his desk, working on the letter he was to send to Bishop Snyder in Berlin, when the cardinal entered the room. He crossed the room to the cardinal and said, "I've finished the letter to Bishop Snyder, Your Eminence."

Cardinal Algado put on his glasses and began reading the two-page letter. After studying the letter briefly he said, "Look at me looking at this bunch of scribbling like I know what the hell it says."

Richard smiled as Father Juan burst out laughing across the room. "Did you put in there what I asked you to?"

"Yes, Your Eminence."

"Well, send it then." Richard started back toward his desk. "Perhaps you'd better write Rome also and see what they might have on this Hitler fellow. At least they can tell us if he is a Catholic or not."

Richard smiled. "I'll see what they know about him, but don't be disappointed if he isn't Roman Catholic, Your Eminence."

"Oh, I won't mind if he isn't, as long as he isn't a Baptist. I never met a Baptist yet that would sit down and have a drink with you. Beats anything I've ever seen," the cardinal muttered as he began sorting papers.

Richard and Juan looked at one another and laughed. It seemed that every time Bishop Flanagan wasn't in the room the cardinal seemed a lot more at ease.

Richard worked on his letter to the Vatican until Sister Carmen entered the room carrying a telegram. Richard and Juan watched as she handed it to the cardinal. Everyone knew it had to be something serious by the expression on the cardinal's face as he read.

Cardinal Algado removed his glasses and laid the telegram on his desk. "I have news from New York City. A few minutes ago, the stock market crashed. There's pandemonium throughout the financial world at this hour. It's reported that people are taking their own lives. Many have lost everything they own."

Richard sat stunned upon hearing the news. Thoughts of Joe ran rampant in his mind. My God, had Joe lost everything? Is he one of the ones that killed themselves or might do so? He had to find out. He had to find Joe. Joe was so high strung and so proud of what he'd accomplished. If Joe had lost everything, he would be liable to do something drastic. These thoughts tore at Richard's mind as he sat oblivious to those around him.

"Richard . . . Richard, my son," Cardinal Algado repeated.

Richard looked up at the cardinal standing beside him.

"I know where your thoughts are at this time, but you must have faith in your brother."

He looked into the eyes of this kind old man who stood looking down at him. Richard had spoken often to the cardinal and Juan about his brother, of how proud he was of him.

"Richard, I'll understand if you must go to New York to find Joe," the cardinal said. "Juan, find out when the next train leaves for New York."

"Yes, Your Eminence." Juan hurried from the room.

Cardinal Algado patted Richard gently on the shoulder. "Joe will be fine, if he's half the man his brother is."

Richard lowered his head in prayer.

"You go pack your things," the cardinal continued. "We'll get you out on the first train to New York. Everything will be fine, my son."

Richard left for his room, packed his bags, then hurried to the cathedral to pray for Joe. He prayed harder than he had ever prayed. Shortly, Juan came for him. In less than two hours, he was on a train headed for New York City.

Chapter Six

Richard checked into the Claremont Hotel in Manhattan and went immediately to Joe's apartment, only to find he'd moved out two weeks before, failing to give a forwarding address. This was Saturday morning. The stock exchange was closed on Saturday and Sunday and according to the latest news might not open on Monday. He found it difficult to believe this was the same bustling, carefree city he'd visited only a few months before. Rumors ran rampant on the streets . . . everything from the president declaring martial law to a military takeover of the government. One thing was certain; there'd been major runs on banks, forcing some to close their doors.

It was misty and cold. Richard walked along the empty sidewalk. He'd just left the office building where

Joe's brokerage firm was located. It, too, was closed for the day. He'd searched all morning for some trace of his brother but to no avail. There was one person who might know Joe's whereabouts.

Richard hesitated a moment, then stepped from the cab pulled up to Elisabeth's apartment building. She might know where Joe was. He paid the driver and pulled his overcoat around his neck. The brisk wind drove the cold air into his face as he walked slowly up the steps, trying to build up the courage to face Elisabeth. Richard knocked lightly on the door and waited. No answer. He knocked harder but with the same results. As he walked away, he felt both relieved that she had not come to the door and disheartened he hadn't gotten to see her after all. For those few minutes, he'd forgotten completely about Joe and his very reason for coming. Once again, he found himself walking alone down one of the thousands of sidewalks that crisscrossed the huge city.

It was after four o'clock when Richard stopped in front of the Forty-Seventh Street mission. He peered into the plate glass window, where a dozen or so men and women milled about the open room.

"Why don't you come in out of the cold, mister?" the straggly middle-aged man said.

Richard turned toward the skinny figure.

"You must be new around here," the man said, "or else you wouldn't be standing out here knowing they got the best food on the circuit in this place."

Richard turned and looked at the man who was busy studying him closely. His pale blue eyes moved slowly from Richard's feet up to his snugly fitted black top hat.

"You sure ain't one of us wearing those fancy

duds." The stranger's gaze moved to Richard's white collar. "Oh, I see you're a preacher. Is this your place?" The man smiled, exposing two missing front teeth.

Richard grinned. "Oh, no, I just happened to stop to see what was going on."

The man laughed. "The same thing that's been going on here for years, preacher man, just feeding us poor wretched people out here on the streets. You see, most of us ain't got no education to speak of or any family . . . that is any kin who cares about us outcasts. But you know, preacher, the way I been hearing folks talk these last couple days, we old outcasts that's been out here alone for years might have to start sharing some of our grub with some of these big city slickers. I hear a bunch of them big shots suddenly ain't big no more. Yes sir, preacher. Who knows, I might be sharing my meal with some bank president before long. Won't that be something?"

The man smelled. Richard's thoughts turned to Joe again. What if Joe were in one of these places?

"You gonna come in and get a bite to eat, preacher man?"

Richard stared harshly at the man, whose only transgression was to speak the truth. Joe was too proud. He would starve to death before he would ask for charity.

"You don't know what you're missing," the old man shouted as Richard turned and walked away. "Say a prayer for me, preacher man!"

The words of the beggar rang loudly in his ears. The long sunny days that had illuminated the city until well after eight in the evening during his last visit had disappeared with the summer. It was just after six o'clock and darkness had swept the city. Richard was cold and tired when he finally stopped at a small restaurant, having not eaten since the day before. He ordered a scotch and water and tried to relax. He'd run out of ideas about how to find Joe. The restaurant was busy. The waitress apologized about the delay in getting his meal. He was in no hurry; after all, he had no place to go except back to his hotel room, where he would only feel guilty and helpless failing to find Joe.

The scotch and water did much to relax his worn-out body and mind. He sat back slowly sipping his drink and watching the scattering of people come and go. He spotted a young woman wearing a bright red dress. At first, he thought it was Elisabeth, but his thundering heart was quickly silenced as the young lady turned out to be someone else. Richard settled back into his chair. His thoughts returned to the first time he'd seen Elisabeth. How beautiful and frustrated she'd looked sitting in that hotel room with that so-called date, totally ignoring her and arguing world politics. Richard sat erect. "My God! How stupid of me not to think of it before." he said to the waitress who'd arrived with his meal.

"Sir?"

"The Plaza Hotel, of course! Room 542. They'll know where Joe is." He bolted from the chair and hastily donned his overcoat.

"But, sir, don't you want your dinner?"

"You eat it. I don't have time." Richard reached into his pants pocket and pulled out a twenty-dollar bill. "Here you are, young lady, and keep the change." He placed the money on the waitress' food tray, then leaned over and kissed the waitress on her cheek.

The elderly lady one table away dropped her glass

at the sight. "My Lord, what is the Catholic Church coming to?" the elderly women said to her husband as Richard passed.

"I don't know, Grace," her smiling husband answered, "but it sort of makes me mad I've been a Presbyterian all these years."

It was a ten-minute ride from the restaurant to the Plaza.

Richard approached the doorway. "Welcome to the Plaza," the young Negro man said.

He thanked the doorman, then weaved his way through the crowded hotel lobby that buzzed with conversations about the stock market's fall. Richard searched the room, his eyes roaming for any sign of Joe or Elisabeth. Unsuccessful, he decided to check room 542. The dimly lit hallway was barren except for one old gentleman that passed Richard in the hallway, heading toward the elevator. He heard voices as he neared the room. He paused in front of the closed door, listening. Sounds of laughter told Richard these could be some of the same young people from before. He knocked on the door. The laughter grew louder as the door opened wider. A young man holding a cocktail motioned for him to enter.

"By yourself, buddy?" the man asked as the closed the door behind Richard.

Richard glanced about the crowded room. "Yes I am." Joe wasn't there. Richard looked closer about the room for any familiar face.

"What's your name, friend?" an attractive woman said, approaching Richard. "I don't remember seeing you here before."

"Richard Carver."

"Richard . . . I like that name." The woman sipped from her drink. "You looking for somebody in particular?" A sensuous smile crept upon her painted lips.

Richard removed his hat, brushing his hair back with his hand. "You wouldn't happen to know a Joe Carver, would you?"

"Joe Carver . . . hmm, the name sounds familiar. He a friend of yours?"

"He's, my brother."

"Your brother—does he look anything like you?"

"There's a resemblance."

"Lordy, I know I'd remember him if he looks anything like you." She held out one arm. "Here, let me take your coat handsome, while I think about your brother."

Richard turned as she took the overcoat off his arms, then turned back facing her. It was as if she'd spied a ghost.

"You're a pr—" The word froze in her throat.

"A priest. Yes, I'm a priest."

The room grew quieter as others began to notice they were in the presence of a Catholic priest. Richard watched in silence, quickly becoming the center of attention; some turned away, as if embarrassed.

A young man in a business suit who'd been standing in a far corner of the room broke the uncomfortable silence. "Aren't you Joe Carver's brother?"

Richard's eyes shifted to the man as he walked toward him. His voice sounded high-pitched and strained. "Yes I am."

"I thought I recognized you from before," the man exclaimed. "We don't get many priests up here."

"I suppose not," Richard answered.

"I'm James Whittaker. I've known Joe ever since he landed here in The Big Apple. Fine fellow that Joe." James swallowed from his drink. By now, most folks had gone back to their conversations prior to Father Carver's appearance.

"I'll lay your coat on the couch, Father," the young lady said.

"Thank you for your kindness, miss."

"Would you like a drink, Father?" James asked.

"Yes, I'd love one." Richard scanned the room.

James handed Richard his drink. The room, once again buzzed with chatter and gaiety, despite the city's recent economic disaster. "So, what brings you here, Father?"

Richard took a sip. "Joe . . . I don't know where he is. I'm worried about him, after what happened to the market and all."

James nodded. "Yes, some of us have lost everything."

"Us . . . you say?"

"Yes, I'm also . . . or I *was* a broker. My company got wiped out, along with a lot of others."

"But you don't seem to upset over it."

James flashed a crooked smile. "Upset, Father? Hell, I've been crying for two days, and so today, I decided to get drunk. One more of these and I will be." James held his glass up. "But at least I won't be in the bread lines by myself. What the hell, Father, I might learn to enjoy poverty."

Richard watched James down his drink. The young man's shoulders hitched, his eyes welling with tears. James lowered his head and stared at his empty glass. This could be Joe standing here. Richard placed his hand on James's shoulder. "Joe . . . do you know where he is?"

James rubbed his eyes. "I saw him last Monday at the exchange. He'd just moved out to the Grove Apartments in Manhattan. Fancy place, I understand. I haven't seen him since the damn bottom fell out."

"Things will get better for you, James."

James looked up at Richard. "Get better, Father? Can they get any worse? I don't have a penny to my name. I've got to go home and tell my wife and little boy we have to move out of our apartment because I don't have the rent money. Tell me Father, what terrible thing did your brother and I do to that God of yours to deserve this? Please tell me, Father."

Richard studied James. Tears spilled from the young man's eyes. Once again the room grew quiet, watching and listening to James and Richard's conversation.

James threw his empty glass across the room. "Well, tell me, damn it!"

"I can't answer you, James. I'm not God."

James stared at him a few moments then walked away. Richard felt a blanket of guilt slip over him as the room of people stood in silence staring him down. "Here you go, Father." The young lady handed him his coat.

He met her gaze. "Thank you for everything. I'm sorry . . . I'm terribly sorry." Richard turned and left the room. He'd gotten what he'd come for: Joe's residence. But it had been costly for Richard.

Just after ten thirty, the taxi stopped in front of the Grove Apartment Building. Richard paid the driver and exited the cab. James had been right about the apartments being fancy. The building looked new. Richard stood in the cold, surveying the ten-story structure. Inside, he proceeded to the four rows of mailboxes at the apartment lobby's south end. He searched residents' names printed below each of the boxes.

"Thank God," he said, reading Joe's name printed beneath box 41. He hurried toward the waiting elevator. The elevator made its way to the fourth floor. Richard read the apartment numbers aloud as he made his way down the hallway, stopping at apartment 41.

"Come on, big brother, be home," he muttered as he knocked on the door. Richard listened intently for any sound behind the closed door, then tried the doorknob. Locked. "Come on, Joe." He knocked on the door. He was about to leave when the doorknob turned from the inside. Richard peered intently into the doorway as the outline of Joe's face developed slowly before his eyes. "Joe, is that you?" He looked closer at the dark silhouette. The door suddenly opened wide.

"Richard," Joe said.

Richard lunged forward, put his arms around Joe and squeezed tightly. "Joe, I've been so worried about you." Joe did not reciprocate his embrace. "Are you all right, Joe?" Richard removed his arms and stood back to get a better look. He examined Joe for the first time, the hallway light illuming his brother's face. "My God, Joe, what's wrong with you?"

Richard stared at Joe in disbelief. His youthful face had aged many years since Richard had seen him last. Joe stared blankly at him, his brown eyes glassed over and streaked in red. Richard grew nauseated. Joe reeked of alcohol. His clothes were soiled and wrinkled. Richard wondered how a person who'd only a few days ago been an up-and-coming executive dressed in the finest clothes, suddenly looked like the bum he'd met earlier at the mission. "Come, Joe. Sit down." He closed the front door and led Joe over to couch.

Richard turned on the lamp next to the couch. He scanned the large room filled with expensive furniture, and the apartment walls adorned with beautiful paintings. It was evident Joe had been closed in for some time. Newspapers lay scattered about the room. News of the crash headlined across them.

"My heavens, man, let's get some fresh air in here." Richard shed his overcoat as he walked over to the closed window. He pulled the curtain back and lifted the window. Richard leaned out the window and took a deep breath. The stagnant, smelly apartment air threatened to make him vomit. Two empty whiskey bottles sat on the coffee table. A half-empty bottle sat on the dining table. Richard took a seat next to his brother.

Joe looked at him, blinking his eyes slowly and deliberately, as if trying to bring the world into focus. "Richard is that you?" he asked pitifully.

"Yes, Joe, I'm here. A weak smile raced across Joe's lips and then vanished. "Richard, I've . . ." he mumbled. The floodgates opened. "Richard, I've lost everything. I'm . . ."

Richard placed his arms around his brother, holding him tightly, as Joe cried like a child. Tears sprung from Richard's eyes as the sounds of Joe's sadness pierced his heart. Joe buried his head deeper into Richard's chest. They stayed that way for the longest time. Joe cried himself to sleep as he lay in Richard's comforting arms. Richard retrieved a pillow and blanket from Joe's bed, then laid his brother on the couch. He made Joe comfortable on the couch and proceeded to clean the apartment. He could find no evidence of where Joe had eaten anything. The milk had gone sour in the icebox. Three more empty whiskey bottles lay atop the smelly kitchen garbage.

Richard cleaned the room as well as he could and proceeded to pour himself a drink from a partially filled scotch bottle. He sat in one of the cushioned chairs facing the couch where Joe lay sleeping. He stared at his brother, a million thoughts passing through his tired mind. How fast the tides of fortune can change. The words of James, the young man at the Plaza, pounded cruelly in his Richard's mind. *What terrible thing did your brother and I do to that God of yours to deserve this?* The words kept repeating. Finally, he forced his exhausted body out of the chair, walked over, and pulled the cover up around Joe's shoulders. "Sleep well, Joe." He looked at him for the last time, then turned out the light next to the couch. He set his empty glass down on the coffee table and made his way to Joe's bedroom. Richard succeeded in discarding his shirt before falling across the unmade bed—asleep before his head touched the pillow.

Richard shivered as the cold air from the open window sent a chill through his body. His eyes opened grudgingly, his body shivering atop of Joe's bed. Bright sunlight shone through the bedroom window as Richard sprang from the bed grabbing his shirt lying wrinkled on the floor. Richard donned his shirt as he headed for the living room and the open window that allowed the cold air to spill into the room. Richard closed the window and grabbed his coat. Joe hadn't moved an inch. Richard placed the cover over Joe's exposed feet, then turned on the heat. Soon the room was comfortable again. Richard sat in the chair and waited for Joe to awaken. Another hour passed before his brother stirred.

Joe held his throbbing head and groaned. Richard smiled as Joe slowly turned toward him. "Richard?" he said weakly.

"Yes, Joe, it's me."

"God, have I died and gone to heaven?" Joe mumbled and rubbed his eyes.

Richard laughed. "No, this isn't heaven, big brother."

Joe moaned. "Damn, I knew I couldn't be that lucky."

"From the looks of you, it looks like you might've been to hell."

Joe looked at Richard. "Huh, you mean I've been *through* hell, don't you?"

The smile disappeared from Richard's lips. "Yeah, that's what I mean, Joe." He rose from his chair and walked to the couch, taking a seat beside Joe. "What's happened to you?"

Joe tried to look Richard in the eyes but turned away instead. "Well, it's like you read in the papers. I, along with a million other fools, have lost every penny."

Richard placed his hand on Joe's shoulder. "You're no fool, Joe. No one could've known what was about to happen. I've some of the best people in the world that do nothing but study the world's economies, and they didn't expect anything like this was about to happen. Lord, if they had, don't you think I would've contacted you before it took place? Damn, Joe, it looks like the whole world could be headed for a depression."

"I don't give a damn about the rest of the world. I only care about Joe Carver. And hell, look what's happened to him." Joe attempted to hide the tears that trickled down the side of his nose.

Richard turned away to let Joe wipe his eyes. "Well, we've to figure out what you're going to do."

"What do you mean *we*? This is my problem. You're safe from this sort of thing. The Catholic Church is the wealthiest organization in the world . . . you're not going to starve to death."

Richard stared at Joe. "No, I'm not going to starve to death, and neither are you. You're my brother. We have to look after one another."

This time Joe made no attempt to hide his teary eyes. "Thank you."

Richard smiled as Joe embraced him. Suddenly, he thought of Lori. In all this worry about Joe's well-being, he'd completely forgotten about their sister. What effect had all of this had on her and her family? What about Jeff's shipyard? Had it failed with the market's crash? He'd waste little time finding out now that he was certain Joe was safe. He called Lori a few minutes later. Fortunately for her and Jeff, the shipyard was solvent at the time of the crash. Jeff's father had prospered in the business during the years of the First World War with the manufacturing of naval ships for the government. Unbeknown to Joe, Richard had told Lori and Jeff of Joe's plight. It took little time for the couple to decide to help Joe in his time of need. Of course, Richard and Lori both knew Joe wouldn't take any form of charity, especially from his sister, but with the help of Richard, Lori and Jeff concocted a plan to lure Joe into Jeff's shipyard business.

***

A week had passed since Richard arrived in New York City. Joe sat at the kitchen table drinking his morning coffee. Richard walked in the front door with Joe's mail, piled up over the past days. He joined his brother. "Morning, Joe."

Joe's head was buried in the morning paper. "Good morning, Richard," he answered, not looking up.

"Looks like you have a letter here from Lori."

Joe lowered the paper. "Lori, you say?" Joe took the letter. Richard laid the rest of the mail on the edge of the table and watched in silence as Joe opened the letter and began reading it silently. Richard knew what Lori was going to write and prayed it would work. He poured himself a cup of coffee. It seemed a lifetime before Joe finally finished the letter. He waited for Joe to say something. Instead, he refilled his coffee cup, then resumed his seat at the table.

Richard couldn't wait any longer. "Is everything all right with Lori?"

Joe took a large swallow of his coffee, then said, "She says Jeff needs help at the shipyard." Joe glanced at the letter. "She says Jeff's father has been feeling poorly lately. Jeff needs someone to help him run the business. Hell, I don't know anything about the shipping business." Joe stood and walked to the open window.

Richard knew by Joe's behavior that he was definitely interested in the offer. "Well, the way I see it," Richard said, joining Joe by the window, "and I'm sure Lori and Jeff see it the same way, a man of your intelligence would have little difficulty in catching onto the business. Besides, I'm sure they want somebody they can trust, and you being part of the family . . . well, Joe, can't you see?"

"You don't think she found out about me losing everything, do you? And she's just feeling sorry for me?" Joe turned to face Richard.

Richard felt his brother's eyes searching deep into his soul. He asked God's forgiveness for the lie before he spoke. "Of course not, Joe. I haven't told her. She and Jeff need help, and they're asking for you to help them. It's as simple as that." Perspiration broke across his forehead.

The sternness in Joe's face softened into a weak smile. "Hell, I suppose it couldn't be that much different than the market. I'm sure it all comes down to buying and selling. The only difference would be instead of pieces of paper you'd be dealing in nuts and bolts."

"I'm sure that's right, Joe." Richard flashed a relieved smile. After a few more minutes of talking, it over, Joe decided to take Lori and Jeff's offer.

***

Richard saw Joe off to Virginia, after which he returned to Baltimore and his evermore emergence into the world of international politics. During the following months, Richard and Juan became close friends.

It had been a long day for Richard, February 5, 1932. The depression had deepened during the last two years and the countries of Europe had fallen into difficult times. Long-standing governments throughout Europe were collapsing or on the verge of collapse. Anarchy had swept through Europe. America was in no position to help, as it, too, was fighting to save itself from the spreading plagues of unemployment and crumbling economic conditions.

Richard had finally fallen to sleep only to be awakened two hours later by a tapping on his door. He slid out of bed, slipped on his robe, and opened the door. Father Genely, the middle-aged Italian priest who'd replaced Bishop Flanagan a short time after his transfer, looked a bit disheveled. "Richard, there's a man at the front door who insists on seeing you."

"What time is it?" he mumbled, brushing his hair out of his eyes.

"It's after one in the morning," Father Genely whispered. The cardinal's room was next door.

Richard wondered who it could be at such an hour. He made his way down the dimly lit hallway, toward the front door. Richard opened the door and peered at the middle-aged man dressed in a heavy overcoat to ward off the bone-chilling cold that had held the city in its icy grip the last six days.

"Father Carver?"

"Yes, I'm Father Carver." Richard watched closely as the stranger reached into his inside coat pocket and produced a leather wallet. To it was pinned a policeman's badge.

"May I come in?" the officer asked.

"Yes, why sure." Richard stood aside as the officer entered the doorway.

The officer followed him into the study. "My name is Jerry Tyson . . . Lieutenant Jerry Tyson, Baltimore Police Department."

"What is it, Lieutenant?"

"Father, do you have a Father Juan Lopez living here?"

"Yes, he's a resident priest. He's asleep in his room.

78

Shall I get him?" A sudden uneasiness swept over him as he studied the lieutenant's expression.

"Father, I'm sorry to tell you this, but I don't believe Father Lopez is asleep in his room. He, along with eighteen others, was trapped in an apartment fire two hours ago, on Ninety-Second Street. He was burned badly, Father. He's dying or perhaps already dead. He asked for you to give his last rights."

Richard stammered, "You're wrong . . . you must be mistaken. Juan is in his room . . . asleep. I'll show you. I'll . . ." Richard started toward the door.

"Father, I'm sorry."

He stared at the floor. "My God, it can't be true."

"I'm sorry, Father, but it's true."

Richard lifted his head, catching the lieutenant's eye. "Ninety-Second Street, isn't that where—"

The lieutenant moved closer to Richard. "Yes, Father, it's the homosexual district." The lieutenant placed his hand on Richard's shoulder. "This is why I came personally, Father. You see, I'm Catholic, and I don't want something like this to get out. Can you imagine what the newspapers would do with a story like this?"

Richard stared in disbelief. He shook his head. "Juan was a ho—" He couldn't bring the word to his lips.

"Please, Father, you must come. I'll drive you to the hospital."

He could only think that it mustn't be true.

"Please, Father, we must be going."

"Yes, I'll get dressed." Richard said nothing about Juan to Father Genely before he left, only not to mention anything to Cardinal Algado, asleep soundly in his room.

Richard was oblivious to the bone-chilling cold as

he and the lieutenant walked up the sidewalk toward the hospital entrance. The lieutenant led Richard to Father Lopez's room. A young doctor stood at the doorway. "Father Carver?" he asked as Richard and the lieutenant approached.

"Yes, I'm Father Carver."

"Father Lopez has been asking for you. He's dying, Father. We've done all we can, which isn't much, except to give him something to relieve the excruciating pain. Please go in Father and I'm very sorry." The doctor placed his hand on Richard's shoulder. Richard walked slowly into the room and began praying to himself as he neared the bed that held his dying friend. A white sheet covered Juan's badly burnt body. Richard took a deep breath, suddenly feeling faint as he looked at what remained of Juan's once handsome face. Juan's dark hair was gone, only red and black streaks remained. The charred lesions cut deeply into his head, exposing portions of his skull. Richard's stomach turned. He turned away from his friend as sickness turned to grief. Tears ran down his beleaguered face.

"Richard is that you?" a faint voice said. Richard gritted his teeth, trying to draw enough inner strength to look down at his dying friend. He turned slowly as his eyes once again, fell upon the charred body that lay before him. "Richard," the voice said again.

"Yes, Juan, it is me."

Juan attempted to look up, struggling to open his charred eyes. "Richard, will you hear my last confession?" he said, his voice barely audible.

Richard fell to his knees next to Juan's hospital bed. "Yes, my friend." He made the sign of the cross as he began to pray for Juan's soul.

Juan finished his confession, drew one last bit of energy, and said, "Richard, I don't know if God will forgive me for the things I've done, but I will know shortly. I ask that you try to understand and perhaps find it in your great and loving heart to forgive me for this great sin I've committed. I wanted to keep my horrid secret away from you but I failed. I'm not as strong as you, Richard. I gave in to human lust. I was weak, while you are strong."

Juan's difficult words rekindled Richard's dark secret; flashes of Elisabeth swept through his tormented mind.

"Richard, please forgive me. I'm sorry for the shame I brought to you and our church. Richard . . ."

He watched helplessly as the breath of life crept slowly from Father Lopez's body, then laid his head on the edge of the bed and cried to himself.

Juan's secret died with Richard. He remained in Baltimore through the early years of the '30s. His role as Cardinal Algado's aid rapidly diminished as Richard's growing allegiances of foreign colleagues agreed he could best serve the church as an American ambassador to the Vatican. The turmoil in Europe took on an imminent danger during the middle years of the decade as war clouds gathered over an increasingly boisterous Germany. Adolph Hitler became the German chancellor, with underlying support from the Vatican, in hopes of keeping the ever-strengthening Communist Party from power. This atheist's movement would flourish, however, and become a dominant force in the years to follow. Meanwhile, Mussolini caused tremors in Italy, much to the dismay of the Vatican, as he, like Hitler, began to show an ever-increasing image of rationalism. Richard was appointed to monsignor in the spring of '34. His knowledge of global affairs proved him a valuable commodity and his time was best spent at the church's nerve center, the Vatican.

On a cold and blustery January day, Richard walked into the cardinal's study. The year was 1935. Cardinal Algado sat behind his desk. Richard approached.

"Good morning, Your Eminence'."

Cardinal Algado looked up at Richard. Light from the small lamp sitting on his desk illuminated his face. Richard noticed for the first time just how much his Italian friend had aged in last few months. He knew this was, in part, due to the cardinal's deep concern for his Italian homeland, caught in ever-frightening turmoil. A faint smile came upon the cardinal's lips. "Sit down, Richard, as this will be our last morning together. Shortly you leave for Rome."

Richard took a seat in front of the cardinal's desk.

"I believe you'll like Italy," the cardinal continued. "The people are so kind and happy." He paused as the glitter in his eyes faded and a sadness swept his face like a wave splashing upon the seashore. "War is about to sweep through my homeland. A terrible war, so Eminence' that man's very existence could be in great peril." Cardinal Algado lowered his head. "I pray I'm not here to see these certain tragic events take place. God has led me through one war. Surely, he will not be so cruel as to let me witness another. But you, Richard, you are young and have suddenly become a very important part of this damn-dabble future. I know not what plans God has for you, but I will pray to him that he spares you from the many horrors of war that lie so menacingly close on the horizon." The cardinal raised his head. "May God go with you, my son.

Spread his divine teachings. I believe you are destined to journey far and wide across this turbulent world of ours."

Part II

Chapter Seven

Richard arrived in Paris January 27, 1935 and had little time to take in the famous city as his train departed for Rome the following morning. He spent most of his time on the journey staring out his window at the seemingly never-ending countryside of France and Italy.

One would never know by looking at these peaceful scenes of rolling hills and endless farmlands dotted by distant villages that war lay just over the horizon. He thought little of war as his train made its way toward Rome. Surveying the alien countryside, his thoughts were between rhapsody and tragedy. Thoughts of his childhood drifted in and out, but, as always, the happy days of childhood ended in tragedy as the horrid flames of death scorched his dreams of serenity. Yes, and there was Elisabeth, the beautiful twenty-one-year-old who'd momentarily stolen his heart and soul from his God. As much as he'd tried to dispel the memories of her, they returned, taking him back to her wanting arms and the night they'd spent together. What had become of her? Had she married that man at the Plaza, her drunken date? Did she have children? As much as he denied it, his heart grew heavy at the thought of her married to another man. Somehow, it wouldn't be right, although he could never admit it to himself.

It was late afternoon when the train pulled into Rome. It was a pleasant day. He stepped from the station onto the streets of the city. It was Saturday, and people were everywhere it seemed, reminding Richard of New York City. The sun sank low in the western sky as Richard waited in front of the train station for his ride to the Vatican. Finally, a voice said, "Monsignor Carver?"

He jumped slightly, turning and eyeing the middle-aged priest who'd so surprised him. "Yes, I'm Monsignor Carver."

"Finally, I've found you. I was afraid you'd missed your train. I'm Father Genere. I'm to see you to the Holy City."

Father Genere helped Richard with his luggage to the awaiting car. The driver loaded the bags as Richard and Father Genere entered the backseat of the long, black limousine. "Did you have a pleasant trip, Father?" the Italian priest asked in terrible English.

"Yes, very nice and such a beautiful country."

Father Genere laughed. "Yes, our people have farmed these lands for centuries. I've also heard a great deal about the beauty of America."

"Yes, we, too, have beautiful farmlands."

Father Genere nodded. "You're a very bright American I am told. You worked very closely with Cardinal Algado."

"Yes, that is so." Richard stared at the balding priest. He wondered what they knew of him and if he'd measure up to their high expectations.

"You look surprised that I know about you?"

"Yes, I'm a little surprised."

"You will learn very quickly, Father, there is very

little that goes on in the world of Catholicism that isn't known within the walls of the Holy City. Do you know which cardinal you will serve?"

"No."

The Italian priest turned to look out the window. The sun was setting as the black car pulled into Vatican City. The dome of St. Peter's Cathedral could be seen in the twilight. Richard stepped from the car.

"I don't imagine you have churches such as this in the United States, do you, Monsignor?"

"Nowhere in the world do they have anything to match St. Peter's."

"Yes, you're right," Father Genere said. "Please follow me. Monsignor Carter and I will show you to your new residence." Father Genre led the way toward a large stone building.

The men entered the building. Like most structures that made up the tiny country of Vatican City, it was built of granite many centuries before. Richard walked beside the Italian priest as they made their way down a long corridor, lined on both sides with closed doorways. Behind these doors were housed the many resident priests and bishops, along with a small number of cardinals. Many of the rooms were empty, used only for visiting clergy who came and went, constantly traveling to and from Rome on official business. Only at the time of a pontiff's death were most of the rooms filled, at which time the cardinals from all points on earth would gather behind the sacred walls of the city to elect a new Holy Father. These high priests were known as the Sacred College of Cardinals. A two-thirds majority of the secret votes cast was needed to elect a new pope from this entourage of over 200 cardinals who formed the Sacred College.

Neither man spoke as they made their way down the seemingly never-ending corridor. Finally, Father Genere stopped in front of one of closed doors. He turned to Richard. "This will be your quarters for the duration of your stay while in the Vatican. I hope that will be for some time, I might say."

"Thank you, Father."

Father Genere opened the door to Richard's room, then stood aside, letting Richard enter the doorway first. Richard entered the rather small room that made up the study and living area. Another, smaller doorway across the room led to the sleeping quarters and toilet facilities. The room had a musty odor to it, due to its long period of vacancy. Richard removed his top hat. He slowly strolled about the room, closely surveying the different artifacts that hung from the heavy stone walls. A desk lamp illuminated the room. A small sofa and matching end tables sat in the center of the room. Richard quickly glimpsed into the adjoining sleeping quarters, then stepped back into the living room. "Very adequate," he said.

Father Genere smiled. "What else does a servant of God need?"

Before Richard could reply, his attention was drawn to the small male figure standing in the doorway holding Richard's luggage. Richard thanked the German priest as he relieved him of the two suitcases. "Welcome to our home," the priest said in broken English. Before Richard could reply, the priest vanished as quickly as he'd appeared.

"I'll give you time to get settled, after which I'll take you on a tour of our facilities. If you look on your desk, you'll find a folder that explains things you must know, such as eating times as well as the different functions that take place in our everyday lives in this small city of ours. Also, if you look in the upper left-hand corner of the folder, you'll find the name of the person you'll be assigned to while you're here. Of course, if you should become a bishop, your duties would change dramatically."

Richard picked up the folder from the wooden desk. His eyes fixed on the name of the superior he would serve. "Archbishop Beroske . . . do you know him?"

A forced smile came upon the priest's lips and his eyes narrowed. "Yes, I know him well, and he is Polish. He was born in Poznan and eventually moved to Warsaw, where he became a strong voice in the church. He became very powerful in church affairs as well as Polish politics. He was brought here three years ago as the political climate in his country began to take on a more hostile flavor. The Holy Father is very fond of the Polish Archbishop and feared harm would come to his boisterous friend."

Richard sensed sarcasm in Father Genere's voice. "Sounds as if the Archbishop readily speaks his mind."

"Ha," Father Genere scoffed. "Perhaps too much for his own safety. If it hadn't been for the wisdom of the Holy Father to bring the Pole to the safety of the Vatican walls, the archbishop might not be alive today."

He stared at Father Genere for a few moments as the words of his one-time friend Father Lopez briefly awakened in the cavities of Richard's mind: *The Italians are the power of the church.* It seemed Juan was correct in his belief that the Italians ruled the church and not the Americans nor the Spanish nor any other nationality for that matter.

Richard grinned at the stern-faced Italian. "I look forward to meeting the Polish archbishop. He sounds like a man of great courage and even greater conviction. I admire that in a man, not to mention a man of God."

Father Genere's eyes looked of fire as he glared at the smiling figure of the American priest. "I believe the two of you will get along fine, seeing how both of you seem to have the same philosophies on how the world, as well as the Church of Rome, should run."

Richard's smile intensified as the Italian priest stressed the word *Rome*. "Oh yes, Roman church. I must keep reminding myself that the church is isolated within the boundaries of Italy." Richard was happy the Italian carried no weapon.

"I hope you enjoy your stay, Father, and may God bless you." The priest's words came out stiff and measured.

"Thank you, Father, and may God bless you also," Richard replied in fluent Italian, leaving Father Genere obviously stunned. "Surely they told you that I speak Italian as well."

Father Genere turned sharply and hustled down the hallway. Richard chuckled to himself as he watched the fleeing priest disappear behind a doorway halfway down the hall.

Richard stepped back into his room and began the task of unpacking. He remained in his room all evening, most of which was spent studying the folder that contained a brief summary of the rules and happenings that took place inside the confines of this tiniest nation in the world. Also, the folder gave a brief history of his new superior, Archbishop Beroske of Poland. It seemed the brash Italian priest had been correct in his appraisal of the archbishop.

He was indeed a vocal opponent of the rising Fascist Party sweeping Italy and the rising Nazi Party in Germany threatening other countries of Europe. Richard was impressed with the report on the Polish archbishop and anxious to meet him.

He finally fell asleep sometime after midnight. He awoke the next morning by a knocking on his door. "Just a moment," he shouted, slipping on his housecoat.

A smiling French priest stood at the doorway. "Good morning, Monsignor Carver."

"Good morning."

"Breakfast will be served for another forty-five minutes," the young priest said.

Richard looked down at the small man. "Father Deboux, isn't it?"

"Yes, Father, I'm to be your guide for the next few days, until you learn your way around."

Richard nodded. "I'm blessed to have such a nice guide as you."

"Thank you for your kind words, Father Carver. I pray I can live up to your praise."

"You speak very good English," Richard said in French.

"I wish my English was half as good as your French."

Richard assured the French priest he'd be to breakfast shortly, then shut the door on the kindly young priest.

***

A chill nipped at the air as Richard and Father Deboux made their way across a courtyard that led to a small chapel. They entered the chapel, dimly lit by large candles that lined both sides of the chapel's walls. Richard followed Father Deboux down the center aisle to a row of pews that ran up and down both sides of the chapel. Richard's eyes were fixed on the chapel's beautiful altar, lit by two large candelabras at either end. Their flickering flames danced upon the white cloth that blanketed the altar. Richard could feel the presence of God as he knelt before the altar and made the sign of the cross. Father Deboux knelt beside him; they bowed their heads in prayer.

The sun was much higher in the clear Italian sky, and the air had lost its chill. Richard paused on the stone steps, looking for the first time in sufficient light at part of the spectrum that made up the Holy City. He surveyed the historic structures surrounding him, his eyes resting upon the great dome of St. Peter's Cathedral, which looked even more impressive than it had in the previous day's twilight. He'd studied it often in the many photos and paintings he'd seen over the last few years. He visualized the great paintings of Michaelangelo, whose artistic genius was sketched across the ceiling of the magnificent chapel.

"Well, shall we go and meet your boss, as you say in America?"

Richard chuckled softly at his new French friend. "Yes, I believe I'm as ready as one can get."

The men started toward a large building that sat diagonally across from the papal apartments. Richard followed Father Deboux into the building. The clatter of typewriters sounded as he and Father Deboux made their way down the corridor. This building housed the main offices responsible for most of the worldwide record keeping needed for the great number of dioceses that formed the colossal church. Also located in this strategic building was the church's political nerve center. Even though the church avoided direct political involvement and attempted to remain neutral in world politics, it was without question that the church had tremendous influence on most of the world's political powers. This was especially true in the heavily populated Catholic countries of central Europe.

The world church found itself, however, in a precarious position as political regimes were crumbling throughout Europe due to mass unemployment and economic hardships, fueling the general populations to search for new forms of government and leaderships. The Catholic Church itself was in turmoil, as the rising Fascist Party led by Mussolini, the same man who in 1929 was responsible largely for setting up the separate state of Vatican City, waited at its doorstop.

Mussolini was now sending shock waves through the same church he'd helped years before with his apparent friendship with Adolph Hitler, whom the Catholic Church had endorsed when his National Socialist Party dueled for power with the Soviet Socialist Party for control of Germany. The church knew all too well that the Soviet Party was an atheist party that would attempt to smother all religious beliefs.

On the other hand, Adolf Hitler and his Nazi party had shown no animosity toward the Catholic Church or any other religious groups. At first, it appeared that Hitler's socialist party was not against Christ and seemed only to want to bring Germany out of its financial depression. Much had changed recently, however, as to Hitler's credibility and true intentions. It grew more obvious by the day that he'd become a real threat to the peaceful coexistence of Germany's neighboring countries. The church feared losing its allegiances and followers. These rapid changes in world events was the main reason Richard found himself standing outside the doorway to one of the major and most secretive political forces in the turbulent world.

Unlike the ground floor, this upper portion of the building was quiet, so much so it unsettled him. He and Father Deboux stood outside one of the many closed doorways that lined the corridor. Father Deboux knocked lightly on the door. It opened slowly. "Father Deboux and Monsignor Carver. We have an appointment with Archbishop Beroske."

The priest studied the men carefully. Richard knew before the priest opened his mouth that he was an Irishmen, having been closely acquainted with two of them before. "Yes, come in, His Eminence is expecting you. Richard smiled at the Irish priest who stood aside the open doorway leading to the archbishop's study. The archbishop sat behind his desk, sunlight streaming from the large window directly behind.

Richard kept close to Father Deboux as they crossed to the famous archbishop's desk. Father Deboux and Richard stood quietly waiting for the Archbishop to look up from the correspondence he was reading and acknowledge them. Richard hadn't known what to expect as to the archbishop's physical features. His reputation as a man of strong will and strong fortitude had painted a certain picture of the man. He'd imagined a figure of great stature, perhaps even muscular. Richard's mental image couldn't have been further from the truth. He marveled at the aging, rather frail figure of Archbishop Beroske with his thinning gray hair, his small, brown eyes still glaring at the letter.

Richard and Father Deboux waited, transfixed on the Archbishop's every move as he carefully laid down the letter, slowly raised his head, and looked at the duo standing in front of his desk. Richard watched nervously as the archbishop laid back in his chair, first looking at Father Deboux then at him. Finally, the solemn-faced archbishop broke the silence. "You must be Father Deboux," he said in French.

"Yes, Your Eminence," Father Deboux answered, also in French.

Then, the archbishop addressed Richard. "I apologize my English is of extremely poor quality. Do you mind if I speak in the Italian language, Monsignor Carver?"

"That will be just fine, Your Eminence," Richard replied in Italian.

Archbishop Beroske turned to the French priest. "Would you mind, Father, waiting in the next room while I and our young American friend have a few private words together?"

"Of course, Your Eminence. I will wait for you, Monsignor, in the next room."

"Thank you," Richard said. Richard's eyes followed Father Deboux out the door.

Archbishop Beroske pointed toward the straight-backed chair next to Richard. Returning to Italian, he said, "Please sit down, Father Carver. I've been reading a little history on you since you were ordained in the church. You've come a long way in a very short time it seems. Already you are a monsignor. I didn't reach such prominence until I was in my early forties . . . very impressive indeed, Father."

Richard didn't know whether to smile at the

cardinal or not. Was His Eminence envious of Richard to have come so far in such a short time? "I see that you were blessed with some fine superiors also. That makes your quick elevation in the church even more impressive." The archbishop hesitated. "Richard . . . may I call you Richard?"

"Yes, Your Eminence, by all means."

"Richard, I don't know what you have heard about me and probably more bad than good."

"Oh no, Your Eminence."

"Richard, you'll learn very quickly that I'm not concerned about my popularity inside these walls. My job is to serve the Holy Father, my people of Poland, and, above all, God Almighty. As long as I feel I'm accomplishing at least part of this, I feel that I'm doing what I was put on this great earth to do, and the hell with all those other glory boys who wait outside this room trying desperately to figure out how they may one day sit behind a desk such as this."

Richard stared at the archbishop whose light complexion had turned harsh red. He was quickly learning the reason for the man's notoriety. It was certain that he spoke his mind, no matter with whom it might not sit well. Richard knew now that he and the fiery archbishop would make ideal working companions.

The archbishop paused as if trying to collect himself. Richard watched intently as the archbishop rose from his chair and walked to an open window. "Richard, before we carry on with this conversation, there is something I must confess. I did not request that you work under me. This was decided by our Italian friends who serve on the Holy Father's special council."

There was that intimation, once again, about the power of the Italians. Richard kept silent and waited to hear more.

"I would've chosen another Pole to help me," the archbishop continued. "After all, we will be dealing with mostly Polish issues . . . and if not a Pole, then at least a European. Yes, even an Italian," His Eminence stated, then added as if by second thought, "but certainly not an American. What does a man know about a country that lies all the way across an ocean from his? But let me say this, Richard, since they have chosen an American, I'm glad they picked someone with your knowledge. At least you have some experience in foreign affairs."

Richard considered the archbishop as he made his way back to his chair, once again taking the seat behind his desk. He expressed no emotion as the archbishop continued. "I am certain that you are a brilliant man. This history on you proves that." Archbishop Beroske lifted the folder that held Richard's background. "And your mastery of certain languages is astounding in itself. I'm sure, however, you are aware by now, as I sit talking to you in Italian, my native language being Polish, that there was either some great mistake made by the Holy Father's council or this was done purposely, considering I'm not the most popular person within the confines of these walls."

Was that it? Had he been brought all the way from the States not for his knowledge but simply as a way to punish the Polish priest who many inside these walls considered a radical? It was obvious to Richard that Archbishop Beroske thought the latter true. Now that he was here, though, what could be done? He certainly did not want to work with someone who did not want him.

Archbishop Beroske continued, "Now that I've laid the cards so bluntly on the table, do you think you might consider working with an old reprobate such as me? Perhaps I may be able to tutor you in the Polish language. I'm certain that a man of your abilities could learn very quickly and perhaps, if you have the patience, you might teach me a little about your language."

Pausing briefly, Richard considered what had been said and the relaxed smile on the archbishop's face, then answered, "Your Reverence, I'm sorry for the apparent error the council made in regard to selecting someone more knowledgeable in your country's affairs. I can assure you I'm not completely in the dark as to Poland's political and financial problems. As far as learning the Polish language, I'm fully confident that with a teacher such as yourself we will soon be conversing in Polish."

Archbishop Beroske squinted his eyes, then exploded in laughter. Richard also laughed, watching the man's sudden change of mood. Richard's laugh faded as the archbishop rose from his chair. "My son, we must believe that God has chosen this union. I must believe, as you must, that he has a good reason for doing so. Perhaps it was done because of your gifted mind and youthful body. It is certain that you will need both of these attributes to endure the troubled years ahead. It could be as the great Cardinal Algado put in his letter about you, believing that the Holy Ghost himself rides upon your shoulders."

Richard squirmed with uneasiness.

"He says that you're a man of destiny. Richard, do you believe that you're a man of destiny?" The archbishop stared deep into Richard's eyes.

Richard muttered something unintelligible, then

said, "Your Eminence, I'm nothing more than a man such as yourself and Cardinal Algado. I don't know what God has planned for my future. I believe that all living creatures have a purpose in life and only the Almighty knows how all will end. I believe this is the way it should be."

"Say no more. Just remember you're still a young man, and even though you wear the garments of the church, you will make mistakes in life, as I'm certain you already have. Life itself is nothing more than trial and error. We do the best we can to help all living creatures for they are the children of God. Help your fellow man and God will reward you forever in the kingdom of heaven."

The archbishop's words rang in his ears: *You will make mistakes in life, as I'm certain you already have.* His mind flashed on Elisabeth.

Archbishop Beroske rose from his chair and walked toward him. "Well, my son, I'm looking forward to our working together. I only wish our work involved something more pleasant." Archbishop Beroske took his hand from Richard's shoulder, returned to his chair, and sat down. "I have papers received last week from Cardinal Jerrod in Warsaw. I've had a copy translated into English for you to study. Also, I've additional papers prepared to bring you up to date regarding recent events in Poland." The Archbishop leaned forward, placing his arms on top of the desk. "I'm sure it goes without saying that everything that transpires between us is of the utmost secrecy. The only other person who is to know anything about what we do is the Holy Father himself, and only then when he asks for such information. The church has no official function in any world politics. We are not to become involved in any form of political controversy. We are only interested in serving

God and the people who follow his beliefs. That is the church's official status. Unofficially, that's a downright lie."

Richard felt the blood rush from his face. In his limited capacity, he already knew that the church was involved to a great degree in world politics. Of course, this was kept under close secrecy. He'd never heard such a harsh word used, though, for this cover-up. A lie? But it was true, and Richard knew it.

"Richard, evil is real. Perhaps God is playing a game with Satan, checkers on a board. Why allow agony and heartbreak? This is not for us to know. God knows. You will find this job is not for glory. It is to be of service. Behind these sacred walls, you will learn what only a handful of others know, but you will never know all. There is one who knows all. That is God."

Chapter Eight

The following weeks and months were hectic for Monsignor Carver. The situation in Poland, as well as all of Europe, had deteriorated. The Japanese in the Pacific were growing more aggressive. There had been sporadic clashes between them and the Chinese. Chiang Kai Shek was creating a more effective army against the increasing danger from Japan. Most the world's eyes, however, were on Germany and its increasingly dangerous leader, Adolph Hitler. The year, 1935, passed swiftly for Richard. His workload left him little time for personal contemplation. He'd received a letter from Lori a few days before Christmas. She, Jeff, and the two children were doing fine.

She wrote that Joe had been performing an outstanding job at the shipyard, so much so that Jeff and his father had decided to extend Joe a limited partnership in the business, which they would give as a present for the holidays. April 4, 1936, the holidays had long passed.

It was another beautiful spring morning when Richard entered his office, which adjoined Cardinal Beroske's. Richard and the archbishop had become good working partners, and as promised, the archbishop had tutored Richard in his native Polish language. Richard, to a much lesser degree, had taught the archbishop a few words in English.

Richard sorted through papers he'd just received from the cardinal in Munich. The cardinal had become deeply concerned with the increased anti-Semitism spreading rapidly throughout Germany and the Vatican's policy of silence as to these increasingly public crimes. Richard read from the letter again. *Surely the Holy Father is aware of what is taking place in my country and the lunacy of its leader, Adolph Hitler?* He'd discussed the matter with Archbishop Beroske the day before. The Archbishop assured him that he would personally take the matter up with the Holy Father. He'd been awaiting word from the archbishop all morning. Finally, just before noon, His Reverence sent word to meet him in his office after lunch. Richard had become acquainted with the resident clergy and was generally well liked by most. A few, however, shunned the young monsignor, mostly because he worked with the not-so-popular Polish archbishop. Richard had discovered through personal observation that most who did not care for the archbishop appeared jealous of Archbishop Beroske's close relationship with the Holy

Father. Of course, there was the highly secretive job that the Pole held and the archbishop's strong will to keep it that way. Richard assumed they knew little about his own deep involvement with the clandestine work.

It was shortly after 2:00 p.m. when Richard entered Archbishop Beroske's office.

"Good afternoon, Richard," the smiling archbishop said in surprisingly good English.

"Good afternoon, Your Reverence," Richard replied in almost perfect Polish.

"Please be seated, my young American friend." This time he spoke in Polish. Richard took his seat in front of the archbishop's desk. Their conversations had been spoken in Polish these last few weeks. Richard had requested this in order to speed up his mastery of the language. He and the archbishop recognized this as a vital priority. It was without question that Richard would soon be called upon to visit the archbishop's homeland. Richard watched intently as Archbishop Beroske paused, as if to consider his words carefully. "Richard, I talked to the Holy Father about the letter received from Cardinal Ornotte. I told him of the cardinal's concern regarding the church's position in this very touchy situation—or lack of a position."

Richard considered the archbishop. It seemed he wasn't the same man he'd come to know. It was as if the Polish fire-eater had been doused with water.

"The Holy Father believes that it is best if the church takes no official stand in this very volatile situation," the archbishop continued. "It seems the church is caught between two evils. On one side stands Adolph Hitler and his Nazi Party. There have been rumors about how they've mistreated a few Jews."

"A few Jews!"

"Please let me finish."

Richard forced his mouth shut. Was he dreaming? This wasn't Archbishop Beroske talking—but a bad dream. Archbishop Beroske knew the facts in Germany and the Nazi's treatment of Jews.

"Richard, as bad as the Germans appear to be, it seems that the Communists might be of a much greater evil. At least the Germans believe in God. These Russian Communists are sworn atheists. Their power is spreading like a rabid disease. If the church should come out and openly take sides with the Communists, what would the Christian world think? That the greatest Christian church in the world endorses a political party that doesn't believe in God?"

Richard settled into his chair. His earlier burst of anger had faded with the archbishop's further explanation as to the church's dilemma.

Archbishop Beroske rose from his chair and approached him. "I can tell by the look on your face you are deeply upset with this news. I know how you feel. I felt the same way this morning when the Holy Father explained this horrid situation to me. I might say it fell upon deaf ears at first. Now, my son, since I've given you the bad news first . . . now for some pleasant news. After further conversation with the Holy Father, we discussed the real issue: the church's unofficial stand. Richard, like us, the Holy Father knows Hitler is nothing more than a depraved maniac, a very powerful and deadly maniac. It is hoped one of his mentally ill followers will take care of him. Of course, the Holy Father didn't say that, I did. If that doesn't happen, perhaps when war commences, the German armies will not persevere for long. Richard, you are to write Cardinal Ornotte and relate the church's official position in the matter. Let me be clear: the official position of the church, not your or my position but the Holy Father's position. Do we understand one another?" The Archbishop returned to his desk chair.

"Yes, Your Eminence."

"Richard, you've dealt directly with many of the dioceses across Europe. What would you say has been one of the most disruptive problems you and the church have faced of late?"

He didn't hesitate. "Getting accurate and truthful information on not only the political leaders but also the party's doctrines, enlightening us as to their true objectives. I'm certain, however, Hitler and Stalin are both evil men. Neither one, I suspect, believes in a Supreme Being. The world is on a perilous course driven by madmen. I honestly believe that every religious group of every denomination will have to rise as one in order to turn back this immoral tide on the verge of ravaging not only Europe but also the world. Those are my thoughts on the matter, Your Reverence."

The cardinal smiled. "Well said, Richard. Well said. However, our church is still in a dilemma and, for now, must sit on the sidelines to witness what is yet to unfold. War could break out at any moment and there's nothing our church can do about it. As has been the case since the beginning of time, God makes the final call. You nor I nor the church can second-guess the Almighty. We must, however, as Christians follow the teachings of the Holy Scripture and do what we can to help save the souls of our fellow man. God will do the rest, I assure you. Having said these things, I must get back to the reality of our jobs. The Holy Father has decided that, for now, the church should remain neutral, siding with no country or political party. He feels, as I do, the best way for us to serve our fellow man is to send a ranking official of our church, representing the pontiff himself, to meet with the top political members of Germany, Russia, and Italy, assuring them that the church will remain neutral if there should be armed conflict. Obviously, the reasoning behind all of this is that it allows us to move about freely and offers protection for our church followers from political or physical persecution from any of the warring parties who might become involved. Once again, our church could be the cornerstone for Christianity, gathering vital information for the God-fearing country or countries that will one day stand up to these barbarians, banishing them from the earth. Who knows, Richard, your country, America, might become the salvation for mankind." The archbishop leaned forward, resting his arms on the desk. "Well, what do you think of the Holy Father's plan?"

Richard pondered the question. "I like it. Sadly, I fear many will pay the ultimate price while we are remaining neutral. Yet, I see no other way. Yes, I believe it is the right decision."

The archbishop leaned back in his chair. "I'm delighted you agree, Bishop Carter."

Richard watched, stunned, as Archbishop Beroske picked up a paper lying on his desk. He'd been made a bishop and, apparently, the pontiff's personal emissary.

"I received this note from Cardinal Gerome this morning," the archbishop said, "asking my permission to give you the next three days off from your duties."

"But that's impossible now," Richard replied, "with all we have to do to prepare for our mission."

"I'm still the boss here, young man," Archbishop Beroske exclaimed. "In any case, we've plenty of time for your mission. I thought you might like to see your sister and her family while they're in Rome."

Richard froze. "Lori is here . . . in Rome?"

"She will be here tomorrow. Her wire came this morning."

"Lori . . ." Richard mumbled, a faint smile spreading across his lips.

"Have fun, my son, and don't worry your mind with what is to come. Think only of your family's love."

"Thank you, Your Reverence," Richard muttered as he stood to leave. Richard's mind was in disarray, torn between the wonderful news that he would see Lori and her family and his upcoming journey as ambassador for His Holiness.

Richard spent the better part of the afternoon meditating, his mind still reeling after all he'd heard. As he often did when he felt the need arising, he proceeded to the small chapel where he'd found such peace the day after his arrival to the Holy City. Usually, the chapel was empty or nearly so. Much different from its two bigger rivals only a short distance away. The Sistine Chapel and the magnificent St. Peter's Cathedral were seldom, if ever, without large congregations. Richard, as always, felt like a renewed man leaving the chapel. He would dine and retire to bed early, after what had been a long and turbulent day. Richard's exhausted body slept well that night.

He arose the following morning thoroughly

refreshed. Thoughts of Lori filled his mind on the otherwise dismal spring morning. The light rain had started just before daybreak and continued to fall as Richard stepped from his car in front of the train station. His driver waited as Richard entered the busy terminal, glancing at the large overhead clock. Lori's train was to arrive at 10:20 a.m. He had ten minutes. He took a seat in the center of the terminal. Time passed slowly. He grew more anxious by the moment. It had been nearly eight years since he'd last seen Lori. A lot had happened. Here he was, sitting in the center of Rome, a ranking member of the world's most influential church, about to embark upon a mission that could affect the peace of all mankind. He felt the weight of it on his broad shoulders.

Lori's train arrived on time. He took her, Jeff, and the children to the Hotel Roma, a grand hotel built in the eighteenth century. Little Richard had shot up like a weed, and Lori's baby girl, Kathy, was a precious doll. Lori and Jeff seemed happy. Richard was happy for them, and he savored every joyful, relaxing moment of their few days together.

He waited until the last day to show Lori and Jeff the Vatican. Lori secured a sitter for the children. They were still too young to enjoy the artistry and history that filled the Vatican, as like no other place on earth. Richard escorted them to St. Peter's and the Sistine Chapel, where Michelangelo's priceless painting covered its breathtaking ceiling. The couple was in constant awe of the untold treasures that surrounded them.

The three enjoyed their last supper together in a small restaurant that had become Richard's favorite. Earlier, when Lori had fed the children at the hotel, Richard had said his good-byes and given each a gift.

"Here's to two of the finest people in the world and the greatest sister and brother-in-law a person could possibly have."

Lori beamed as she lifted her wine glass.

"We haven't had much time to talk about Joe. How's he doing at his job?" Richard asked.

Lori cut a glance toward her husband.

Jeff set down his wine glass. "Lori wrote you and told you about Dad making Joe a partner in the business, correct?"

"Yes, and I want to thank you for doing that."

"To the contrary, Richard, I and my father, and Lori of course, want to thank you for putting us on to him. He's done wonders with that business. My father says he's never seen a finer mind for the business world."

Richard agreed. "Yes, Joe has always been a go-getter and not a lazy bone in his body either."

Jeff nodded in agreement and sipped deeply from his wine. Lori looked Jeff's way and frowned.

"Are there any ladies in his life?" Richard asked.

Lori shrugged. "Nothing serious yet, I don't believe. He leaves no time for socializing. But there has been some woman from New York City who's writing him quite regularly. He's never said whom. I've bitten my tongue and haven't asked."

Jeff laughed. "You know how difficult that must be for Lori?"

Richard smiled. "Yes, I can imagine."

"Oh, you two men," Lori fussed. "You know that it doesn't bother me in the least what Joe does."

"Sure," Jeff said, winking at Richard.

106

"I'm beginning to think Joe might end up a bachelor," Richard concluded.

"Oh, I doubt that," Lori said. "There are too many lonely women who'd give their souls for a man like Joe."

Richard laughed. "I hope Joe finds the right girl, but not for the price of her soul."

After dinner, Richard saw them to the hotel. Little was mentioned about the turmoil sweeping Europe. Jeff mentioned casually that Joe had visited Washington D.C. a few times on the possibility of acquiring naval contracts, but Richard didn't press the subject. He was involved enough in the world's problems and wanted to enjoy these few days together with his family. After all, the United States and his family were far away from the mess in Europe. The depression was worry enough for the Americans, never mind what was taking place all the way across the ocean.

Richard saw Lori and the others off. Their European vacation did not last long, and they returned safely to the States.

The following months were chaotic for Richard and Archbishop Beroske. The intricate and highly secretive arrangements required seemed, at times, virtually impossible. Finally, in the middle of June, the complexity of the problem was resolved. Richard was to meet with a high-ranking German official in Munich on July 18 and then with the Russians the following week.

Chapter Nine

Time passed swiftly for Richard and the Polish archbishop. They worked long hours, finalizing their plan as to what and to what degree the church's position would be based, mostly on hypothetical situations. The day arrived for Richard to leave for Munich. Richard and the archbishop waited until the final hour, awaiting word from Berlin as with whom Richard would meet. Word never came, and it was time for his departure.

Richard boarded his train in the late afternoon. Archbishop Beroske had traveled with Richard to the station, briefing him up to the last minute. Richard had never seen His Reverence so nervous. He understood the archbishop's apprehension, as both knew much hindered on the outcome of the upcoming meetings for the Catholic Church and mankind. The journey to Munich was long. Richard paid little attention to the beautiful villages and countryside he passed through on his way to Germany. His mind was filled with more urgent things, growing nearer at hand with every revolution of the great locomotive's wheels. They passed through Austria during the night. Richard woke shortly after daybreak.

The train pulled into the Munich station in the mid-afternoon. It was a gorgeous day. Temperatures hovered in the mid-seventies, quite pleasant for mid-July. Bishop Stein from St. Matthew's Church had a car awaiting Bishop Carver as he exited the terminal. To Richard's surprise, the driver was a young priest from Concord, New Hampshire. Richard and the young priest, who appeared to be in his mid-twenties, had a fine conversation on the way to the rectory. St. Matthew's Church and its rectory were located on the northern edge of the city. Munich was a fun metropolis. Its vibrant youth and rich heritage made it one of Germany's most proud and prestigious cities. Richard helped the young priest carry the heavy luggage into the building that housed Cardinal Stein, who headed the diocese in this part of Germany. Richard was shown to his small but adequate room. He'd communicated with the cardinal for over ten months. Richard felt he knew the man quite well, even though they'd never met in person.

A knock at the door broke his thoughts.

It was the young priest from Concord. "The cardinal will see you in his study at your convenience, Bishop Carver. And welcome to Munich."

"Thank you, Father," Richard replied.

He unpacked a few things before going to meet the cardinal. The young priest had waited outside Richard's room to escort him to the cardinal's study. The cardinal, having heard Richard advancing down the hallway, stood to greet him as Richard entered the room.

"Your Reverence." Richard bent on one knee and kissed Cardinal Stein's ring.

"Welcome to Germany, Bishop Carver."

"Thank you, Your Reverence."

"I feel as if I already know you, my son." The cardinal's dark brown eyes surveyed Richard. "You're even younger than I'd pictured . . . very young indeed to have come so far in the church in such a short time. So young," the elderly cardinal reiterated, nodding his head. "Come sit down and tell me a little about yourself." Cardinal Stein made his way to a cushioned chair that sat next to a large wooden rocker. "Sit down, my boy." The cardinal motioned toward the high-backed rocker.

Richard took a seat next to the cardinal. "A

beautiful city you have here, Your Reverence."

"Thank you, Bishop Carver, but it grows uglier every day." The cardinal's smile slipped away. "You no doubt noticed on your travel through the city the large banners draped from buildings?"

Richard nodded, having seen the banners with their swastikas that appeared to be draped on every building, along with German phrases that praised Adolph Hitler. Richard looked hard at the seventy-three-year-old German who sat across from him. His face showed the same telltale signs as that of Archbishop Beroske. Yes, the price of worry and skepticisms of what lay ahead were deeply etched into this kind old man's face.

"You come here on some sort of secret mission, I suspect?"

Richard realized it would be foolish to try to deceive this wise old man. He'd seen too much in his life to try to fool him now. "Let's just say it's a rather important meeting that I must attend."

"I see. Well, I'm sure it's for the betterment of the church and our people, whatever the reason for which you've come. I know that if my longtime friend Archbishop Beroske has a hand in it, then it must be good. He's one of the last from our old school who still stands for what he believes and the hell with those who disapprove."

Richard stared at the red-faced German cardinal who reminded him of the fiery Polish archbishop, although their physical features were in no way similar. Cardinal Stein was a fine example of German manhood: strong willed and resolute.

"God help my country and Archbishop Beroske's country and all of the countries of Europe. My people, the

German people, are worshiping a false God—a God so evil that I fear for all of mankind as long as he lives." Tears welled in the cardinal's eyes. "He's wicked and insane, and my people have no better sense than to follow a crazy man like this. I've failed them. Our church has failed."

Richard watched intently as the cardinal slowly rose from his chair. "We men of God have failed our people. If we cannot teach them what is right and what is wrong, then what good are we? My congregations have left our church in droves. Do you know where they attend church now, Bishop Carver?" The cardinal towered over Richard. "They attend church at Nazi rallies. Their God wears a mustache and a swastika on his arm. My people . . . yes, the German people, who are supposedly intelligent and not aborigines in some jungle, for heaven's sake. At least if my people were ignorant, it would help ease my burden and guilt." Cardinal Stein leaned over, his face inches from Richard's. "If you, have it in your power, Bishop, destroy this beast, Hitler. Kill him with your bare hands if you can. If he is not destroyed soon, it will be too late. I fear he may be the Anti-Christ." The cardinal returned to his seat.

Richard shivered with the cardinal's warning. A Catholic cardinal had asked him to take a man's life, a mortal sin of the worst kind. Was Hitler the prophesized Anti-Christ, the one to bring the Christian world to the verge of collapse? Richard asked his God if this could be true. He studied the silent cardinal. Neither spoke. The redness had disappeared from the cardinal's face, his eyes mellowing into a stale darkness. Richard was lost for words.

Finally, the cardinal said, "Your mastery of the German language is quite phenomenal. I had even forgotten you are an American."

"Thank you, Your Reverence. I'm glad to have this opportunity to practice. I'm afraid of my skills going stale."

The cardinal smiled. "A man that speaks German as well as you needn't worry."

Over the course of the evening, the elderly cardinal briefed Richard on Germany's many problems and a multitude of concerns the church, indeed the world, necessarily faced in the not-so-distant future. Richard absorbed the cardinal's knowledge like a dry sponge. The men talked well into the night. It was after 2:00 a.m. before Richard fell asleep in his quarters.

The men continued their conversation in the cardinal's study the following morning. The cardinal was alone. Though they spent the morning discussing certain of the church's current troubles, Germany was not mentioned by name. After lunch with the cardinal, Richard retired to his room, spending the afternoon reviewing the vast array of notes he'd brought with him on his journey. It was 4:15 p.m. when the young American priest knocked on his door. It was nearing time for Richard to leave. The American would drive Richard to his meeting. At 5:15, Richard exited the rectory. Rain had fallen steadily all afternoon and showed no signs of slowing. He pulled his hat down low and dashed toward his awaiting car.

"I thought it only rained like this in Louisiana," Richard said, sliding into the front seat and slamming the door shut. The American bishop laughed. "I know there's no need in asking you if you know where we're going."

The young priest smiled. "Bishop Carver, I wish I knew the alphabet as well. You don't want to know how many times the cardinal has had me make this practice run the last three days."

Richard laughed. "I thought as much."

The long black automobile made its way through the heart of the city. He had never visited Munich. His eyes were on the beautiful buildings that lined both sides of the vibrant city. The heavy rain didn't damper the vast number of people leaving work on the dreary Friday afternoon. Richard's eyes were also on the large colored banners hanging from many of the buildings. The black swastika appeared wicked to Richard. Although his eyes had been fixed on the sights of Munich as the car made its way to its destination, his mind had not. His full attention was on but one thing: the person or persons he was to meet. The larger buildings became scarcer as Richard's car made its way from the city's core, where the beautiful office and government buildings morphed into ugly, rundown tenements. The heavy clouds brought an early darkness.

"Your Reverence, the Shultz Theatre is just around the block."

Richard beheld the harsh surroundings. Trash cans and overflowing garbage littered the sidewalks and streets. Graffiti covered the neglected shops and apartments. Anti-Semitism was certainly an issue in this part of the city. Richard read some of the slogans as the car moved slowly down the street; Down with the Jews, one sign read. Kill the Jewish Swine, read another.

"Here we are, Bishop Carver—the Shultz Theatre." The priest stopped the car in front of the dilapidated playhouse.

Richard stared out the window at the ruinous structure. "Doesn't look as if they're going to have a show tonight, does it, Father?"

The American smiled as he peered at the crumbling stone building, its double doors coated in red paint and anti-Semitic slogans. "A Jewish family once owned this theatre when it was one of the finest in Germany. As you can see, Jews have suddenly become very unpopular in Germany."

Richard watched a hungry dog scavenging for food. Within minutes, a black limousine pulled behind their car. Richard and the American watched in silence as two men dressed in dark trench coats and black visor hats exited the limo. The two men carefully surveyed the area. Apparently satisfied they were alone, except for Richard and the American priest, one of the men opened the back door to the limousine. He observed in the mirror as the third man exited the limousine, dressed in the same attire as his fellows. The driver of the limousine stayed in the car. The three men headed toward the theatre, passing Richard's car without glancing their way. At the theatre's entrance, one of the men unlocked the door and the three entered.

"That must be the other party," Richard said.

The American priest looked troubled. "So, it seems."

Richard reached for his briefcase and opened the car door. "Wish me luck."

"God go with you, Bishop Carver."

"Thank you, Father Hoover. I fear I'll need all the help I can get." Richard exited the car.

The rain came down in a light shower and darkness blanketed the deserted street as Richard attempted to open the theatre's doors. Locked. He knocked heavily on the solid doors, pulling his topcoat tightly around his neck. The drizzle turned to a downpour. Richard moved to knock again when a door cracked open. He stared at the man who stood in the darkness of the doorway. "I'm Bishop Carver. I have an appointment," he said in German. The man squinted at him, his face stone cold.

"Come in," the man commanded. The man stood aside to let Richard pass. Dimly lit wall lights lined the small, musty lobby. Richard glimpsed a large rat scurrying beneath a stack of old chairs. His eyes returned to the cold figure who'd let him in. He'd little trouble telling the man was German, dressed in his military uniform and holding a pistol in his right hand.

The soldier ordered, "Follow me, Bishop Carver."

Many rows of wooden seats lined both sides the main theatre's center aisle. Like the lobby, dim lights ran the length of both walls. Richard followed the solider down the center aisle, to where a lone figure sat in the front row. A second soldier stood next to the exit door, brandishing a rifle. Richard kept his gaze on the man who sat alone down front. He smiled wide as Richard approached.

"Good evening, Bishop Carver. My name is Hermann Goering, personal representative of the führer, who sends his regrets for not being able to be here himself. He was unavoidably detained in Berlin. I'm sure you realize that he is a very busy man these days."

Richard considered the smiling German officer. "I've heard of you. You were quite a hero in the first World War, weren't you?"

"Oh, I was lucky enough to shoot down a few of the enemy planes."

Richard knew that Field Marshal Goering was more than just lucky, having proven himself an expert pilot. Currently, he was the second most influential man in

Germany and, perhaps, one of the wealthiest. Goering was a striking figure, dressed in his German uniform, a large man with a pleasant face and striking blue eyes. His image mirrored a man of great courage and strong conviction. The man with whom Richard was presently standing face-to-face was no maniac or fool, unlike Hitler. This knowledge troubled Richard.

"Please, Bishop Carver, sit."

Richard took his seat next to the cordial general. The soldier who'd led Richard down the aisle had left and stood guard at the front entrance to the theatre. "So, you're from America, Father. From the state of Louisiana?"

The general knew he was from the South. What else did he know about him?

"I'm confident you know much about me, and that is as it should be. Please, Richard, I bet you can tell me the last time I enjoyed the sexual pleasures of a woman—and probably her name." The general's grin returned.

"I'll give you this much, General, she was a pretty woman."

Field Marshal Goering's eyes widened slightly, then he tipped back his head and laughed. "I like you, Bishop. I see why they chose you for this kind of work." The laughter faded, and a mood of seriousness swept through the theatre. "Just what is it the leaders of your church wish of us?"

"We wish to know what your party's intentions are and what role it will pursue with the German people and its European neighbors."

"Bishop Carver, our führer and his German followers have no qualms with the Catholic Church . . . any church for that matter. We understand the church's concern

116

in this matter. There have been many lies written about our party. My führer wishes only to help his people out of the serious poverty brought on by greedy capitalists on one side and Communist idiots on the other. Surely, you know the Communists position on religion?"

Richard nodded.

"Atheist dogs!" the general spat. "All our people want is to have what is rightfully theirs. Some of these things are openly disputed by other countries. We are willing to negotiate a fair compromise in these areas."

Richard understood the general's reference. Germany wanted Poland badly, as well as Czechoslovakia and Finland, as these countries possessed large areas of farmland. Poland had many important factories. Germany needed room for Hitler's obsession on German domination. If Germany was to come out of its severe economic problems, Hitler would have to find jobs for the hundreds of thousands of unemployed Germans. If he didn't accomplish this quickly, the people would soon turn on his party, as he had against the previous one. It appeared building war machines was Hitler's answer, accomplishing two feats at once: putting his people back to work and enlarging the German empire to include all of Europe.

"The führer has no quarrel with the Catholic Church," Goering continued. "He understands the church's power over its followers, especially here in Bavaria. The führer told me to tell you personally that you have his word; there will be no action taken against your church whatsoever in Germany or anyplace else our people might be."

Richard noticed a twinkle in the general's eyes with his last caveat: *or wherever our people might be.*

117

"All the führer asks in return is that the leaders of your church take no official public stand against him or our party. For that simple gesture, we promise to keep hands off the Catholic Church."

"What about other Christians? What about the Jews? Will you interfere with them?"

Once again, Richard had succeeded in wiping the smirk from the German's face. "We must deal with them on an individual basis, such as we are doing here with you. I see no problem with being fair with the others, except maybe the Jews."

Richard's eyes had little trouble seeing behind the general's German mask, to the Nazi underneath. "You seem confident that the Holy Father will agree to this compromise your führer offers. Please don't deceive yourself into believing this has been accomplished by this meeting. I'm only a spokesman for my church . . . the Holy Father has the final say in this matter. I can promise, however, if Hitler or your armies show hostilities toward any sect of people, be it for religious or ethnic reasons, no matter what agreement made today between your leaders and mine, all will be wiped out with first drop of innocent blood spilled. I do have the authority of the Holy Father to assure that if you and your party agree to certain conditions today, you have the verbal word of the Holy Father that the Catholic Church will in no way interfere in your country's politics. The pontiff will send out an order to all clergy of the universal churches to refrain from any position on the political affairs of the Nazi party. This, the Holy Father promises, but only on certain conditions."

"Name them," the smiling general said.

"The Nazi party promises not to interfere in any of

the church's business. The Catholic Church will be off limits to any interference from your political party."

"Agreed."

"Also, the promise that your government does not harm any individual simply because of his religious or ethnic beliefs." Richard watched as the general's face soured.

A few quiet moments passed before the general said, "Agreed."

"That is all that the Holy Father asked." A surprised smile reappeared on the general's lips. Richard wiped it away with his last words. "General, if these simple steps are followed, you will have no problem with my church."

"Good."

"However, if in any way or form these promises are broken, the power of the church will come down upon you and your party with all the peaceful force it can muster. Let me remind you of this fact. Many governments have risen and fallen over the past centuries, along with their followers and leaders. One has only to look at the Roman Empire, one of the greatest powers the world has ever known. Like the sands in the desert, the dunes build mightily and then blow away. Yes, the Roman Empire no longer stands, but the founding church of Jesus Christ remains. The Catholic Church lives on in Vatican City, which was once the heart of the mighty Roman armies. The Holy Father still rules and our followers' number in the millions. As God is my witness, if your party or Adolph Hitler violates these two simple requests the Holy Father has made, God forbid, my church will come at you with all its force. The mighty wind will come and blow you and your followers away—just like the dunes in the desert. This

I can promise. Don't ever underestimate the faith of man, General. Napoleon did. Consider what happened to him."

The general sat back in the theatre seat, seemingly dumbfounded, his mask of cordiality ripped from his face by the American priest. The bishop was no old, feeble cardinal, sent by an ineffectual pope. Richard thought he glimpsed humility flash across the general's face, a fleeting glimpse. He wondered how long this temporary peace treaty would last.

Chapter Ten

Richard returned to St. Matthew's in Munich. After a night in Munich, he left for Vienna and a brief meeting with Cardinal Solovh, the next day flying to Warsaw and a meeting with Cardinal Sarkoski. For a while, Richard had been communicating with the Polish cardinal weekly. The cardinal had been a crucial source of information as to what was taking place in this strategic country bordered by Germany to one side and Communist Russia to the other.

Poland was a vital piece of real state for both the Soviet Union and Germany if they were to increase their borders, which, by this time, Germany was leaving little doubt it intended to do. The big question throughout Europe was *when*. Richard hoped to answer this question on his current trip; the meeting with the Germans had not. He tended to believe that even the rulers of the Nazi party, especially Hitler, weren't sure when, precisely, this would occur. It seemed a case of wait-and-see, waiting for the right moment to seize the opportunity. One thing of which

Richard was certain upon leaving the Polish capital and Cardinal Sarkoski was that the Catholic hierarchy in Poland was certain Germany would invade Poland. The big question, once again, was *when*.

Richard left Warsaw and flew to Moscow, meeting with the commissar of foreign affairs, an intellectual Jew, and a remarkable man for the job. The commissar expressed his concern for the Nazis, fully aware of the rumors leaking out of Germany about their inhumane treatment of his people. His fear seemed to be more concentrated on what the Germans would do with Europe's Jewish people than on the fate of the Soviet Union. Richard left Moscow with a somewhat better feeling than the one he'd experienced in Munich with the Germans. The Soviets had also agreed to the same demands exhorted by the Catholic Church for peaceful coexistence to which the Germans had consented. He felt that the possibility of these demands being upheld by the Soviets was better than that of the Germans.

Richard perceived that the new Soviet regime, threatened by the mobilizing German Army, was unprepared for a major war with the Germans. The Soviets were deeply concerned that if Germany invaded Poland and was victorious, it would place the aggressive German Army on the border with Russia. Richard knew it was this fear, and this fear alone, that made the Soviet leaders willing to cooperate with the Catholic Church, fully realizing the power the Vatican held over the Catholic state of Poland. If Poland were to fall to the Germans, all bets would be off as to the Soviets' further cooperation with the church. Richard knew the Soviets hadn't accepted this agreement with the Vatican because of their love for the church or God. To the contrary, they didn't believe in either one.

Richard returned to Rome. He, along with Archbishop Beroske and, at times, the Holy Father, reviewed what had occurred at the meetings. The archbishop and the Holy Father were thrilled with what the young American Bishop had accomplished.

Richard spent the rest of 1936 traveling extensively throughout the countries of Europe. His art of diplomacy mushroomed during these months of increasing turmoil throughout the European theatre. Richard received bimonthly letters from Lori during the following year. She'd read the newspapers about the increasing dangers spreading through Europe and was deeply concerned for Richard's well-being. Unknown to her, she'd no idea just how deeply involved her beloved brother was in certain stories of which she, and the rest of America, had begun to take serious notice.

The war clouds gathering throughout Europe were all but ready to burst. Thunder, in the shape and sound of war wagons, had rolled into Austria. The invasion of German troops and equipment had been a quiet one with neither side firing a shot. Many of the Austrians were German speaking, welcoming the German Army into their country. Czechoslovakia would also yield to the Germans in the coming months. During this time of German expansion, the French and English were thrown into near panic, ill-equipped to take on the Germans. Great Britain saw the handwriting on the wall. Poland must take a stand against the Germans. Prime Minister Chamberlain, against the wishes of Great Britain's military advisors, signed a guarantee with Poland to render whatever kind of aid necessary to rebuff any German offensive Hitler might throw at the Polish state. This treaty between Britain and Poland had started World War Two. Richard learned that Hitler, upon discovering this agreement, flew into a rage, swearing to make the two countries pay dearly for the pact and making plans for the Polish invasion.

Richard studied the rapid turn of events with cautious skepticism. He and Archbishop Beroske understood the dilemmas facing most of the countries of Europe, especially those bordering Germany and her newfound territories. England and France had backed themselves into a corner, having supported the German takeover of Austria and Czechoslovakia in hopes of appeasing Hitler.

The first part of 1939 was quiet of any major events. It seemed Hitler was at a stalemate with Russia and held the key as to what would transpire next. In early May of that year, Richard, and Archbishop Beroske witnessed the key fall. Stalin had replaced Litvinov, the Jewish commissar with Molotov, one of Stalin's most trusted comrades. Richard and the cardinal saw this as an open invitation for the Germans to approach the Soviets to form some type of peace treaty between the two countries. Molotov was not a Jew and had already displayed bad overtures toward the British and French. Hitler liked this move. It showed that the Soviets didn't want to enter an armed conflict with Germany. If Stalin had only known that he had stymied Hitler's aggression for the past few months, he could've probably hammered out a much better agreement with the Germans than the one for which he settled.

On August 23, 1939, a top official from Germany landed in Moscow. A meeting was scheduled with Stalin and Molotov. The following day, it was announced that the Russians and Germans had signed a mutual non-aggression pact. A clap of thunder rolled through the European countryside with the news. The storm clouds were about to burst. Richard and Archbishop Beroske weren't surprised by the happenings, having speculated something similar would occur months before. But, again, the big question of *when*. When would Germany invade Catholic Poland? Since the signing of the pact, Richard had been in almost constant contact with Cardinal Sarkoski in Warsaw. The cardinal had reported a huge military buildup of the Polish army along the German border. Richard had been at his desk all morning when Father Stalleto, Richard's private secretary for the past three months, entered the room.

The young Italian priest carried a telegram. "It's for you, Bishop," the Italian said, handing the sealed envelope to Richard. The word *Urgent* was printed in large black letters across the front. The Italian priest stood next to the desk peering at Richard as he opened the gram and read it silently.

"Inform Archbishop Beroske I wish to see him immediately," Richard said, never looking up from the paper.

"Yes, Bishop." The priest exited quickly.

He returned in short order. "His Reverence will see you now."

"What have you that is so urgent?" the archbishop asked as Richard crossed to the archbishop's desk.

"I just received this telegram from Berlin, Your Reverence. I believe you should read it yourself."

Richard handed the archbishop the telegram, then took a seat across the desk. He watched the wise, old archbishop's eyes as they slowly scanned the German letter. The archbishop could speak very little German, but he could read and write it like a German scholar. The archbishop looked up from the paper, removing his reading spectacles. "What do you make of this?"

Richard paused, then said, "I'm not certain, Your Reverence. As you can read for yourself, the letter is very vague as to what this is all about."

Archbishop Beroske grunted as he glanced back at the short message. "I would say very vague." The archbishop read from the note. "'Meet me at our last place of encounter. Eight o'clock on the night of August 25th.' Signed 'Lucky.' I don't remember you mentioning anyone by the name of Lucky when you were in Munich."

Richard smiled. "I've never met anyone by that name, Your Reverence, but I have a hunch as to whom Lucky might refer."

The archbishop leaned closer. "The suspense is killing me."

"Hermann Goering."

"Goering," the archbishop repeated. "And what's so lucky about that German swine?"

"I happened to mention something about his war deeds during the First World War, and he called himself lucky."

"I see," the archbishop said, slowly leaning back in his chair. "And what do you suppose Lucky wants with you, Richard?"

Richard thought briefly. "Your Reverence, I truly don't have the faintest idea. I'm as baffled by this as you are. I would think that a man of his military importance would be in Berlin planning the invasion of Poland."

The archbishop examined the paper again. "You must go immediately. I, like you, have no idea as to what this could refer. I am, however, certain this important German figure wouldn't be asking to meet you in Munich to hear his last confession."

Richard laughed.

***

Richard made the arrangements, leaving on a private plane that night and arriving in Munich the following morning. The young American priest, Father Hoover was waiting for him at the airport. Unlike his previous visit, the weather was clear and warm. Richard saw no signs of troop movements or any soldiers for that matter. Father Hoover told Richard a large, armored convoy had moved through the city the night before and appeared to be heading toward the Polish border. Cardinal Stein would later confirm this, along with other needed information pertaining to the German Army. Richard would carefully document these military happenings. He'd sworn not to use them against Germany up to this time, but, if and when, the first German shot was fired at a Pole, then the oath would be terminated; at that point, Germany would unofficially become an enemy of the church.

Richard arrived at St. Matthew's. He had lunch with Cardinal Stein and then settled in for a long meeting in the cardinal's study. Cardinal Stein updated him on the latest German military movements and the latest political happenings taking place within the Nazi Party. Richard learned there had been much military activity in last few days, most of which under the cover of darkness. The cardinal also felt that Poland would be invaded at any moment. Richard, of course, hadn't told the cardinal why he'd come. For certain, Richard wasn't sure himself.

The two men enjoyed an early dinner, after which Richard retired to his room. Shortly, the American priest informed him it was time to leave for the theatre. It was late in the afternoon when Richard walked out the rectory door. It was a beautiful Bavarian night.

"Much better weather than your last trip," Father Hoover said, holding open the car door.

Richard smiled. "It's truly a beautiful night, Father." Richard took his seat in the car. Within moments, the twosome was on its way.

"I see you forgot your collar again," the smiling priest said.

"Yes, I did."

The car moved at a moderate pace through the core of the city. People strolled leisurely about on this perfect August night. Richard caught Father Hoover watching him from the corner of his eye. "War is close at hand, isn't it, Bishop Carver?" Richard turned, momentarily startled by the young priest's unexpected question. "War is on our doorsteps, isn't it?"

Richard considered the question briefly, then stared back out the window at the fading city. "Yes, Father, I'm afraid so. It appears man hasn't learned his lesson about war. Why would anyone in their right mind want to foul God's clean air with deadly smoke spewing from the barrels of man's weapons? Heavens, how much tragedy awaits mankind?"

The young priest spoke matter of fact. "You're a man deeply involved in all of this, aren't you, Bishop Carver?"

"I'm nothing more than a man trying to do God's

127

will. It is very disheartening to deal with such powerful men who seem to have no mortal soul."

Father Hoover said nothing else to Bishop Carver, as there was no need; the Bishop had said it all.

The black limousine pulled up next to the theatre. This time, the two priests were not the first to arrive. The auto they'd seen the last time was parked in front. Father Hoover stopped the car a few feet behind the first vehicle. As before, the street was dark and deserted.

A German soldier stood guard next to the automobile, staring at the black limousine. Richard nodded toward the armed soldier. "Well, it looks like we're either real safe or real dead, wouldn't you say, Father?"

"I pray it isn't the latter," Father Hoover whispered, his eyes fixed on the soldier.

"I'll be as quick as possible." Richard exited the limousine.

He felt the steady watch of the soldier as he walked toward the theatre. This time, the door opened. Richard entered the theatre, where another soldier stood guard by the swinging doors leading to the main theatre. "I'm Bishop Carver," Richard said to the guard.

"Follow me," the stern-faced soldier said.

Richard followed the solider through the swinging doors and down the aisle to where the familiar figure sat alone. "So we meet again, Bishop Carver. Please sit." Goering's smile seemed more sincere than their initial encounter.

Richard sat beside the general. The guard had returned to the front of the theatre. "You're much too handsome to be a Catholic, Bishop. I'm sure the women are envious of God."

The general's words spiraled violently in Richard's mind as images of Elisabeth invaded his thoughts. He believed he'd prayed her out of his life, but like a bolt of lightning, her face illuminated his mind.

"Are you all right, Bishop Carver?" the general asked the second time.

"Yes, General, I'm fine."

"Good, you looked pale for a moment. I imagine, Bishop Carver, you've been wondering why I requested to meet with you again in this deserted theatre."

"You might say the thought has crossed my mind."

Goering laughed as Richard's smile faded from his lips. A seriousness formed on Goering's face as he suddenly stood, shouting at the two frightened soldiers. "Leave the two of us alone. Stay in the front lobby!"

Richard tensed, shocked at the general's sudden outburst. The two young German soldiers scurried toward the lobby. The General stood until the men disappeared behind the swinging doors. The red rage coloring Goering's face drained away as his eyes fixed on Richard. A weak smile appeared upon the marshal's face as he sat back down. "If one is to be a leader of men, he must have their respect." The general took a short breath. "Now, for the reason that I've asked you here. Perhaps you will not think of me as a complete barbarian after what I have to tell you. Remember the deal we made, Bishop, at out last meeting?"

"I do, General, and the church and I have kept our word."

"That you have, Bishop Carver. I much admire a man of his word. What a pity that a man such as you couldn't have been born a German. On second thought, though, perhaps it is for the best. You might have my job if you were a German."

"I doubt that."

Goering chuckled. "Well, in any case, can I still depend on your secrecy if I were to give you some important information?"

"You can, if nothing is done to force me to rescind my word."

Richard felt the general's warm breath on his face as he leaned toward him.

"This information that I'm about to give to you, use it as you wish within the church—but you must promise me it is to go no further," Goering said. "By that I mean to any parties who are enemies of Germany or the führer. Will you agree to this?"

Richard looked hard into the general's eyes. "You have my solemn word."

The general smiled. "That's good enough for me, young bishop. Are you aware of the treaty my country has just signed with the Russians?"

Richard nodded.

"The Polish issue has been settled," the general continued. "In time, the Soviets may have eastern Poland. Germany will have the west."

"Will Poland have anything to say about this deal?"

"Bishop, they don't even know they have been divided up yet."

Richard wasn't amused by the general's quip and his eyes showed it.

"Bishop Carver, I don't make the rules. As a general, I only enforce them. If it were up to me, I would invade Russia tomorrow. I hate the Communist bastards. But I don't make the rules. Bishop Carver, Poland will be invaded on the first day of September. The exact time has yet to be settled."

Could this be so . . . that a Nazi general was sitting here telling a Catholic priest one of the most secretive and vital pieces of information an outsider could possibly know? Richard peered at the general for the longest time. "Why would you tell me something of this great magnitude? You're speaking of war, General. Why would you tell me this?"

The field marshal stared hard, unblinking; the smile erased from his lips. "I speak to you now as a mortal man, Bishop, and not a military general. Perhaps history will make me out a barbarian, a tyrant. Or, perhaps, even a hero. These things only your God knows. Your face tells me you're surprised that I speak of God. Perhaps I speak to God more often than you would imagine. Remember this, Bishop, whatever history will have to say about me, I'm not a tyrant but simply a servant in the German Army fighting for his fatherland. Perhaps our people will rule the world one day as the führer says. Perhaps not. These things are of little importance to me. What is important is that I perform my duty to my country. But remember, Bishop, I will personally take no part in treachery. I'm a warrior, not a butcher. You asked why I tell you these things. Perhaps the great Marshal Goering is nothing more than a scared human being, masqueraded by this uniform. Perhaps I'm bartering with your God for my soul. I hope this information will benefit you in some way, Bishop Carver. If by chance it should get out that I've told you these things, you know what will become of me."

"I know," Richard said. "Don't worry yourself about that, General."

"I won't, Bishop Carver." The field marshal stood. "Well, I had better be going. You're a fine man. The Catholic Church is lucky to have a man like you on its side."

"I'm on God's side, Field Marshal Goering."

"Yes, Bishop Carver, you're definitely on God's side. I must be going. Perhaps destiny will have us meet again. I only hope it will be on a friendlier basis."

"It will always be on friendly basis as far as I'm concerned."

"Good-bye, Bishop Carver."

"Good-bye, General. I will pray for your soul."

The general turned. "Pray for yours also, Bishop. I feel your God will test you many times before your life is over—many times." The general proceeded toward the swinging doors.

***

Richard was silent on the drive back to St. Matthew's. It was well after 11:00 p.m. when they arrived at the parish. He went straight to his room; his body was tired, but his mind spun. What should he do first? Awaken the cardinal and tell him of his meeting with Field Marshal Goering? That he couldn't do. He'd given his word to the general. The German cardinal might not be trusted. But of course, he could, he reminded himself. After all, he'd wanted Richard to kill Hitler. Still, this was something much too big to chance. These were but a few questions that ran through Richard's mind as he attempted to sleep. On this night, however, sleep would be hard to come by. His thoughts turned to the little chapel in Vatican City, where he felt closer to his God than in any other place. If he were there now, he would know what to do.

It had been a long night. Richard thought the light of day would never come. He spent an hour in solemn prayer at St. Matthew's awaiting a divine direction, but none came. Before daylight, he'd awakened Father Hoover to make arrangements for a private flight back to Rome. Richard's plane was to leave at 10:00 a.m. It had been a quiet breakfast that morning. Cardinal Stein hadn't asked Richard any questions about his meeting the night before. He said his farewells to the cardinal. Father Hoover drove Richard to the airport. He liked the young priest and felt sad knowing the atrocity in which he'd soon be caught. A heavy, unexpected downpour delayed Richard's flight.

It turned out to be a beautiful flight to Rome. Richard dozed for a while in flight and felt rested by the time they landed in Rome. He hadn't had time to notify Archbishop Beroske of his early return and caught a cab from the airport to the Vatican. It was after 9:00 p.m. by the time he reached his quarters. This was already August 26. September 1 was close at hand. This lack of time played heavily on Richard. It seemed to him that time was one of his greatest enemies.

Richard's thoughts were on but one thing as he threw his suitcase on top of his bed and hurried out his room. It was raining hard when Richard dashed from the rectory building toward the small chapel. He hadn't bothered to wear his overcoat or top hat and was dripping wet when he entered the chapel. In his left hand, he clutched a bronze rosary Lori had given him two Christmases ago. He always brought it with him when he came here alone, as was the case tonight. The dimly lit chapel was empty. Flickering flames of sacrificial candles danced on the chapel's stone walls as Richard made his way to the altar and the silver chalice resting on its bed of white silk. Richard knelt at the altar and began to pray. This was a special prayer that his friend Bishop O'Toole had taught him, a prayer Bishop O'Toole had learned from his mother while the bishop was still a child in his native Ireland.

As far as Richard knew, Bishop O'Toole and he were the only two in the world that knew the special prayer. Perhaps to others the prayer would not be special, but to Richard it was a great gift. He finished reciting the imploration and began to say the rosary, his eyes fixed on the small altar as his fingers worked the rosary's beads. His large fingers had tarnished the small bronze beads over the last two years, affording evidence of their heavy use.

He was a halfway through the rosary when he suddenly stopped and took note of the large crucifix hanging on the wall behind the altar. Richard's dark eyes radiated in ecstasy and his turbulent mind rested. Was this one of those times that his God was actually speaking to him, or was it just his mind playing tricks? One thing was certain, whatever it was, it was very effective.

Richard finished his prayers and walked out the chapel a much different man than the one who'd entered. He knew what he had to do and wasted little time doing it.

"Yes . . . yes, I'm coming," Archbishop Beroske muttered, slipping on his housecoat as he made his way to the door. "What is it that is so important one must wake a man this time of the night . . . and an archbishop at that?" Archbishop Beroske struggled with the door lock. "Richard, is that you?"

"Yes, Your Reverence, it's me. May I come in?"

"Sure, come in my young friend. What time is it?"

the archbishop asked as he made his way to his soft cushioned chair. "Sit down, my son." The archbishop pointed to the empty chair. "I didn't expect you back from Munich this quickly. Perhaps you didn't expect to be back this quickly either, Richard? By your expression, I see the meeting was more than just a confessional, is this not so?"

Richard leaned closer in his chair. "I have some grave news, Your Reverence."

"That's obvious. I've seen this look before. It's the look of war."

Richard peered at the archbishop. "Yes, Your Reverence."

"And somehow you know when it is to begin?"

"Yes, Your Reverence—the very day it is to begin."

Archbishop Beroske slowly leaned back into his chair. "I feel that somehow there is something more to this story than you knowing when the war is to begin, correct?"

Richard hesitated and then answered, "Yes, Your Reverence, there is."

"I thought so. There's a price you must pay for such important information."

"Yes, Your Reverence, and a very heavy price."

"I see, and you come to me for an answer to your dilemma?"

"To you and the Holy Father, Your Reverence."

"You wish to have council with the Holy Father?"

"Yes, Your Reverence. Tonight, if possible."

"Tonight! My, I believe you're brasher than I was at your age. Not only do you want to have council with the pope, but right now besides."

"I wouldn't ask if I felt it wasn't extremely important."

Archbishop Beroske stared at Richard for a few moments. His stern face began to wane into a kind smile. "I'm certain you wouldn't, my son. Go to your room and wait to hear from me. The Holy Father has been sleeping too much anyhow."

"Thank you, Your Reverence."

"Don't thank me yet. I just hope what you have to tell him is important enough to arouse him this time of the night. Because if it isn't, you and I might find ourselves being field missionaries in Timbuktu."

"I'm confident that won't be the case, Your Reverence."

"Well, I'm glad you are. I know some of these people around here would be more than willing to vote for my transfer."

Richard returned to his room and waited word from Archbishop Beroske. He wouldn't have to wait long. Not quite an hour had passed when the archbishop sent word to meet him in front of the building. He was waiting for Richard when he arrived outside the building. The rain had ceased, and stars were beginning to break through in the eastern sky.

Richard and the archbishop walked together to the Sistine Chapel where the pontiff was awaiting the two men. They entered the back of the chapel and headed to a large meeting room usually used by the pontiff or cardinals for private business, such as was the case tonight. Even though Richard had been in the pope's company a number of times, he remained somewhat apprehensive, especially about tonight's meeting. Two Vatican guards stood on either side the doorway. The archbishop introduced Richard and himself to the guards, asking for permission to meet with the Holy Father. The guard entered the room and returned within moments, stating the pontiff would see them.

One could feel the presence of history as they entered the ancient chamber. Richard and the archbishop were no different, though they'd been in the room many times before. Large wooden chairs lined both sides the room, used by the church cardinals on special occasions, such as the voting for a new pope. At the end of the long room sat another wooden chair, draped with an overhead canopy. This was the pontiff's chair and where the Holy Father now sat.

Archbishop Beroske was the first to approach the Holy Father. He made his way up the two steps, knelt before the Holy Father, and kissed the pontiff's ring. Richard followed the same ritual. The pope was an imposing figure sitting in the large wooden chair, wrapped only in a white robe. It was a feeling of great excitation whenever Richard stood before the Holy Father in this sacred room.

The two priests stood silently side-by-side before the Holy Father.

"Please be seated my children," the pope said. He was Italian but spoke in Polish, for benefit of the archbishop.

Richard and Archbishop Beroske took their seats beside one another, looking up at the smiling pope.

"So, it seems we have some sort of important information from Munich. Is that so, Bishop Carver?"

Richard glanced quickly at his friend the archbishop, then back at the pontiff. "Holy Father, while in Munich I met with a high-ranking German officer—"

Richard paused, glancing at Archbishop Beroske for reassurance.

"Go ahead, Richard," the archbishop urged.

Richard continued, "The general told me when the invasion of Poland would begin."

The pontiff glanced at the archbishop, then at Richard. "Isn't this a little unusual for a general to tell the potential enemy when he's going to attack before it occurs?"

Richard paused. "Holy Father, he doesn't recognize us as the enemy."

"But surely, Bishop Carver, he knows the moment his army crosses the Polish border that the church will rescind its neutral position and immediately become an enemy of the church."

Richard considered the archbishop. His expression was the same as that of the Holy Father's, one of confusion. He was aware of the believability of the story. He too, at first, could not understand why Goering would go out of his way to notify the church of an oncoming battle, especially one that would go directly against the church. Yet, without doubt, Richard knew Field Marshal Goering was telling the truth. He also thought he knew why. The general thought that by doing this the act would save his soul. Richard knew this, but he would never try to explain this to the archbishop or the Holy Father. He couldn't explain such a thing if he wanted. It was as if Field Marshal Goering had given Richard his last confession, and his penance for doing what he was set to do was to confess to Richard the grievous sins to which he'd committed.

"Holy Father, I know the general was telling the truth, no matter how bizarre it must sound."

The pontiff narrowed his eyes. "Apparently there's something else to this story, Bishop Carver, I haven't heard. You haven't come forth with the specific day and time of this invasion."

"Holy Father, the general asked that I give my word not to notify Germany's enemies as to the day of the assault. The church may use this information, however, to alert our churches inside Poland of the oncoming conflict."

"I see," the pontiff said. "It's obvious that you gave your word, Bishop Carver, because my ears still haven't heard the date of this coming invasion. It's obvious that you gave your own word on the secrecy of this information knowing that you couldn't swear the church to such secrecy without confiding with me first." The pontiff cut his gaze to Archbishop Beroske.

"That's the problem, Holy Father. I've sworn to secrecy as a priest. Only if the church were to take the same oath would I be unbound to tell this information that is crucial for the security of the church. Hitler knows once they invade Poland the church will become his enemy. The cloak of protection that we bargained for in the previous months will no longer exist. Hitler's irrationality could spell peril for all religions inside Poland and, of course, the Catholic Church."

The pontiff leaned back in his chair, peered intently at Richard. "Bishop Carver, knowing the great importance of this information to the church and the people of Poland, if neither I nor the archbishop agrees to give our word on the secrecy to this information, would you come forth with this information given my decree?"

A sudden warmth spread over Richard's body as two of the most powerful church figures fixed their gazes upon him. He breathed in deeply before answering. "Holy Father, I would give my life for you or the church, but I cannot go back on my word. My word was given as a priest and as a man, neither of which I can go back on—no matter the consequences."

"That's your final word, Bishop Carver?"

"Yes, Holy Father, that is all I have to say."

"Archbishop Beroske, what do you think of our young American's stand on this matter?"

The archbishop turned slightly to Richard. "Holy Father, I couldn't be prouder of this man if he were my own son."

"I see," the Holy Father said. "He could easily pass for your son, Archbishop Beroske. Goodness knows he's inherited your same attributes." The pontiff rose slowly from his chair. Richard and the archbishop watched as he made his way down the steps, stopping in front of the nervous Bishop Carver. "My young American bishop, you are obviously a man of your word . . . and also a man of God. Tonight, you've proven this beyond a doubt. Any lesser of a man would've broken under my pressure. You simply got stronger, a magnificent quality very few men in this world possess. Here I am blessed with two of these men before me at one time. I understand the importance of the information that you alone possess in this room. I will not ask that you break your word to the general. I already have and you refused me." A small smile appeared on the pontiff's lips as he placed his right hand on Richard's shoulder. "I give you my word and the word of the church that I will not reveal this information to anyone save selected members of the church of which this information would benefit in regard to clergy safety. I give you my solemn oath, Bishop Carver. As head of the Roman Catholic Church, I swear it. Will you tell me and the archbishop when this invasion of Poland will begin?"

Richard looked up at the humbled pontiff and said, "The invasion will begin on September 1. The field marshal wasn't certain of the exact time."

The pontiff looked at Archbishop Beroske. "Not much time for your people to prepare, Archbishop."

"Your Holiness, my people would have no time to prepare if it weren't for Richard."

The pontiff nodded. "You're a remarkable young man, Bishop Carver. It seems that you are able to accomplish such difficult task with remarkable ease. I'll leave the problem of notifying the proper parties inside Poland to the two of you."

"We will begin tonight, Your Holiness," the archbishop said.

"Yes, I will pray for Poland this night," the pontiff said as he walked back to his chair and sat down. "Enough bad news for one night and now for a little good news." The pontiff's eyes shifted to the archbishop. "Since I've both of you here at once I think it's only fitting to let Bishop Carver be the first to know of our archbishop's new status in the holy church. From this night on Archbishop Beroske will be known as Cardinal Beroske."

Richard looked at the stunned bishop. It was apparent that it had come as a great surprise to the aging bishop. Richard thought the bishop should've been chosen a cardinal long before now. "Congratulations, Cardinal Beroske," Richard said, smiling at the startled cardinal.

"Your Holiness, I don't deserve this."

"Cardinal Beroske, no man has ever deserved it

more."

"Thank you, Your Holiness," the cardinal said, rising from his seat and kneeling before the pontiff.

The pontiff's eyes switched to Richard who had remained seated. "Perhaps one day you'll also be chosen a cardinal, Bishop Carver."

"Oh, I doubt that Holy Father."

"It seems you have an excellent start. Already at your young age, you're a bishop and the Vatican is your home. You have a brilliant mind, young American. All that you lack is experience and that will come with time. God has given you the ability to accomplish whatever you wish in this life. It now depends on what you do with this gift. Perhaps you're still uncertain that the church is your calling. I've seen this many times in men such as yourself. Your handsome looks and high intelligence can be a great hindrance to men like you. The outside world can become a demon as it tries to pull you away from these human confines that the church demands of its servants. I've seen great men falter by the wayside from these tremendous pressures of the world's promiscuous societies. It would be a great loss to our church and our God if this were to happen to you, Bishop Carver. Until you are certain of your calling, the confines of our church can become a living hell for men such as yourself. But once a man turns his life and soul over to his church and his God, then will he find peace, a peace and love so great it will allow him to live the solitary life of a priest without any thought of remorse. Jesus is our mate in this life, we who walk alone."

Richard considered the pontiff and at the elderly cardinal who knelt at his feet. Yes, this was truly a lonely job, and two prime examples were before him. These men had given their lives to their church; here they were at the far edge of life alone, except for their God. Their God who couldn't hold them at night when they were lonely. Their God who'd never borne them a son or daughter to love and care about them or a mate with whom to grow old. These two men had none of these things, but they had something else. They had a soul filled with love and caring for their fellow man. They possessed a love that most men would never know even existed in this life. Their love rose above that of mortal man. Yes, their love was infinite and was never more evident than in this holy chapel on this late August night. Within a matter of hours, Nazi Germany would invade Poland and begin a war that would change the world forever. The three men who occupied the historic chapel on this night would be no exception. The roar of firing cannons would soon drown the peaceful sounds of church bells. War was at hand!

Chapter Eleven

Four forty-five on the morning of September 1, 1939, German troops crossed the border into Poland. Unlike Austria and Czechoslovakia, Poland fought for its homeland. Two days later, Great Britain and France declared war on Germany. The Second World War had begun in earnest. The Poles, though brave, were little match for the German war machine with its well-trained troops and superior weapons. Neither Britain nor France was of much help for Poland. Polish dreams of British and French equipment quickly turned into a notorious nightmare. The two superpowers of the First World War were only that.

They hadn't prepared for another war as Germany had. They couldn't defend their own homeland against the advancing Germans, much less save Poland from the hands of defeat. Within three short weeks, the Germans swept through Warsaw.

Because of Richard's advance information on the upcoming Polish invasion, the church had adequate time to prepare for the invaders. The church's great art treasures had been packed and shipped to Rome before the Germans could take them for themselves. Many of the church's outspoken critics of the Nazi party were also safely transported to neighboring countries. Richard's information had been much more rewarding than he or the Holy Father could've ever imagined. No one besides the three men in the Sistine Chapel that night would ever know from where or whom the advanced warning had come. Richard's word to Field Marshal Goering had been kept. Of course, the moment Germany invaded Polish territory, the Catholic Church denounced the Nazis as a serious threat to its church and all Christian peoples of the world.

As Germany swept through Poland, Richard and Cardinal Beroske studied the German advances, attempting to outguess Hitler's next military move. For certain, France would be invaded; the famed Maginot Line in which the French had placed their faith during the First World War would be of little consequence for slowing the rapidly advancing Germans. Richard and Cardinal Beroske had seen this some time ago. Richard became quite a military tactician as he followed Germany across Europe. His uncanny ability to predict many of the upcoming battles would prove beneficial for the church in the months ahead.

The latter part of 1939 was one of grave concern for

Europe. Germany had asserted itself as a formidable foe, having conquered Poland in record time, doing so against one of the finest equipped armies in Europe. This sent terrifying chills throughout Europe. In early 1940, Europe watched and waited for Hitler's next move. It had become clear by most military experts that Germany was virtually unstoppable. They would show this to be correct on May 10, when Germany invaded Holland and Belgium. Russia, who'd sat back and watched Germany's dramatic advances, was showing signs of irritation with Hitler's increased wielding of power. Russia had hoped the French and British would have checkmated the Germans, but this hadn't occurred, as they, too, had greatly underestimated the German war machine. Stalin was growing uneasy with Hitler's antics.

To this point, the United States had stood back, watching the rapid turn of events spreading through Europe, its eyes fixed on another aggressor, this one in the Pacific. The Japanese had swept through China with almost the ease with which the Germans were racing through Europe. President Roosevelt tried desperately to keep the United States out of the European war, but every new battle and German victory drew the war closer to America.

The year 1940 passed; Richard and Cardinal Beroske watched helplessly, along with the rest of Europe, as Hitler moved unchecked wherever he pleased. The Vatican kept a close eye on its nearest problem. Mussolini, it seemed, had grown captivated with Hitler's powers, as he too wanted to be another Napoleon. The Vatican was aware that Mussolini would only become a threat to the church and the Italian people if Hitler continued to go unchecked in his march through Europe, eventually drawing the childish-thinking Mussolini into some sort of German-Italian pact. Richard observed this tactic taking shape over several months, as Hitler publicly flattered the Italians and their great leader Benito Mussolini.

It was New Year's Eve 1940. Richard and his friend Cardinal Beroske sat in his room enjoying a glass of wine and discussing the ongoing war. They both agreed that if Hitler were to be defeated the United States would have to enter the war. Richard, in his correspondence with Lori, wasn't certain if America would freely enter the war. The Americans were still licking their wounds from the last war. They'd grown weary of fighting in Europe.

Cardinal Pacelli had been elected pope shortly after Pope Pius XI's death in 1939. Pope Pius the XII had been a close friend of Pius the XI, who handpicked Pacelli to be his successor. Since becoming the new pope, he'd altered his predecessor's doctrine to some degree. He wasn't as openly critical of Hitler and his Nazi Party—that he condoned the Nazis' barbarianism or the Communists, also cited for atrocities against humanity. The new pope found himself caught between two great evils. To condemn one was to help another. To condemn both would place the church and its followers in grave jeopardy from both sides. The church found itself more and more fighting against both evils through the church underground that grew larger by the day. Richard and Cardinal Beroske were well aware that their office had become the nerve center of the underground itself.

It was a few minutes after midnight, New Year's Day. Richard and the cardinal were finishing the last of their New Year's toast when the cardinal's telephone rang. "Richard, the call is for you," the cardinal said looking across the room.

Richard went to the phone. Who could be calling at this time of the night? "Lori is that you?" he asked. Richard had not heard from Lori since Christmas.

It was Lori, calling to wish him a happy New Year. Richard had forgotten just how much he'd missed her until he heard her sweet voice over the phone. Joe, who was spending New Year's Eve at Lori and Jeff's, also got on the phone. Richard let loose a cascade of tears as he spoke to his loved ones. They talked for some time before he reluctantly hung up.

The cardinal poured them each another drink. Richard wiped his tears as he took his seat next to the cardinal.

"Tears of joy," the cardinal said. "No man deserves to wear them more than you, my friend."

Richard smiled at the cardinal as he sipped the wine. "My family is happy and well. I forget at times how much the Lord has blessed me."

The cardinal nodded. "Yes, indeed you have been blessed my son. Look at you, still only a child. You've accomplished so much."

Richard's smile disappeared as he said, "Perhaps, but there's so much more to do, Your Reverence, and never enough time. At this moment, as we sit in our comfortable surroundings, people are being persecuted, put to death for being born of a certain race. Murdered for believing in God. Murdered for having different political beliefs. Many times, a day I ask God how this can happen. How could such great evils be possible in this day and time? This isn't the dark ages. This is the twentieth century. It seems the world has gone completely mad."

"Enough about the problems of the world. These are difficult times, but we put our faith in God. We know not his plan." The cardinal lifted his wine glass. "To your happiness and your family's happiness, Bishop Carver."

A smile returned to Richard's lips. "To a great man and a true friend." Richard touched his glass against the cardinal's.

So it was on this New Year's Day 1941. The winter of 1941 left most of Europe shivering. Not so much from the cold, but from the forceful aggression Germany continued to pursue through central Europe. Not only were the Germans persistent in their attempt of world domination, the Soviets and the Japanese were also on such a course. Mussolini continued to make trouble for the Italian people, as he, too, had dreams of bringing Italy back to military prominence. Never in the history of the world had four individual men controlled the destiny of so much of the world's population, and all four were maddened with world domination. Richard kept busy throughout the winter and spring. Germany now held a strong grip on half of Poland while the Soviets controlled the other half. In April of '41, Germany attacked Greece and Yugoslavia and, once again, the battles were swift and victorious. Germany now poised its guns at France, the Netherlands, Belgium, and Luxemburg. On May 10, Germany invaded all the countries at once. Again, the outcome was swift and decisive. France fought courageously, but, like the others before, was no match for the superior Germans. Richard was certain now that Hitler had Russia in his gun sights. Word had come to him that Field Marshal Goering was having frequent bouts with narcotics, to which he'd become addicted following a severe leg injury in 1923. Richard was convinced it was during one of these times that the general, under narcotic influence, had confessed of the upcoming battle with Poland. Whatever the reason for such strange behavior, it was to happen again in the form of a secret message, delivered to Bishop Carver on June 2, 1941. Upon reading the message, Richard asked for a joint meeting between Cardinal Beroske and the Holy Father.

The meeting was set for that same afternoon, at which time Richard read aloud the unbelievable information received from Berlin. Cardinal Beroske and the Holy Father sat together as Richard read the letter aloud.

"'Dear Father Carver, I thought I might pass on a little information of possible interest. The last great hurdle ensuring the Fatherland's greatness is about to begin, three days before Napoleon's anniversary. Germany will prevail where Napoleon failed. In less than a month after our armies cross the vast border of the Soviet pigs, the führer and I shall be dining in the palace of the Czar in Moscow. Good-bye, my friend. Again, all I ask for this information is a word from you to your powerful God, as another payment on my soul.'" Richard looked up. "Signed, 'Lucky.'"

The pontiff sighed. "Amazing!"

The strong impression Richard had made on Field Marshal Goering was evident. The information, though, was not of any grave importance to the church as far as church matters inside the Soviet Union. The Communists had long ago suppressed the Catholic Church, and all churches for that matter, to such a degree that their members had decreased to a point of insignificance. As many times before, however, the church was trapped between two evils. Communism was in fact a serious threat to the church, but the Nazis were turning out to be even worse. The church was committed to helping the west and its democratic governments. The Holy Father and his two disciples, Richard and Cardinal Beroske, quickly decided that France and England be given this information in hopes of helping their cause. For the first time, it became imperative to the church that the United States be given such information. From Richard's correspondence with Cardinal Algado of Baltimore and other high-ranking church officials in the United States, as well as information from Lori and Joe, there had been a dramatic increase in military production of naval ships and supplies. It was evident to Richard that America was in the process of preparing for war.

The Holy Father decided that Richard should deliver this information in person. He would leave for England the following day, then move on to Washington. He would serve as the pontiff's personal attaché. Cardinal Beroske would deliver the information to the French underground, leaving the following afternoon for Paris. Richard was concerned for the safety of the aging Cardinal Beroske, as more and more horrible tales came daily out of German-occupied countries. Stories of mass executions by the Germans ran rampant throughout the underground. Most of the victims had been Jews, but scattered stories of the slaughtering of Christians were surfacing. The Holy Father was confident the Germans wouldn't dare harm a high-ranking member of the Catholic Church. Richard disagreed, believing this wasn't based on sound judgment. His close relationship with the French underground had warned Richard of possible repercussions against the church for not giving Germany and its führer more public support, especially after the invasion of Poland. Richard told the pontiff and cardinal about this retaliatory possibility, but both passed it off as nonsense.

***

Richard left for England the following morning. It was shortly after midnight when Richard's plane arrived in London. Bishop O'Hare had an automobile in waiting for Richard's early-morning arrival. A middle-aged priest by the name of Father Shaw was to be Richard's official escort to the ultra-secret meeting, scheduled to take place within the hour. Father Shaw, an Englishman, had served in and about London since joining the priesthood, the last two years serving as secretary to Bishop O'Hare. The bishop would see Richard later that morning, clueless as to the details of Richard's critical meeting. The limousine made its way through the war-torn city of London in the early morning hours. Richard witnessed the damage inflicted on sections of the city as his car made its way along the ravaged streets.

"You looked surprised, Bishop Carver?" the English priest said.

"Your people have great courage, Father, to withstand the decimation and carnage the German Luftwaffe has inflicted on this great city."

"My people are a proud people, but we are a badly battered one also. Yes, my people are proud and strong, but they are also only human. How many more bombs will it take before we have no city left in which to clear the remains? Not many more, I fear. You're an American, Bishop Carver?"

Richard looked at the priest. "Yes, I'm an

American."

"Why is it your government doesn't hear the cries of her friends across the Atlantic? Aren't they aware of our struggle? Will they continue to turn their heads until the butcher Hitler himself reigns over parliament? That is, if there's anything left to reign over by the time the bombs cease. I don't know what brings you here to my country, but I know it must be of great importance. Please, Bishop, you're a man of God such as myself. Carry the word to America and the world leaders of what you've seen this night. Surely, you're a man of great power in our church, or else you wouldn't be representing the Holy Father. Please, I beg you. For my people, tell the pontiff what you've seen. Tell him his people are dying by the thousands because of that bastard Hitler. Tell him if we can't quiet the bombs before long, there will be none of the church's children left to bury. I know I've overstepped my bounds by saying these things to you, Bishop Carver, but I'm not sorry for what I've said. Please help my people."

Richard looked into the teary eyes of the priest. He placed his hand on Father Shaw's shoulder. "I'll tell the Holy Father the horrors I've seen tonight, Father. I'll also tell of the great courage these people are showing in such a dark hour of man's history. I'll do what I can to help these people, but, Father, you must remember these bombs aren't only falling on British soil. They've already blackened most of Europe's countryside with their clouds of death. The whole world is on the verge of war. I assure you the Holy Father is working night and day to do what he can to bring peace back to these lands. I'll pray hard for your people tonight." Richard stared out the car window, at the rubble and ruin. Nothing else was said by either man as the motor car continued its journey through the decimated city. It was evident as the motor car moved through the core of the city and into the residential districts that the meeting wasn't to take place in any of the government's official residences. The area reminded Richard of his Munich rendezvous with Field Marshal Goering. Here, too, the streets were nearly empty; of course, it was nearing two o'clock in the morning.

"You'll be right on time, Bishop Carver. I've driven it twice since you gave me the address last night," the English priest said as their car turned off Liberty Street, onto what appeared to be a back alleyway. Both sides of the dark alley were bounded by warehouses. The alley was wide enough for just one car. They traveled a short distance then stopped behind another car that blocked the alleyway. Richard watched as a man exited the front seat of the parked automobile and made his way toward their car. He was a rather large man, dressed in a dark brown overcoat and wearing a black hat pulled low over his forehead.

He walked to the car and addressed the French priest chauffeuring Richard's auto. "What is it that the three of you want?"

Richard never hesitated. "I'm Bishop Carver."

The man looked long and hard at Richard. "You're expected Bishop Carver." A friendly smile appeared on the man's lips, much to the obvious relief of Father Shaw and the cleric chauffeur.

"Wait for me," Richard said, exiting the car. The two priests hadn't noticed that Richard wasn't wearing his white collar or his bishop's ring, the only visible markings identifying him as a priest. He was never to wear any type clothing that identified him as a Catholic clergyman. This was done for added secrecy for the church as well as the escorting party. Certain individuals and many governments would have liked evidence of such meetings as was soon to take place. Such information could be worth millions to certain governments, not counting the untold lives affected. If Hitler knew of such a meeting, there would surely be extreme, negative consequences against the church and its followers under his armed control.

Richard followed the man. The moon was half-full and cast enough light onto the darkened alley for the two men to make their way with little trouble. He followed the man up the three concrete steps to what appeared to be an abandoned warehouse. The man smiled at him as he opened the warehouse door. Richard followed. The large room appeared empty, except for a few crates stacked in a far corner. Overhead lights, suspended from the three-story ceiling by heavy drop cords, dimly lit the room. Richard focused on two men at the room's far end.

The man beside him motioned toward the two men. "Shall we?"

Richard started toward the male figure as his newfound friend walked by his side. As he grew nearer, he caught the faint whiff of tobacco smoke that fouled the already stale air. He'd gotten close enough by now to recognize the famous face that silently peered at him as he approached. Richard stopped in front of the wooden crates. The pudgy man sitting on the crate smiled warmly at him.

"I'm here on behalf of the Holy Father, Pope Pius XII, who sends his blessings to the people of England. I'm Bishop Carver and honored to be here, Mr. Prime Minister."

Churchill looked Richard up and down. His round

154

face looked more aged than it had in recent news releases. He puffed on his cigar and laid it down on the edge of the wooden crate, then glanced at the man who stood next to him and proceeded to stand. He was dressed in a dark suit. He wasn't tall but was portly in stature and every bit the imposing figure Richard had seen so many times in the papers and newsreels.

"Bishop Carver, I would like to welcome you and your esteemed church to our country. I'm honored that you have come here. Please be seated."

Richard took a seat on a crate across from the prime minister.

"I understand that you are an American, and from the South, I believe?"

"Yes, Prime Minister, that is true."

"You know, of course, my mother was an American also."

"Yes, I do, Mr. Churchill. I, too, have done my homework on you."

"Ha, of course you have, my son." Churchill chuckled. "Isn't it a bit unusual for the Vatican to have an American doing such important work?"

Richard paused and then said, "Perhaps they couldn't find a foolish enough European to do such devious duties, Mr. Churchill."

The prime minister laughed. "Thank you, my new American friend. Do you know how long it's been since I've laughed?"

Richard's smile faded as he considered the suddenly solemn-faced prime minister. "By the looks of your city, it has surely been a long time."

"You've observed evidence of our people's courage

as you rode through the streets tonight, no doubt."

"Yes, Mr. Churchill, I have. You must be proud of your people."

"Proud, Bishop? That's hardly the proper word for such courage and fortitude these people have shown."

Richard watched and listened as Churchill's words revealed his great emotion regarding his people. He could easily see and feel how this man was such a great motivator for the people of England.

Churchill appeared as if he were about to become enmeshed in his own words, as he often did when he talked of England and war, which was almost constant these days. Instead, Churchill retrieved the partially lit cigar. "You didn't come here to be entertained by my long-winded outburst, Bishop Carver . . ."

"To the contrary, Mr. Churchill, I'm fascinated by your oratory skills."

Churchill snorted as he took a puff. "You call it oratory skills. Most of my colleagues call it blabbermouth."

Richard smiled. "They're just jealous, sir."

"Enough, Bishop Carver if I'm not careful, you'll have me converted to Catholicism before you leave. I'm assuming that our meeting must be of some grave importance to the church and England, or else we certainly wouldn't be foolish enough to be sitting here in the middle of a warehouse swapping compliments, even though I do find it a much welcome change."

"May I ask, Mr. Prime Minister, that the remainder of our meeting be held between just us?"

Churchill seemed surprised at Richard's request. He looked to his two comrades. "If you gentlemen would wait outside the doorway while the bishop and I have a little

156

private conversation." It was apparent that the man who'd been standing next to the prime minister all this time was huffed at Richard's request. "Don't worry. I'm among safe company."

Richard watched as the men left the room.

"OK, Bishop Carver, what brings you here?"

Richard laid his hat atop the crate, his dark eyes fixed on Churchill's. "Mr. Prime Minister, the church has come about what we believe is vital information. How important it may be to you we have no way of knowing. We are priests, not generals. Before I'm privileged to reveal this information to you, the Holy Father asks only two things. First, that you never reveal your source of this information. Before I can continue, will you agree to the first request, Mr. Churchill?"

"Of course, do you wish me to sign something?"

"Your word is good enough for the Holy Father. Mr. Prime Minister, our church has been informed by what we believe are reliable sources the exact day the German Army will invade Russia and the Soviet Union."

Churchill looked hard into Richard's unwavering eyes. "You know what?"

"It's true, Mr. Prime Minister. On June 22, the German military will attack Soviet Russia."

"How can you be sure of this?"

"It came from a very reliable source. Neither I nor the Holy Father would have requested this meeting on unreliable hearsay. You can expect the Germans to cross Russia's border on June 22 of this year, less than three weeks away."

"Who else knows this besides me, Bishop Carver?"

"No one at this time."

"But you're on your way to America with the same information?"

Richard hesitated and then said, "Yes I am. The Holy Father has deemed it important that America should also be given the same information."

"I see," Churchill answered, looking down at the floor. "Why hasn't your country come to England's aid, Bishop Carver?"

"The Holy Father believes this is about to change."

"He does, does he?" Churchill barked. "Well, I wish I could feel as confident as the Holy Father about what America is about to do. I pray to God your pontiff knows what he's talking about."

"He usually does, Mr. Churchill."

The prime minister looked sharply at Richard. "I imagine he has some excellent advisors such as you, Bishop Carver."

"At times I'm of benefit to the Holy Father."

"I imagine many more times than you realize. Too bad that's not a British uniform you're wearing. I could surely use a man like yourself right now."

Richard smiled. "I pray against war, Mr. Churchill, not support it."

"I also pray against war, but I don't have the luxury to turn my back upon it while my people perish in the streets of London . . . and your second request, Bishop Carver?"

"Mr. Churchill, the Holy Father realizes you must relate this information on to the Soviets. He asks as you do so that you make a simple request of the Soviet government—a small compensation for such a valuable piece of information."

"Go on, Bishop."

"The Holy Father asks that the Soviets loosen their grip on the church's freedom inside its Soviet boundaries. They've openly depressed religious orders since the establishment of the Communist's doctrine. We realize their party is atheist, and all we ask is for those who wish may still have the freedom to pray in their churches and synagogues without reprisal from the government."

A smile spread across the prime minister's face. "This is why you didn't deliver this news to Stalin himself, because he's an atheist. The Christian world would look down upon your church for dealing with an atheist state . . . correct, Bishop Carver?"

Richard looked at the smiling Churchill. "No comment, Mr. Churchill."

"I'll try my best with Stalin as far as the religious freedom for the Russian people. However, don't hope for much. I feel if it weren't the Germans, we were fighting today, it would be the Soviets tomorrow. They're a dirty bunch themselves. Tell the Americans and their president not to wait much longer before joining us in this struggle. If they do, they'll find themselves fighting the Germans on American soil."

"I will, Prime Minister."

The two men shook hands and Richard left the room.

Richard left for Washington the following morning.

***

Father James reached into his coat pocket, retrieved a small, sealed envelope, and handed it to the guard.

The guard opened the envelope. "You're expected Mr. Carver."

159

Richard and the young Father James—Bishop Carver's latest cleric chauffeur, a freshly ordained priest from rural Georgia assigned to St. Mary Mother of God Parish—stared at the magnificent mansion until a doorman made his way to the parked car.

"Good evening, gentlemen. Welcome to the White House." The doorman opened Richard's car door. Father James joined Richard's side. "Follow me, gentlemen." The doorman started for the White House porch.

Richard was dressed in his traditional black suit, white shirt, and black tie, and, as always, his narrow-brimmed hat. Absent was the briefcase, as there was no need of it on this journey.

A second doorman greeted the two priests at the front doorway. "Good evening, gentlemen, and welcome to the White House." The doorman escorted Richard and Father James into the large foyer.

"They don't have places like this in Georgia," Father James whispered as his eyes swept the giant room. Richard smiled.

A distinguished looking man approached the two priests. "Good evening, gentlemen." The man turned to Richard. "You must be Bishop Carver."

"Yes, I'm Bishop Carver. This is my close friend Father James of St. Mary's Parish."

"Good evening, Father," the smiling man said. "My name is Dean Jacobs, special secretary to the president."

"An honor." Father James shook the gentleman's hand.

Dean Jacobs turned to Richard and shook his hand. "The president is expecting you, Bishop."

"Have you someplace for Father James to wait

while I speak with Mr. Roosevelt?"

"Certainly, Bishop. Henry, would you show Father James to the waiting room while I accompany Bishop to the East Room? Bishop, follow me please."

Richard walked beside the secretary down the corridor, finally stopping in front of a pair of closed double doors.

"Please, Bishop, if you would wait here for a moment."

Richard smiled as Mr. Jacobs entered the room, closing the door behind him. Richard looked up and down the hallway, barren and quiet.

The door opened. "The president will see you now, Bishop." Mr. Jacobs motioned for Richard to enter.

The room was large, its walls spotted with assorted portraits of past American presidents. Heavy drapes covered a large window. Behind a massive wood desk sat a male figure reading a sheet of paper. Richard's eyes settled on the figure. The man at the desk looked up from his papers. "Bishop Carver, I assume?"

"Yes, Mr. President."

"Well, come in young man and let's get acquainted."

Richard felt Mr. Roosevelt's eyes on him as he crossed the room and stopped in front of the desk. "It is an honor to meet you, Mr. President."

"It's also an honor to meet with the man representing the pope," the president reciprocated. "Please, Bishop, have a seat."

Richard took his seat directly across from the president.

President Roosevelt removed his metal-rimmed

glasses. "Bishop Carver, it seems you've been a busy man these last few days by these papers I received from your boss. You don't mind if I call the pope 'boss,' do you?"

Richard laughed. "No, Mr. President, 'boss' is just fine."

Roosevelt paused, as if studying the young bishop. "So, you were recently in the company of the prime minister, I see."

"Yes, Mr. President, I was."

"Obviously, whatever it is you met with him for is the same reason you're here with me."

"Yes, Mr. President, that's correct."

"I see, but before you tell me whatever it is you came here to tell me, let me ask you a personal question."

Richard was taken aback at the president's request. "If I can answer it, Mr. President, I will."

"In your opinion, can England survive the German attacks?"

Richard laid his hat in his lap. "Mr. President, I'm a disciple of the Roman Catholic Church and can report the things that I've seen only as an observer."

"I understand, Bishop Carver, and that's why I want to hear from you. I've enough political and military advisors and every one of them has a different opinion as to what is occurring over there."

Richard looked at the frustrated president. "Mr. President, I'll first tell you what the prime minister asked me to pass on to you. Mr. Churchill said that if you don't join the battle shortly over there you will soon be fighting the Germans over here."

Roosevelt studied Richard. "You agree, don't you?"

He nodded. "The Germans are on a roll, Mr.

President. They've swept through central Europe with virtually no resistance. Fear grips all of Europe. Such fear has only added to the ease by which the German Army marches. The will to fight is being slowly drained from the German resistance. Only England has managed to ward off total defeat, mainly due to the geographic location of the country. True, I've witnessed great courage from the English people. But, Mr. President, I also witnessed great courage from the Poles and from the French and from the Czechoslovakians. They, too, had great courage before the German war machines ground them into the smoldering dirt beneath the treads of their tanks. Mr. President, only a miracle will save Europe from German domination, and I fear that miracle lies in the image of the United States." Richard rubbed the brim of his hat and leaned forward. "Mr. President, what I've told you is only my opinion, not the church's and not the bishop who sits here tonight before you. I've spoken only as an American who loves his country dearly. I've also learned, however, to love those countries that lie over the water and the people who live there. And, Mr. President, they're being murdered in large numbers. Horrid stories are seeping out of Poland and other German-occupied countries. Someone or something has to stop this great tragedy before it sweeps the world like a horrid plague. If it isn't stopped soon, the plague will cross the ocean and land upon our shores. This is that of which the prime minister speaks, Mr. Roosevelt, the plague . . . and I agree with him."

The president pulled away from his desk in his wheelchair, bowed his head, and stared at the floor. A few silent moments passed before he lifted his head and looked at Richard. His voice was low and soft. "And what have you come here to tell me, Bishop Carver?"

"Mr. President, I have to ask that you give the Holy Father your word that you will disclose to no one where you have received this information."

Roosevelt made his way back to the desk. "Did the prime minister also swear to secrecy?"

"Yes, Mr. President."

"You have my word."

"Mr. President, we have reliable information that on June 22 Soviet Russia will be invaded by the Germans."

Roosevelt's face was blank. "You're certain of this, Bishop Carver?"

"Yes, Mr. President."

Roosevelt pounded his fist hard on the desktop, startling Richard. "Best damn news I've heard in a long time," he bellowed. "Excuse my language, Bishop, but do you know what this means? It means this might be the thing that finally pisses the American people off enough to get involved in this damn war."

Richard nodded. He hadn't thought of that possibility. "One more thing, Mr. President, the pontiff also asks that when you talk to Stalin, you ask that he might strongly consider relaxing his anti-religious doctrines that have suffocated the Soviet churches."

"Tell the pontiff that I'll demand it if we are to save their ass from Hitler." Roosevelt laughed. "Perhaps I'll rephrase it just a little."

"I must be going, Mr. President. I've been honored to have met you."

Roosevelt smiled. "Bishop Carver, you have honored our great country by your work. May God lead you on a safe journey through the troubling years ahead. I don't suppose you would tell me how you managed to become the pope's personal emissary being an American and all?"

"I told them my mother was Italian, Mr. President." Roosevelt laughed.

Richard returned to St. Mary's that night. His train would leave from Union Station at eight o'clock the following morning.

Chapter Twelve

The trip to Baltimore was pleasant, and he enjoyed his brief reunion with Cardinal Algado. For the last two years the cardinal had been in ill health. He would briefly improve the next five months, then fall gravely ill and return to Rome and the Vatican.

After his brief stay in Baltimore, Richard left for Virginia to visit Lori and Joe. It'd been nearly six years since he'd seen his brother and sister, which, at the time, was probably the lowest point in Joe's young life. It was dramatically different for him now, as the vice president of Jeff's newly acquired Norfolk Shipbuilders International.

Richard's train arrived in Norfolk shortly after four o'clock in the afternoon. During the trip, his mind had been filled with memories of Lori and Joe and their childhood in Louisiana. It had been over three years since Richard had been tormented by the horrid nightmare of his parents' deaths. This dark memory reoccurred whenever he was with Lori or Joe, which was soon to be the case. His siblings ran toward him in the sparsely crowded station.

"Richard! Richard," the familiar voice cried.

He turned toward his quickly approaching loved ones. A broad smile swept his face as he opened his arms, grasping Joe's sudden embrace. Joe held him fast, Richard's tear-laden face resting against his brother's chest.

"Lori," Richard muttered, taking hold of her with his free hand and pulling her close.

The three Carver children held one another, sobbing like the children they once were. Lori's husband, Jeff, waited patiently for Richard's release from his loving captors, so he, too, might welcome his brother-in-law to their home.

Shortly, the four were on their way to Jeff and Lori's home. Their children had left already for summer camp in upper New York State before learning of Richard's upcoming visit. Lori had been extremely upset that the children wouldn't get to see their wayward uncle while he was in the states. Jeff sat silently up front with the chauffer. In the backseat, Lori and Joe took turns quizzing their brother about his quiet and mysterious life in Europe and, like everyone else, finding little success wrestling free much information. He would mostly smile his handsome smile and say nothing of any great importance to satisfy their curiosity. Lori still lived in the beautiful house at Virginia Beach. They'd added on a large wing in hopes of luring Joe to live with them but to no avail. He had a nice apartment in Norfolk not too far from the shipyard. Lori grumbled that Joe was still a bachelor. There was that pretty, young girl from New York City who'd moved to Norfolk to become Joe's private secretary. Maybe she'd become Mrs. Carver, Lori joked. Joe was tight-lipped, giving away nothing. Richard leaned back in the car and enjoyed the conversation and laughter as they traveled to the Virginia Beach home. It was good to be with family.

It was nearly seven o'clock when Richard finally unpacked and settled into his room. Lori and Jeff waited for him in the library. Joe had gone to Norfolk to finalize some sort of documents for the navy. The government had placed several orders with the shipyard over the past several months, ever since Roosevelt had agreed to sell Great Britain war supplies through the lend-lease program. All of America's shipyards were working at full capacity, twenty-four hours a day.

"I feel much better now," Richard said upon entering the library. Rows upon rows of books lined the oak paneled walls.

"Richard, you're more handsome than ever," Lori said, taking her husband's hand.

Richard nodded. "You're a lucky man, Jeff."

Jeff smiled as he looked at his beautiful wife, kissing her softly on her cheek. "Yes, I know." He kissed her again.

"Fix Richard a drink, Jeff, while we're waiting on Joe. I thought we would wait on Joe before having supper, Richard, if you don't mind waiting."

"No, not at all. It feels good just to relax again." Jeff handed him his cocktail. "What's this in your letter about Joe getting serious over a woman? You must be tickled after all these years worrying over having another bachelor brother."

Lori's expression lit up. "I'm hoping this is the girl for Joe. Goodness knows he isn't getting any younger, turning thirty-three soon. And, Richard, this woman is really a knockout, isn't she Jeff?"

Jeff grunted his approval and sipped on his drink. "She's beautiful, Richard, simply beautiful." Jeff winked.

Lori cut her eyes at her smiling husband. "One beautiful is sufficient, Jeffrey."

"I look forward to meeting this lady," Richard said just as the front doorbell rang.

He could see their butler, Jeremiah, walk by the doorway on his way to answer the front door. "That must be Joe and Elisabeth now," Lori said.

Richard stopped mid-sip with the mention of the name Elisabeth. It couldn't be. The striking couple appeared in the double doorway. Richard's eyes widened and his jaw slackened. To anyone watching, he looked as if he'd witnessed the Virgin Mary herself. The woman he was presently staring at was definitely not the Virgin Mary; no one knew this better than he.

"Elisabeth, I'd like for you to meet Richard, my brother."

A sudden, unease fell over the room. Lori's and Jeff's proud smiles faded. The color had completely drained from Richard and Elisabeth's faces.

Joe broke the silence. "Lori, I didn't tell you before because I wasn't sure if Richard would remember meeting Elisabeth back in New York."

Richard's and Elisabeth's eyes were transfixed on one another.

"It appears obvious they do remember," Jeff said, taking another sip of his drink.

Lori forced a smile as she continued to look at one and then the other. Richard turned briefly to his sister. He could sense her mind working. He tried not to imagine what she thought as he turned back and stared quietly at his

Elisabeth. She was even more beautiful than he'd remembered if that were possible.

"Hello, Bishop Carver, it's been a long time."

Richard heard the words clearly, having never forgotten the softness of her voice or of her arms by which he suddenly and without warning wanted to be held.

Lori broke in. "Well, Richard, what do you think of your brother's choice in secretaries?" She walked briskly to Richard's side, taking his limp right arm. "Well?" she said again, looking up at Richard and smiling.

"She's beautiful. I think Joe has great taste." Richard brought the half-full glass of scotch and water to his lips, downing it all.

Lori glanced nervously at Joe, who'd remained quiet. "Fix Elisabeth and yourself a drink for goodness sake."

"Oh yes, I'm sorry, Elisabeth."

"That's all right, Joe, I knew you would get around to it sooner or later." Her emerald eyes stayed on Richard.

As if by instinct or nervousness, Richard's hand rose to touch his clerical collar. He stopped short, remembering he hadn't worn it this evening.

"How about you, little brother? You ready for another one?" Joe took the empty glass from Richard's hand.

He lowered his hand. "Please, Joe, don't mind if I do."

"I think I could stand one myself," Jeff said as he and Joe walked across the room to the portable bar.

Lori's eyes followed Elisabeth as the woman crossed the room to her little brother.

Elisabeth spoke in barely a whisper. "How have you

169

been, Richard—you don't mind if I call you Richard?"

Richard looked at her.

"Richard, aren't you going to answer Elisabeth?" Joe handed Elisabeth her drink. Jeff handed Richard his drink as he joined the circle.

"Sure, Elisabeth, you can call me Richard. I'm with my family. All formalities go out the window when I'm with family. And I've been fine . . . the church keeps me pretty busy." Richard took a swig of his liquor.

Apparently, Lori had been the only one to take notice of the couple's strange behavior toward one another. Perhaps Joe might have if he hadn't been drinking for the last couple of hours, celebrating Richard's homecoming and the recent navy orders for two medium destroyers.

After Joe broke the news about the navy's ship order, everyone had more rounds of drinks before dinner. Joe and Jeff ate little and drank much more. Richard and Elisabeth picked at their plates, for understandable reason of their own. Lori wouldn't eat because of the combination of the two. Before long, Lori was as drunk as Joe and Jeff.

Richard tried with all his will to keep his eyes off Elisabeth during the dinner, but inevitably, he'd find his eyes locked with hers. Finally, Jeff put an end to the miserable situation, recommending they retire to the living room for a few after-dinner drinks. Richard tried desperately to ignore Elisabeth as the five gathered in the spacious living room, even to the extent of acting interested in Joe and Jeff's conversation about shipbuilding matters. Lori, perhaps sensing Richard's plight, kept Elisabeth entertained with female talk, but this too began to unravel. Lori's nervous thirst had about done her in as far as sober reasoning was concerned. After an hour in the living room and four drinks later, she joined Joe and Jeff into the world of intoxication, and so went Richard's last buffer between him and Elisabeth. He would never admit it, but deep down he'd been hoping for such an opportunity all evening. Lori joined Joe and Jeff on the settee, where the three passed out in drunken slumber.

Richard fixed himself another drink and walked out on the large stone patio that fronted the living room. The half-moon hung high overhead. Its silver light shone through the leaves of the estate's towering maples. Richard gazed at the rolling hillside.

"You've been avoiding me tonight, Bishop Carver."

Richard turned slowly toward the familiar voice, his breath nearly stolen. He stared at the most beautiful woman he'd ever seen. "Yes, and I've failed miserably, haven't I?"

Elisabeth drew nearer to him. "It seems you've done a poor job of hiding your true feelings about me."

Richard turned away. "I thought so."

He sensed Elisabeth moving closer to him. "Aren't you going to ask how I've been all these years, Richard? Aren't you curious how I ended up here as Joe's secretary?"

He pivoted slowly to face her. "How did you end up here, Elisabeth?"

"Do you remember our last night together in New York?"

How could he forget?

"When you left our room that night," she said, "you took my heart with you. Do you know to this day you haven't given it back?" Richard started to speak, but Elisabeth continued. "All these years, I've been searching for love, unable to find it. Several months ago, out of sheer desperation, I called Joe from New York and asked if he might be in need of a good secretary. He hesitated at first, perhaps remembering the somewhat strange relationship you and I had those few days in New York. I convinced him the only thing you and I had between us was like a brother-sister relationship. Then one day, I just happened to be in Virginia, and so I looked Joe up. We had dinner together . . . and here I am."

Richard considered Elisabeth and her half-hearted smile. "But why did you come here? Why Joe?"

Elisabeth sighed. "I finally decided I'd probably never see you again, and surely never hold you in my arms." Elisabeth's voice faded to a whisper. Tears welled in her eyes. "So, I made up my mind to have Joe. He's the closest thing to you . . . his being your brother."

Richard started to speak but Elisabeth raised her hand, placing it softly against his lips. The warmth of her hand melted his heart.

"Please, Richard, let me finish while I still have the courage." Gently, she removed her hand from his lips. "After being here for a while and being around Joe most of the time, I soon learned that my love for you couldn't be passed onto someone else, especially Joe. He's so much like you in so many ways and yet so different. My guilt began to get the best of me for what I was attempting to do. In fact, I felt so guilty, Richard, I went to one of your churches. I wanted to go to confession. Not being a Catholic, I didn't know how. I simply went to my knees in that large church hoping to talk to that God of yours. I don't know if he listened to me, but I told him everything. I cried in that church, Richard. I cried as I did the night you left me in New York. But you know when I left that church,

I felt so much better." Her tears sparkled in the moonlight. "I made a promise that night in your church. I promised I would never pass my love for you onto someone else, especially Joe who's so kind, Richard, you can't imagine."

Softly, he whispered, "I know Elisabeth."

"After all these months with Joe, I believe I love him. One thing is certain: I can never love another man as I love you. That was proven again tonight. I thought maybe after all these years of not seeing you that my love would fade away. Oh, but it hasn't. You know that I actually prayed when I saw you again that you'd have grown fat and baldheaded? Do you believe that?"

Richard tried to hold back his chuckle but couldn't. Elisabeth began to laugh and cry at the same time.

"I've put on some weight," Richard said rubbing his stomach.

The laughter suddenly stopped. "You look gorgeous, Bishop Carver." Elisabeth stepped closer. Richard moved to drink from his empty glass, but she stopped him, placing her hand on his. He froze as she took a tiny step closer. The sweet smell of her perfume filled his senses. She leaned slowly into him, her soft lips meeting his. Her warm breath and pounding heart electrified his body. The glass dropped from his hand and onto the stone patio. He wrapped his arms around the petite body of his Elisabeth. They kissed passionately, a raging warmth flowing between them.

The sound of nearby laughter brought Richard back to reality. He pulled away from Elisabeth, though she tried desperately to hold their embrace. Richard stepped back just in time. Lori and Joe walked through the double doorway onto the patio, arm in arm. They laughed loudly as they attempted to hold one another steady.

"We've been looking for you two," Lori said. "I guess everyone passed out on the couch except you two. Jeff's still on the couch."

Richard glanced at Elisabeth as she composed herself. He couldn't help but laugh at Lori and Joe as they tried to steady one another.

"Well, little brother, what do you think of my little secretary here?" Joe staggered over and placed his arm around Elisabeth's shoulder. Elisabeth managed a strained smile.

"As always, Joe, I believe you made a splendid decision," Richard said.

Joe winked at Elisabeth. "You heard that, didn't you, Elisabeth? If my brother thinks you're all right, then, by God, you're all right. You know he's got personal contacts with the Man Upstairs." Joe pointed toward the moonlit sky. "Maybe, in the near future, we might ask him for one of his services, if you know what I mean, Elisabeth." He winked again at Elisabeth.

Elisabeth's smile vanished, as did Richard's.

"Come on, Elisabeth, it's time we were going. I've a big day at the shipyard tomorrow."

Richard looked sharply at Joe. "Surely you're not driving."

Joe laughed. "No, little brother, that's what our sister has Barry for."

Richard's eyes revealed his confusion.

"Barry's our cook . . . and also Joe's chauffer on nights such as these," Lori said.

Joe laughed. "It cost me five bucks, but he saves my ass from getting killed."

The foursome made their way to the front porch where Barry had the car waiting in the driveway. Elisabeth held Joe steady.

"Richard, you're coming to the shipyard in the morning with Jeff, aren't you?" Joe said.

"Please come, Richard," Elisabeth said. "You'll enjoy seeing how they build those gigantic boats you see floating around the ocean."

"Boats? For Christ's sake, they're ships, Elisabeth," Joe muttered.

"Yes, I'll come with Jeff tomorrow," Richard replied. "Perhaps I'll finally find out how those heavy hunks of steel are able to float in the first place."

Elisabeth smiled an approving smile at Richard. Barry and Elisabeth helped Joe into the backseat of the car.

"We'll see you tomorrow, Richard," Elisabeth said, glancing at Lori who was watching her closely.

"Yes," Richard replied.

Barry helped Elisabeth into the backseat, next to the already sleeping Joe. Lori and Richard watched as the limousine drove away into the darkness. Richard placed his arm around Lori, pulling her close. They walked slowly toward the house.

"You seem to like Elisabeth quite a bit, Richard."

"She seems like a fine lady, Lori—a fine lady, indeed."

"If you'd met a girl such as that before you became a priest, would you be a bishop today?"

His body stiffened. After a brief pause, he answered, "Perhaps not, Lori, but that's of no consequence now. I'm an ordained minister of the Church of Rome. My vows have been consummated. I can share my life with no one except Jesus Christ."

Lori stopped as they reached the front steps. "You're a fine man, a man any woman would love to call her own. I believe you when you say these things about your church. I believe with all my heart you're exactly what God intended you to be. But one thing is for certain, my handsome brother, there are many people in this world who would fight your God for the right to your soul. Just look at you. Without question, you'd decorate any woman's home. I don't know what transpired between you and Elisabeth before. If it weren't for the drinks, I wouldn't have the courage to say this to you. Richard, a blind person can see the attraction you two have for one another. Surely, if Jeff or Joe hadn't been so heavy in the bottle tonight, they would've seen it also." Lori shook her head. "You and Joe are my only brothers, and I love the two of you dearly. It would break my heart to see something like this come between you both. Richard, you're a priest, and as you said, you've taken your vows to your church and your God. You mustn't place that in jeopardy, much less your brother's love."

He knew Lori spoke the truth. He mustn't grow anymore involved with Elisabeth than he had tonight. He'd keep his meeting tomorrow with Joe at the shipyard and leave the following morning for Rome. Richard reached out, taking both of Lori's hands. "I will not become involved with this lady or any other woman, Lori, especially if she might become Joe's wife. That would be a mortal sin of the worst kind. Rest easy, my loving sister. This is my wedding ring." Richard lifted his hand, showing her his bishop's ring.

A smile crept upon Lori's lips as she said, "I'm

sorry I even brought up such a crazy thing. That damn scotch, that's what did it. No more scotch for me . . . ever!"

Richard laughed as he placed his arm over Lori's shoulder and walked into the house. He slept little that night. Into the early hours, he prayed to his God, asking for the courage to repress his manly attraction for the woman he loved.

***

"Good morning, Richard. I hope you feel better than me and my sickly-looking spouse." Lori glanced toward Jeff.

Richard joined Lori and Jeff at the breakfast table.

Lori's cook, Manny, poured Richard a cup of coffee. "They sure look rough, don't they, Preacher Richard?"

Richard poured cream into his coffee. "They sure do, Manny."

Conversation was scarce during breakfast. Jeff wasn't feeling that well to talk much and Lori knew she'd already said too much the night before. Soon, breakfast was over. Richard and Jeff readied themselves to leave for the shipyard in Norfolk.

Jeff kissed Lori good-bye. "We'll try and be home before dark, dear."

"I hope so. I'd like to spend a more time with my brother before he leaves for Rome tomorrow."

Richard leaned over and kissed Lori's cheek. "See you tonight." He followed Jeff to the waiting car.

It was just after seven when the car pulled out for the drive to Norfolk. The bright morning sun shone brilliantly in the clear Virginia sky on the scenic ride to the shipyard. Jeff educated Richard a little on the history of the

177

shipbuilding business and offered his opinions on the
European war. Richard said little as his thoughts were
mostly on his upcoming meeting with Elisabeth. He recited
many Hail Marys along the way. The long limousine pulled
through the guarded gate, passing the many sizable
buildings that were but a part of Norfolk Shipbuilders
International, currently the largest maritime yard on the
East Coast.

Richard watched curiously as their car made its way
along the wide paved road. "This is extremely impressive,
Jeff."

"Yes, isn't it?" Jeff's tone denoted his pride.

Outside the car, a miniature city bustled with
hundreds of workers kept busy by numerous naval projects
the company had been afforded over the last several
months, most of which were being rushed to completion for
shipment oversees to the war-torn countries England and
Soviet Russia. The limousine pulled to a stop in front of a
large two-story building. The brick structure housed the
architects, engineers, secretarial, and other white-collar
workers who formed the brains of this large operation.

Jeff pointed to the red brick building. "This is where
your brother and I spend most of our long hours."

The men exited the car. Richard looked toward the
bay front several hundred yards to the north. The outer
shells of several massive ships sat perched side by side in
their large steel cradles to be assembled and finalized
before their final slide into the Chesapeake Bay. After
completion, the ships would sail across the Atlantic to
countries battling the onslaught of the ever-advancing
German Army.

Richard followed Jeff into the building and down a

long hallway lined on both sides with assorted offices. "This is mine and Joe's office," Jeff said as he opened the door, letting Richard enter first. Jeff joined Richard inside the doorway where Richard's eyes had already discovered Elisabeth sitting behind her desk. Jeff nodded toward her and smiled. "I see you recognize someone in the room."

"Good morning, Mr. Roberts."

"Good morning, Elisabeth," Jeff replied.

"Good morning, Bishop Carver."

"Good morning, Elisabeth," Richard answered, smiling politely. Richard touched the white collar around his neck.

"Please, Richard, come into my office. Elisabeth, please inform Joe that Richard and I have arrived."

"Surely, Mr. Roberts," Elisabeth said.

"This is my office on this side of the room and Joe's is on the other."

Richard noted the closed door across the room. Jeff's office was a rather impressive room, its walls sprinkled with a scattering of photos of mostly ships built in the boatyard. A wide window behind Jeff's desk afforded a great view of the shipyard itself. Richard took a seat in front of Jeff's desk as Jeff took his seat across from him. No sooner had they sat than Joe entered the room, showing no signs of a hangover from the night before.

The day was delightful. Occasionally, his thoughts turned to Elisabeth, but he'd been kept busy by his guided tour of the shipyard. It was almost four o'clock when the men returned to Jeff's office. Richard looked for Elisabeth when they first entered but she was gone. He sighed with a mixture of relief and remorse. He'd have perhaps only one more chance of seeing her, tomorrow morning before he

179

left for Rome.

The three men capped their day off by having a cocktail in Jeff's office. "Elisabeth and I have decided to take the two of you and Lori out to dinner. Elisabeth talked with Lori around midday today and got the OK from her. The two of us will meet y'all at Lori's house around seven tonight. We've made reservations at Frankie's Place. Jeff can tell you, Richard, they have the finest seafood in all of Virginia."

"Yes, they do," agreed Jeff.

"But—"

"No damn *buts*, little brother. It's all set." Joe placed his arm around Richard's shoulder.

"Sounds great to me," Jeff said. "Let's get going, Richard. You know Lori's waiting anxiously on your return."

Richard forced a smile as his thoughts were once again on Elisabeth. He attempted to carry on a conversation with Jeff on the way home, failing miserably. There was still plenty of daylight left when the black limousine pulled into the circular driveway of Jeff and Lori's home. Richard could feel Lori's uneasiness as he entered the house. He knew that Lori hadn't wanted such a farewell dinner tonight, sensing there was great risk involved with such a close union.

The early evening passed swiftly. Richard caught Lori watching him nervously as he calmed his nerves over several strong drinks.

At half past seven, Barry went to the door to let in Joe and Elisabeth. Lori glanced at Richard anxiously as the sounds of Joe's and Elisabeth's laughter could be heard in the hallway. Richard downed the remainder of his fourth scotch as Joe and Elisabeth entered the living room. He watched Elisabeth's every step, looking like a princess in her flowing blue gown, its low-cut bodice revealing the best of Elisabeth's physical qualities. Her long, brown hair flowed softly over her tiny shoulders, accented by a string of gorgeous white pearls that adorned her bosom. Yes, she was dazzling in Richard's eyes—the most beautiful lady his God had ever placed on this earth and his for the taking.

Elisabeth flashed a radiant smile. Richard noticed that Lori also kept her eyes on Elisabeth as she and Joe made their way toward them. Elisabeth left little doubt as for whom she wore the smile. The drinks Richard had purposely consumed to help ward off his weakness for this woman had worked against him, adding fuel to the already smoldering fire. Lori looked agitated, crossing, and uncrossing her arms. Jeff and Joe were comparatively sober at first, making their capacity for observation much keener than the night before.

Everyone had another round of drinks. Lori made it an obvious point to stand between Richard and Elisabeth as they stood in a tightly closed circle, carrying on idle conversation. Elisabeth remarked subtly that Richard hadn't worn the white collar, which caused a slight huff and crossing of arms from Lori. Richard, though, had trouble keeping his eyes and thoughts off Elisabeth. Finally, Lori forced the group to leave for Frankie's Place. The limousine waited out front. Lori insisted on the seating arrangements. Jeff and Elisabeth were to sit up front with the chauffer; Joe and Lori would sit on either side of Richard in the backseat.

It was a twenty-mile ride to Frankie's, which had been an old antebellum plantation before the Civil War.

The white column mansion stood nestled beneath ancient oak trees. Two elderly Negroes dressed in butler uniforms met Jeff's limousine in front of the home, opening the car doors for the sharply dressed patrons. A mammoth chandelier hung from the two-story ceiling lit the sprawling front porch and entrance to Frankie's Place.

"Shall we." Joe took Elisabeth by the arm as they began up the brick walkway.

Lori watched Richard's expression as Joe walked with Elisabeth, then broke the momentary silence. "Would you two gentlemen care to escort this lady to the house?"

"It would be an honor, my lady." Jeff took her left arm in his. Richard took her other arm.

"Welcome to Frankie's Place." The black butler opened the door to the mansion. They followed the maître d' to their table. At one time, the room where their table was located had been the library. On one wall, the custom-made bookcases were still in place, along with priceless books left behind when the plantation owners were forced to flee from the advancing Yankees in the spring of 1862. Everyone took their seats at the circular table covered by a fine white tablecloth. An antique kerosene lamp sat in the center of the table. Shortly, the waiter took everyone's food order, and they enjoyed their first round of drinks.

Richard had become much more reserved since arriving. Elisabeth, who sat directly across from him, had also mellowed to some degree. Their eyes seemed to become tangled quite often though. Again, no one seemed to notice except Lori. Everyone appeared to enjoy the meal. They sat at the table, sipping after-dinner drinks. Soft music drifted down the stairs from the upstairs dance floor. Unbeknown to Lori, Joe had also reserved a table upstairs for after dinner. Lori tried in vain to persuade the others that they should leave, but it was of no use. Joe wouldn't hear of it, and within a few minutes, they were sitting at a table next to the dance floor.

The entire second floor was one large room. A ten-piece orchestra played on a slightly elevated stage, easily viewed from anywhere in the room. Joe ordered a round of drinks when they first sat down. It was evident that Joe liked this sort of thing. Richard watched his brother keep time with the band by tapping his spoon on his crystal water glass.

"Here's to Richard," Joe said, raising his whiskey glass in a toast.

Everyone smiled at Richard as their five glasses touched over the center of the table. He grinned. His eyes darted at the others before settling on Elisabeth.

Soon they were on their third round of drinks. Until now, no one at the table had danced. Richard knew Jeff wasn't much of a dancer. Lori had told him years before that Jeff had to get half smashed before he could build up enough nerve to dance with her. Richard wasn't sure about Joe. He'd never known Joe to dance. Joe leaned toward Elisabeth, whispering something in her ear. She smiled and glanced at Richard. Joe stood, took Elisabeth by the hand, and proceeded to the dance floor. He watched the couple glide effortlessly across the floor. Joe was a terrific dancer all right, and so was Elisabeth. By far, they were the most impressive couple on the floor as far as Richard was concerned. He watched closely their every move. Elisabeth's eyes were rarely off Richard as she danced.

After several songs, Joe and Elisabeth took their seats. The band played another song while the couple rested. Then, Joe whispered once again in Elisabeth's ear. He turned to Richard. "Little brother, dance with Elisabeth."

Lori nearly choked on her drink. Elisabeth was all smiles.

"But I'm not much of a dancer, Joe."

"Oh, go ahead, Richard, dance with the beautiful lady," Jeff chimed in.

"I'd love to dance with you, Bishop Carver," Elisabeth said softly.

Richard took the last gulp of his drink, then stood and escorted Elisabeth to the dance floor. Briefly, he glanced back at Lori's sour expression and Joe and Jeff's approving grins.

Richard brought Elisabeth close as they began to dance. Elisabeth closed her eyes and laid her head against Richard's chest. Effortlessly, they drifted across the dance floor. Richard succumbed to this wonderful moment in time; thoughts of war and his priesthood washed away, pushed aside by a giant wave of love and passion for the beautiful lady who filled his arms.

The band quit playing but the magnificent couple kept dancing to the music of their hearts. It was the sound of applause that brought Richard and Elisabeth back to realities of the moment. Both appeared embarrassed and astonished as they looked about the dance floor at other couples who'd stopped dancing and clapped for them.

Elisabeth looked into Richard's eyes. "You know how much I love you. Tonight, you showed me how much you love me. Richard, take a leave of absence from the church and spend time with me. Please, I beg you." Before Richard could answer, Elisabeth placed her tiny fingers against his lips. "Please, think about it before you give me your answer. I know you leave for Rome tomorrow, but promise me after you get there that you'll consider it. Don't tell me no now. I don't believe I could stand that right now, not after I've felt you in my arms again."

Richard wiped a tear from Elisabeth's cheek. "Please don't cry here, Elisabeth. Joe and the others are watching."

"I don't care, Richard. I love you and you love me, and I want to shout it out to the world. Perhaps, then, your God will hear me and understand that he's made a mistake. I need you, Richard, not the damn crazy world. Let the world solve its own problems. You're my world. Please don't leave me alone in a world without you—please."

He pulled her to him. She buried her face into his chest. He glanced about the dance floor as the orchestra struck and couples began to dance. Richard didn't need to look at their table to feel the eyes of Lori upon them. Joe and Jeff were nowhere to be seen. Elisabeth was in no condition to return to the table now. Richard led her away, melting into the crowd on the other side of the dance floor, giving Elisabeth time to compose herself before they joined the others.

The thought of taking a leave of absence from the church weighed heavily on his mind. After a few minutes, he led Elisabeth back to their table. Lori sat alone.

"Where's Joe and Jeff," Richard asked. He and Elisabeth took their seats at the table.

Sternly, Lori answered, "Two men from the navy department recognized Jeff and your brother, and I coaxed them into going outside while they talked about building more naval ships—thank heavens they came by." Anger flashed across her face. Before Richard could say anything, Jeff and Joe returned to the table.

Joe nudged his brother in the arm. "I must say, Richard, if you weren't my brother and a priest, I might've gotten jealous with the way you held my girl out there."

Lori cut her eyes at Richard. Elisabeth's eyes were red from crying. Joe seemed not to notice. They had one more round of drinks. Joe was about to order another when the waiter came to the table with a young man, carrying what appeared to be a telegram. "Bishop Carver?" the waiter asked.

"Why, yes, I'm Bishop Carver," Richard replied, at which time the other man stepped forward addressing Richard.

"I'm sorry to bother you, Bishop," the nervous courier said. "But I've an urgent telegram for you." He handed Richard the brown envelope.

Richard tipped the courier, and both he and the waiter left the table. Everyone's eyes were on Richard and the telegram he held.

"Must be important to track you down here this time of the night." Joe polished off the last of his drink.

Richard opened the envelope and began reading to himself. His expression changed as he made his way through the telegram. His face went slack, and his eyes filled with gloom as he finished the message, then placed it in his coat pocket.

Joe looked about the table, as everyone seemed scared to ask the inevitable question. "What's wrong, Richard?" he said finally.

"My friend Cardinal Beroske . . . it seems the Germans have taken him prisoner while in Paris."

Elisabeth's voice shook. "Surely, they won't harm a Cardinal of the Catholic Church."

"What will you do, Richard?" Lori asked, concern showing in her dark eyes.

"I must find him. He's a proud man that speaks his mind. I fear for his life." Richard lowered his head. "I must be going back to your house, Lori. I have things I must do." Richard rose from his chair, not even looking to see if the others were doing the same. It made no difference to him; he would leave without them. He had to find the cardinal while there was still time.

There was little conversation on the way home. The limousine sped through the Virginia countryside. Elisabeth was quiet, making no mention of Rome or his returning to the States.

Richard said his brief farewells to Elisabeth and Joe. Jeff and Lori took him to the airport in the morning. He had a short flight to Baltimore where Cardinal Algado awaited inside the airport. The news of Cardinal Beroske had spread throughout the world's Catholic clergy. Richard had spoken to Cardinal Algado the night before, trying to talk the aging cardinal from meeting him at the airport, knowing of his recent ill health, but the cardinal had insisted.

Richard hoped for more news on Cardinal Beroske's arrest, but there was none. Cardinal Algado had received a telegram from the Holy Father that morning, requesting Richard proceed directly to Rome, where upon Richard and the pope would confer in private as to what could be done to free the Polish cardinal. Richard and Cardinal Algado met for over an hour in the private lounge of the Baltimore Airport, after which Richard said his farewells to his great friend. Richard would spend the next twenty-four hours in either the air or awaiting another flight in one of the many airports in which he'd find himself on the long trip to Rome.

Richard arrived at the Vatican in the early morning. He'd gotten very little rest the last twenty-four hours, but a fresh bath would go a long ways of relieving his fatigue. He'd sent word to the pontiff that he'd arrived, and within the hour, he received a reply from the pope requesting a private meeting between the two forty-five minutes later. That time had come as Richard entered the small chamber where he and Cardinal Beroske had spoken with the pontiff often on top-secret matters such as this. Even though the world clergy was aware of the dilemma, the press had not picked up the story as of yet. Richard crossed the room to the pontiff. He bent on one knee, kissed the pope's ring, and took a seat beside him. After a brief summary of Richard's trip back to America, the two men got down to the business at hand.

The Holy Father looked worn sitting in his wooden chair, wrapped in his traditional white robe. The strain of the spreading world conflict and now the added worry of Cardinal Beroske were taking its toll on the pontiff. His eyes were sunk deep into his head, dark circles encompassing them. He seemed to have aged many years since Richard had seen him last, not long ago. Richard would discover later that the pontiff hadn't lain down upon first hearing of the cardinal's arrest.

"There's very little news to report on the disappearance of the cardinal," the pope said. "All we know for certain is that he was arrested by the German SS sometime after midnight, as he slept in an old friend's small farmhouse outside Paris."

The pontiff had to stop speaking several times as he told Richard the story, struggling to control his emotion. Richard had also cried for his friend as he knelt by his bed that last night at Lori's, asking God to please return the cardinal to the safety of the Vatican. The pontiff looked at him with the eyes of a child. Richard could not conceal his feelings as the holy old man took his hand and begged, "Please, my son, go forth and find our friend. Save him from the evils that hold him. Bring him back safely to his home. He's old like me. Let him journey into the heavens with the dignity of the great cardinals before him and not by the hands of barbarians. Find him, Richard. You're the only one who can manage such a task. Go tonight. Don't wait. I'll pray long and hard until the two of you return. Go, young bishop of Almighty God, and let the sword of Jesus lead the way."

Richard didn't answer, as there was no need. The pontiff's eyes had already spoken for him. He kissed the pontiff's ring for the last time and slowly exited the chamber. He knew not where he was going but knew he must go, and with all possible haste.

Chapter Thirteen

Richard spent the rest of the day making

arrangements for his urgent trip to France. There was the task of making the necessary clearances into the German-occupied country. Of course, he had the necessary passports and his Vatican papers that marked him as a personal representative of the pontiff. Unfortunately, certain officers of the German Army had taken matters into their own hands without the knowledge of the führer. Richard felt the current situation with Cardinal Beroske could very well be the work of one of these renegade officers of the German Army, probably SS officer. The führer still wanted the cooperation of the Catholic Church, realizing the great power it wielded with the people of Europe. The führer wouldn't have allowed such action against the Catholic Church and certainly not against such a powerful figure as Cardinal Beroske. The Poles were difficult enough to manage during the occupation. If the news were to circulate about their cherished cardinal, they would certainly make it more difficult for the Germans and their occupation. It appeared that Hitler was concentrating all his attention to the upcoming Russian invasion and certainly couldn't afford a Polish uprising over a Catholic cardinal.

Richard had given thought as to letting the word get to Hitler about the cardinal's detention but had second thoughts as to what those responsible for the action would do to the cardinal in a final reprisal. He decided against such action, at least for the time being, until he was able to assess firsthand the circumstances surrounding the cardinal's detention. Richard contacted Cardinal Renau in Paris, informing him of his arrival time but not mentioning his reason for coming. Cardinal Renau decided it would be in Richard's best interest not to meet with him right away.

Too many eyes watched the cardinal's every move. The Germans were paranoid of the organized resistance to their occupation from the French underground and certain high-ranking officers believed the Catholic Church was actively involved, thus adding to the reasoning behind Cardinal Beroske's arrest.

Richard caught a flight out of Rome late that evening, arriving in Paris the following morning. The cardinal had arranged transportation for Richard upon his arrival and had no trouble checking through German customs. To Richard's surprise, his chauffer wasn't part of the church clergy, or even male for that matter. Her name was Claudette. She gave no last name. She was French and spoke both French and German. It was agreed that they would speak in French.

Richard had no idea where he was going; Cardinal Renau had arranged this trip strictly on the limited knowledge that had filtered to him mainly through the hands of the French underground of which he had close ties, much different from the rest of the Catholic clergy spread throughout France. The underground had taken a dim view as to the pontiff's tolerance of the Germans until now, believing he should take a much tougher stand against Hitler. There were even rumors to the effect that the pope had made a deal with Hitler that the church would not condemn the Nazi Party if, in return, the Germans did not interfere with the workings of the Catholic Church. For this reason, Richard was to tell no one that he was here on behalf of the Holy Father. Such information, if it were known, could be catastrophic to Cardinal Beroske's welfare.

Richard sat alone in the backseat of the car as the

woman driver made her way out of the city. He attempted several times to carry on some type of conversation with the driver but to no avail. Eventually, he fell asleep in the backseat, having gotten little rest since hearing the news about his friend. His life had become one of a world traveler spending most of his time in and out of train depots and airports, not to mention backseats of automobiles.

Richard slept for several hours as Claudette pushed relentlessly across the rich wine country of eastern France, stopping only for petrol. Midday passed into early evening, and Richard finally stirred in the backseat.

He sat up and rubbed his aching eyes, focusing on Claudette. "Where are we?" he asked, looking out the car window at the rolling countryside.

"We will be at our destination soon, Father."

He settled back in his seat. There was little traffic on the narrow two-lane road. At one point, a small convoy of German trucks passed the opposite direction. Richard noticed a roadside sign that read Strasbourg 200 Kilometers. He knew by his knowledge of European geography that Strasbourg was a good-sized city located near the French and German border in eastern France. Claudette had brought rations, so there was no need to stop for food. Richard offered to take the wheel for a while, but Claudette refused.

During the next several hours, they passed through small towns and villages with little or no signs of German troops. The sun had set some two hours earlier when they entered a small village by the name of Les Frances, midway between Paris and Strasbourg. Richard watched quietly as Claudette turned onto a narrow side street. The street was dark except for the scattering of light shining through the villagers' windows. The car neared the end of the winding dirt road, finally pulling off and stopping in front of a desolate-looking farmhouse. Claudette killed the car's engine. A peaceful silence filled the cool night air. She turned to face Richard. "We'll stay here tonight."

Richard opened his car door, overlooking the rifle lying on the front seat next to Claudette. Claudette took the rifle by its shoulder strap and slung it across her right shoulder. She blended in well with the dark surroundings in her gray pants and black pullover sweater. She was an attractive, dark-complected woman in her early thirties. Richard imagined she had a beautiful smile—but she wasn't smiling tonight

Claudette motioned for Richard to follow her. They walked to the front of the house, moving stealthily in the dim moonlight. It was evident to Richard that Claudette had journeyed this path in darkness before. The house was a single-story wood structure in bad need of repair. Richard noted the two boarded up windows in the front of the house. He watched and listened as Claudette tapped gently on the front door—some kind of secret code, tapped out in a strange rhythm. The door cracked opened. He glimpsed a person's face as they peered through the small opening. "It's Claudette," she whispered. Then, the door opened wide enough for her and Richard to pass. Claudette removed the rifle from her shoulder and handed it to the young man who'd let them in.

Richard's attention was drawn to the two figures standing beside one another, next to a table with a kerosene lamp that gave off a faint glow to the barren room. The men looked to be in their early to mid-twenties. Richard followed Claudette to the table.

"Is this him?" one of the men said, dropping the butt of his cigarette on the floor and mashing it out with the heel of his boot.

"Yes, Pierre, this is the priest from Rome," Claudette said, glancing at Richard.

Richard spoke in French. "I'm Bishop Carver." He extended his hand and smiled. The smile slowly dissipated as Pierre ignored Richard's kind gesture.

"You aren't French, are you?"

"No, I'm an American."

"I see," Pierre answered. "And you are here about the cardinal?"

"Yes."

"Please sit down, American bishop." Pierre pointed to a chair sitting next to the table. Richard complied. Pierre did likewise, facing him across the table. They stared intently at one another. Pierre appeared the typical Frenchman, dark hair, dark eyes. He was quite a handsome lad, even with the deep scar that ran from the corner of his left eye down to the bridge of his narrow nose. Pierre fetched a pack of cigarettes from his shirt pocket. "Care for one, Father?" He offered Richard a cigarette.

Richard declined.

Pierre lit the cigarette. "Please, Father, take your hat off and stay awhile."

Richard removed his hat and laid it on the table.

"Claudette, bring us wine."

Richard watched Claudette as she quickly responded to Pierre's command. Claudette and the other two men took their seats around the table. Perhaps it was the fact that he was an American that they studied him so, but whatever the reason, it made Richard nervous.

Pierre quizzed him for some time, mainly question-answer style. He did a remarkable job of avoiding the papal issue, saying only that he'd spent some time at the Vatican working directly with Cardinal Beroske. It was common knowledge that the French underground thought highly of the Polish cardinal due to his strong and unbending stance against the Germans. The wine relaxed Richard to such a point that he was finally bold enough to ask the question for which he'd traveled the long distance. "Do you know where the cardinal is being held?" He fixed his dark eyes solidly on Pierre.

The young Frenchman eyed his three comrades as he sipped the last of his wine. "We knew where he was yesterday morning . . . but that doesn't mean that he's there tonight." A weak smile bent Pierre's lips. "But we intend to find out if he's still there before this night is over, Bishop Carver."

Many thoughts raced through Richard's mind. The cardinal must be close. Perhaps in this village. Perhaps he . . .

Pierre derailed Richard's train of thought. "Claudette will stay here with you while we go to this place."

"No, damn it! No, Pierre, I'm going with you." Claudette's loud outburst startled Richard.

"But Claudette . . ." Pierre couldn't finish.

"I'm going with you and that's it," Claudette demanded.

"All right, you can go," Pierre said. "Josh, you'll stay with the bishop."

Richard turned his attention to the man standing next to Pierre.

"You know I must go with you, Pierre. My brother and I will not stay behind."

Richard studied the other young man who, like Josh, brandished a rifle.

Pierre's gaze shifted from one brother to the other and back again. Richard imagined that the brother—as with everyone else in this room—had his reasons for being here. Pierre relaxed his shoulders and turned to Richard. "It looks as if you'll accompany us on our little journey, Bishop Carver. It could be dangerous—perhaps even deadly."

Richard considered carefully the four French patriots. Surely, if these four young people were willing to die for a man they'd never met, then there was no way he could refuse.

"I'll go with you," he said as another thought struck him. Perhaps they weren't risking their lives for the cardinal. Maybe they had other reasons—perhaps a hatred for the Germans beyond anything of which he was privy.

Pierre smiled as he leaned across the table, holding his pistol in his outstretched hand toward Richard. "Would you care for a weapon, Father?"

Richard recoiled slightly from the pistol and Pierre. "I need no weapons, my friend. God is my shield."

Pierre grunted. "I hope the bullets meant for you don't ricochet off your shield and into us."

A hush fell over the room as the two men glared at one another for a few anxious moments. A smile suddenly appeared on Richard's lips. "Pierre, if you and your friends are as good with those rifles as I believe, you needn't concern yourself with ricocheting bullets."

Pierre hesitated, then burst with laugher. The laughter was short lived as, once again, the business at hand fell over the small farmhouse.

Richard wasn't allowed to participate in the final plans. He realized they were protecting him in case of capture. The Germans were severe on their captives, especially when it came to the French underground. The less Richard knew about the French underground the better for him as well as the French resistance.

He watched as the four plainclothes soldiers checked their weapons one last time. "Are you ready, Bishop Carver from America?" Pierre said as the other three filed out the front door.

"I'm ready." Richard walked ahead of Pierre through the open doorway.

The five of them filed into the car that had brought Richard. Pierre drove while Claudette sat next to him in the front seat. He sat between the other two Frenchmen in the backseat. He figured it was close to midnight, as the car sped out of Les Frances. An hour into their trip, the rolling countryside was well hidden within the night's blackness. Forty more minutes passed, and Pierre turned off the main road and onto a narrow dirt road.

The car traveled three or so miles down the dirt road, then Pierre stopped the car and killed the headlights. "We'll get out here," Pierre whispered, still peering into the darkness up ahead. "Bishop, be as quiet as an angel. Our lives depend on it." Carefully and quietly, the Frenchman opened his car door. The rest followed suit.

The night was still and quiet as Pierre stood in front of the car, staring at the faint silhouette of a farmhouse a short distance ahead. He bent over, grasping a handful of the rain-soaked dirt. "Close your eyes," he whispered, rubbing the black mud onto Richard's face. "Now you're not such a fine target, Father. You push God's protection to the limits." Pierre smiled and Richard reciprocated. Pierre's smile dropped. "Follow close behind us, American priest."

The five advanced cautiously toward the distant house. The tall weeds offered good cover most of the way, before finally breaking into a small clearing only 100 feet away from the house. They crouched close to the ground. Pierre and the other three Frenchmen scanned the area around the house with their well-trained eyes. He motioned for Richard to come to where he knelt. "You stay close behind us, Father. There's liable to be some activity before this is over." Pierre made one last survey of the area, then motioned for the others to follow. They remained low as they made their way over the open field to the farmhouse.

Richard sighed with relief, crouching with the others against the house. They listened with strained ears to hear the voices and laughter coming from inside. The voices were German. Pierre glanced at Richard, then moved slowly along the edge of the house; the others followed on his heels. Richard suddenly wished he'd taken Pierre's pistol. Pierre stopped at the edge of the front porch. Richard noticed the outlines of two automobiles parked some fifty feet in front of the porch. The sounds from inside grew louder as the five made their way to the front of the house. There were female voices mixed in with the male. Everyone held their positions as Pierre slowly made his way around the side of the porch, his trained eyes looking for a guard or German sentry.

Being the last in line, Richard had lost sight of Pierre but felt the tension rise as Claudette and the others readied their rifles. The silhouette of a soldier carrying a rifle rounded the far corner of the front porch. Richard said a quick, silent Hail Mary. He started a second, hardly thinking the word *Hail*— when another figure appeared behind that of the German soldier. A quick lunge and a hollow thud ended Richard's and the others' eminent danger, at least for the moment. He watched with mixed emotions as Pierre, who'd grabbed the German from behind and plunged a twelve-inch knife into the man's abdomen, slowly lowered the soldier's body onto the porch.

He'd little time to dwell over the situation. Pierre motioned for them to advance and follow behind him. He stayed close behind on Claudette's heels as they single-filed past the German body. Richard glanced at the blood-soaked solider, saying a brief prayer for him as he passed. Pierre motioned for them to get down and crawl underneath a window draped in a red and white cloth. Richard had only crawled a few inches when the figures of Pierre and Josh suddenly appeared standing on opposite sides of the front door. The window was directly above, the laughter and loud voices seemingly inches from his ears. He heard the click of Claudette's rifle safety as he scanned the darkness for another German soldier. But she had not readied her rifle for a guarding soldier.

Richard laid on the porch, witnessing the sudden turn of events. Pierre backed away from the door, then kicked it with all his seeming strength. The door flew open. Pierre and Josh rushed through with guns at the ready. At the same instant, Claudette and the Frenchman in front of her leapt to their feet. The Frenchman dove through the glass window, followed by Claudette. The sound of gunfire mixed with terrifying screams pierced Richard's ears as he lay frozen, spellbound by the horror before him.

What seemed an eternity as he lay listening to the

sounds of death was actually over within a matter of seconds. Richard looked toward the open doorway, praying as he heard the heavy sound of footsteps cross the wood floor inside and make their way toward him. He sighed deeply and lowered his head to the floor when Pierre appeared in the doorway.

"It's all over, Father. You can come in now."

Richard stared at the Frenchman, astonished at the young man's complacency. How could he stand there so calm having just killed a man?

Richard stopped at the doorway believing his eyes were betraying him as he looked into the blood-splattered room. "Welcome to the real war, Father—welcome to France." Pierre's words were as cold as the cooling bodies would soon be. Richard slowly entered the room; his eyes focused on one horrifying sight after another. The partially clothed bodies of four German officers lay on the floor, each one soaking in their own pool of blood. Additional bodies were sprawled on the couch next to the window, where Richard, moments earlier, had heard the sounds of laughter. They would laugh no more. The Nazi officer and scantily clothed young Frenchwoman lay across one another, their bullet-riddled bodies still draining blood.

Richard had been so involved with the dead bodies that he hadn't noticed the absence of Claudette and Josh. A sudden, pain-riddled scream quickly brought them to his attention. He turned toward the open doorway leading to one of the two bedrooms. He made his way toward the doorway. Richard stood in the doorway staring at the most horrible sight he'd ever seen. His mouth dropped open as he stared at Claudette. She smiled, holding a scrotum sack complete with two testes. Richard's eyes then shifted to the naked German tied to the soft feather bed soaking in his own blood. Beside him lay the bullet-riddled body of a young Frenchwoman, apparently in bed with the soldier when Claudette and Josh entered the room. Richard watched as the castrated German made a feeble attempt to free himself. Josh, who was standing next to the bed and the tormented man that it held, finally did the humane thing by placing his pistol to the soldier's head and pulling the trigger. Richard watched the merciful execution, unable at the time to pray for the young soldier's soul; this he would do many times later. At the moment, he struggled to digest the barbarism he'd witnessed, his eyes shifting from the dead solider to Claudette who knelt beside the dead woman. He watched with added horror as she pried open the woman's mouth with her long blade knife and stuffed the soldier's testes into her throat. His strength drained from his body. Pierre's arms embraced him, guiding him out the front door where he proceeded to vomit.

Richard sat alone on the edge of the porch while the others searched the bodies of the dead soldiers for any useful information. Pierre came out and sat beside Richard. With him, he carried a bottle of wine and two glasses. He poured Richard a glass full of wine, then filled the other glass. The two men sat on the edge of the porch silently staring at the blackness of the night.

Finally, Richard broke the silence. "I don't understand how people can be so cruel and heartless to another human being." He hung his head.

"Father, what you've seen tonight puts my people in a very bad perspective. I know we appear to be nothing but bloodthirsty barbarians. True, American bishop?"

Richard nodded. "Yes, it does."

"Mister holy man, if you're fortunate to live long enough into this war, you'll soon learn what brings people to this point. Each of us has our own personal reasons for doing what you have witnessed tonight. You hear some say they do it for the love of France. They're liars. To do these things isn't out of love, it's out of hate. You see that woman named Claudette that only a few moments ago castrated that German officer . . . you saw it, didn't you, bishop of God?" Pierre's voice rose with anger.

"Yes, I saw it."

"Did you know that when the Germans invaded our country that she was living in a Catholic convent?"

Richard's eyes showed his surprise.

"She was going to be a Roman Catholic nun. Then the bastard Germans came. Her father was a powerful and well-liked man in the French government who spoke out loudly against the Germans and its Hitler. The SS came for him one night. Claudette happened to be home. They took all of them to a house, something like this, and there they tortured Claudette's mother and father before taking them away the following night, never to be heard from again. Claudette and her young sister weren't so lucky. They stripped them of their clothes, and the officers took turns raping the girls as they lay in bed next to one another. Claudette's sister finally went delirious and took one of the German's pistol's laying on the bedside table while she was being raped by a German pig. She raised the pistol to the German's head, blowing his brains out all over the bed and all over Claudette, who was being raped at the same time next to her. She turned the pistol toward the German who was momentarily startled atop Claudette and shot him in the head. Claudette's sister then placed the gun next to her head and blew her own brains out. Claudette watched the entire ordeal, her sister's brains splattered on her face."

Pierre's stoic expression melted as he wept openly retelling the story of Claudette. Richard placed his hand on Pierre's shoulder and wept silently with the Frenchman.

"Pray for us, priest of God, and ask that He forgives us for the things we've done and shall do. Beg Him to send the German invaders of our land to everlasting hell. I'll gladly take my place alongside of them for the things I've done. All I ask is take the Germans from my country and leave our people alone. Please, American priest, pray hard for Claudette and the French people . . . please."

Pierre wiped the tears from his cheeks as he rose to his feet, tossing his empty glass into the darkness of the night.

Richard stood beside him. "Your good people fighting an evil war. God will govern your actions knowing of the evils you face."

Pierre smiled. "Perhaps I and my friends here tonight will see you in heaven, my friend the American priest."

Richard returned the smile. "Let's hope it isn't too soon."

There had been no sign of the missing cardinal. It seemed the Germans were one step ahead of the French resistance. Pierre and the others assured him the cardinal had been there, and not too long before their arrival. The Germans were aware of the importance of their captive. It wouldn't be simple finding the cardinal.

Later, Richard met with certain leaders in the resistance, then with Cardinal Renau in Paris. After a lengthy discussion, it was decided that Richard should return to Rome and await further word, being of little use in France and needed more than ever back at the Vatican. The absence of Cardinal Beroske and Richard had left the Holy Father virtually void of inside information concerning the deepening war.

Richard reluctantly returned to Rome. His heart was heavy, failing to find his friend. The hunt, however, was far from over.

Chapter Fourteen

Richard conferred with the pope immediately upon his return to the Vatican. It was decided that Richard would carry on the secret work alone, at least for now, until the pontiff decided who would take Cardinal Beroske's place. All hoped the cardinal would be found safe and returned to his duties before replacement became necessary.

Richard remained in daily contact with assorted informants inside France. At first, optimism remained high about the chances of finding the Polish cardinal, but as the days faded, so did the hope of ever seeing the cardinal again, alive that is. Richard's optimism, however, never faded, and for some unknown reason, he was certain the cardinal remained alive. He prayed many hours for his friend as the burdens of war grew heavier on his shoulders.

It was June 21, 1941, the day before the planned German invasion of Russia. Richard met early in the day with the pontiff, then spent the evening in the small chapel. The Holy Father wanted to know if Richard had heard of any change of plans about the German invasion; he had not.

Richard's prayers had been threefold this night. He prayed for those who would die in the eminent invasion of Russia and for the safety of Cardinal Beroske. Also, he prayed for Claudette, the young Frenchwoman. He'd gotten word this morning she'd been killed in a skirmish with German soldiers just outside Strasbourg five nights ago. Pierre had been badly wounded in the same skirmish but escaped along with the others who made up the small group of the French underground. Richard left the chapel feeling confident God would take her tormented soul to heaven. She, like so many others, had become a victim to a hideous war. Richard sat alone in his room that evening awaiting word on the German invasion.

The knock-on Richard's door came early. He'd fallen asleep in his chair sometime during the long night. Father Gioloni carried the news for which Richard had waited. The Germans had crossed into Russia, and from first reports, it seemed the Soviets had been ill-equipped or prepared for the invasion. The Germans were meeting only token resistance, which had been expected by most of the military allies. The Soviet military was antiquated in comparison to the well-equipped Germans. Richard continued to receive updates throughout the following day. The news didn't get any better as the Germans advanced deeper into Soviet territory at will. It appeared nothing and no one could slow the German onslaught. Roosevelt's hopes that the invasion would ignite the American spirit into entering the war with full effort were dashed as the days passed. Americans appeared reluctant to enter such a war, unwilling, as of yet, to feel personally endangered by Hitler and his German war machine. Churchill seemed to take America's reluctance to enter the conflict hard.

Reports to Richard indicated that Churchill was certain that if Germany took Russia, Great Britain would surely fall in time, as would the last democracy in Europe. If the invasion had done nothing else, it had elevated the Vatican to a prominence never before experienced in the major capitals of the world. The church's support was even more crucial to these governments.

Days rolled into weeks as the German Army advanced and conquered vast regions of the Soviet Union. Hitler's determination to defeat the Soviet Union had taken pressure off Great Britain, at least temporarily. The vastness of Russia was overwhelming, and at one point, the Germans were forced to fight on a 200-mile front. By all indications, Hitler planned to be in Moscow and Leningrad long before the Russian winter set in. Richard knew what happened to Napoleon's army when it became trapped in the unbearable Russian cold. The first few weeks after the invasion, it looked to him that Hitler would have little to worry about; the German Army had been advancing at nearly fifty miles per day. As the Germans made their way deeper into Russia, however, reports from the French underground stated that the German Army was experiencing difficulty receiving much needed supplies. By November, Germany's advance had slowed to a crawl as the Russian winter settled in. By December 1, the Germans were still many miles from Moscow. The Russians, who at first were no match for the advancing Germans, had managed during the following weeks to regroup and were better supplied than during the initial invasion. The Soviet Army had struggled terribly during the first weeks following the German offensive, but Hitler had failed to cast the killing blow and Moscow remained in Soviet hands. No one had foreseen such an unbelievable accomplishment, as most military strategists believed Germany would be victorious in a matter of weeks.

It was the morning of December 7, 1941. Richard studied information he'd received the night before regarding Germany's advance on Moscow. The Soviets were still holding the Germans in a stalemate less than twenty miles from Moscow. A knock sounded on his door. A middle-aged priest entered Richard's study carrying a telegram. He'd grown accustomed to such messages, averaging better than twenty a day from all parts of the world. He took this one expecting it to be from his friend Cardinal Renau in Paris. Information had come in over the last several days suggesting Cardinal Beroske might've been moved to Poland. Richard had cabled Cardinal Renau as to the authenticity of these rumors. The priest waited as Richard opened the telegram. His face grew pale as his eyes scanned the unbelievable words printed on the coarse vanilla paper.

"Something wrong, Bishop?"

"The Japanese have bombed Pearl Harbor . . . the American base in Hawaii."

The priest blinked rapidly at Richard. "What will happen, Bishop Carver?"

"America, my country, will now fight," Richard replied matter-of-factly. "God help these people who have openly provoked the United States. The Americans are a free and proud people who believe in God and his infinite power. God and America will prevail once again." His voice shifted with a sudden urgency. "I must see the Holy Father immediately."

The priest hurried from the room. Within the hour,

Richard and the Holy Father were conferring with one another in yet another of their secret meetings. They, like most everyone else in the world, had been caught off guard by the surprise Japanese attack. The world's attention had been centered on the European conflicts. The overnight surprise attack changed everything, especially after it was learned that the Americans had lost most of its Pacific Fleet. Richard imagined Hitler rejoiced upon hearing the news. The Japanese had taken Germany's concern of America entering the European war and fighting against them. The attack would allow Hitler the much-needed time to finish off the stubborn Russians and then the equally stubborn British. America could surely not fight on two different continents at once; Germany wasn't even capable of such a thing.

This was December 1941. The democracies of the world trembled this winter, as all of Europe was on the very threshold of being overrun by two fanatical leaders: Hitler of Germany and Mussolini of Italy. In the Pacific, another fanatic by the name of General Tojo, the prime minister of Japan, and his military were racing through the Pacific Islands as swiftly as Hitler had swept through Europe. Richard prayed hard the night of December 7, but he wasn't alone. The peoples of the free world prayed with him, especially in America where the tragedies of war had been cast so violently into their faces.

The following morning on December 8, 1941, the United States declared war on the Empire of Japan. Great Britain declared war on Japan a few hours later the same day. On December 9 China declared war on Japan and Germany. On December 11 Germany and Italy declared war on the United States. In a matter of four days, the whole civilized world was thrown into a massive conflict.

The rapid chain of events affected the church and especially Richard's unique position of being an American bishop, which allowed him to move rather freely throughout Europe and Germany, considering America was still neutral in the European war. This advantage changed overnight with Hitler's declaration of war against America and in Italy where Mussolini declared America an enemy. Richard's only hope was that Germany and Italy would still recognize the Catholic Church as neutrals, allowing him to continue traveling about these countries with the same ease, as of which was yet to be seen.

***

For the first part of 1942, Richard remained in Vatican City. During this time, Germany still hadn't taken Moscow, as the Soviets had even managed small counterattacks against the stymied Germans. England was more determined than ever, holding out hope that America's arms buildup would be enough to counter Germany's war machine. The information Richard was receiving from Lori confirmed that, indeed, America had shifted into full-time war preparation. It seemed that Joe and Jeff were working day and night at the yard putting all their efforts into the united cause. Lori had also taken work in an ammunition factory outside Norfolk. She, like the rest of the country, had become totally dedicated to the war effort. "Remember Pearl Harbor" had become America's war cry. Lori hadn't mentioned Elisabeth in any of her letters. Richard hadn't mustered the courage to ask about her, trying desperately to focus his full attention on the war. He failed miserably, though, at this as thoughts of Elisabeth filtered through his shield at different times, especially when he was alone in his room at night rereading Lori's letters.

The escalating war alienated Richard more than ever from the mainstream of the Vatican. His guarded work and long, tedious hours spent alone in his office left him little time for socializing with other residents of the Holy City, and with the absence of Cardinal Beroske, Richard had no other close relationships. This period of isolation continued for a short time before, once again, making many, mostly covert journeys throughout Europe. This, within itself allowed Richard to make few friends inside the Vatican; in great contrast, however, his friends outside the Vatican walls continued to multiply.

These first months of 1942 were bitter ones for the United States and its allies. Like most other countries drawn into the conflict, America found itself almost totally underprepared in both armaments and trained military personnel. The United States was to taste many bitter defeats by the battle-hardened Germans and the fanatical Japanese, well trenched in most of the South Pacific Islands by the time America fired its first shot.

It became apparent to Richard that the Europeans in general were disillusioned by America's seeming insignificance in this early part of the war, somehow expecting much greater impact militarily from the Americans than, as of yet, had been the case. The United States' reluctance to enter the war had hampered the country's preparedness for such powerful enemies. Likewise, it never anticipated fighting on two global fronts: Europe and the South Pacific. It quickly became evident that America had no magic tricks for a quick duration of the war.

As had been the case all along, the Vatican kept a low-profile during Hitler's rampage across Europe, but as more horrid stories began to filter out of Germany and Poland about the great atrocities committed against religious groups and, especially, the Jews, the Catholic Church's voice grew louder, speaking out against the Germans and, for the first time, against Mussolini and his renegade army. But the pope continued to be defiant, refusing to publicly condemn the Nazis or Mussolini.

Until now, Richard had gone along with the pontiff's decision, aware of the political tightrope on which the church balanced. During the last months, however, two events forced a change on Richard's continued support. First was the unprovoked kidnapping of his friend Cardinal Beroske by the German SS; second was the unprovoked attack by the Japanese against the peoples of his homeland. The pontiff avoided asking Richard his opinion on the matter, likely aware of Richard's change of attitude on the subject.

***

The day was April 15, a little over four months since the Japanese had bombed Pearl Harbor. Richard wrote Lori once a week on average since the bombing, keeping abreast with his family in these crucial times as well as he could. Until the last five weeks, she'd written as often; since then, there'd been no word. Richard was beginning to grow concerned about the drop in communication.

It was Sunday 4:00 p.m. when Richard received a telegram from Joe, who was in England. It seemed that six weeks prior he and Jeff had come to a mutual decision. With the war deepening and America badly in need of men to serve in the military, Joe would join the navy. Being short of qualified naval officers to man the growing flotilla of military vessels, the navy offered Joe the rank of full captain if he would pilot one of the ships they were producing for the navy. This seemed reasonable, as Joe was more knowledgeable of these vessels than was probably anyone else. The German U-boats had been playing havoc with English shipping, sinking large numbers of cargo ships on their way from America to Great Britain. It was for this reason that Joe and other American captains were sent to this part of the world to rid the seas of these underwater killers, so, once again the free world could control the high seas. Joe also stated in the telegram that he would be in London for sixteen more days, and if it were possible, he hoped Richard could come join him for a few days. After conferring with the pope, they decided that there was no pressing reason to keep Richard from briefly visiting London. Richard wired Joe after making the travel arrangements that had become almost an impossible ordeal during this stage of the war. Most commercial craft had been confiscated by the ruling countries, converting them into military aircraft of one sort or another. Finally, Richard arranged a flight on a Swiss plane whose government had remained neutral to the warring countries that virtually surrounded it.

Richard arrived in London on the afternoon of April 19, 1942, at 3:30 p.m. This was Richard's first aerial view of the bombed-out city; the last time he was here was under the cover of darkness. The city looked decimated from the air, but once on the ground, it was apparent the British were still quite alive. Richard had transferred onto a small plane on the coast of France and landed on a short, grassy airstrip outside of London.

Joe had arranged for a military jeep to bring his brother into London. Richard's chauffer was a young army corporal from Abilene, Kansas. The young nineteen-year-old kept Richard entertained as they made their way toward London. A light rain had moved in from the channel. He pulled his overcoat tightly about his neck. The damp air flowed freely through the open jeep as it made its way through the English countryside. It was nearly dark by the time the jeep reached the core of the city, and the fog had thickened with the setting sun. Richard watched with strained eyes as the driver made his way along the London streets.

"Here we are, Padre," the corporal said, stopping the jeep.

Richard attempted to make out the building that sat only a few feet away, but the heavy fog would have no part of it.

"Welcome to the Blake Hotel," the doorman said, holding the door open for Richard and the corporal as they entered the plush establishment carrying Richard's luggage.

Checking in with the hotel clerk, Richard and the corporal were off to room 312. "This looks like it, corporal." Richard placed his luggage down and entered the room. He called out Joe's name. No reply. Then, he thanked the young soldier, tipping him five dollars for his help. The company and entertainment had been worth that much. Richard spotted a note on the coffee table. *Stepped down to Kellies Pub for a few beers. I'll be back around ten o'clock, Joe.* Richard glanced at his watch; it was almost nine now, and he was very tired, having journeyed a long distance these last several hours.

Richard forced himself to unpack, then took a soothing bath that helped revive him. After the bath, he fixed himself a mixed drink from the scotch bottle Joe had graciously supplied and made himself comfortable upon the large couch that sat beneath a heavily draped window. Richard studied some of the notes he'd brought with him in reference to his meeting with Archbishop Shannon later in the week. His eyes grew heavy. He'd fought off sleep as long as he could. He pulled the quilt that lay on the back of the couch over his outstretched body and within moments was sound asleep.

Richard hadn't heard the tapping on the front door, but the sound of Joe's voice and the closing of the door awakened him. He lay watching as Joe set the canister of hot coffee on the table next to the window. So far, Joe hadn't noticed Richard's presence, and he called from the couch, "Aren't you going to ask your brother if he'd like to have a cup of coffee?"

Joe turned, almost spilling his coffee. "God, Richard, you startled me." He took a deep breath. "Damn, Richard, I'm glad to see you." Joe sat his cup of coffee on the table and took Richard into his arms.

After a long embrace, Richard poured himself a cup of coffee. Then, both men sat on the couch and caught up on each other's lives. Richard told of his failure to this point of locating his friend Cardinal Beroske but never went into the horrid details of his search. Joe spoke of the war effort taking place back home, how everyone seemed eager to do what was necessary to defeat the Japanese and Germans. Joe briefed Richard on the booming shipping business. Joe hated leaving Jeff and his ailing father-in-law behind to run the ever-emerging shipping giant. But they'd all agreed that he could do more to benefit the country than if all three stayed at home. Joe spoke of Lori's sacrifice working at the munition's factory, how she never complained about the long hours she put in and her lost hours with her children.

Richard waited anxiously for Joe to mention something about Elisabeth, but he never said a word. Finally, Joe said he'd an errand to run and would like Richard to come along. Richard had finished dressing and was finishing the last of the coffee when Joe entered the room. He stared at his handsome brother decked out in his naval captain's uniform. "Impressive, big brother, to say the least. I'm proud of you, Joe . . . if only Mom and Dad were here to see you now. How proud they'd be."

Joe beamed. He placed his hand on Richard's shoulder. "How proud they would be of both of us, Richard. Look at you, a man of the cloth. And as Lori and I have said before, there's no telling how much power you wield in that secretive world you live in. We're not complete fools, little brother, your sister and I. Simple observation would tell one that you're no ordinary church preacher, not a man that travels the world as much as you do. Tell me, Richard, exactly what is it that you do? I can keep a secret. You're my brother."

Richard smiled. "I follow orders, brother Joe, just like you."

Joe laughed. "I supposed I asked for that."

Joe had borrowed a car from a shipmate whose brother lived in London. The misty fog of the night before had lifted, and the bright sun shone overhead. It was almost noon when they left the hotel. The city bustled with activity. If it weren't for the remnants of earlier bombings, one would probably never realize that these same people were caught up in a life and death struggle of a severe war. The narrow body of water separating this island from the French mainland had probably been the salvation that had kept them, so far, from a similar fate endured by the French across the English Channel.

The moderate traffic began to thin as Joe drove down Covertly Street to Piccadilly Circus. "Where we heading, by the way?" Richard said, staring out his window.

"There's a field hospital set up on the edge of the city. It's a US military hospital that's been operational for two months now. Most of the wounded are British civilians. We haven't been in this war long enough yet to fill it up with American wounded." Joe's smile disappeared as he glanced at Richard's stern face. "OK, bad joke."

"That answers my question as to where it is we're going, but why are we going there?"

"Oh hell, Richard, she wanted me to surprise you but what the hell."

Richard's voice rose slightly as he turned sharply to Joe. "She . . . who is she?"

"Elisabeth, she joined the Army Nurse Corps a week after Pearl Harbor was bombed. She's been stationed here in London for almost five weeks now."

Richard sat stunned. Never in his wildest dreams would he have guessed Elisabeth would join a nurse corps and much less stationed in London. This couldn't be.

Joe broke the prolonged silence. "What's wrong, little brother? You act as if you wish Elisabeth wasn't here."

He tried to recoup from his shock. "Oh no, I think

it's quite admirable for such a fine lady to sacrifice herself this way."

"That's what I told Lori you would say. She was all upset about the whole thing for some reason, especially when I wired her telling her about you coming over and spending a few days with me. Damn, she wired back and told me to wire you back telling you to stay in Rome. It was too dangerous for you to come to England. Women, I'll never figure them out."

Ten minutes later, Joe pulled onto a narrow side road. Richard spotted the hospital. A white banner with a huge red cross was draped over the front half of the two-story stone building. This was done in the hope of a German bombing raid they would spare the medical facility. The maneuver, it seemed, had little effect as the cross offered only a better target for the bombardier.

The two-story structure sat out amidst a large clearing surrounded by thin forest. Joe pulled the car to a stop in the rear of the compound. It was mid-afternoon, and many of the staff and more able wounded were scattered about the grounds enjoying their lunches and taking advantage of the weather on this gorgeous April afternoon.

Richard and Joe walked side by side toward the rear entrance to the hospital. Richard's eyes were in constant search for any sign of Elisabeth. Even at this moment, he fought with everything he had inside to cast his feelings about Elisabeth to the wind. With every step, though, the wind grew calmer, no more than an uneasy lull by the time they entered the building. They walked down a long corridor. Unlike the serene life forms that had greeted the two brothers outside, the world they entered was a truer image of the horrid war.

The sounds of hurried footsteps and the clatter of pushcarts carrying medical supplies from one room to another—this was the real world and some of the real people who'd taken part in it. Some of these victims of war would be lucky and recover from their wounds, but many would die—or even worse, live. Many were maimed horribly for the remainder of their agonizing lives. For others, the physical wounds would heal, but their minds, much more delicate, would be scarred forever; for them, the war would never end.

Joe acted as if he knew where he was going, and Richard kept pace as well as he could. "There it is." Joe pointed to the small overhead sign hanging above the double doorway.

Richard looked at the sign that read Nurses Duty Station.

They entered the office. Joe and Richard approached the counter on the far side of the room where a woman nurse seemed busy with some sort of paperwork.

"Excuse me," Joe said finally, after the nurse failed to acknowledge their presence.

"Yes, what is it?" she grumbled, then looked up at the naval captain. Richard watched with silent amusement as the sour-faced nurse transformed into a sweet, helpful lady. "Yes, Captain, may I help you?"

"Yes, could you tell me where I might find the nurse Elisabeth Downs?"

The woman ran her finger down a long ledger. "Yes, Captain, she's at the far end of this hallway, in ward G."

"Thank you." Joe and Richard started back down the hall, toward ward G.

218

The large wards that made up most of this first floor seemed well occupied. Richard and Joe glanced into the rooms as they made their way down the hall.

Joe stopped at the entrance to ward G. "Here we are."

Richard took a deep breath of courage as he followed Joe into the room. It was a massive, open room with a wide corridor running down the center. Rows of metal-framed beds lined both sides. Large, open windows ran across the length of the east wall, lighting the room brilliantly from the midday sun. Some of the more fortunate wounded sat in the numerous chairs scattered about the room while the less fortunate wounded lay in their beds.

The two brothers stopped in the middle of the corridor, searching for Elisabeth. Nurses moved about the room performing their particular duties, tending patients. Neither brother spotted Elisabeth.

"Richard, you search that side of the room. I'll take the other." Joe pointed Richard to the window side.

Both men started down the wide corridor in opposite directions. Richard who was wearing his priest clothes was well received by most of those he passed. Joe also seemed well received. Richard could hear wounded soldiers thank his brother and America for coming to help eradicate the evils of the German Empire and their leader Adolph Hitler.

Richard stopped to say a few words to a young British officer who'd lost his right arm in a bombing raid four months earlier. The faint call of "Father . . ." disrupted the chat. He looked across the room at another young man who stood beside a bed motioning to him. Richard excused himself from the British officer and started toward the excited man who motioned for him to hurry. He approached the young soldier who was looking down at the bandaged body lying motionless in the metal bed. The young soldier whispered in Richard's ear, "Father, I'm afraid this young chap isn't going to make it. He's from County Cork, Father. I told him you were here. He asked that you give him his last confession."

Richard looked down at the soldier whose body was wrapped in gauze and white tape except for his eyes, nose, and mouth. Richard bent over and whispered something to the dying man, then knelt beside the bed, making the sign of the cross. He prayed for a few moments, then stood and sat close to the man on the side of the bed. He listened closely as the young man labored to speak his last words that would free his soul on his final journey to his awaiting God. Richard looked into the young man's blue eyes, death upon them. He wiped the tiny tears from the corners of the soldier's eyes. Within a matter of moments, the soldier was dead. Richard looked at the young man's eyes one last time, as they remained open after his passing. The look of death had transformed into one of serenity. Richard smiled to himself as he gently closed the soldier's eyes with his fingertips. Once again, he knelt beside the soldier's bed, saying one last prayer. Finishing his prayer, he stood and turned away, continuing his journey down the corridor.

He'd walked only a few steps when the most stunning nurse he'd ever seen captivated him. Her beautiful smile whisked the previous moments of sadness into eternity.

"Hello, Richard."

"Hello, Elisabeth. It's so good to see you again."

"Do you really mean that Richard?"

"Elisabeth, I mean that more than you'll ever know."

It was a moment frozen in time. She was radiant, dressed in her white uniform, her flowing brown hair and green eyes glistening in the brightness of the room. It was as if they were suddenly without words, or perhaps it was that words would simply be foolish. They spoke to one another at this very moment, and the spoken word *love* could never compare to the silent love flowing between them. They were alone in this moment of many.

Joe's voice returned them back to the horrid reality of their real world. "Hello, Elisabeth." Joe approached the couple. "I see Richard found you first."

"Yes . . . Oh yes he did," Elisabeth said, glancing at Richard.

Joe's voice softened. "Have you missed me?"

"Yes, Joe," she said, stuttering a little as Joe leaned over and kissed her on the lips.

Richard turned away, unable to bear watching someone else touch Elisabeth intimately, especially his brother.

"Joe, please, not here while I'm working," she whispered.

Richard heard her terrible whisperings. Thoughts of her and Joe together flashed through his mind like an awful dream. He shook his head violently, trying to cast out the wicked scenes.

"Richard, are you all right?" Joe asked.

"Oh, I'm fine. My mind drifted off somewhere else."

"Damn, little brother, you keep that up and Elisabeth will find a bed for you in here."

221

Richard considered that possibility.

"Well, we'd better be getting back to the city," Joe continued. "You're going to meet me at Kelsey's around eight tonight."

Elisabeth glanced at Richard, who was looking down the corridor, doing a lousy job of trying to act unconcerned. "Why yes. Will you be there too, Richard?"

"Who . . . me? Oh no, I have work tonight."

"Hell, don't worry about it, Richard." Joe placed his arm around Elisabeth's shoulder, pulling her to him. "We still have a few more nights before we head our separate ways. Anyhow, I'm sort of glad you're not coming tonight. I'd like a little time alone with my girl here."

Richard forced a smile as he looked at his brother holding firmly to Elisabeth. Her beautiful smile had faded, but he saw something working behind her eyes. Then, a look came over her, one Richard was unsure of just how to read, a slow smile that grew until she beamed. Yes, a new, splendid smile creased Elisabeth's lips as she looked at Richard. "I'll see you again, Richard, before you leave for Rome."

"Yes, I hope so. I'll be leaving for Dublin on the night of the ninth, but that's a few days away yet."

"Good," she said quickly, as if Richard might decide to change his mind.

Joe removed his arm from Elisabeth's shoulder. "Well, let's get back to London, old boy, and let this little lady work on these poor folks."

Richard had temporarily forgotten where he was, but a quick glimpse around the room reminded him of the terrible surroundings.

Joe kissed Elisabeth again. "See you tonight."

Richard smiled weakly. "Good-bye, Elisabeth."

"Good-bye, Richard, and I'll see you soon," she said softly.

Richard and Joe were fairly quiet as they made their way back to London. Richard went with Joe to Kelsey's Bar. They had a few beers and listened to some Englishwoman attempt to sing American songs. Richard watched and listened as the young soldiers sang songs of war and glory as if it were something magical and good. He imagined most had yet to feel the earth tremble beneath their feet as bombs and mortar shells exploded about them. They hadn't seen their friends drop in the fields; their heads blown from their shoulders. They hadn't yet heard small children cry for their mother as she lay beside them, a bullet through her brain. No, they hadn't seen these terrible things Richard was thinking as he looked about the room filled with gaiety and laughter. How many of these same young men would be laughing in a month? Better yet, how many of the ones in this room tonight would be alive a month from now? Richard's eyes rested on Joe. A sudden chill ran down his spine as he glared at his laughing brother, as Joe, too, had never experienced the sting of battle. Richard was certain Joe would survive the war but said a Hail Mary anyway.

They had their final beer and headed back to the hotel room. Joe took a bath and once again was ready to meet Elisabeth. He entered the room decked out in a clean officer's uniform. "How do I look, little brother?"

"You make America proud. The women won't be able to resist you."

"Elisabeth is the only woman I care about. You know, I wasn't certain before how I really felt about

Elisabeth. You know as well as I she's the prettiest woman God ever let set foot on this planet . . . and smart, Whooee. But I was never sure about marriage and all until I set eyes on her at that hospital this afternoon. I knew then she was the one for me. What do you think, Richard? You think she loves me?"

Richard's stomach turned and small beads of sweat popped out on his forehead. Clearing his throat, he said, "Well, Joe, I can't speak for her, but she apparently has feelings for you, still seeing you and all."

"Yeah, I guess I'm just a little scared, that's all. I've never had a woman affect me this way, and I haven't slept with her either . . . and that's something that's never happened to me, at least after the first date. Sorry, brother priest, about talking of such stuff."

"That's OK, Joe. I'm a man also."

"Oh yeah, I forgot," Joe laughed. "Well, time to go. See you later, brother." Joe positioned his naval captain's cap on his head and made his way out the door.

Richard stared at the closed door for the longest time. Joe's words rang loudly in his ears. This was the first time Joe had ever opened up to him about how he really felt about Elisabeth. Before, Richard could only surmise Joe's feelings, always playing them down to ease his conscience. He knew this but couldn't bring himself to admit it fully, until now. There was no more game of charades. Joe had ended that game. Richard was left with no choice; he couldn't and wouldn't ever see Elisabeth again. Rising from the couch, he put on his hat, wiped the tears from the corners of his eyes, then walked out the door.

He walked the busy streets of London for hours it seemed, not really going anywhere, just walking and thinking. Finally, he came to a Catholic Cathedral. He entered the church and took a seat in the front pew. A handful of worshipers occupied the cathedral as Richard went to his knees and prayed harder to his God than he'd ever prayed, asking forgiveness for what he'd done and strength for what he needed to do. He spent two hours in the church, arriving back at the apartment an hour after Joe.

Daylight broke when Richard finally drifted off to sleep. He slept until late morning. Joe dozed on the couch, a book lying face down on his chest. Richard's stirring roused him.

Richard joined him in the living room. "I didn't hear you come in last night," he said, not aware Joe had been asleep on the couch by the time he'd returned.

"Yeah, it was late."

The two sat around not saying much. Richard was anxious to discover what had occurred between Joe and Elisabeth the evening before. Finally, he brought up the subject. "Did you have a good time last night?"

Joe yawned. "We had drinks at Kelsey's and a nice dinner after, then pretty well walked around the city."

Richard awaited word on Elisabeth's response to perhaps Joe's marriage proposal. "Did you ask Elisabeth to marry you?"

Joe smiled and set the book on a nearby table. "You know it seemed like every time I was ready to ask her, she would get off on another subject. After a while, I got paranoid and was embarrassed to ask. You know how easily I get my feelings hurt." Joe smiled.

Richard tried to smile back. "Yeah, Joe, you're just one big, wrapped package of emotion."

Joe laughed. "I wouldn't go that far. But seriously,

it did seem she was deliberately avoiding the question."

Richard paused to consider that, indeed, such was probably the case. He reminded himself this quest for the same woman had to end, especially when it should never have begun. He was a priest; he'd taken a vow to his church and the Almighty. He recalled the night before, roaming the streets, warring with his own consciousness and convictions, only to reach this final, inevitable conclusion.

Joe interrupted Richard's thoughts. "Maybe I'll ask her tonight. Elisabeth made reservations at The Harbor for dinner tonight for the three of us."

Richard sat up straight. "No, I can't go . . . I have important work to finish tonight on my upcoming trip to Ireland."

"Come on, Richard. You can't do this to Elisabeth. She went to a lot of trouble to make these reservations. It's one of the finest restaurants in London. She likes you a lot, I can tell."

Richard had difficulty clearing his throat. "She's a beautiful woman, Joe. The two of you will make a fine couple and bear many children together."

Joe smiled and said, "How can you marry us and be the best man at the same time?"

"We'll work it out when the time comes. But I can't go with the two of you tonight, and this will be the perfect time for you to propose to her, a romantic candlelight dinner just the two of you. Think about it, Joe, no woman could say no to a marriage proposal under those conditions." Richard watched as Joe's attention drifted, perhaps imagining dinner with Elisabeth at the Harbor restaurant. "Even to someone as ugly as you," he added.

Joe threw a couch pillow at him. "Why you smart ass."

Finally, he persuaded Joe into going alone to the dinner. Richard did not intend to set eyes on Elisabeth again, at least not until she'd accepted Joe's marriage proposal. Then, and only then, would he feel confident enough to stay out of Elisabeth's arms, having given up on trying to convince himself that he didn't love her.

Joe and Richard cleaned up, then decided to go down to Kelsey's for a bite of lunch and a few beers to help pass the afternoon. It was another beautiful spring day. Richard noticed the headlines on one of the London newspapers as he and Joe walked to Kelsey's: GERMAN U-BOATS CAUSING HAVOC WITH ALLIED SHIPPING. His thoughts turned to Joe as he read the words. Joe never paused to look at the papers.

It was a little after four in the afternoon when they left Kelsey's. A brief shower thirty minutes earlier had cooled the afternoon air, providing a very comfortable walk back to the hotel. Richard and Joe were well received by the English people as they ambled down the street.

They entered the hotel lobby. Before they could catch the elevator, a desk clerk called Joe over. Richard followed and watched as his brother opened a telegram. He knew by Joe's expression it wasn't good news.

"What is it, Joe?"

"I have to get back to the ship immediately. No reason given. Damn!" Joe crumbled the dreaded paper. "Well, you'll have to go to dinner tonight and tell Elisabeth of my predicament. Tell her I'll be in touch as soon as possible."

Richard couldn't refuse.

Joe hurriedly packed his things and was shortly off to his ship. Richard's well considered strategy was maimed badly with Joe's unexpected orders. He rehearsed his new course of action as he bathed, dressed, and rode in the taxi. He was still rehearsing when he entered The Harbor, overlooking the Thames River that ran through the heart of the city. Richard arrived a few minutes early. The reservations weren't until seven thirty, and it was only a few minutes past seven. A small lounge sat off to the right of the dining room. He decided to have a cocktail while he waited on Elisabeth to arrive.

Richard wasn't wearing his priest vestments, dressed in a dark suit, white shirt, and tie. This wasn't unusual for him to dress this way in a strange city, having grown accustomed to it in his line of work. This absence of vestments, at times, posed other problems in the form of flirting young ladies, as was the case now. Two young English ladies had already set their aim on the striking young American who sat alone at the bar.

An attractive, young woman took a seat on the bar stool next to Richard. "Hello, handsome. By yourself?"

"I'm—"

"No, the gentleman is with me."

He was as shocked as the as Englishwoman to find Elisabeth standing behind them.

"Well, handsome, you do have good taste."

Richard smiled at the woman as she rose from the bar stool and whispered something in Elisabeth's ear. Elisabeth looked at the woman a moment, then smiled slyly as the woman left, joining her other companion at another table.

"I can't trust you alone by yourself for one moment.

The very idea of a woman trying to pick up a priest . . . that is, if she knew he was a priest." Elisabeth touched her neck as if to indicate she noticed he'd not worn his collar.

"You look beautiful tonight, Elisabeth, as always." Richard gazed upon Elisabeth's green eyes and wavy brown hair.

"Thank you, Richard." She took a seat next to him. "Where's Joe?"

"He's very sorry, but late this afternoon he received emergency orders to return immediately to his ship."

"You mean he won't be here tonight?"

"Yes, I'm sorry."

Elisabeth's eyes sparkled. "We'll just have to make the most of it, I suppose. Please order me a drink, Richard."

They finished their one drink—saying little. When their drinks were empty, they moved into the dining room.

It was a lovely place overlooking the river. Several military men, mostly officers and mainly American, dined with their dinner guests. Richard had been uncharacteristically reserved back at the bar, and this continued at the dinner table. Elisabeth seemed somewhat unnerved by his aloofness, shifting in her seat, barely picking at her meal. Occasionally, she would laugh extra loud or lean forward, attempting to engage him further, but he remained as stoic as possible, struggling to keep his thoughts on Joe and Joe's feelings for the woman they each loved.

Toward the end of the meal, Elisabeth laid down her napkin and looked him squarely in the eyes. "Richard, where are we going after we leave here?"

He looked at her as she sipped on her glass of brandy. "Elisabeth, I really have to get back to the hotel. I have some last-minute things I must finish before my trip to Ireland day after tomorrow. I hate not seeing you back to the hospital, but you'll have no trouble driving on your own."

Elisabeth pouted slightly. "I don't have any way to get back to the hospital. I caught a ride with a couple of army doctors who happened to be coming this way, thinking Joe would see me back. You surely wouldn't leave me stranded in a city like London, would you? There might be another Jack the Ripper out there lurking beneath the bomb debris."

Richard couldn't hold back his smile as he looked at Elisabeth's saddened face. "Honestly, I don't believe it's a good idea for us to be alone together. Not that I don't trust you. It's me I don't trust."

"Please."

Richard shook his head and smiled. "I don't suppose that even I'm capable of doing such a thing. I guess you could sleep in Joe's bed tonight, seeing how he won't need it." Elisabeth's puckered lips softened with Richard's words. They finished their drinks and started back to the hotel.

It was a beautiful evening for a walk through the London streets. They left the restaurant around eleven o'clock, but the streets were filled with people strolling along, enjoying the nice evening and the peaceful serenity that draped over the city. Quietly, they walked beside one another, glancing at the passing sights. Elisabeth slipped her hand into Richard's. At first, he pulled slightly away, unnerved that his hand had gained a silent partner, then he tightened his grip. She reciprocated, squeezing his hand. Her walk took on a strut and a fiery heat poured into his heart.

They arrived at the hotel after midnight. "This was Joe's room and now your room," Richard said, showing Elisabeth the large bedroom adjacent to his.

She looked about the room. "Very nice. You wouldn't happen to have an extra pair of pajamas, would you? You see, all I have is what I'm wearing. Of course, I could always sleep in the nude."

Richard's face grew flush, and Elisabeth chuckled softly.

"Yes, I have an extra pair. I'll go get them." He left the room.

Elisabeth walked back into the living room, to the small dinette table where Joe had left a bottle of scotch. She grabbed a glass sitting next to the bottle and poured herself a drink. Richard exited his room carrying a pair of plaid pajamas.

"I hope these will do. This is all I have."

Elisabeth smiled as Richard handed her the pajamas. "Pour yourself a drink, Richard, while I go bathe and freshen up."

He started to reply but couldn't find his voice, standing so close to her beauty. "I should—"

"Oh hush," she interrupted, taking Richard's hand and gently squeezing it. "I'll be right back. And don't worry, I won't seduce you, even though I must admit it has crossed my mind more than once this evening."

Richard felt somewhat relieved by Elisabeth's remark, and, yes, somewhat disappointed.

He skimmed through a magazine, his back to her. "Well how do I look?"

Richard turned. His weak smile turned to laughter

231

as Elisabeth slowly turned around, modeling the pajamas that all but dwarfed her beautiful body. "You look gorgeous." His laughter gave way to sincerity. "Absolutely ravishing."

The pajamas did an excellent job of disguising Elisabeth's body, but nothing hid the radiant beauty of her face. Elisabeth stopped modeling the pajamas. Their eyes locked, as they had the day at the hospital. Yes, and the invisible vibrations had returned, wavering violently between them. Elisabeth raised a hand and placed it over her heart, as if to feel it race. Then, she lowered it to her side, and he pulled her to him. He'd fantasized about this moment, tried to pray his desires for her away. What good were his prayers now? He heard her moan softly as she wrapped her arms tightly around him, their lips lingering upon one another. They embraced for the longest time, then Elisabeth surprised him, pulling away. He tried to kiss her again.

"No, Richard, not now, not tonight."

He stepped back, his confusion written plainly across his face.

"Richard, I'm going up to York the day after tomorrow. We have a new hospital there. I have three days leave coming, and I want you to meet me there after your trip to Ireland. I've already rented a cottage in Pickering. It's in the countryside. Richard, it's beautiful. Just me and you, alone together for three whole days."

He froze, confused and dumbfounded by her sudden turn. "But I can't."

"Yes, you can—if you really want to. Please, Richard, I know how much you desire me at this moment, and I want you more than you'll ever know. But let's wait until we can be alone together, no time schedules or important meetings hanging over our heads."

Richard turned his head, running his hand through his hair. "Elisabeth, I'm a priest."

"I know what you are better than anybody in this world. Don't you know that? Listen, if you wish, we won't have to do anything except be together. You have my word that I won't try and force myself on you . . . my solemn word, Richard." She crossed her heart.

"I don't know, Elisabeth."

"Richard, please, you owe me three days of your life. My Lord, I've given up so many of mine waiting for you."

He looked at Elisabeth, the tears tumbling down her cheeks. Gently, he wiped her tears with his fingertips. "I guess I do owe you that much."

Her face brightened. She threw her arms around his chest. "I love you so much."

Richard gently pushed her away. "Remember, you promised."

She smiled and said, "Good night, my precious Richard."

"Good night, Elisabeth," he replied as she turned and walked to her room.

He stared at her door a few moments, then poured himself one last drink and went to bed.

Richard's mind twirled. His life was suddenly one large mess. Only hours before, he'd sworn never to set eyes upon Elisabeth again. Then, at the next moment, he agreed to spend three days alone with her. He couldn't even consider the consequences of such a thing as he lay in bed staring into the blackness of the room. He would tell no more lies to himself or his God. "I'll be gravely punished for what I've already done and for what I'm about to do. But I will not deny Elisabeth these three days, or myself," he said aloud in the quietness of the room. As if for God's benefit, he'd convinced himself to a degree that he was not betraying Joe in any way. Joe hadn't asked Elisabeth to marry him . . . yet. "I'll spend three days with Elisabeth and treat her as I would my sister," he said to the dark. "Just a nice, pleasant vacation away from war. I will not break my vows to the church or God. I promise." He was exhausted and his plea-bargaining between himself and his God would have a short trial as he drifted off to sleep.

With daybreak, the sun's rays shone through the corners of the bedroom's heavy curtains. He rubbed his aching eyes as pulled the curtain back, allowing sunlight to fill his room with the warmth of a new day. The clock on the fireplace mantel read 9:15. He couldn't believe he'd slept so late. He dressed quickly, then entered the living room. Elisabeth wasn't to be found. On the edge of the couch, he found his spare pajamas neatly folded, a note attached. Richard picked up the note.

Richard, I peeked in on you early this morning and wanted terribly to wake you, but you were sleeping so sound I just couldn't. You're cute when you're sleeping. I'll catch a ride back to the hospital. I know plenty of people who live here in the city and drive to the hospital every day. I've written the address of our cottage in Pickering and directions of how to get there from York. I'll arrive in Pickering the day of the 12th. In case you should arrive before I do, I put the name under Mr. and Mrs. Richard Carver. I hope you don't mind me putting it that way, but it sounds terrific to me. Have a safe trip, Richard. I love you so.

Elisabeth
P.S. I promise . . . I promise.

Richard laid the note atop the pajamas. His flight to Dublin wasn't until nine tomorrow morning, and he decided to take in a few sights of the great city while he had the spare time. He would avoid looking at a newspaper these next few days, having decided the war would have to rage without him for this short time he'd be with Elisabeth, sensing it would probably be his last, as it was becoming more evident than ever that destiny wouldn't include his love for Elisabeth. Not only was his religion against him, but also the war and his dangerous involvement in it. If these things weren't enough within themselves, his brother still loomed closely in the background. Yes, God would allow them these three days together, but they would have to last a lifetime, as the world around them was growing angrier by the hour.

Richard toured London that day, then had a quiet dinner that evening. He was off to Dublin the following morning. He had a safe and pleasant flight, making a quick stop on the coast of Wales for fuel, then across St. George's Channel to Dublin. The weather was terrible by the time Richard arrived in Dublin late in the afternoon of May 10. He'd never met the bishop personally but having had many hours of correspondence with the bishop. Like most of the clergy Richard had been in contact with recently, the bishop wanted to know the reason behind the Holy Father's restraint from condemning Hitler and his Nazi Party, especially after the apparent abduction of Cardinal Beroske.

Ireland had been spared any direct combatants from the Germans up to this point, although their merchant ships had been hit hard by the German U-boats in the North Sea but had at least been spared from any raids from the German Luftwaffe. Richard got along well with the rather rough-spirited Irish bishop, promising him that he would personally relay his message to the pontiff on his opinions of Hitler and Mussolini and wondering to himself how much longer the pontiff could ignore the rising outcry of his Catholic camaraderie.

Chapter Fifteen

Richard's mind shifted from world happenings to peaceful, private thoughts as he flew over the Irish Sea to York, situated in northern England. Thoughts of Elisabeth replaced those of Hitler and Mussolini. The screeching sounds of the plane's tires touched on the English runway, jolting him into reality. Richard's plane had been delayed for over three hours before leaving Dublin after reports of German U-boats attacking an Australian troop carrier inside the North Channel; the reports later proved to be false. An Australian merchant ship had been hit, however, by a German torpedo 100 miles north of the channel. An American ship rescued the crew before the merchant ship sank.

The weather was much better in northern England than it had been his recent days in Dublin. Though the sun shone brightly, the air was chilly. He was thankful he'd carried his overcoat with him on the plane. He slipped on his coat as he walked from the plane to the small terminal. Richard retrieved his baggage and caught a cab. He showed the cabbie the crude map Elisabeth had drawn.

"Yep, I know where that is." The elderly English driver handed the map back. "You're a Yank, aren't you?"

"Yes," he answered as the cab pulled away from the terminal. They'd traveled a short way when Richard asked, "How far to Pickering?"

"About 25 kilometers, I guess. It'll still be daylight time we arrive. Got one of those London ladies waiting on you feller, I bet?"

Richard looked at the cabbie, at first insulted before realizing he wasn't wearing his priest vestments. The heavy frown wilted as Richard said, "No, she's American."

The cabbie smiled. "I see."

It was a little after 6:00 p.m. when the cabbie said, "There she is, the village of Pickering."

The small village was nestled in a shallow valley. A single main road ran through the village's center. The streets were all but deserted as the cab rolled slowly through, passing small shops and the town's only hotel. It seemed they'd just entered one end of the village when they were exiting the other end.

Richard was about ready to ask the driver if they'd passed the cottages when he spotted a large stone house, four smaller houses clustered around it. "That's the place, Shattering Cottages. The cabbie turned off the main road and onto the narrow dirt drive leading to a row of cottages set on a hillside.

Richard's heart quickened as the cab slowly made

its way up the hill. The sun was getting low, and within moments, it would begin to dip behind a distant hill, signaling darkness was at hand. The cabbie slowed in front of the large cottage sitting in the center of the clearing. Smaller cottages were positioned a quarter mile apart on either side of the main cottage. "Wait," Richard said, his eyes fixed on the distant figure waving frantically in front of one the smaller cottages. His voice lifted. "There, that's it."

The cabbie drove toward the cottage and the excited young woman standing at the cottage door. "Can't blame you, lad, for coming this far. I'd swim the bloody channel for a pretty lady as she."

The cabbie's words fell upon deaf ears as Richard's whole being focused on the green-eyed woman that stood smiling at the front entrance to the dainty stone cottage. A trail of smoke rose from the cottage chimney, as if reaching for one of the distant stars peeking out in the clear evening sky.

The cab stopped in front of the narrow stone walkway that led to the front door of the cottage. Elisabeth waited at the edge of the walkway. Richard exited the cab.

"Hello, Richard," she said smiling.

"You're lovely, Elisabeth, and this place is lovely."

"I'd hoped you'd like it."

"How could I not like it—you're here." She took his hand in hers. "I'm glad I came." He felt the tightening of her grip.

After helping the driver with the luggage, Richard paid him and he left. The sun had disappeared, and darkness clothed the English countryside. Richard quickly scanned the living room of the cozy cottage as Elisabeth took his top-coat from around him. He moved to stand in front of the fire, turning and examining the room in more detail. The warming fire from the stone fireplace felt good.

Elisabeth fixed them a drink as Richard warmed himself. The room was furnished superbly in rich English traditional, a large couch in the center of the room, a pair of matching chairs at opposite ends. On the far wall next to a window sat an antique desk with a bright bouquet of assorted flowers decorating its center, adding a freshening scent to the room. A kerosene lamp offered enough light, with the help of the fireplace, to adequately light the room. The room's two windows were draped in handwoven, auburn-dyed wool, adding further depth to the room.

"I'd no idea places like this still existed," he said.

From the sofa, Elisabeth patted the cushion beside her. "Come, Richard, sit next to me."

Richard took the seat.

"For heaven sakes," she said, "you're not in some important meeting now. You're with me. Make yourself comfortable . . . so I can get comfortable." She handed him her drink, bent down, then untied and removed his shoes. Looking him up and down, she unbuttoned the top two buttons to his white dress shirt. "Now that's much better." She took back her drink. "Isn't that better?"

He laughed. "Much better."

"See what you've been missing without me?"

"I'm beginning to."

Elisabeth took the drink from Richard's hand and placed their glasses on the table next to the couch. He watched as Elisabeth leaned forward; the heat of her body ignited untold passion within him. Their lips met. He gently lowered her to the couch. Their passion grew as they disrobed one another. Soon, they lay upon the couch making love, bathed in the warmth of the fireplace and their own heat. Slowly, the passion subsided into contentment. Elisabeth fetched a nearby blanket, and they snuggled together on the couch, gazing at the dwindling flames in the fireplace.

Elisabeth snuggled closer to Richard as they lay side by side, her back to him, both staring at the fire.

"I love you so much, Richard," she said drowsily.

"I love you too," he muttered, as he, too, surrendered to sleep. She would awaken him twice more during the night; twice more, they would make love.

Richard awoke to the smell of freshly brewed coffee and sweet rolls Elisabeth had bought in town. She placed the tray of coffee and rolls on the table in front of the couch. "Did you sleep well, my lovely?" She leaned over and kissed him on the cheek.

Richard sat up on the couch, wrapping his naked body in the blanket. "I don't know if I've ever slept better in my life." He smiled up at his love as she handed him a cup of coffee. She took her seat next to him, then enjoyed the coffee and rolls.

Elisabeth rekindled the fire, and the room was filled once more with warmth. Outside, the morning sun burned brightly. A scattering of white clouds dotted the blue sky, offering a beautiful day. After breakfast and a bath, they decided to do a little local sightseeing. Elisabeth managed to talk the innkeeper into borrowing his two bicycles during their stay. This would be their only mode of transportation, which was fine since Pickering was just over the next hill. Richard wore a light gray cardigan sweater, long trousers, and, of course, his black hat. Elisabeth wore brown English riding pants that flared out at the thighs, and a long-sleeve white shirt. A blue scarf covered her long, lustrous hair.

He straddled the bike. "Well, I hope I can still ride one of these."

Elisabeth laughed. "It's easy, don't you see?" She pedaled her bike in a small circle in the middle of the stone drive. Richard started out the bike, a little wobbly at first. Shortly, the two were making their way up the roadway toward the village of Pickering. Richard stole glances at Elisabeth as she pedaled her bike up the ancient stone road, looking so beautiful against the rolling landscape, her golden complexion, accented by her emerald eyes and lovely smile, made a magnificent picture in Richard's mind—one to which he'd hold tight.

They stopped as they topped the hill, pausing to look at the breathtaking beauty of the Yorkshire landscape. The village of Pickering was less than a meter away, nestled snugly in a shallow valley, surrounded by rolling hills. Stone fences ran up and down the green countryside. A light breeze blew across the cold North Sea, fifty kilometers or so from Pickering, chilling the air. "Shall we go into the village for warm tea?" Elisabeth laid her hand against his cheek. "The wind is a bit chilly." He took her hand, then kissed it. She smiled warmly. "My precious, I've never been happier in my life than I am at this very moment."

"I love you, Elisabeth. My mind and body cries out for you at this very moment," he whispered in all sincerity. They held hands, lingering atop the picturesque hill. He wondered if this were but a dream, being here alone together, but he knew a dream could never be as real as the warmth and love that swept through their bodies as they kissed atop the hill on the chilly spring day. Finally, they started down the hill toward Pickering.

They cycled down the main road of the quiet village, passing shops along the way. Richard followed Elisabeth to the small bakery shop at the edge of town. The smell of fresh bread filled the air. Richard and Elisabeth parked their bikes in front of the bakery and went inside. The aromas were even more scrumptious as they entered the land of sweets and breads. The countertops and glass casings were filled with every type of bread and pastry imaginable. The couple made their way about the room oohing and awing at the different bakery masterpieces that filled the room. A tiny, gray-haired woman took notice of the two visitors as they approached her standing behind the counter.

"You made all of these beautiful pastries and bread yourself?" he asked.

"My husband and I did. He's out sick today though," the baker lady said, flashing a nearly toothless grin.

"I'd have to say you might have a little Michaelangelo blood running through your veins to create such a treasure," Richard praised the woman.

A look of pride filled the old woman's face. "I've just finished baking some of my finest apple turnovers. They'd be a treat with a warm spot of tea on a chilled day such as this. Would the two of you care to try one?"

Richard turned to Elisabeth, who seemed overjoyed by the whole carryings-on. "My lady friend and I would be honored to try one of your turnovers, madam."

Richard's words and warm smile caused the baker lady to blush. She pointed to an empty table in the small dining area. "Take a seat then."

"You're such a kind man, Richard. You've made that woman feel so proud and important."

Richard sat at the small table, then sighed and took Elisabeth's hand in his. "That's what's wrong with the world today, Elisabeth: people don't stop and talk to the other person. If they did, they'd find most people are the same as them, thoughtful and loving, only wanting to love and be loved in this short time we have."

She leaned forward over the table. Her eyes looked into his. "What you just said is true—to love and be loved, like we feel for each other. That's the way God intended us to be and not sworn by some manmade oath to remain a hermit. If God had intended that, do you think he would make us the way we are? You can't deny our love for each other anymore. You've had time to experience just a small pinch of what our lives will be like together. No one's love or hate is strong enough to break the bond between us. We are one, Richard. When you lie with me, our bodies become one and our bodies and mind are absorbed into one another. No love could be stronger than the one we possess. People live all their lives never imagining a love like ours could possibly exist between a man and a woman." Elisabeth paused, looking into Richard's beleaguered eyes. "Richard, you belong to me now, and I won't let you leave me again. Will you stay with me until the end of time . . . please?"

He looked into her misty eyes. "I too adore you, Elisabeth. Yes, I'll stay with you." She gently squeezed his hand upon hearing his final submission. His God had given him finally to the woman who adored him. She smiled at him as renegade tears of happiness trickled down her cheeks.

The little baker woman broke up the intimate conversation. The two feasted on the turnovers and warm tea, spending better than two hours in the bakery shop, chattering idly and enjoying the moment together. They spent the rest of the day touring the countryside on their bikes, stopping at intervals to walk and run through the rich hills and meadows, pausing at times to embrace like the lovers they were. They made their way back to the cottage as the afternoon sun fell behind the distant hills.

It was after dark when they finally made their way back to the cottage. The lamp had been left burning but the room was cold. Richard began the fire-building task as Elisabeth heated the last of the soup on the stove. Within a short time, the warmth of the fire filled the room. They finished their soup. Richard gathered more firewood while Elisabeth enjoyed her evening bath. Richard bathed while Elisabeth fixed hot chocolate. They took a seat on the thick carpet in front of the heavy stone fireplace that spread warmth throughout the cozy room. The couple sat next to one another, wrapped warmly in their fluffy robes, sipping the hot chocolate.

He studied her; Elisabeth's gaze fixed on the flickering fire. "This has been the most wonderful day of my life."

She turned slightly to him. "And mine also, my darling Richard," she whispered, taking his hand in hers and raising it to her lips. "If I should die tonight, all these years of waiting would've been worth these last precious hours we've spent together."

Richard looked longingly into her eyes. "Can it be possible for a man to love a woman the way I love you?"

"With all these past years wasted," she said, "we mustn't allow a moment to pass without expressing our love for each other." She leaned over and kissed him softly on the lips.

Richard sighed. "These years that have passed us by weren't wasted, Elisabeth. God has a purpose for what he did. No mortal can or dare question the works of God in heaven. Anyway, that's all in the past. The future is ours together."

A look came across her face: sad and sullen and defiant. He wondered what she thought of God. Was she jealous of God's place in his life? He kissed her again, hoping to erase the look. Their passion rose to that of the burning embers. Again, they made love in front of the fire. Their flames were slowly extinguished as they lay naked on the thick rug, bodies entwined. Richard ran his fingers through Elisabeth's ruffled hair.

She broke the silence. "Richard, what are you going to do about the church?" She sighed. "You know what I mean."

Richard smiled as he caressed her hand. "I'll resign from the church, explaining my reasons to the Holy Father."

"Does this mean you'll still return to Rome?"

"Why yes, Elisabeth, I owe the church that much." She gently slipped her hand from his lips and fetched a blanket from the couch. Returning to him, she paused, as if considering the act, then covered Richard's naked body and laid down, snuggling next to him. Soon they lay sleeping in front of the dwindling fire.

They were up early the next morning. Elisabeth fixed hot tea, served with the sweet rolls from the bakery.

Richard had mentioned he would like to visit the fishing village of Staithes where Captain Cook supposedly found his love for the sea. Elisabeth thought that would be a wonderful journey, only some fifty kilometers away. They rode their bikes down to Pickering and found Harvey Jenkins who owned the only cab in town. It wasn't a real cab, so to speak; it was his private car. He was the local cobbler, becoming a cabbie only when the need arose, as was the case today. Harvey was a weasel-looking chap around forty with thick black hair, receding chin, and long, sharp nose. Quiet by nature, he rarely spoke, only muttering, "bloody Germans" every now and then, for no particular reason, as he drove Richard and Elisabeth through the Yorkshire countryside. A bright sun bore down on the green countryside.

After their scenic journey, they arrived at Staithes. It was easy to understand the young Mr. Cook's love affair with the quaint fishing village nestled in a natural harbor. The town breathed of the sea, small fishing boats lining the beach. On both sides of the village, steep cliffs overlooked the sea and harbor. Richard gave the cabbie sufficient funds to do what he liked while he and Elisabeth took in the local sights. They were to meet the cabbie back at the car in six hours, which should be sufficient time to see the village and stroll along the beach. This was a Saturday and many of the markets were closed, for whatever reason Richard did not understand.

They strolled along the cobblestone streets peering into store windows. It seemed most of the villagers were patronizing the town pubs that day. The narrow streets were especially barren, except for children who played and laughed in the streets. Richard and Elisabeth stopped in one of the pubs for a beer. He noted the men in the pubs were mostly elderly and asked the bartender why this was so.

The bartender stared at Richard as if he had asked a rather stupid question. "The young men are out there somewhere killing the bloody Germans, of course."

Richard felt embarrassed by such a stupid question. He should've thought of that himself. But during the last two days, he'd forgotten a war still raged with greater ferocity than ever. Richard downed his beer. Elisabeth left most of hers. "How stupid of me!" he muttered, stepping out of the pub.

Elisabeth tried consoling him. "You had no way of knowing where the young men were, Richard."

He glared at her. "Why sure, I should've known. My God, I just gave last rights to one of those young men a few days ago. He might've been that man's son."

"Don't be silly. You meant no harm by what you said."

Richard ignored her comment as he walked down the street. His blundering comment to the bartender rattled him. As they walked along the beach, under the shadows of the giant cliffs, Elisabeth tried again to offer consolation, but he could not shake the incident.

She held his hand as they walked next to the edge of the sea. Richard paused, looking out over the great North Sea. A distant fog bank hung over the water like a giant curtain, waiting on the wind to change before rolling in like some magic carpet to engulf the tiny fishing village in its mysterious mist. Richard stared intensely at the endless sea. It seemed some power pulled at his soul, beckoning him beyond the fog to a far-off land. The great power tugged violently at him.

After what seemed like an eternity, his mind returned to the seashore. He turned to Elisabeth, whose appearance had changed. He could tell he'd somehow frightened her. He watched her nod and then shake her head as if in disbelief. He realized she was responding to something he was saying. His full awareness returned; he'd been talking to her, explaining the force in the fog—or what he could understand of it. "Cardinal Beroske is alive," he said. "He's in a Polish prison camp. I just saw him. He spoke to me, Elisabeth."

"No! No! You're wrong, Richard," Elisabeth cried out, tears rolling down her flushed cheeks.

"Yes, Elisabeth, it's true. I know exactly where he is. He told me only moments ago," Richard muttered. His words became almost inaudible as he again looked to the distant sea. He turned back slowly to Elisabeth who, by this time, sobbed uncontrollably. "I must go to him, Elisabeth. He has called for me. He's slowly dying. I must get to him quickly." Richard's eyes went hollow as he looked down at the sand.

"No, Richard, it's just a dream. You're imagining this. You're still upset about what took place in that pub. You're mine. You promised me. You can't leave me like this." Her tears ceased as her voice changed from sadness and remorse to anger. "Look at me," she said, lifting his head so his eyes met hers. "If you go looking for this pipe dream of yours, I won't be waiting for you when you return." Her voice faded from sternness back to sadness and heartbreak. Once again, tears cascaded down her cheeks as she tried to finish her ultimatum.

Richard placed both hands on her trembling arms. "This is something I must do. I've just experienced a vision from Christ himself. Don't you know what that means?"

She looked at him and shook her head violently. "Too hell with God! I wish God would die and leave you alone. He's nothing but an Indian giver!" She fell to her knees on the sand.

Richard looked down at her as she wept. "I'm so sorry, Elisabeth. I love you so, but—"

"But nothing!" Her face flushed red with anger and grief as she looked up at him. "You go. You go now. Find your precious cardinal and see if he can love you as I can. See if he would die for you as I would. See if he can bear you a son as I can. Go! Get out of my sight. I'll stay here tonight."

"I can't leave you here. How will you get back to the cabin?" He stepped toward her.

"Don't come any closer. I'm a grown woman and damn sure able to take care of myself. You go find your cardinal before he dies. Leave me here to die by myself. You've destroyed my soul for the last time, Bishop Carver. It has no life left. Go, I said." Richard started to speak. "Get the hell out of my sight!" she screamed.

He looked at her one last time. "One day you'll understand my leaving."

"That's what I think of your Cardinal Beroske," she said.

"I love you, Elisabeth, and I always will." Richard turned and started back down the beach, toward the village and the awaiting cab.

The crushing words echoed in Richard's ears as streams of tiny tears ran down his drawn face. *I hate you*! *I hate your Cardinal*! *I hate your God*! He paused for a moment wanting to go back to Elisabeth and try to explain, but he didn't. Finally, the distant sobbing sounds were smothered by sounds of the rolling sea.

Richard returned to Pickering that afternoon. He composed Elisabeth a short letter, trying to explain the thing he must do, telling her once again how much he loved her, promising her that he would resign from the church as soon as his mission was over. He knew she wouldn't believe him—and with good reason. Already, he'd broken his word to her twice. Still, he prayed she would wait a little longer. After the letter, he gathered his belongings and took the cab to York. He made arrangements for a flight to London and then back to Rome.

Chapter Sixteen

Having returned to his ship, Joe had since been ordered to Londonderry in Northern Ireland. It was a new facility for allied shipping, much safer from German air attack and easy access to the North Atlantic. The Germans had continued to sink many ships with their U-boats. Richard arrived back in Rome on the morning of the sixteenth. He'd read every newspaper he could get his hands on since leaving Pickering. Nothing of any major importance had occurred during Richard's brief absence from the war, except the encouraging reports that Russia still held the Germans at bay, allowing the United States and England more time to strengthen their forces to combat the battle-hardened Germans.

Upon arriving at the Vatican, Richard proceeded directly to his office. He'd many things to do before going before the Holy Father with his dangerous and highly bizarre plan to free the cardinal. Richard remained in his office the entire day and most of the following night, having his aide fetch food and drink from time to time. The young priest kept busy delivering numerous telegrams.

It was after midnight when Richard finally left the confines of his office, making his way out the building and across the courtyard to his living quarters. He'd walked this corridor many times as others had slept. His steps were a lonely sound, echoing off the heavy stone walls of the empty corridor. Richard and Cardinal Beroske had made this walk together countless times during the early stages of the war, when Hitler's army swept across Europe. Richard was alone now: his vigil solitary and lonely—oh so lonely, especially now. Those precious hours with Elisabeth, fantastic and rewarding, were history. Now, he was alone once again. Only one man was left in whom he could confide. The Holy Father was the only one Richard could feel free to tell the many things he carried within him. Even the Holy Father, though, couldn't share in some of Richard's well-tunneled secrets, not his love affair with Elisabeth. For the present, only his God could be aware of Richard's human emotions. He wondered at times— especially when lying in his bed at night, Elisabeth burning in his mind—if the Holy Father had ever had such thoughts about a woman. Surely, he wasn't the only priest who'd ever slept with a woman, especially one they deeply loved, as he did Elisabeth. Richard's body and mind were near total exhaustion when, finally, he fell asleep, but his troubled, confused mind would give him little rest for the Eminence' challenges that lay before him.

This was the morning of May 18, 1942. The war

had reached a fevered pitch. In the Pacific, the Japanese continued to dominate, well prepared for such conflict. The green Americans we're being bathed in hard-learned lessons about this mostly amphibious war in which they found themselves engulfed. The steamy, partially inhabited islands of the South Pacific were well entrenched with fanatical Japanese soldiers. American blood colored the beachheads of the decimated islands dark red, as the brave marines clawed their way up the beach inch by inch. The Japanese soon learned the Americans were brave and as determined as they; defeat was not an option.

Richard found comfort in the small chapel early that morning, spending over two hours alone. As was the case most often, he left the chapel mentally refreshed and at peace. He'd need all these things this morning as he'd arranged a private meeting with the Holy Father on this clear, sunny Roman day.

He met with the pontiff in their usual place behind St. Peter's.

"Welcome back, Bishop," the pope said as Richard knelt before him, kissing his ring. Richard took his seat next to the pope. "So, I trust you had a fine trip to London and saw your brother?"

"Yes, Holy Father, it was a rewarding trip." Images of Elisabeth flashed in his mind.

"You look refreshed, my son. You needed a rest from this horrid war. We all need a rest from this horrid war."

"Holy Father, I've asked for this meeting for an urgent reason."

The Holy Father nodded. "I see the urgency in your eyes, and I hear it in your voice. What can be so urgent to

252

excite a man like you who isn't easily excited anymore, not after all you've seen and done?"

Richard leaned forward, looking the aging pope squarely in the eyes. "I know where Cardinal Beroske is."

The pontiff leaned back in his chair. "How do you know this?"

"Your Holiness, I saw him in a vision while I was in Staithes on the beach. He appeared in a distant fog bank over the North Sea." Richard looked at the pontiff timidly, knowing what he'd said sounded crazy.

The pontiff's stoic expression stayed steady. After a moment, he leaned forward, eye to eye with Richard. "You say you saw him in a vision, in a distant fog bank?"

"Yes, Holy Father, I swear it," Richard added in defense.

"Are you certain that Irish whiskey didn't help you see this mirage?"

In the moment, he forgot himself and his position. "I had nothing to drink except one beer. I know what I saw, and I know what I heard! The cardinal is alive inside a Polish prison camp. The cardinal even told me the name of the camp: Auschwitz. That's the camp's name!" Richard realized he was standing and yelling at the surprised pontiff. "I'm sorry about my outburst, Holy Father, but I'm telling you the truth." He took his seat.

The pontiff's golden eyes sparkled in the overhead light. "Richard, for a man to act as you have, who am I to say it isn't true? You know I saw a vision once. I was only a child, living with my uncle in Milan. I was playing alone in the back of my uncle's store. It seems I was always alone as a child. It seems most of us priests spent our childhoods alone, doesn't it?"

Richard lowered his gaze. "Yes, Your Holiness, it does."

"Must be we were marked for solitude long before we were born." The pontiff paused as if deep in thought, then continued. "As I was saying, I was playing alone in my uncle's yard . . . some silly child's game, I don't remember what. Without warning, the yard grew dark. I was terrified at first. After all, this was the middle of the day and not a cloud in the sky. I began to tremble, wanting terribly to call for my mother, but remembered my mother had died a year earlier, during childbirth. The infant was stillborn, and my father blamed himself for the tragedy, having gotten her with child. No one ever knew for sure, but he began to drink heavily and soon left the village, never to be seen again. And so, I went to stay with my uncle, where I was at the time of the vision. I trembled and fell to my knees. Then, out of the darkness, appeared two images. At first, I couldn't discern them, but slowly my vision focused. They were smiling at me. My mother held the infant in her arms, wrapped in a white cloth. Next to her was my father. He was happy, as before my mother had died. My trembling vanished as I gazed in wonderment at my beautiful family. A few moments passed and my mother spoke to me, just as I'm speaking to you now." Richard smiled as the pontiff continued, "She called my name as only a mother can call her son's name properly. I answered. She told me of my destiny that day behind my uncle's store. She told of my calling to God. She said I'd been chosen to lead this great church within my lifetime. She told me the task would be a difficult one. She told me of a great war that would rage during my time as church leader. She told me of my time of death when I would join them in heaven. I watched as my family faded into the darkness. The darkness faded into lightness. Within moments, the sun shone brightly again. I knelt there for the longest time, trying to absorb in my adolescent mind what had taken place. I finally decided it was only one of my daydreams. I fantasized much in my youth."

Richard chuckled softly.

"I got up from the hard ground," the pontiff explained, "wanting to run tell my uncle of the strange thing that had happened to me. But I knew better, as he already thought I was a little light in the head, the way I stayed to myself and all. I told myself it was only make-believe, and I began playing again. In a short while, I noticed something white lying in the corner of the yard. I had an uneasy feeling as I walked across the yard, picking up the white cloth that had held my infant brother only moments earlier. Do you know you're the only person to whom I've told this story?"

Richard hesitated, not knowing what to say. Finally, in desperation, he said, "I'm honored that you confided in me, Your Holiness, and I believe every word of it."

The pontiff smiled. "The only reason I told you, Bishop, is I know you won't tell anybody else, worrying that I would do the same to you. They would lock us both up as looney birds."

Richard laughed. "Yes, Holy Father, that is true."

"But we know these things we saw are real, don't we, Bishop Carver?"

Richard's laughter ceased as he looked into the pontiff's serious eyes. "I know what I saw, Your Holiness."

"I know, my son, and I believe you saw what you said. I also believe a man who is blessed with such visions will one day inherit this chair."

Richard swallowed hard.

"Yes, my son, I firmly believe you are chosen by God to sit upon his throne before you leave this world."

Richard attempted to speak but couldn't.

"Don't worry about that matter now. The Almighty will handle all of that in due time. So, what are we to do about Cardinal Beroske?"

Richard thought a moment. "I've been working on a plan since returning to the Vatican, Holy Father. I believe I've put together one that will work."

The pope hesitated, then asked, "Who will rescue him, Bishop?"

"I will, Your Holiness.

"This could be highly dangerous for the both of you."

"Yes, Your Holiness, extremely dangerous, but I want to try. He would do no less for me."

"Yes, I'm confident he would. How long will this take?"

"I don't know for sure . . . perhaps only a few days. Perhaps weeks."

"You have my permission to do what you wish in this matter. But remember, the rules are the same if you are revealed."

"Yes, Your Holiness, I've done this on my own accord, the church knew nothing about it."

The pope smiled. "Go with God, young American Bishop. I will pray hard for your success. But before you leave, I want to tell you that if you indeed make it back, successful or unsuccessful in your quest to rescue Cardinal Beroske, I'm strongly considering elevating your status to cardinal, yet another steppingstone to what I spoke of earlier." Richard started to reply but the pope raised his hand not to speak. "Good luck, my American friend, and may Gabriel and all the angels in heaven watch over you as you journey into the valley of death in search of a friend and colleague. I ask this in the name of the Father, Son, and Holy Ghost. Amen."

"Thank you, Your Holiness." Richard knelt and kissed the pontiff's ring.

He'd walked halfway to the door when the pontiff called out, "Bishop!"

Richard turned back to the pope.

"Remember that vision I told you about?"

"Yes, Your Holiness."

"This is my brother's blanket I found that day."

Richard looked in amazement as the pontiff held a tattered white cloth over his head. "Put faith in what you've seen and heard, Bishop Carver, for you've heard the voice of God. Only the chosen few hear and see what you have, visions from the Almighty. Find our brother and bring him home."

Richard nodded and walked away.

Part III

Chapter Seventeen

The freedom Richard and the other Catholic clergy had enjoyed during the early days of the war had greatly diminished, especially for an American priest like Richard. Hitler's declaration of war against America changed Richard's immunity status virtually overnight. In addition, the fact that the führer turned his full attention to defeating the Russians increased the dangers to such men as Richard. Himmler's SS forces gained Eminence' power under the German rule. Their internal duties within Germany and its captive states went virtually unchecked by the German high command. Even Hitler himself rarely interfered with the workings of the SS. Himmler's storm troopers that were eradicating Europe of its Jews as fast as was humanly possible. Hitler was well satisfied with Himmler's leadership in such an important matter. Fear of the German SS sent most of the Christian clergy into the underground. No one was safe from the deadly SS troops, almost a million strong by this spring of '42.

Richard had boarded a train for Bern, Switzerland. He would journey through Italy and into Switzerland as Bishop Carver. Even though Mussolini was a tyrant like his hero Adolph Hitler, he still had enough wits about him to keep hands off any official of the Catholic Church, knowing the Italian people wouldn't tolerate any harming of their sacred church leaders. Switzerland had remained neutral in the global conflict, allowing Richard easy access to the country. It had been a long and tiring journey, but his body had learned in recent months how to savor strength and quickly recoup from such treatment.

Richard entered the Grand Hotel, inside the beautiful city of Bern, in midafternoon. The picturesque, snowcapped Alps rose majestically around the alpine city. Richard checked into his hotel room, a luxurious space. The double doors in his bedroom led onto a large terrace, affording an unspoiled view of the towering Alps. It was a beautiful spring day, and the air was cool. He unpacked and changed into fresh clothing. Noticeably absent from his belongings were his church garments and his beloved rosary from Lori. Nothing marked him as a man of the church, except for the passport he carried in his coat pocket. Within a matter of minutes that would also change. Tapping at the door disturbed the moment. He glanced at his watch: 4:15. Right on time.

The three men briefly studied one another. "Father Carver?" One of the men asked.

"Yes."

"I'm Lorenzo and this is Heinz. We're here at the request of Bishop Rutgers."

Both men were dressed in dark suits. Lorenzo, who'd done all the talking so far, looked every bit Italian as the language he spoke. He was an average-sized, relatively young man with dark wavy hair. The other man looked more Aryan, with short blond hair and square facial features, and appeared to be in his late twenties. Richard invited the men in. They took seats next to one another on the couch, gracing the north wall of the room. Richard sat directly across. The men stared silently at Richard for what seemed an eternity. Then the Italian said, "Excuse us, Father, for staring at you. We're simply trying to figure your chances of pulling off such a scheme. Surely you understand the great odds against you?"

"Yes, I'm aware of the consequences of failure."

The blond man spoke for the first time in German. "How fluent is your German, Father Carver?"

Richard looked at the solemn-faced German. "Enough, Heinz, to pull this thing off," Richard replied in flawless German.

Heinz's deep blue eyes were etched in hardness. Richard wondered what terrible things had happened to this young lad in his early years of life.

Heinz turned to Lorenzo. "His German is sufficient to pass."

Lorenzo, who hadn't taken his eyes off Richard since being seated, said, "Give me your passport, Father."

Richard took his passport from his coat pocket and handed it to Lorenzo who quickly scanned through it . . . after which he handed it to Heinz, nodding his head as he did so. Heinz got up from the couch and headed for the front door. Richard looked at the fleeing German carrying his passport.

"Don't worry, Father," Lorenzo said. "He'll be back shortly with your new passport."

The uneasiness slipped from Richard's face. "Would you care for a glass of wine while we wait on your friend's return?"

Lorenzo agreed and had two glasses of wine before Heinz returned.

Richard watched with eager eyes as Lorenzo studied the passport Heinz had given him. Finally, after careful study, he turned to Richard. "Here, Claude Schmitt. Here is your new passport and identity." Richard took the passport from Lorenzo. "Study it well, Claude, your life depends on it."

Richard looked at the smiling Lorenzo and then back at his new passport. Lorenzo and Heinz sat quietly as Richard studied his newly printed documents. "Incredible piece of work."

Lorenzo and Heinz smiled at Richard showing their

gratitude. "We must be going Fath—I mean Heinz," Lorenzo said. "See how quickly I would get you killed."

Richard smiled. "God bless you for your assistance and thank Bishop Rutgers for what he's done to help."

"God go with you, Father. We all pray that you find Cardinal Beroske and bring him safely back to Rome." Heinz broke a grin for the first time, noticing Richard's surprised look as Lorenzo mentioned the cardinal's name. "Surely, Father, you didn't think we were ignorant of your intentions. Cardinal Beroske is deeply loved by my people and the peoples of the church. Heinz and I are here for one reason and one reason alone: to help you find the cardinal and bring him safely back to his homeland and to his people who so dearly love him, like me and Heinz." Richard nodded his head as he affectionately looked at the two. "Thank God there are people like you in this world, Father. We will see Hitler and his butchers to their deaths. There are millions of us out there abiding our time, waiting for the right moment to arise and crush the devilish bastards. You were surprised that we knew of your mission, Bishop Carver. You would be more surprised how much our people know about you. Your deeds are well circulated among our people. You've become an inspiration to them. Millions of our people walk proudly beside you—even if they can only offer their spirits. I promise you, Bishop Carver, one day soon their bodies will walk where their spirits only tread today. God bless you, Bishop, and good luck on your search for Cardinal Beroske."

Richard shook Lorenzo's hand. Heinz extended his hand and Richard took it firmly. Unexpectedly, Heinz placed his arms around Richard and hugged him. They embraced for a few moments before Heinz released his grip, turning away to hide his watering eyes. Richard watched as the two turned and headed down the hallway.

Richard went to the train station to make arrangements for the second portion of his journey, perhaps being the most dangerous and uncertain of the whole bizarre plan. He boarded the Munich-bound train two days later, venturing little from his hotel room during his visit in Bern. The stopped at the Swiss-German border. The soldiers checked the passenger's passports. Richard passed the first barrier. The train traveled through the German countryside under the blanket of darkness, stopping intermittingly to load or unload passengers. He slept most of the night, arriving in Munich mid-morning of the next day.

The Munich station brimmed with activity, German soldiers arriving and departing the station in large numbers. Richard walked among them, making his way through the depot on the way to his luggage. He was awaiting his luggage when a middle-aged man approached, dressed in a dark suit and donning a hat.

"Claude Schmitt?"

Richard considered the stranger. This had been the first time anyone had addressed him by his new name, sounding odd even after the many hours he'd spent rehearsing the name. "Yes, I'm Claude Schmitt," Richard replied in German.

"I have a car waiting for you."

Within a short while, Richard was sitting in the passenger side of the black limousine. The car moved briskly through the city with virtually no conversation between Richard and the driver. The weather was fine, slightly overcast, but a comfortable temperature for this late in the spring. The city of Munich was alive with activity. Truck convoys streamed in every direction carrying troops and large gun batteries. Large banners displaying the German swastika seemed to hang from every building tall enough to drape the huge emblem.

Richard's driver had said nothing since leaving the depot, his eyes fixed on the road ahead. They drove through the heart of the city and onto a two-lane road heading north, still within the outer suburbs of Munich. Within a short while, the car stopped in front of a vacated storefront. A scattering of people could be seen meandering about the sidewalks. Most appeared to be elderly and impoverished.

The driver remained silent as he exited the car, walking to Richard's side and opening the door. Richard exited and took a better look of the neighborhood. He followed the driver into the two-story building. They walked up a narrow stairway and down a short hallway, stopping in front of a closed door. The driver tapped lightly on the door and the door opened slightly. The driver whispered something to the person inside. The door opened and the two men entered the room.

The room was rather dark. He strained his eyes, attempting to focus on the two figures sitting across the room at a wooden table. Richard felt the man's presence who'd opened the door as he walked up behind him. Richard peered at the two men across the room, his eyes finally adjusting.

"Please come forward, Mr. Schmitt," the older of the two said. Richard walked to the two men sitting at the table. He studied the well-dressed men as they studied him. "I'm Bishop Rutgers," the man said. He stood and extended his hand.

Richard felt great relief upon hearing the bishop's name. A smile bent his lips as he shook the bishop's hand.

"And this gentleman is Harold Dziobak," the bishop said. The serious-faced, bearded man stood and shook Richard's hand. "Harold is a highly respected rabbi from Warsaw."

Richard looked at the bishop and then back again at the stone-faced rabbi.

"Bishop Carver, I had nothing to do with the rabbi's coming today."

He looked again at the German bishop, unable to conceal his surprise at the rabbi's presence.

"Please, Bishop Carver, take a seat." Bishop Rutgers pointed to the empty chair next to Richard. "I can see you're uneasy about the rabbi being here. Perhaps he can explain better than I why it is he wished to join us today."

The rabbi wore thin metal-rimmed glasses that fit snuggly against his drawn face. His graying hair was long but well kept. "You speak Polish as well as me, Bishop Carver."

"Perhaps not that well, Rabbi," Richard answered in fluent Polish.

A hint of a smile could be seen on the rabbi's lips. "Cardinal Beroske taught you well, my son."

Richard was taken aback by the mentioning of Cardinal Beroske by the rabbi.

The rabbi seeing his reaction leaned over the table and took Richard's hand into his. Looking him straight in the eye, he said, "My young American friend, Cardinal Beroske and I were children together. We're like brothers." The rabbi's grip tightened on Richard's hand as he spoke of the cardinal. His dark eyes glistened in the faint light of the lamp that sat in the middle of the table. A renegade teardrop fell from the rabbi's eye onto the heavily stained table. "I'm also aware of your great friendship. The cardinal wrote several times telling me how proud he was of you and the great future you have in the church. These are great compliments he bestowed upon you, Bishop, and they come from a great man. You're surprised at my being here today. Better yet, you're surprised at my knowing you were to be here to begin with."

Richard nodded. "Yes, Rabbi, I'm surprised in both cases."

"I thought so," the rabbi said, taking his hand away from Richard's and leaning back in his chair. "My American friend, you'll soon learn there are very few secrets in this land of war." Richard started to speak, but the rabbi interrupted. "I don't care to hear idle words of modesty, young bishop. There would be no purpose in such idle rhetoric if it weren't true. Perhaps you've stayed secluded behind those Vatican walls for too long, not even aware of your well-known deeds in such important matters as world stability, such as advanced knowledge of the Russian invasion for example . . . should I say more?"

Richard felt his bottom jaw droop as the rabbi spoke of the invasion. "How did—"

The rabbi interrupted Richard once again. "You see, Bishop, more eyes are on you than you could ever imagine. Don't fret, only those of us in certain positions know of your secret deeds, such as the one you've traveled here to do."

"You don't know why I'm here." Richard's voice was just below a shout, feeling both anguish and embarrassment. "I'm certain of that."

The rabbi looked at Bishop Rutgers. "Perhaps you'd better answer that question, Bishop. It seems I've already said too much to our American friend as it is."

Bishop Rutgers smiled as he looked at Richard. It was evident Richard didn't consider this a smiling matter. "Bishop Carver, we know why you've came here. Only Cardinal Beroske would bring you here at this time. I've been in communication with the Holy Father since you left Rome."

"The Holy Father told you the reason for my journey?"

Bishop Rutgers looked at Richard then at the rabbi who'd become rather amused at Richard's childish antics in such a trivial matter. "Yes, he told me. He's concerned about your well-being. He loves you very much. You should feel honored by such a love. We, too, want you to find Cardinal Beroske. Heavens, the rabbi has told you of their friendship."

He shook his head. "I understand, but I'm concerned about the secrecy of this matter."

"You miss the point, Bishop Carver . . . we're the ones who receive such information from the Germans. The Germans are too stupid to gather such information on us."

Richard considered what the bishop had said. His main concern was if such information filtered into the wrong hands, it would be instant death. Even his own comrades weren't to be fully trusted, especially many of the German clergy who felt Hitler was right in his treatment of the Jews. Richard was confident that Bishop Rutgers was aware of who these few were, feeling safe in the bishop's hands. After a little more conversation, the rabbi got down to the purpose of his inclusion in their meeting. Surmising Richard would in some way encounter a high German source, the rabbi asked if he would propose to the Nazis the prospect of swapping Jews for gold. The rabbi shared with Richard that he was in a position to acquire large sums of gold for the swapping of Jews being shipped to Auschwitz and other death camps. Richard said that he would if afforded the opportunity, figuring it would cost the Catholic Church some sort of monetary outlay for the release of Cardinal Beroske. But he would know nothing for sure until his scheduled meeting set three days hence.

He ended his meeting with Bishop Rutgers and the rabbi with both men saying they would pray hard Richard would find Cardinal Beroske alive and bring him back home to the church. He'd reserved a hotel room at the Steinwartz Hotel in the center of Munich. He scheduled another meeting with the rabbi and Bishop Rutgers in five days, giving Richard sufficient time to study the outcome of his meeting with the Germans. Perhaps he would be arrested on the spot and that would end it all. Richard thought of such things from time to time.

He ventured very little from his hotel the following days, only leaving from his room for something to eat and a daily newspaper. When he grew tired of reading war news, he prayed for long periods. He had no rosary or Holy Book to comfort him in these long hours of loneliness—just the comfort of his God. Late at night, though, his thoughts returned to Elisabeth. The memories were still fresh in his mind of those precious days in Yorkshire. He wondered if she had forgiven him for leaving her. He wanted to write but knew it was too risky. Perhaps he was being watched by the SS; they seemed to be everywhere. He spent long hours peering out his fourth-floor window. Richard stared below at the never-ending flow of German soldiers and weapons moving day and night through Munich. Hitler had done a masterful job of brainwashing the German people, making them believe they were the super race and one day would dominate the world. As of now, there still remained a broken spoke in Germany's war wagons. The pesky Russians still held on.

Chapter Eighteen

The days and nights drug by for Richard as the walls began to close in on him. Finally, the time arrived for his meeting with the Germans. Richard paced the floor of his room for over two hours. Glancing at his watch once again, he muttered, "Damn it" as he paced anew. It was a quarter after six in the evening. The meeting was scheduled for four o'clock. Something was wrong. His mind spun. Another hour passed. He peered out his window. Darkness. Richard had almost lost hope. Then, someone knocked on the door. Hesitantly, he opened it.

A German officer stood in the center of the doorway. "Claude Schmitt," he said.

"Yes, I'm Claude Schmitt."

"May I come in?"

"Yes."

Richard stepped aside as the officer stepped into the room. Another soldier took the officer's place in the middle of the doorway. The officer walked about the room making certain Richard was alone. After the officer had thoroughly searched the rooms, he nodded his head at the soldier standing in the doorway. The soldier disappeared.

"One can't be too careful these days, even in Germany," the officer said.

Richard forced a smile. "Yes, one never knows who might be lurking in the shadows."

The sound of footsteps came from down the hall. The officer stood erect, his boot heels clicking as they came together. He extended his right arm into the air. "Heil Hitler!"

"Heil Hitler." Richard raised his arm to greet the German officer.

The officer left the room when yet another officer appeared in the doorway, looking even more important than the first. The blue-eyed colonel was tall and lean, impeccably dressed in his German uniform, marking him as the epitome of a German soldier. Richard watched in silence as the colonel removed his cap; the officer's blue eyes locked with his. The colonel's short hair was blond and squared at the top. Richard's eyes fixed on the terrible looking scar that ran from the corner of the man's right eye down to the contour of his lower chin, distracting from his otherwise handsome face. Only a few moments passed when another German officer entered the room, taking his place beside the colonel. Then, without warning, another figure entered the doorway. This officer wasn't as spectacular looking like the other officers. His body wasn't nearly as trim and fit as the colonel's, and his somewhat pudgy face wasn't nearly as aristocratic looking. But none of these things really mattered; the field marshal was still the number two man in the Nazi party.

A smile creased Goering's lips as he met Richard's

gaze. The guarding soldier closed the door. Richard smiled as he shook the general's hand. "So, we've gotten even more secretive with age. Claude Schmitt it is now."

"Yes, General, it seems I've become a man with many names."

Goering smiled as he took a seat in one of the chairs sitting next to the sofa. "Claude Schmitt, meet my most trusted officer, Colonel Herman Zooke." Richard extended his hand to the colonel, who silently refused to shake it.

"As you can see, Father Carver, Herman is not particularly pleased with shaking the hand of an American, especially an American priest."

"So, I see.

"The colonel does have, however, one weakness that might be helpful to your foolish cause."

"And what might that be, General?"

"Gold."

Richard looked at the grinning general, then at the colonel.

"Sit down, Richard, and let's discuss just what it is you're after."

Richard took his seat. The colonel stood during the meeting. Richard had informed the field marshal of his reason for coming in a secret letter delivered as the field marshal was on the Russian front, indicating his willingness to pay dearly for assistance in returning Cardinal Beroske to the Vatican. The field marshal had researched the missing cardinal's location. Richard had been correct as far as the cardinal having been sent to Auschwitz, but that had been two months ago. There was very inadequate record keeping at the camp and none of Goering's contacts knew for sure if the cardinal still survived. It was very doubtful that he did. One's life expectancy was short in the camp, especially in the last few months with the addition of needed gas chambers and ovens to dispose of the bodies. Goering expressed his uncertainty of the cardinal's well-being, explaining to Richard that even if he still survived it would be almost impossible to sort him out from the thousands of others. No one in the camp knew what the cardinal even looked like, and after a short period in Auschwitz, a prisoner seldom looked as he or she had upon entering.

Richard still insisted on searching for his friend, reiterating the fact that money was no object. The church would pay any price for the chance of finding the cardinal. This, along with Richard's mentioning of striking a deal on the purchasing of Jews with gold, had caused the general and the colonel to give the possibilities added thought. Finally, after an hour of figuring and discussing the situation, Goering made his astonishing proposal. Goering, who didn't trust Himmler to begin with and despised Himmler's free hand in running the SS, was anxious to get something on the führer's pet. Auschwitz was Himmler's pride and joy; his finest SS troops were there. Perhaps this opportunity offered two chances at once for Goering: an opportunity to make a large sum of money, which he would have if Germany won or lost the war, and, perhaps more important, to make a fool of Himmler and his righteous SS. Richard and Colonel Zooke listened carefully as Marshal Goering told of the bold plan. Colonel Zooke was obviously astonished. Such a plan risked his life. Of course, Goering risked death, as well. Richard listened. At first, the idea seemed complete lunacy, but the more he thought about it, the more feasible it sounded.

Goering awaited Richard's response. "Do I understand you correctly, Marshal Goering," Richard said, "that you'll pass me off as a German officer, of which I will be under the direct command of Colonel Zooke? And the both of us will be special attachés of yours inside Auschwitz, reporting directly to you as to the operation of the camp?"

"Yes," Goering confirmed, "this way it'll give you time and the opportunity to look for your cardinal, while at the same time give Colonel Zooke the opportunity to make the proper contacts for a possible Jew-swapping deal. Of course, before any of this can be done, we have to have the colonel's approval. It won't work without him."

Richard and Marshal Goering looked at the colonel, who for the first time since being in the room showed signs of human emotion. Zooke rubbed his hands together. His hard look turned to one of concern.

"Well?" Goering asked again.

The colonel cleared his throat. "What you're suggesting, Field Marshal, is extremely dangerous. We could all be easily killed. What you've suggested would be difficult enough with one of our own officers. To attempt such a thing with an American priest . . . Field Marshal, I believe it would be suicidal. This priest has never seen the inside of one of these camps. Field Marshal, I feel no remorse in watching these Jews go to their deaths, but what about him." Colonel Zooke pointed to Richard. "One slip or false move on his part would spell death to us also. If I could be certain of his actions once inside the death camp, I possibly would consider it . . . if the reward made it worth the risk."

Goering nodded at the colonel, then turned to

Richard. "What the colonel says is true, Father. You're a man of saintly idealisms, and the taking of a life is a grave sin in the Catholic doctrine isn't it, Father? In this camp, death is everywhere. How could you stand by and watch?"

"I'll do what is necessary to make this mission successful," Richard assured Goering. "I know people will be murdered all around me. I've heard many of the horror stories. But I also know this is a chance to save some of them. Just one life saved would be more than is being saved at this moment. Remember, also, I'm only a priest. I'm no martyr. I want to live as badly as you. I will not be the cause of this failing. I swear to my God on this."

"If it became necessary for you to kill someone in that camp in front of everybody—if Colonel Zooke ordered you to kill one of the Jews and perhaps it might be a child, would you do it?"

A chill swept through Richard's body. Goering and the colonel stared at him. He knew the importance of this horrid question and probably the ultimate future of this entire mission. "I would kill if so ordered." Richard stared resolutely at both men.

Goering turned to the colonel. "You've heard the priest answer. Will you risk such a plan with him?"

Colonel Zooke looked at Goering for a moment, then back at Richard. "The price will be high."

Richard sighed. "I'll pay your price."

Goering smiled as he stood. "You'll remain here until you're contacted by the colonel. Say nothing to anyone about this matter. Only we three are to know about what's taken place here. There are certain things about the military that you must know before we dress you as one of its finest officers. The colonel will return tomorrow to begin your crash course on German soldiering. He'll also need your clothes sizes. All of my officers wear only the finest tailored uniforms, as you can see." Goering opened his arms to show off his uniform. "Also, you'll be furnished with new papers and documents. Claude Schmitt has led a short life . . . let's hope your next life survives much longer. After all of this is done, you and the colonel will be transferred to Auschwitz. There's one other thing, young American priest, you should know. I've given the colonel direct orders that if you should in anyway, at any time jeopardize his or my welfare, he is to kill you on the spot."

Richard considered Goering's words carefully, his forehead breaking into a sweat.

"Also, Richard, tomorrow the colonel will tell you how much this escapade will cost you and your Jewish friends and the arrangements on where the gold will be deposited, and, of course, this will be done before any goods are delivered."

Richard nodded. "Fair enough, Marshal Goering, and I thank you for your cooperation."

Goering smiled. "Father, I don't know what strange fate has brought us together. Perhaps it's your God's doings, but for some reason, I've always liked you when I have every reason not to like you. After all, you stand for everything I stand against, such as the Jews. I'll see to it that that Jews will be eradicated from Europe. But in any case, I feel this will be our last meeting, and I feel sad about that. Because that tells me one of us is going to die before this war is over, and it has to be you that will die. Germany will win the war, and I will more than likely be the next leader of Germany and possibly the world after Hitler leaves us. I do hope you find your missing cardinal.

Surely if your God is as powerful as you and your church believe, he will lead you to the cardinal. Good-bye, Richard, Heil Hitler . . . and please say a prayer for me."

Richard didn't return Goering's salute to Hitler. They shook hands and departed ways.

The colonel was back the next morning, bringing with him the monetary fee in gold it would take to free Cardinal Beroske if he was still alive, and the fee required to free some of the Jews incarcerated inside Auschwitz. The price for the cardinal's return seemed very reasonable, if one could put a dollar figure on an old man's life. The price for the Jews was quite a bit steeper, but obviously the risk much greater of freeing untold numbers of Jews from the camp in comparison to one old man, Cardinal Beroske.

Richard was to meet with Bishop Rutgers and Rabbi Dziobak the following evening to discuss the financial arrangements ordered by Goering. The Catholic Church would pay for Cardinal Beroske's ransom, and the rabbi would stand good for the Jews. During the next five days, the colonel spent many hours tutoring Richard on the basics of the German military. Richard absorbed the knowledge like a dry sponge. The colonel remained astute through these sessions; Richard made it obvious they would remain ideological enemies, bonded only the monetary gains on the colonel's side and the spiritual, humanity factor on his side. Richard knew he would have to fear this man as much as the SS at Auschwitz. His life had suddenly become very expendable.

During this time, he was fitted with a German uniform and his head shaved. Also, he was issued new papers and a new name: Captain Stefan Reiner from Nuremburg. The time had finally come for Richard and

Colonel Zooke to depart for Auschwitz. It was quite a journey from Munich to Warsaw. Richard was a bit frightened his first time out dressed in his German uniform but quickly adapted to his new identity. If only the Holy Father could see him now, in a Nazi uniform. Surely, he'd be excommunicated.

The pope knew nothing about his mission. Bishop Rutgers and the rabbi had sworn a secret pact to keep this deadly quest secret. Possibly thousands of lives hung in the success or failure of the mission. The plane made three brief stops as it crossed Germany into Poland. It was around five in the morning when the plane finally reached its destination, a large German airfield some twenty kilometers northwest of Warsaw. Richard and Colonel Zooke disembarked the plane along with eight other Germans, pilots in Goering's air corps on a brief furlough in Munich. They were on their way back to the Russian front where they were badly needed. The stubborn Russians had temporarily stalled the German advance yet again. Germany's titanic struggle with the Soviets was approaching a critical stage if the Germans were to defeat the Russians. The Soviets had entered the war vastly unprepared but had managed during the preceding months to reorganize their outdated factories while still holding the Germans from outright victory. This wasn't accomplished without sacrificing a severe loss in life and property. Millions of Russians paid the ultimate price.

Colonel Zooke arranged a ride for them to a train terminal just outside Warsaw. Their train, unbeknown to Richard, was loaded with boxcars full of Polish Jews. Richard and the Jews shared a common destination— Auschwitz. Unfortunately, the Jews' journey to the camp was radically different from that of Richard's and the other handful of German SS soldiers also on the train. He was unaware Colonel Zooke had been stationed at the first Auschwitz One, located only a short distance from Auschwitz Two where Richard's train was presently headed. The second camp was constructed after Himmler's visit to Auschwitz One a year earlier. Himmler had been dissatisfied with the slowness and expensive extermination procedures, which, at the time, was done mostly by firing squads and mass burials. Himmler ordered Auschwitz Two to be constructed with its modern gas chambers and crematorium ovens. Auschwitz Two was still in its infancy when Richard arrived. The camp wouldn't reach full operational status until late 1943 and early '44. The ovens would still be warm when the allies invaded the camp at the close of the war.

Richard, still unaware of the reality of the boxcar cargo, would soon come face to face with his fellow passengers. Richard and Colonel Zooke sat alone on the journey from Warsaw, sitting across from one another. The other SS men who shared the same compartment with Richard and the colonel kept to themselves. He and the colonel carried papers verifying the two men as special attachés of Marshal Goering, which proved to be a help as well as hindrance, quickly isolating them from the other SS troops. The SS men considered them nothing more than spies for Goering.

Sunrise was still some two hours away when Richard and the others disembarked the train, exiting onto a large unloading ramp that ran the distance of the boxcars. Large overhead flood lights lit the ramp and surrounding area nearly as well as the Polish sun. This area was designated for the unloading of prisoners, its location centered halfway between the old Auschwitz One and the new Auschwitz Two, only a mile and a half separating the two camps. He followed Colonel Zooke into the small station, and the colonel arranged for their baggage to be transported to the camp. Richard quietly studied the strange surroundings, still feeling uneasy about his German masquerade. Richard was beginning to build a false impression of these handpicked killers, appearing nothing like the steely-eyed colonel meant to be Richard's ally but displayed more of a brute nature than any one of these young SS men. Richard's false impression of the young Germans would soon be righted with the rising of the Polish sun.

Richard and the colonel milled around the outside loading deck waiting on sunrise. He'd assumed the boxcars were filled with war supplies. The stillness that enveloped the Polish darkness began to awaken shortly before sunrise as the tall pines that surrounded the area swayed in the breeze. Richard took a seat in front of the depot, silently watching the first rays of light slither between the tall pines. He watched with great interest as Colonel Zooke paced back and forth along the edge of the ramp, stopping occasionally to stare at the boxcars. His imposing figure and solitary impressions had already alienated him from the other soldiers who shared the ramp with the stern-faced colonel. His appearance and actions had also segregated Richard from the others, perhaps sensing he was as antisocial as the colonel.

The western sky began to lighten; with this came heightened activity on the ramp. The once jovial soldiers took on a more serious and professional demeanor. More

SS men arrived mysteriously from the surrounding darkness. A sudden uneasiness swept through Richard's body. He sensed something was about to happen. The red western sky began to fade into silver as the sun rose above the Polish farmlands—and with the sun came Richard's first clear view of his surroundings. The tall pines had changed from darkened silhouettes into large living things. Looking closer now, he spied a tall chain-link fence encircling the pine forest and train terminal. His first inkling of what was in the boxcars came when an overhead loudspeaker burst to life, instructing the awaiting SS troops to man their posts.

Armed soldiers scurried down the length of the train facing the boxcars. Within moments, another order blast over the speaker, informing them the unloading was to begin. Richard stood and peered down at the far end of the train as a solider unlocked a boxcar and slid open the door. The overhead speaker again came to life. This time instead of speaking in German, the words flowed in Polish. Richard was astonished as he watched the first of the Polish Jews exit the wooden boxcar. He glanced quickly at Colonel Zooke who'd stopped his pacing to watch the pitiful sight of the haggard-looking Jews as they stumbled and fell from the car. The colonel's face no longer looked hard and taut. An evil smile filled his dry lips; his steel-gray eyes sparkling ungodly-like in the morning sun. Richard continued to watch in utter disbelief as the unloading process continued down the line, until the last car was emptied only a few feet away. He watched in horror as the Germans entered the cars, dispelling the ones who were unable to exit the car on their own accord, mostly the elderly and the noticeably young. Others arrived dead from the terrible journey. These unfortunates were thrown from the cars like dead animals, their bodies landing on the ramp at the feet of their terrified countrymen. The crying of children mixed with the sounds of German Lugers, scattered shots from inside the boxcars, soldiers executing the dying. Standing only a few feet from the last unloaded car, Richard looked into the faces of the terrified Jews; the look of fear and death obvious in their eyes. All of these Jews were from Poland; they had, at least, been spared the long journey some of their predecessors had endured, as would millions to follow.

Richard listened to the voice on the loudspeaker shout orders and rules to the terrified Jews, assuring them they would soon be showered and afforded a change of clothes and then positioned in their appointed work camps. All of this was done in order to control the Jews with a minimum amount of manpower, allowing more German soldiers to be on the Russian front. The Jews were to be exterminated with a minimum of cost and personnel.

Richard was as dazed and confused as the Jews, having never expected such a horrible welcome. He watched as the Jews were escorted off the ramp, forming a long triple file along the tracks, guarded on both sides by armed SS men. Colonel Zooke got Richard and boarded an open troop carrier, a SS guard manning a machine gun centered in the rear of the truck. He sat on the truck's right side, facing the lines of Jews still being formed into long columns. Colonel Zooke sat in the cab of the truck next to the driver. Richard and the machine-gunner watched in silence as the other SS guards finished forming the Jews into ranks. Small children clung to their parents like frightened animals. The young and strong Jews helped the elderly with their belongings. It was obvious to Richard the truck would follow alongside the lines of Jews to the main camp. There were two similar trucks behind them, evenly distanced along the line of Jews. The three machine guns were aimed at the helpless prisoners only twenty yards from their ranks. Richard prayed for strength to watch and bear such tragedy, constantly reminding himself of his purpose. The line of Jews began moving toward the camp. An occasional cry of a child disrupted the otherwise somber sound of weary feet trudging their way to the death camp. Richard's stomach turned, but he was successful in hiding his sickness, throwing up over the side of the truck when no one was looking.

Finally, the truck entered the main gate to Auschwitz as the trail of prisoners followed. The truck continued on, leaving the Jews behind as they struggled forward. The sight of them quickly faded into oblivion and Richard's eyes turned to other aspects of the camp. The truck made its way to the center of the compound.

The morning sky was clear, and the sun shone brightly as the truck continued along the unfinished railroad tracks. Jewish men and women dressed in striped clothes worked diligently laying the heavy trestles. Little did they realize they were laying the track to speed up the extermination of millions more like them. Richard's truck passed the large unloading ramps also under construction, where the actual unloading of prisoners would take place once the train track was laid. Directly across from the ramps stood one of the gas chambers, and next to it stood a large building, a chimney with smoke bellowing . . . a crematorium.

Richard's truck turned onto another road that led to

the SS headquarters. Here, Richard and Colonel Zooke would be assigned to their barracks. The two soldiers who'd manned the machine gun were the first to exit the truck, Richard following behind.

Colonel Zooke joined Richard behind the truck. "Well, Captain Reiner, what do you think of our Jewish detention camp?" Richard only stared at the colonel. The colonel laughed. "Follow me, Captain."

He followed the colonel into the main office, a large room with several desks occupied by the German military. No one seemed to pay any attention to the two men as they walked through the room to a small office located on the opposite end of the building. They stopped in front of the closed door. Colonel Zooke knocked. A deep voice called for them to enter. Richard followed the colonel into the small office, closing the door behind him. The room looked unimportant. A poster of the führer hung on the wall behind a wooden desk. Sitting behind the desk was a rather distinguished gray-haired man with blue eyes fixed on the two strangers approaching his desk.

Richard and the colonel stopped simultaneously as they neared the front of the desk. "Heil Hitler," the colonel and Richard boasted in unison, extending their right arm and snapping their leather boots together.

Colonel Freud returned the salute remaining seated behind his desk. "So, the two of you have been sent here by the Field Marshal?"

"Yes, Colonel," Zooke replied. Zooke took their papers from his coat pocket and handed them to Colonel Freud. Richard watched nervously as the seated colonel inspected the papers carefully, repeatedly looking up at the two men.

After a thorough inspection, he handed the papers back to Colonel Zooke. "I didn't realize Marshal Goering had an interest in Auschwitz. I assumed he would be too busy trying to destroy the Russian Air Force than to worry himself about a bunch of Jews."

Colonel Zooke remained calm. "Begging your pardon, Colonel Freud, Field Marshal Goering concerns himself about all aspects of the Third Reich."

Colonel Freud's taut face softened to a frigid smile. "I'm sure he does, Colonel." Colonel Freud's eyes shifted to Richard. "Well, Captain Reiner, what do you think of our institution?"

Richard glanced at the calm Colonel Zooke, at his plastered, hollow smile. "Colonel, I haven't had much of an opportunity to inspect the facility as of yet."

"I see," the colonel said. "I'm confident you'll find our facility and personnel here very professional and highly productive. Perhaps if our army and air corps were as proficient, we'd be inside the Kremlin by now." This stinging remark by the SS colonel received no reaction from Colonel Zooke, whose grin remained steadfast on his scarred face. "I hope the two of you enjoy your stay. If there is anything you need, please do not hesitate to ask. We want you to report to Marshal Goering that all is running in the finest traditions of the Third Reich." Colonel Freud stood for the first time. "Corporal Zorn will see you to your quarters. I do hope you don't mind sharing quarters with officers of the SS, as we have no private quarters here . . . even for Marshal Goering's emissaries." Colonel Freud smiled at the two and then abruptly snapped to attention. "Heil Hitler."

Richard and Colonel Zooke answered his salute and

left the room.

The corporal led the way, pushing a wheelbarrow brimming with the two men's luggage. They walked briskly toward the row of long buildings, passing soldiers along the way. Richard looked back toward the camp's entranceway as more Jews were arriving. There was no sign of those who'd ridden the same train as Richard and Colonel Zooke.

Richard and the colonel arrived at their barracks. Building H2 was a long wooden building divided into small rooms, each room housing two men. Colonel Zooke was the ranking officer in this particular building. In all, forty-eight officers occupied barracks H2. All officers and enlisted men were members of the SS except Richard and Colonel Zooke. The colonel was no more talkative than he'd ever been. Richard was thankful for this, utterly despising the colonel.

It was afternoon when the two men exited the barracks for the first time. The strong north wind had abated as the sun shone brightly in the overhead sky. Richard couldn't believe his eyes as he looked toward the tracks at the long line of Jews being marched into camp. He and the colonel started down the grated road toward the distant tracks. Richard was openly confused why he hadn't seen any other Jews except the ones extending the railway. Finally, he asked Colonel Zooke, as the colonel walked briskly toward the lines of Jews streaming into the camp, why this was so.

The colonel never altered his stride. "Why, Captain Reiner, I'm surprised a man of your intelligence hasn't figured that out yet. I'll be glad to show you where our arriving guests are taken to rest after their long, tiring journey."

He looked again toward the Jews. Now, he witnessed clearly what was taking place at the front of the two lines. On one side, women and children stood in a single row that formed a line along the gravel road nearly a quarter mile long; men and young boys extending about the same distance as the female line formed the other row. At the front of the two lines stood two SS soldiers holding walking canes. Additional soldiers stood on either side of each line, keeping the Jews moving. As the prisoner or prisoners (mothers carrying small children) approached the officer holding the cane, the officer performed a brief visual inspection, then, pointing either right or left with his cane, directed the prisoner in that direction. As Richard examined this process, it became clear all the old and very young, as well the women with young children, were directed toward the left, while the younger and stronger males and females were turned to the right. This strong group was then led further down the far side of the road.

Richard watched as this line stretched beyond the main yard, reaching beyond the far end of the main camp. Another high fence could be seen lining a different part of the camp. He did not know that these were the lucky ones. They would be housed in special barracks until they could be dispersed to the labor camps, where they would be put to use in the war effort. Then, the other line made its way along the high fence, toward distant brick buildings. Black smoke bellowed from one of the building's massive chimneys. Richard viewed the scene in disbelief. How could human beings, even the SS, be so brutal to old men and women, to young children, beating them with their swagger sticks if they fell to the ground? Other, stronger prisoners helped the weaker ones, too weak to go any further. Those too far gone would be left simply to lie there in the sun. Eventually, a SS soldier would check if the person was still alive. If not, one of the "Canada" men would throw the corpse into a wheelbarrow and hurry down the fence toward the distant buildings. The prisoners who still breathed were shot in the head, then they, too, would be loaded in a wheelbarrow and hurried off to the ovens.

Richard felt dirty and evil as he stood there in his Nazi uniform watching these inhumane deeds, especially when one of the elderly or young children looked at him as they passed a few feet away, their eyes piercing his soul. He cringed at the sound of Colonel Zooke's voice.

"Come, Captain Reiner, I'll show you the Jewish welcoming center."

The colonel started toward the fence where the Jews walked in silence toward the smoking chimney. Richard hesitated, drawing inner courage as to what horrors might yet face him.

The colonel walked a few feet. When Richard did not follow, he turned sharply and demanded, "Come, Captain Reiner."

Richard stood his ground.

The colonel's face turned red. SS officers were nearby. "Captain Reiner, if you're not by my side within ten seconds, I'll kill you."

The colonel's voice could be heard throughout the main yard. All eyes turned toward the raging colonel. Even the Jews stopped to take notice. Colonel Zooke unsnapped his holster, took the pistol in his right hand, and pointed it at Richard. Reluctantly, Richard joined the colonel. Colonel Zooke holstered his weapon.

Richard followed Colonel Zooke down the edge of the fence, forcing his eyes to look straight ahead at the gravel road paralleling the fence. Apparently, they were heading for the brick buildings about 200 yards ahead. Richard glanced quickly at the scattering of SS men who stood watch over the unending line of Jews making their way slowly along the edge of the fence. They reached the end of the tall fence, affording a close view of the three buildings erected only a few feet apart. As they grew nearer, he could see a large gathering of Jews standing in what appeared to be a large courtyard directly in front of one of the buildings. Richard kept stride for stride with Colonel Zooke as they neared the courtyard where three or four hundred Jews stood in front of a large wooden platform. On top of the platform were armed SS guards.

Standing in the front center of the platform was a SS officer. The officer shouted to the Jews in their Polish language. "You're about to enter the showers. All are to strip off their clothes where they stand. New clothes will be issued after your showers."

Richard heard the low roar of Jewish voices as they talked amongst themselves about the terrible orders. These were proud and highly religious people and their morality unquestionably high. To be ordered to fully disrobe in front of others was total embarrassment, especially for the very old and young adults.

Richard followed the colonel up the concrete ramp, to the solider holding the megaphone. He now had a firsthand view of the encircled Jews. He'd never seen such a more disturbing sight, the fear and anguish. They stared in silence at their German captures of which Richard was now one. Only a handful of Jews removed their clothes.

Richard had been here only a short time, but already he'd witnessed the impatience of the Germans. He'd also taken notice that the line of Jews was beginning to back up along the edge of the fence. These people in the circle were taking too much time.

No sooner had the thought entered Richard's mind, when a woman screamed. A guard pulled a teenaged girl from the circle. Why had she not been chosen for the labor camps? The girl attempted to escape the laughing solider but was no match against the 200-pound guard. He tore the clothes from her body. Then, another guard joined in the melee, holding her wailing arms as the first guard continued to disrobe the screaming girl. Within seconds, the girl stood naked in the bright sun. Adding insult to tragedy, the huge SS guard fondled the young girl's breasts. Her screams were drowned by the megaphone. "Everyone will be naked within one minute or this girl will die."

Richard watched with the others as the big SS guard pulled his pistol from his holster, holding the barrel next to the terrified girl's temple. The gathering of Jews began to strip with all the speed they could muster, tearing the clothes from their bodies and those standing near them. "You must learn that time is of great importance while you're here at Auschwitz," the guard with the megaphone said. "Bring the girl up here!" He motioned for the guards to bring the naked girl up the ramp.

An uneasy silence fell over the compound as the two guards brought the girl up the ramp; her resistance was in vain. The guards positioned her in the center of the platform where she could be easily seen by both groups of Jews . . . those who'd already stripped and those who still waited in line. "To show you that we mean what we say, we must give you an example." The SS officer laid the megaphone down on the ramp and walked over to where the naked girl stood, trembling in fear. Richard watched in horror as the officer unsnapped his holster and removed his pistol. Before he could perform his duty, Colonel Zooke hurried to the girl. Richard sighed with relief as he watched the colonel stand before the girl, blocking the young lieutenant. Zooke would stop the senseless murder.

Richard began a short prayer thanking God for sparing the young woman's life, then stopped in disbelief as the colonel drew his pistol from his holster and placed the barrel between the eyes of the terrified girl. He witnessed the unholy look in the colonel's eyes as the cracking sound of the exploding shell pierced the air. The dead girl fell to the floor. Smiling, the colonel proudly placed his pistol back into its holster, then turned to Richard. "One less Jew to feed, Captain Reiner." Richard's gaze returned to the dead girl lying on the floor. Richard walked to her and bowed his head, praying for her soul as she journeyed to heaven.

Colonel Zooke and the SS guards turned their attention to the remaining Jews yet to be processed, paying little attention to Richard. While Richard prayed, he'd missed that the other Jews had already been ushered into the building for their showers . . . or so they'd been told.

The Canada group scurried about the empty courtyard, picking up the piles of discarded clothing. The Canada group, as they were called, were other Jews who'd been chosen to work about the camp, performing various duties. They were fully aware of the atrocities happening in the camp and, indeed, played an important part in speeding up the extermination process. But this way, they were surviving. Richard watched as two Canada men picked up the murdered girl, placing the body in a wheelbarrow and hurriedly pushed it down the ramp, heading for the building with the smoking chimney.

"Come, Captain, let's go see our friends as they exit the showers." Richard turned to the smiling colonel. Hate filled Richard's heart, a new emotion for him. He drew a deep breath and reluctantly followed on the heels of the colonel.

They rounded the far side of the building, on the opposite side of where the naked Jews had entered. As they neared the rear entrance of the building, Richard noticed a large number of the Canada group milling about a large concrete ramp that extended all the way across to the building with the smoking chimney. He followed the colonel up the ramp and onto the concrete platform, where a scattering of SS guards carried on idle conversations and smoked cigarettes. It was obvious to Richard that they were only taking a break in between some duty.

The colonel stopped in the center of the concourse and pointed toward the large door, presently closed and centered in the middle of the building. The door was at least twenty feet across and half as high. "That's where our showered guests will exit from in a very short while," Colonel Zooke said, glancing at his timepiece. Over half of the Canada group had gathered at the front of the large door, including at least fifty members spread about the platform. Richard noticed a half dozen Canada men standing behind a small concrete wall centered halfway between the two buildings, about twenty yards from the door. The two-foot-high wall ran some fifteen feet across. Standing behind it were six Canada members puffing on cigarettes. Some type of tools lay on the long wooden table directly behind the six Canada men with metal boxes stationed along the table.

Once again, Richard turned his attention to the closed door. Canada men with wheelbarrows began gathering in front of the door. He felt nauseated again with the sight of the wheelbarrows and the gathering of the SS guards moving toward the door. His heart raced as the large door cracked open. Richard looked into the massive entranceway brightly lit by overhead lights. Centered in the huge room were the naked bodies of the Jews he'd seen in the front of the building only minutes ago. The blood drained from Richard's face. Colonel Zooke laughed. The bodies were piled on top of one another, forming a large pyramid—the elderly and young closer to the bottom, the strongest on top of the pile, as they had tried to climb above the deadly gas as it filtered into the room. The action was futile, as the thirty-foot ceiling was unreachable. Even if it had been, it was only a matter of minutes before the gas reached the ceiling. Perhaps the ones crushed on the bottom of the pile were the lucky ones after all, as they, at least, died swiftly, many by suffocation instead of gas.

Richard wanted to turn away, but his eyes would have no part of it. He watched in dreaded silence as members of the Canada group rushed into the opening, each grabbing a body, children cradled in their arms and adults slung over their shoulders, utterly racing toward the center of the concourse where the other five members of Canada stood at the ready with their pliers. It was a horrid dream. If only. Six Canada men held the limp bodies as they probed the corpses' mouths for gold teeth and fillings. They moved swiftly, extracting the gold teeth and placing

291

them in the metal boxes beside them. When finished, they dropped the bodies into the awaiting wheelbarrow. Another Canada member held the wheelbarrow in waiting, then, when fully loaded, hurried off toward the building with the smoking chimney. This terrible ordeal continued until all of the bodies were disposed of at the other side of the building were more Jews awaiting their welcoming showers. Richard's stomach did painful somersaults. Colonel Zooke leaned over, his cold lips brushing Richard's ear as he whispered, "If you show any kind of weakness to this, you'll place us in a very precarious situation. They will begin to wonder about your allegiance to their proud group. You may not have the chance to find your friend, much less save any of these sorry bastards."

Richard realized he spoke the truth. Nevertheless, he felt the puke rising in his throat, filling his mouth. He looked about; three SS men peered at them and spoke amongst themselves. He closed his eyes and swallowed hard, forcing the vomit back down into his stomach. He asked God for help as he held his breath, afraid if he breathed the vomit would force its way back up.

Richard opened his eyes slowly and looked at Colonel Zooke, at the ugly scar that ran the length of Zooke's face. Richard's mind was diverted from his weak stomach to the Satan bastard who stared back at him. He would think later that God had done this to keep his mind off being sick, but whatever the reason it worked.

"Follow me, Captain Reiner, for our last stop of the day."

Richard glanced at the gas chamber, the last of the bodies had been removed and the door was closing. His mind flashed a picture of naked Jews who he knew were awaiting their turn on the other side of the building to enter, repeating the same grotesque events that had just ended.

He trailed behind the colonel as they walked toward the other building, glancing at the small piles of gold sitting in the metal boxes next to the six Canada members who puffed on cigarettes and awaited another batch of bodies with their trinkets of gold. Richard and the colonel entered the large, open doorway as three Canada men exited pushing wheelbarrows. The dramatic rise in temperature gave Richard the first inkling of what was to come. The roar of the second story fans drowned out most of the other sounds that echoed along the brick walls of the crematorium. Bright overhead lights lit the entryway and long, wide corridor that ran the entire length of the building.

Richard could easily see from where the massive heat originated. Both sides the hallway were lined with Canada slaves in the process of shoveling coal and other burnables into the open doorways of the crematorium. Other Canada members scurried up and down the wide corridor pushing wheelbarrows. It was evident that the raging fires weren't particular about what they burned, using everything imaginable for fuel. Richard's eyes settled on one of the barrows that brimmed with old clothes. Their own clothing had become fuel to cremate their bodies. Richard and the colonel had only been in the building about a minute and already their bodies were wet with sweat. His attention was gotten by Colonel Zooke as he pulled at Richard's uniform sleeve. Richard read his lips as he told him to follow. The two men walked to an elevator. It was a very large elevator, able to hold some fifty bodies at the time, more if they were small children. The elevator began to rise toward the second floor where the roaring of the fans had reached their maximum.

There were no wheelbarrows on this floor, only larger four-wheeled pushcarts able to hold three times as many corpses as the barrows. Colonel Zooke exited the elevator. His glassy steel eyes peered into Richard's dazed ones as he watched the Canada slaves throw naked bodies into the ovens.

"Oh my God," Richard said aloud.

"Come," Colonel Zooke shouted, waving his hand for Richard to follow.

Richard hesitated for a brief moment praying—God how he prayed—that this was just a horrid dream, but he knew as he began to walk down the corridor a few steps behind Colonel Zooke that dreams weren't equipped with smells. The awful smell of burnt flesh filled the corridor. The great fans above them couldn't draw the odor out fast enough. Richard had reached a point of being beyond sick; his mind shut down the reality around it, as if simply going through the motions of being alive. Just then, Colonel Zooke motioned that it was time to leave.

Outside, the fresh air and afternoon sunlight was a welcome relief to Richard's body and mind. Both men's uniforms were saturated with sweat. Canada slaves still hurried back and forth, to and from the quickly emptying chambers. Another group of Jews waited around the front of the building, patiently awaiting their turn in the chambers. This process would continue until just before dark. The sun was already below the tops of the towering pine trees that surrounded the camp, as if nature, too, was attempting to hide the great atrocities taking place in the murder camp. The roar of the crematorium fans faded as

Richard and Colonel Zooke walked toward their dorm.

The sudden burst of machine-gun fire ended the few brief moments of silence. Richard and the colonel looked in the direction of the noise. Only sporadic rifle fire was heard now coming behind a large cluster of tall pines that stood some 300 yards beyond the crematorium.

"Tomorrow we'll visit that part of the camp. Too much excitement in one day isn't good for you, Captain Reiner." Richard glared at the laughing colonel. "Come, Captain, my stomach is begging for food, and I'm certain that you must be ravished also after the wonderful things you've seen today."

"Welcome to Auschwitz. We're here to help you start a new and productive life. Heil Hitler."

Richard looked toward the tracks, to where the young German guard shouted these words to the hundreds of Polish Jews just arrived. He shook his head as he stared at the pitiful sight. He wanted to shout at the Jews, warn them of their plight. The unexpected words from Colonel Zooke took his voice away.

"Tomorrow, Bishop, we'll begin to search for your friend. Perhaps he's one of those who still live. Even we heathens aren't so barbaric as to destroy the strong. They're our cattle, and don't eat near as much as a bull."

"What about your contacts and the gold that awaits the freedom of some of these poor people?"

Colonel Zooke laughed, looking carefully about him before answering. "This all takes time, Captain Reiner. Don't worry about these Jews who are here now as their deaths are already assured. Even your God couldn't rescue them." Colonel Zooke placed his right hand on Richard's shoulder. "Don't worry yourself, Bishop. There are many more Jews in this world than there are gold bars. Even Jewish and Catholic treasures combined couldn't pay for them all." The colonel walked toward the barracks, occasionally glancing up at one of the many guard towers scattered about the massive grounds. "Tomorrow we'll find Cardinal Beroske."

Chapter Nineteen

Richard awoke just after daylight, terrified by the muffled roar that came from overhead, believing he'd awoken inside the crematorium. He sighed with relief as his drowsy brain acknowledged the sound was only that of heavy rain falling on the overhead roof. Faint light shone through the nearby window. He could make out Colonel Zooke as he slept. Richard laid there a while longer praying for the strength to get through another day inside this dreadful place. His thoughts turned to Elisabeth, wondering again if she'd forgiven him for leaving her as he did. How he wished he were with her now back in the serene Yorkshire countryside. He promised himself that if he survived this, he'd never leave her again. The stirring of Colonel Zooke interrupted his thoughts of the future.

Richard got up and headed for the showers, passing other rooms of sleeping SS men along the way. Only one other man was in the showers, a young lieutenant from Berlin. At first, he was reluctant to talk to the good-natured German. He was still uncertain of his acting abilities. Speaking fluent German was one thing but playing the role of a German officer was something else. Richard's fears were quickly washed away like the soil from his body. He couldn't help but wonder how it could be that a seemingly nice and intelligent young man like the lieutenant, who spoke warmly of his family back in Berlin, could walk from this building and help perform such terrible crimes on innocent people.

The shower accomplished more for Richard than just cleaning his filthy body; it gave him the confidence needed to communicate openly with other SS men. Richard was already having serious doubts as to Colonel Zooke's bargaining ability with other members of the SS, as surely there would have to be mutual trust among the two parties if any kind of deal could be made for the release of Cardinal Beroske and who knows how many Jews. Richard knew that Colonel Zooke's arrogant behavior would win over few friends with most members of the SS and surely none with prisoners of the camp, who must also be involved if the bizarre plan were to succeed.

The tall watchtowers were clearly visible now. Two men neared the outer perimeter of the high metal fence topped with barbed wire. Richard counted six watchtowers as he and the colonel finally reached the main entrance where three SS guards occupied the small wooden guardhouse that sat next to a closed gate.

"We wish to inspect the quarters," Colonel Zooke said to the rifle-bearing guard, his voice short and direct.

The guard stared at the rigid colonel, then at Richard who stood behind him. "You're the Goering spies, aren't you?" the brash captain said.

Richard felt unnerved by the man's confrontation, all too aware of Colonel Zooke's short temper. Richard's stare froze on Colonel Zooke's right hand as it slowly moved toward his holster. He felt himself begin to sweat as the colonel's fingers unsnapped the top of his holster. A deadly quiet enveloped the small perimeter when a familiar voice broke the uncertain silence.

"Hello again, Captain Reiner," the smiling lieutenant said as he walked out of the guardhouse, positioning himself next to the captain.

Richard stepped in front of Colonel Zooke. "Good morning. Lieutenant Steiner, we wish to visit your camp. Field Marshal Goering is considering taking some of these prisoners off your hands, as they could be useful on the Russian front cleaning up the remains of Stalingrad and Moscow after our troops secure the cities."

The lieutenant paused, then said, "Yes, that's a clever idea. Good idea. Yes, Captain Reiner." The lieutenant patted the captain on the back.

Richard looked at the captain with guarded apprehension. After a few tense moments, the captain's posture relaxed. Richard's eyes settled on Colonel Zooke, his hand remaining on the handle of his pistol.

"You're free to inspect the camp," the captain said flatly.

All eyes turned to Colonel Zooke who still showed no sign of backing off. Richard's heartbeat in a steady rhythm again as Colonel Zooke slowly lowered his hand from the pistol. The captain also watched with noticeable relief as he stood back, letting Colonel Zooke and Richard pass.

Colonel Zooke's irrational behavior only deepened Richard's concern about the chances of the mission's success. Richard and the colonel walked across the open field toward the first of many wooden huts that housed the male prisoners. He followed Colonel Zooke into the first dwelling. He prayed that his eyes deceived him, but they didn't. The long, open room was poorly lit. Filtered sunlight shone through the row of small windows lining both sides the open corridor. The smell was atrocious, perhaps even worse than the crematorium.

Richard and the colonel hadn't moved since entering the building. The dark maze of silhouettes began to clear as the two men's eyes slowly adapted to the dim light. The room was uncomfortably quiet, sporadic coughing coming from all directions. The once blurry figures became living creatures in Richard's eyes . . . at least most of them. He walked slowly down the center of the room, careful not to step on one of the hundreds of bodies that seemingly took up every spare inch of the room's floor. Colonel Zooke, who followed on Richard's heels, had pulled his pistol from its holster.

"My God," Richard mumbled as he looked into the eyes and faces of the Jewish men, their starving bodies sprawled on the damp floor. It wasn't difficult to tell how long each had been incarcerated in the camp, as the newest arrivals still showed signs of health and their clothes still conformed to their bodies. The ones that had been there the longest were either dead or near death and lay partially dressed in rags that had once been their clothing. The bulging eyes of the starving followed Richard and Colonel Zooke as they slowly made their way through the quarters.

His eyes at floor level, Richard startled when he brushed into the body hanging from a makeshift rope tied to an overhead rafter. His muffled shriek had also startled the already frightened colonel who spontaneously fired his Luger into the swinging corpse. Richard's vision sharpened further as he counted at least seven other bodies hanging from the rafters throughout the room. The stench of sour skin filled the room with a noxious, invisible cloud, but it wasn't the odor that turned his stomach, it was the sight of these retched souls lying pathetically before him.

He made his way slowly toward the back of the room. Colonel Zooke had retreated out the front door, asserting that he wanted a cigarette. They both knew the real reason . . . Colonel Zooke had become terrified in the midst of the Jews, virtually alone in the company of his enemies. There were no SS men nearby; they entered these huts only when absolutely necessary, when the Canada men removed the bodies from the rafters and the dead who lay upon the floor.

Richard quickly realized his search for Cardinal Beroske would be much more difficult than he'd imagined. All the faces looked the same; he peered at their protruding eyes and starving bodies. As he neared the back of the building, he noticed a man who lay on the bare floor trembling violently. The others who'd lain next to him had moved away. They, like everyone else in the room, watched Richard's every step.

Richard walked to where the man lay. There was no doubt the dying man was a veteran of the camp, nothing more than a skeleton covered in thin, jaundiced skin. He lay shivering on his side, his legs pulled to his chest. His closed eyes were sunk deep into his head. Saliva rolled from the corner of his mouth. Richard knelt on one knee next to the man and forced his hand to the man's cheek. His fingertips felt the chill of imminent death. Essentially, the man's body had died already, having survived this long only because his thirty-year-old heart wanted so much to live. Knowing the man was near death, Richard knelt on both knees, removing his officer's cap and laying it on the floor beside him.

The eyes of the room watched in disbelief as Richard made the sign of the cross and recited aloud a Latin prayer. A younger man who lay closest to Richard watched in dazed wonderment as Richard performed the ritual of last rights over the man. The man's well-fitting clothes were evidence he had recently arrived at the camp. A short time before Richard finished his prayers, the sickly man died. He paused a moment after finishing his prayers and, to the further astonishment of the Jews, unbuttoned his trench coat and lay it over the dead man's body.

Richard started to stand, but a gentle hand held his arm. He looked at the newly arrived Jew and thought how wonderful it felt to see a warm smile on one of these thousands of faces. Richard smiled back. Hesitant, at first, the Jew said in broken German, "Why would a German officer pray for a dying Jew?"

Richard looked at the Polish Jew who'd just attempted to speak to Richard in German, "Perhaps some of us who wear German uniforms aren't at all what we appear to be."

The young Jew's eyes told of his astonishment as Richard had responded to him in fluent Polish. The Jew shook his head slowly. "Who are you—how can this be?"

Richard leaned closer to the man. Colonel Zooke reentered the front of the building. "Never mind who I am, friend. I'm here looking for a man in his late fifties. He's a Polish cardinal. I need to find him before he ends up like this poor man. I'm also here to attempt the release of some of your people. I have no more time today." Richard's dark eyes glanced at the impatient Colonel Zooke, who paced along the front of the doorway. "I'll be back tomorrow. The Catholic cardinal's name is Beroske. Please find out what you can."

The young Jew smiled. "I'll do my best, Father."

Richard's eyes widen at the religious title. He smiled as he gripped the man's hand tightly, then stood and headed for the doorway.

"Here," a Polish voice said.

He turned and looked at the elderly Jew lying close to the dead man. He held Richard's trench coat above his head. Richard walked back to him.

"Take this," the starving man said, handing Richard his overcoat. "Garments like this are to be worn by the living. Dead men have no need for them."

Richard glanced at the body; a tattered shirt now covered the dead man's face. It had been the old man's pillow, and it would again be his pillow as soon as Richard turned and walked away. He looked at the old man. "Thank you and God bless you," he whispered.

The old man took Richard's hand, holding it tightly. He cried as he said, "Please, Father, survive this camp so you may go forth and tell the world of our peoples' plight. Our very race might depend upon it."

He glared into the old man's eyes. His cold hand told Richard that the old man would soon end up like his neighbor. Richard's trance was broken by the shouting voice of Colonel Zooke. The colonel had regained his bravery; beside him stood two-armed SS men. Richard winked at the old man, stood, and walked toward the three Germans.

The rain hadn't let up. Richard pulled his cap low over the front of his forehead as he and Colonel Zooke sloshed through the water and mud from one hut to another—but they were all the same. All the faces soon blended into one. Some of the dwellings were empty, their occupants sent out on some kind of work detail. Those that survived the day would be back in the hut by nightfall. Richard and Colonel Zooke visited eight of the huts, with many more yet to be searched. The occasional burst of machine-gun fire sounded beyond the timberline. The colonel had promised him a look at the area the day before. He prayed the colonel would forget. The colonel wouldn't take him there today—but hadn't forgotten about it. The sun broke through the clearing skies as Richard exited the last of the huts that formed the first line.

It was after one o'clock when the two men started back toward the SS area. Colonel Zooke complained about his hunger, but Richard had no appetite. He felt no different than most, as even the majority of SS men felt this way the first few days in the camp. But even the severe horrors of the camp would mellow in time. The everyday treacheries would gradually become just another routine of camp life. Richard felt this complacency already creeping into his mind and prayed to his God that he'd never grow used to the killings and torture, giving him the inner strength to do what he could to free as many as possible. He prayed he would not lose his compassion for every soul in the camp. The dying Jew who took Richard by the arm inside the first hut would become a constant reminder of the importance of his surviving this place. Every passing moment meant more murders of innocent people. He need only look at the distant chimney that poured the black smoke as a reminder.

A week passed. Having been forced to spend two days in bed, he'd fallen behind on his quest for the cardinal.

Even now, on the eighth day, he forced himself from one hut to another, though he was terribly sick. Colonel Zooke had stopped tagging along on the wild-goose chase. The colonel spent most of his days around the tracks or at the gas chambers. The word had spread throughout the Jewish work camp that Captain Reiner was a priest and searching for a Polish cardinal. This could help his search for the cardinal—or be deadly if leaked to the SS. There were, indeed, informants among the Jewish prisoners. A secret of such importance to the SS could be worth much to a starving man.

The bright midday sun had reached its apex in the sky two hours before. Richard was about to enter his seventh hut of the day and his last until tomorrow. He stopped in front of the hut. Leaning against the edge of the doorway, he removed his cap and wiped beads of sweat from his pale forehead. The hot sun played havoc with his already feverish body, and his nagging cough was no better.

Richard took a deep breath of fresh air and placed his cap back on his head. As always, he paused to ask God for strength before entering the hut. This dwelling was no different than any of the others. The place smelled of filth and rotting bodies. Faces—always the same faces. Richard slowly made his way down the center of the room. No bodies hung from these rafters, but there had been four the night before. He couldn't understand why suddenly he was receiving such friendly welcomes to the huts. He wore the same German uniform when the Jews would shiver at his very presence. Strangely, these dying men found a smile for Richard as he walked among them.

The bright June sun afforded more light than usual

in this hut. Its silver rays pierced the small windows that ran the length of the building, offering Richard a much better view of the endless faces and revealing more vividly just how gruesome the place. The noises were always the same in the huts, scattered coughing intermingled with pitiful groans and the occasional snoring. Presently, another sound, different than the ones he was used to hearing, came from the middle of the south wall, midway between two windows.

Richard made his way toward the high-pitched squealing sound as hundreds of eyes followed him to the edge of the wall. The Jews knew the sound, hearing it often during the long nights. The noise silenced as Richard approached the middle-aged man who sat leaning against the wall. Fear gripped the starving man's face. His protruding brown eyes looked up at Richard. He watched the man's body shake with fear. Richard wanted to assure the frightened man that he wouldn't harm him. He knelt on one knee. The man, who'd been holding the front of his coat tightly, tightened it more with Richard's nearness. He reached out to calm the man.

"No it's mine!"

Richard's hand stopped with the man's words. He was confused.

A Jew sitting close by said, "He's afraid you'll take it from him."

"Take what?"

"Show him, Karl," the man said.

Karl looked cautiously at his comrade.

"He won't take it from you," the man assured.

Karl looked back at Richard. "You promise?"

"I promise," Richard said.

He watched with great curiosity as Karl slowly opened the front of his coat. His body, already weak with fever, suddenly felt faint as the smiling Karl took the still warm rat from his jacket, holding it up proudly by its hairy tail. Richard lowered his head and closed his eyes. He drew enough energy to look up. Karl placed the rat back into his jacket for safekeeping, as such bounty wasn't safe to lay around. Karl stared at Richard, a strange smile on his face.

"Karl is one of the oldest survivors in the camp. Some say he's been here for six months," the man sitting next to Richard said. "He, like many others, has survived off things like what he now has in his coat. But survival has cost him his mind. There are no winners in Auschwitz."

Richard looked at the man, then at the smiling Karl still clutching his jacket. Richard bowed his head and said a prayer. Then, he stood. A sudden rush of vertigo nearly brought him back to his knees. He removed his cap, his face and body wet with sweat. The heat inside the hut was high, and so was Richard's fever. He started toward the front entrance, his legs rubbery. The room spun. He felt his legs giving way and was near collapsing when a strong grip grabbed him under the arms. His eyes tried to focus on the strong, young Jew who held him up.

"Come, Father, I'll help you to the door."

"How do you know I'm a priest?" Richard muttered at the man.

"It doesn't matter, Father. Your secret is safe with me." Richard rested his weight on the young man's body as they walked toward the door. The man stopped just short of the doorway. "Listen to me, Father. I know you're looking for a Polish cardinal."

Richard's weak eyes strained to see the man who

spoke of Cardinal Beroske. "You know where he is?" Richard asked weakly.

"Listen, Father, you come back here in two days."

Richard tried to speak but couldn't.

"Two days, Father. You get some rest, or you won't be alive in two days." The Jew helped Richard to the front door.

He sat on the edge of the hut's small porch. The Jew disappeared back into the dreariness of the hut. The fresh air revived Richard, and he was able to get back to his barracks. He was deathly sick, sleeping for the next twenty-four hours. Colonel Zooke brought him a small amount of food the next day. As Richard's body grew stronger, so did the urge to return to hut 42, where the young Jew had spoken of Cardinal Beroske.

Richard wracked his brain most of his waking hours, wondering if the young Jew had meant Cardinal Beroske was still alive, or if he knew when and where the cardinal might have died. Richard would've given the cardinal up for dead shortly after he arrived if it hadn't been for the vision, he'd seen on the beach that day with Elisabeth. That day seemed three lifetimes ago. That world was only a wonderful dream. Auschwitz was the real world now, and, again, Richard was one of the main characters in this bizarre game of life.

***

He awoke early the morning of the second day. His fever had broken sometime during the night. Although extremely weak, he'd crawl to hut 42 this morning if need be. Colonel Zooke would sleep later than normal this morning. Zooke and three other SS officers had stayed up late the night before emptying a fifth of Russian vodka brought back from the Russian front.

Richard dressed and went to the mess hall. Still having no appetite, he forced food into his stomach, attempting to regain some of his lost strength. He sat next to Lieutenant Steiner, one of the guards at the prison gate, the same man who'd probably saved the disastrous confrontation between Colonel Zooke and the captain at the gate. Richard had eaten breakfast with the lieutenant three times previously and found the lieutenant a likable young man. The lieutenant had turned twenty-two the week prior. He was a highly intelligent German, born in Munich, his father a respected surgeon, who, like his son, had been caught up in Hitler's war, serving presently somewhere along the 2,000-mile Russian front in one of the field hospitals. The lieutenant told Richard he'd received a letter from his father ten days ago, telling of heavy losses on both sides and a growing concern the German forces were now incapable of defeating the Russians.

The lieutenant never spoke to Richard about the treatment of the Jews, leaving Richard to believe the lieutenant was here for only the purpose of serving his country and not for the elimination of the Jews. Richard's growing friendship with the lieutenant was already paying dividends as far as his goings and comings inside the Jews' work camp, allowing him to move about the huts and grounds with ever-increasing ease. Even the guards in the tower would wave at Richard as he made his rounds to the huts.

He and the lieutenant finished their breakfasts. The two men walked together to the hut area, and the lieutenant asked why he spent so much of his time in the Jewish quarters. Casually, Richard passed it off as being a simple study of how to improve the sanitary conditions of the labor camps. Berlin was concerned about the recent outbreaks of cholera and similar diseases found in camps. Richard hoped the lieutenant would pass this information to the other SS personnel in the area, hopefully frightening them even further about the possibility of catching a fatal disease from the prisoners and keeping them even further away from the Jews' living area than was already the case. This would allow the prisoners a little more freedom and perhaps even cut down on the labor details.

The sun was hot and bright as the two men neared the hut area. Countless Jews were lined, as always, along the tracks. The smoke from the crematorium rose straight up on this still, clear morning. Along with the usual Polish words that blared through the German megaphones, two long bursts of machine-gun fire sounded through the distant pines as the two men approached the guardhouse. Richard asked the lieutenant what was taking place in the wooded area.

The lieutenant passed it off saying, "I don't know what goes on in that section of the camp and could really care less."

He could tell by the lieutenant's voice that he did know what was taking place in the tall pines but didn't want to talk about it.

Richard left the lieutenant at the guardhouse and proceeded toward hut 42. His thoughts were only on Cardinal Beroske as he made his way across the open area. One of the huts had just been emptied. SS guards were lining up the Jews to get a head count. Even from this distance, Richard could see some of the men, barely able to stand. He knew many of these men would never return from their work area that day. He prayed for their souls as he neared hut 42.

Richard paused at the doorway, asking his God to let the cardinal be inside and alive. He breathed deeply and walked in. He stood just inside the doorway, allowing his eyes to adjust to the dim lighting inside the hut. He had no trouble seeing the bodies hanging from the rafters. He would never know that the Jew hanging from his neck in the far corner of the room was Karl, the same man who'd captured the rat two days earlier.

Richard began to make his way through the crowded room, careful not to step on any prisoners lying on the floor. The scene never changed: the skinny bodies, the bulging eyes and protruding cheekbones, and, of course, the ever-present faces of death. Richard's eyes searched for only one face this morning: the face that had told him to come back today. But as he looked from man to man, he grew terrified. They all looked the same.

Richard's heart pounded as he made his way down the center of the room. Had he come all this way to only lose him now? Face dripping with sweat, he was near panic as he neared the back of the room. He paused, ready to make his way back toward the front of the room, when he noticed a man waving his arm, motioning for him to come where he and another man sat leaning against the wall.

Richard approached the two men cautiously. He recognized the face of one, the same Jew who'd helped him out the other morning. His eyes shifted to the other man who sat next to him. His pounding heart suddenly went lame as he looked at the second prisoner that wasn't Cardinal Beroske. Richard knelt beside the man who'd told him to come back today.

He removed his officer's cap and wiped the perspiration from his forehead with the sleeve of his army jacket. Looking into the eyes of the Jew, he said, "The cardinal's dead, isn't he?"

"No, Father, he still lives."

Richard's heart raced again as he looked at the other man, making sure it wasn't the cardinal. "Where is he, then?"

The two men's eyes shifted over to the small figure that lay next to the Jew who'd spoken. Richard stared at the motionless figure, then back at the two Jews. "Yes, Father, it's the cardinal you've been searching for."

Richard's eyes shifted to the child-sized body. Could this really be the great Polish cardinal lying on the filthy, damp floor? Slowly, he stood, his eyes fixed on the body that showed no life. He took tiny steps toward the pile of rags, his face riddled with anxiety.

The face that had been hidden from Richard by the bulge of the worn clothing covering the man's body began to slowly appear as he grew nearer. He knew instantly by the dark cancers that marked the hairless scalp that it was, indeed, Cardinal Beroske. The cardinal's face began to unfold before Richard's unbelieving eyes. He stood beside the cardinal, his eyes not wanting to see the terrible picture that lay before them. He forced his eyes open, wiping the tears from his cheeks as he did so.

Richard knelt next to the cardinal, who lay on his back facing the overhead rafters. His face looked no different from the others who shared this camp with his protruding cheeks and skeleton body. His sixty-year-old face had lost all its character, his once-wrinkled brow stretched into a smooth, thin, grayed sheet of skin.

Richard's eyes shifted to the cardinal's chest. He was still alive! The cardinal's shallow breathing barely lifted his heavy coverings.

He glanced toward the two men who silently watched the unhappy reunion and whispered, "Can he hear?"

"Yes, he can hear and speak slowly. He lost his sight about two months ago."

Richard swallowed. "He's blind?"

"Yes, Father."

"But how has he been able to survive the SS?"

The Jew smiled. "Our people have been persecuted for centuries, Father, and by better men than the SS. We've still found ways to survive. Great men as the cardinal should never die at the hands of such trash. He, along with certain others in this camp, will never die at the hands of the German swine. One of our people will kill him before the butchers can add another notch to their pistols."

He leaned over the cardinal, his face within inches of the great man's sunken cheeks. "Your Imminence, it's Richard." He searched for any sign of response, but there was none. Richard repeated the words, this time louder. He hadn't noticed the entire occupant population of the hut had become his audience.

The cardinal's lips showed signs of movement. Richard placed his hand on the side of the cardinal's cheek, touching him softly with his fingertips. He leaned closer as the cardinal began to speak, his voice barely above a whisper. "Richard, is that really you?"

A smile creased Richard's lips as he answered, "Yes, Your Imminence, it's Richard."

The cardinal seemed to draw strength from

Richard's voice. He spoke again, this time loud enough for those around to hear . . . though they had no clue what he said, speaking in Latin instead of Polish. Although he was near death, he still was no fool. If this man who called himself Richard was really him, then he could answer the question the cardinal had asked in Latin.

Richard answered in Latin. "Yes, I'm fine, Your Imminence. I've come to rescue you from these German devils."

The cardinal appeared to ponder Richard's words. "No, Richard, I will die in this place. I've lingered too long already. Help these people who need it so. Help the young and healthy, not the old and dying like myself."

"But, Your Imminence, I had a vision from God. He told me you were here and sent me to save you."

The cardinal forced his eyelids open. He moved his right arm, his trembling hand searching for Richard's hand. Richard took the cardinal's hand in his. It was cold. He'd felt the hands of death many times since arriving in this ungodly place but never the hand of a dear friend, as he now held. A chill passed through Richard's body. He looked down at the dying cardinal who again spoke, this time in his native Polish. The room listened.

"My son, listen to me. You've underestimated the wisdom of our God. The vision of me that has led you here . . . God knew that you would come for me, as I would have for you. If it had been the face of a Polish Jew instead of me in your vision, do you think you would be here now?" The cardinal turned his head toward Richard. "Until now, I could never figure God's purpose for letting me linger on such as I have." A weak smile came upon the dying cardinal's lips. "But now, with my blind eyes, I can see the whole plan that was masterfully laid out. My only purpose for being here was so you would follow. Our friend Cardinal Algado was right after all when he spoke of you as a man of great destiny. Who would've ever guessed it would've brought you here into this valley of death?" The cardinal paused, drawing on all of his remaining strength. The grip of the ailing cardinal tightened on Richard's hand, and his voice took on an air of urgency. "Listen to me, Richard. You must do whatever is necessary to save as many of these people from the hands of Lucifer as you can. The Almighty chose you to do this. Fear not for your life, my friend, as this time you do not walk alone. The power of God walks with you. Use this power to the fullest. Only a chosen few are given this gift." The cardinal's strong grip slowly eased while the chill of his hand grew colder. "Richard, the Lord finally calls. Please hear my last confession."

Richard glanced up momentarily, meeting the eyes of the two Jews who'd sat next to the cardinal and listened intently to their conversation. Being respectful of such a great man, the two men backed away. Richard knelt on both knees next to the cardinal's side. Making the sign of the cross, he leaned his head close to the cardinal's trembling lips. The room was solemnly quiet except for an occasional cough. The confession was short. Cardinal Beroske was near death when Richard took his hand and began to pray for his friend's soul. Tears trickled from the corners of Richard's closed eyes as he knelt praying for his friend. The two men who sat next to the cardinal also grieved openly for the man of God. Then, the cardinal's hand went limp. Richard opened his eyes. He looked down at his dead friend. He knelt for the longest time, staring at the cardinal's lifeless face.

As if a voice called him, Richard looked up toward the overhead rafters, making the sign of the cross. Hundreds of Jewish eyes locked onto him as he bent and removed some of the tattered rags that covered the body of the dead cardinal. The room watched with astonishment as he placed his arms underneath the cardinal, cradling him in his arms. Richard stood. Then, he started for the front of the hut. The two Jews who'd been seated next to the cardinal glanced at one another, their eyes showing fear for Richard's life.

Someone shouted, "Father, I know how you grieve for your friend, but you can't walk out with him like this. The SS will kill you."

Richard turned. His voice cold and resolute, he said, "A man who has done so much more for the betterment of this sick world will not lie on a cold, rat-littered floor awaiting the word from some SS bastard to dispose of the body like some animal as himself. I will bury this holy man such as he is entitled, and if I'm to die doing it, so be it. I can think of no prouder way to die than by the side of such a man as this. Now if you please, I'll carry out my task."

The entire room watched as the bishop who was clothed in a German uniform carried the body of his friend, and one of the greatest men Poland had ever known, out the front entrance of the hut. The sun bore down on this midmorning day. Two nearby huts had just emptied their prisoners. Several SS guards shouted orders and obscenities as they attempted to form the Jewish prisoners into some sort of military alignment.

Richard walked toward the two groups as his destination lay beyond where they stood, next to the far fence and the pinewoods. As Richard neared the newly regimented groups, the shouting of the SS guards began to fade. All eyes turned to the German officer who carried the remains of a stinking prisoner. Even the guards in the surrounding towers turned their full attention to the German captain who boldly walked across the prison yard cradling the body of the condemned—and in the presence of other prisoners no less.

Richard stared straight ahead, as he passed in front of the first group of Jews. The SS guards studied him in silence. He felt the cold eyes of the German SS as he passed. He was nearly beyond the second group when a SS guard jumped before him. The nervous lieutenant clutched his pistol in his right hand. Richard stopped, his dark eyes glaring.

"Captain, where are you taking this body of a Jewish swine?"

Richard's voice was clear and deliberate. "I'm going to bury him with the dignity he deserves."

A second SS guard took up station next to his comrade. Perhaps feeling bolstered by the appearance of the second guard, the nervous lieutenant's voice steadied. "He'll be carried to the incinerators like the other Jewish pigs of this camp."

Richard's eyes looked of fire, never responding to the lieutenant. Again, he moved toward the distant pines. The lieutenant grudgingly stepped aside as Richard walked unwavering, the cardinal cradled in his powerful arms.

"Halt or I will fire!" Richard stopped as the SS voice sounded in the tense air.

He felt the judging eyes of the camp. He looked at a nearby tower and the two German guards pointing a machine gun directly at him. He did not look back, however, at the guard who'd ordered him to stop. Again, he walked toward the pines. He felt the presence of the two pistols pointing at his back, held by the two SS guards: the lieutenant and his comrade.

Richard recited the Lord's Prayer as he proceeded forward, knowing death could come at any moment. His body, however, never felt the sting of heated bullets. He neared the edge of the fence. The ground was soft and covered in afternoon shade from the nearby pine trees that laid just beyond the high fence. He spotted the ideal place to bury his friend. He laid the body gently on the ground, next to the chosen spot. Richard felt the presence of someone behind him. He turned slowly, expecting the SS to kill him where he stood. Instead, standing only a few feet away, holding a shovel in his hand instead of a German Luger was his newfound friend Lieutenant Steiner. They studied another briefly. Finally, the lieutenant smiled. "You're a complete fool for doing what you've just done, but I'm a bigger fool for standing behind you with this shovel. I only hope your departed friend here is worth my dying."

"He's worth your life, my German friend. He's just won you later entrance into heaven."

The lieutenant considered Richard. "You're not a German. I'm certain of that now, just as your friend here wasn't a Jew. Whoever you are, I wish to never know, as I feel certain our friendship would have a terrible ending. You're either very foolish or very lucky. But with moves such as this, I feel certain none of these things will spare you for long." The lieutenant moved closer. "You've now placed yourself on center stage, and you'll be watched like a hawk. So, will I. You and I have embarrassed the others. To show compassion for prisoners is nothing short of treason in the eyes of the SS. To bury one in sight of the whole camp is even worse. Please, my friend, I know that you'll want to mark the grave, but for my sake, don't. This will mean certain death for me."

Richard looked at his friend who'd laid his life on the line for him and the dead cardinal. "I'll not jeopardize your life any more than I already have."

The lieutenant handed Richard the shovel. "This man will never know how dear a friend he had in you."

Richard smiled. "Yes, he will, lieutenant, as surely as I know how dear a friend I have in you."

The lieutenant grinned and nodded. "Bury your friend, Captain, so we might get on with living."

The lieutenant started back across the open field. The barrel of an overhead machine gun followed his every step but did not fire. The ringing sound of the working shovel sounded across the field and yard, all the way to the huts.

Richard buried Cardinal Beroske that morning, marking the grave with a simple cross in the sand, drawn by the end of his shovel.

Chapter twenty

The days passed slowly for Richard, spending many hours in the confines of his room and never venturing beyond the SS living area. At times, he'd find a secluded spot and stare for hours on end at the endless rows of Jews that formed the ever-present death line. The smoke from the crematorium never faded now as other figures besides the Jews arrived at the camp by the trainloads. Russian soldiers captured at the front appeared; they, too, awaited their turns for the brief walk to the death chambers.

These were times of self-pity for Richard, who awoke every day into a world of never-ending death and suffering, having journeyed to rescue a great, loving friend only to have him die upon discovery. And, of course, there were the ever-lingering thoughts of his beloved Elisabeth, who would probably never speak to him again. These thoughts were always followed by another thought: he wouldn't have to worry about that anyway. Within a short time, they would figure out who he was, then he, too, would be sent to the gas chamber. Perhaps, Richard told himself, he would rather die in the death camp than return and find Elisabeth would no longer have him.

Ten days had passed since Cardinal Beroske had perished. Colonel Zooke, having learned about the cardinal's death and the subsequent event of Richard burying him, decided it best to stay away from the captain as much as possible. Richard was now an open target. Colonel Zooke had virtually become a one-man show for the SS, displaying his talent of finding different ways of torturing and killing Jews. There was no talk between the two men of Goering and the gold-for-Jewish-lives arrangement. Up to this point, Richard could have cared less about Colonel Zooke's actions, as Richard was drowning in his own self-pity. Very soon, this poison would begin to dissipate from the bishop.

Richard had been sitting on the pine stump all morning. The early summer sun again bore down on the stinking camp. It was nearing one o'clock. He stared at another group of arrivals at the distant end of the camp. The pounding of hammers and buzzing of saws seemed never ending in his ears. The killing never ending—the expansion of the facilities never ending—the smoke from the furnaces never ending—the smell of death never ending—rat-tat-tat-tat, the sound of machine-gun fire never ending.

"No-no-no!" Richard screamed. Jumping to his feet and holding his hands over his ears, he tried to block the sounds of death from entering. He stood, body dripping with sweat. He slowly lowered his hands from his ears. His dazed eyes scanned the camp, finally settling on the large pine forest and the home of machine-gun fire. Richard's inner fear had kept him isolated from the pinewoods since his arrival. Something about the area caused him to tremble every time he looked that direction. He knew that death lay there as with the rest of the camp, but could it be any more horrible than that to which he'd already been witness? As he stood there now, a sudden urge pulled at him to see what was hidden in the pinewoods. For reasons unknown, he started toward the distant pines. Later, he would try to recall what had made him take the long journey to the pines, but his mind would remain blank. He would not even remember the walk.

After twenty minutes, he approached the outer edge

of the wood line. He stared into the dark forest. Blasts of machine-gun fire halfway across the camp yard marked the direction he must walk. The sound of a tractor led him to the spot. He entered the woods. His eyes danced like a ballet star, looking for the slightest of movements. He moved deeper into the woods, spotting a clearing in the same area where he'd heard the tractor's engine. Movements near the clearing caught his eye, then came the familiar sound of SS guards shouting orders over a megaphone.

Richard broke into the large clearing. Two hundred meters from where he stood were several hundred naked Jewish women and children. Twenty or so SS men moved around the group, beating the Jews with their canes and whips. Richard's eyes searched for the machine gun as he made his way across the open field toward the prisoners. There was no machine gun visible. He neared the group, the tractor's roar coming from behind another section of pines some fifty meters in front of the prisoners.

A German captain approached. "Come to join in the fun, Captain Reiner?"

"Colonel Zooke, is he here?" Richard scanned the area.

"Yes, he's beyond the trees, in his usual spot."

Richard looked in the direction of where the captain had pointed. The roar of the tractor's engine stopped.

"Just in time, Captain, for another show. You'd better hurry before the show begins without you." Richard walked toward the trees. The laughter of the German captain rang loudly in Richard's ears as he entered the thin line of pines. He had only walked some 200 meters when, again, he spotted a clearing and people moving about. Only these were armed SS men, some thirty of them. He made his way toward a small gathering of officers.

Colonel Zooke stood amongst the SS men. "So, my captain friend, you've decided to join us."

Richard stared at the smiling colonel and the other five officers gathered around him. He spotted the two machine guns mounted in the center of the open field, some ten meters apart, two Germans manning each. The large scattering of spent shells that surrounded each weapon was evidence enough to tell Richard these were the same culprits he'd heard since arriving. Beyond the guns, some twenty-five meters away, sat the tractor, now quiet, its Canada driver resting against the wheel. Before the tractor, some ten meters away, was a long, open trench, roughly 100 meters long and ten wide. In front of the trench stood some forty Canada men, dressed in their striped shirts and bright gold star, marking them as prisoners of the Third Reich.

"Let the show begin!" Colonel Zooke shouted. Without warning, he raised his pistol, firing into the air. Shouts of SS men sounded from the nearby pines. Human images began to appear under the shadows of the pines. The crying of women and children taunted at Richard's soul as he watched the young, whipped and poked by the relentless SS men. All of God's mighty power would be called upon to hold Richard back from trying to stop the oncoming slaughter. He clenched his fist, witnessing the tragedy unfold. Within moments, some 300 naked women and children lined up along the side of the deep trench. The crying women held their young while many of the older children stared innocently at the men behind the machine guns as they laughed and joked, getting the guns at the ready.

The Canada group took their place at the side of the trench. Their faces showed no emotion for the surrounding carnage. Once again, Richard reached his breaking point as he watched the SS guards place their machine guns in position.

"No, don't do this!"

Richard's cry went unheard as the deafening noise of the exploding shells drowned out his final plea. He watched and cried as the helpless women and children were slaughtered that day in the open field—watched as the Canada men walked along the edge of the trench, throwing the dead and dying bodies inside, only to be covered by the Polish soil shoveled by the waiting tractor. Richard bowed his head, crying and praying for the wasted lives of these beautiful people.

Then, Richard lifted his head, donned his cap, and started back across the field toward the camp. As he walked, he decided he'd wasted enough time; he'd attempt to save as many Jews as possible. Every moment he wasted would cost others their lives. Deeply absorbed in prayer, he made his way to his room. Alone, he knelt by his bed and prayed to his God for help and guidance in the days and weeks ahead. He knew he'd need all of God's help to pull off the impossible task that lay ahead. He swore another oath to his God and mostly himself that afternoon. If by God's grace he survived and completed his task, he would return to Rome and resign his priesthood to the Holy Father. Then, he would return to England, find Elisabeth, and ask her hand in marriage. If he accomplished the task for which he was sent by his God, then he should be allowed to spend the remainder of his life with the woman he loved.

Richard retired early; his mind afire with plans of saving the Jews. He awoke when Colonel Zooke entered hours later. Richard had hoped to confront the beast about the plans to help with the Jewish exchange.

"Wake up!"

Colonel Zooke opened his aching eyes, attempting to focus on the tall figure staring down at him. "What the hell do you want, Captain?" Colonel Zooke snorted, sitting up on the side of his bed.

"Today we start saving people."

Colonel Zooke slowly raised his head and glanced up at the stern-faced bishop. A sadistic smile formed on the colonel's lips. "What's wrong, holy man? You don't like watching the slaughter of pigs?"

Richard's dark eyes widened, rage rising to his face. He reached down, grabbing the colonel by his wrinkled coat collar. With the strength of five men, he lifted the colonel from the bed, shoving his limp body against the side of the wall. Richard felt the pounding heart of Colonel Zooke as he pressed his trembling body flat against the wall. "Listen to me, you son of a bitch, either we start this minute on what we came here to do, or I'll walk out this door and tell the first SS officer I see who you are and what purpose you have for being here. And after I tell him that, I'll tell him who I am. Then, we'll both face the firing squad together."

Colonel Zooke stared at the wild-eyed priest. "You don't want to die any more than I do, Priest." Colonel Zooke forced a smile on his scarred face.

Richard grinned. "You're a fool, Colonel. You see, I'm ready for death. I've seen enough of man's butchery.

I'm ready to join my God in heaven. I have no fear of dying. That's the difference between me and you. You're trembling in your boots this very second just thinking about it. Of course, I can't blame you for wanting to stick around here on earth as long as you can with only the fires of hell awaiting your arrival."

The smile evaporated from Colonel Zooke's lips as fear boldly replaced it. "OK, Captain, we'll begin today on saving some Jews."

He released his grip. "I'll wait for you outside . . . and don't be long." He exited the room.

Richard sat on the tree stump in front of the barracks. The sun had broken above the horizon. The first group of Jews was already on their way to the killing station. The rising smoke from the crematorium chimney had a sharp bend in it as a warm summer breeze had risen with the sun. The distant sound of machine gun fire bellowed through the morning air. Richard made the sign of the cross upon hearing the awful sound. Moments later, Colonel Zooke walked out of the building.

"Follow me, holy man."

He'd no idea as to where Colonel Zooke was taking him but had no other choice than to trust the colonel with this part of the plan. His only hope was he'd frightened the colonel enough as to go through with it. Colonel Zooke would never know that Richard's confrontation with him that morning had only been a well-played act. Only the day before, when walking from the killing fields, had he realized how much he wanted to live. The thought of spending the rest of his life with Elisabeth had suddenly made him realize how much he wanted to live. The two men proceeded down to the train tracks and caught a ride on the back end of a military truck. The truck was headed to the train terminal that had been their first arrival point. Colonel Zooke remained silent during the ride. It was quite apparent that Richard had gotten the colonel's attention.

A newly arrived train rested at the terminal, the SS busy unloading its cargo. These weren't Polish Jews, however; they were more Russian soldiers from the eastern front, many wounded, their wounds untreated by their German captives. Many remained inside the boxcars, dead upon arrival. Still, the Germans had not taken Moscow or Stalingrad. Germany had taken an awful beating, and German casualties were enormous, already approaching the million mark. The huge German losses, however, only hardened the depraved Hitler, more determined than ever to see the Russians defeated. Plans were underway for a full-fledged German assault on Stalingrad in the early summer.

Richard paused at the entrance to the terminal, pondering the state of the defeated Russian soldiers. "Poor bastards," he muttered. He turned and followed Colonel Zooke into the terminal.

Unbeknown to Richard, Colonel Zeffler, whom he was about to meet, had been part of the plan since the very beginning. Colonel Zeffler and Marshal Goering had grown up together as children. The purpose of this meeting was to set the already existing plan into motion. This had been worked out before Richard's arrival at Auschwitz, and no changes in the format had occurred since his incarceration at the camp. Richard's basic job was to witness and verify the freeing of the Jews, then notify Bishop Rutgers in Munich. The bishop would, in turn, notify Rabbi Dziobak in Zurich, Switzerland, where he'd taken up temporary residence, of the verifiable release of Jewish prisoners. A simple code had been worked out between Richard and Bishop Rutgers to ensure the Germans couldn't falsify any of Richard's correspondence. There would be large sums of money involved in these transactions; Goering had placed a price tag of $200 American dollars for each Jew's release, payable in gold. To further ensure the security of the transfer, only Bishop Rutgers knew both secret codes—the one between himself and Richard, to be written entirely in Latin and to include the name of a predetermined Saint affixed to each message; and the second code, to be employed between the bishop and Rabbi Dziobak. Richard wasn't to know the second code used during the transfers.

The Germans, too, took precautions in the deal. A trusted attaché of Marshal Goering's had taken up residence in Zurich. His real identity would remain unknown to everyone except Goering. Only the fictitious name of Hans Brock would hint to his real existence. This was the name utilized for his secret account in a Zurich bank. Besides the fictitious Brock and Marshal Goering, only Rabbi Dziobak knew of this account. The rabbi would deposit the gold into the account once word of the amount came from Munich. As added security, the account was set up in such a way that no withdrawals could be made without the twin signatures of Brock and Goering. Once the deposit was verified by Hans, he would, in turn, notify Colonel Zooke at the train station, after which Richard and Colonel Zooke would arrange another drop of Jews in a small village that bordered the tracks from Warsaw.

Ostrow, located halfway between Warsaw and Auschwitz, was heavily wooded, affording the prisoners temporary sanctuary while Polish sympathizers worked to relocate the escapees. Many would filter into

Czechoslovakia and Italy while others would be recaptured by the Germans or killed attempting to flee. But almost all would remember the man dressed in the German uniform the night of their escape. Yes, that was all most of them would see of their modern-day Moses, his tears of joy hidden in the darkness of the pines.

Time passed slowly for Richard as thousands died before his eyes awaiting the night to save a mere 300. But, if successful, that was 300 more that wouldn't perish in the gas chambers or feel the burning bullets of death.

Chapter Twenty-One

The sun seemed extra bright this morning as Richard and Colonel Zooke boarded the train for Warsaw. Richard wouldn't ride the full way, disembarking at a small station in Ostrow. A long line of empty boxcars made up most of the train, except the two passenger compartments riding behind the locomotive, one occupied by Richard, Colonel Zooke, and a dozen or so SS men who frequently made this run. They would be the ones loading the Jews once they reached Warsaw. Most, if not all, would then make the return trip the day after, loaded with Jewish prisoners. This was just one of many trains that rolled these rails night and day, capturing Jews from the Warsaw ghettos. They would succeed in killing over two and a half million Jews of the three million who occupied Poland before the war was to end. Because of their proximity to Auschwitz, the Poles were first to die.

The ride had been a rather pleasant one for Richard; just being away from the sight of death and the stench of decaying bodies was a welcome relief. He'd spent the entire morning sitting alone by an open window enjoying the fresh country air that brushed against his worn face. An evergreen forest blanketed much of the Polish countryside, broken by large areas of rolling farmlands. Richard dozed off briefly, then was awakened by the noticeable slowing of the train as it pulled into Ostrow Station, which amounted to no more than a one-roomed frame building that sat along the edge of the track somewhere between Auschwitz and Warsaw.

The depot was manned by three local Poles who lived in the nearby village of Ostrow. The men were in their sixties, and their only usefulness to the Germans was their ability to send and receive telegraphs to Auschwitz when trains left or arrived. Richard was the only one to disembark the train, as Colonel Zooke and the SS would travel on to Warsaw where they would pick up more Jews, returning to Ostrow around midnight the following day. Richard watched as his train bent slowly around a widening curve, finally disappearing behind the distant forest. He was free to do what he wished, which, in essence, was very little. The village of Ostrow sat some four kilometers away. He would make only one visit to the village though, spending nearly all of his time in the nearby fields and forest. At first, he wished to stay in the small village but quickly learned that Germans weren't welcome there . . . especially German soldiers. A single cot located inside a small room of the depot served as his sleeping quarters over the next few weeks. He did not return to Auschwitz sometimes for weeks on end, then only to visit the camp doctor who formulated some sort of medicine to help relieve his increasingly nagging cough.

Colonel Zooke brought him needed supplies from camp and exchanged his soiled uniforms for clean. A freshwater stream ran behind the depot approximately 400 meters into the woods. Richard used the stream for bathing water and for sanitary purposes. Over a period, Richard became fairly good friends with Otto, the night clerk at the depot. Occasionally, Otto brought him a hot meal prepared by his sister, which was always a welcome change from the canned meals Richard ate at the other times.

Richard grew nervous the second day at the depot as time grew nearer for trains to return. Already ten trains of Jews had passed through since early in the morning, Colonel Zooke's was the next scheduled to arrive. Occasionally, Otto glanced up from his novel to follow the pacing captain as he walked back and forth across the small wooden porch that faced the tracks.

Richard glanced regularly at an overhead clock mounted over the doorway. Afternoon passed into early evening with still no sign of Colonel Zooke's train. The stars twinkled brilliantly on this cool summer night. His mind ran rampant with bad thoughts as he continued pacing the depot floor. Where were the partisans that were to lead the Jews away? Had Bishop Rutgers failed in his attempt to recruit enough patriots for the Jewish cause? It remained a well-known fact that many gentiles had bitter feelings toward the Jews and many even agreed with Hitler's tactics on eliminating them. Richard knew this too well as he searched the darkness for any telltale signs of those who would help the condemned Jews, risking their own lives in the process. War had always been cruel in this respect with brother against brother or father against son.

This war was no different than the ones before it. Some of these would die attempting to save the Jews while other members of their family were busy murdering them. Like Richard, these men and women who hid in the forest tonight would remain faceless to the outside world. Only their darkened silhouettes would be seen as they roamed the forest of the Polish hillsides. They would sleep by the light of day and roam the hills in the darkness of the night. Richard, too, would become a legend of these hills, known as the smiling German. Years later, after his identity was to be known and as the stories of his great deeds swept throughout the world, he was to become known by those he'd helped save as simply Cardinal of the Forest.

The overhead clock showed 12:15. Richard paced the depot floor. Otto had walked around to the back of the depot to smoke a cigarette, perhaps to escape the anxious bishop. A distant train whistle broke the quietness of the night. Richard turned toward the whistle, a smile slowly forming on his lips. The distant sound of spinning wheels grew louder as the train from Warsaw neared the distant curve. Shortly, the faint light of the steaming locomotive could be seen as it rolled down the tracks toward Ostrow Station. He watched with great anxiety as the great locomotive came to a stop a few meters beyond the depot. A burst of steam shot from a huge stack, reminding him of a winning racehorse snorting victory after a championship run. Richard's eyes followed the line of wooden boxcars into the blackness of the night. One would never know by the quiet stillness that hundreds of living souls were jammed into the forty cattle cars that sat motionless on the tracks.

Otto never rose from his seat, deeply engrossed in a Robert Louis Stevenson novel. The passing moments seemed like hours to Richard as he frantically searched for Colonel Zooke. He sighed with relief as the tall, lean figure of the colonel appeared out of the darkness. Richard stepped from the small porch and hurried toward the motioning colonel.

"Come, we have little time," Colonel Zooke said.

The two men walked briskly down the side of the track. The stench of human excretion filled Richard's nostrils as he walked past the seemingly endless boxcars. An occasional sound of a crying infant or cough from the sick and elderly came from inside one of the forty cars.

"Listen, Priest," the colonel said. "We have very little time, so understand what I say." Richard looked sharply at the colonel as they continued their journey toward the end of the train. "Your cargo lies in the back two cars. There are 150 Jews in each. Young—old—male—female. They were all alive when we loaded them this morning, so if any are now dead, we still get paid for 300, understood, Priest?" The colonel looked coldly into Richard's eyes.

"Yes, I understand."

"Have you the note authorizing payment?"

"Yes, I have it, and I'll give it to you after I witness the release of the Jews."

"You're worse to deal with than the Jews. By the way, Priest, where are your helpers?" The colonel turned toward the black forest that lay only a dozen meters beyond the tracks.

Richard glanced at the tree line. "They're out there waiting."

332

"You better hope to hell they are, Priest. If not, these stinking bastards we're about to turn loose won't be alive tomorrow."

Richard's voice hitched slightly. "Yes . . . I know."

As the two men approached the last two cars, Richard noticed another solider exiting from between the second and third car from the end.

"These two cars will stay here tonight. We'll pick them up tomorrow on our way back to Warsaw. Stay here," Colonel Zooke commanded.

Richard watched as the colonel walked over to the other soldier who'd disconnected the back cars from the others. He couldn't hear their brief exchange. The colonel walked back to where Richard stood. The other soldier hurried over to the last two cars, apparently removing the padlocks from each of the large sliding doors. "I strongly suggest it would be best that you're not seen by these Jews, Priest. If they're captured, they'll probably squeal like the pigs they are."

Richard gritted his teeth as he looked at the smiling colonel. He fought back his anger, realizing his personal hate for this man wasn't worth the lives of those waiting in the boxcars. "I'll wait next to the woods," he said, turning and heading for the edge of the trees.

"Don't let the boogey man get you, Priest," the colonel whispered.

Richard paused. He watched from the nearby trees as the colonel and the other German slid open the heavy wooden door. At first, no movement was visible in the blackened entrance of the car. Then, figures of all shapes and sizes began appearing in the doorway. The two Germans helped the first few down from the train, a three-foot drop from the car to the ground. The young and strong got off first and then helped the others, mostly older or very young. The two Germans had already moved to the last car and here, too, the Jews began to exit.

Richard's heart pounded ecstatically as he watched the men, women, and children start for the cover of the woods. The German soldier worked to convince the terrified Jews to enter the forest, not knowing what terrible fate awaited them. As the German led them to the forest's edge, Colonel Zooke checked inside each of the two cars, making sure they were empty. He closed the doors and started toward Richard.

Richard caught movement within the depths of the forest, reassuring him that the bishop had been successful. He smiled amidst tearing eyes as the last of the Jews entered the woods, thanking his God as they did so.

"You only lost five, Priest. Four were already dead. I put the small girl out of her misery." The colonel wiped the blood from his knife blade. "Got the note, Priest?" The colonel put his knife away.

Richard glared at the colonel, reaching inside his coat pocket to retrieve a small, sealed envelope.

"Pleasure doing business with you, Priest." The colonel placed the note in his pocket. "Be back with more pigs four nights from now." The colonel started to walk away, then stopped to look back at Richard. "By the way, Priest, have you been to town yet? Understand these Polish farmwomen love to have sex with American men. Oh, that's right, all you priests are virgins, aren't you?"

Richard took a step toward the grinning colonel, then stopped.

"Good-bye, Priest." The colonel laughed as he

walked toward the waiting train.

Richard watched in silence from the porch of the depot as the train pulled away, slowly disappearing into the darkness. Tears streamed down his cheeks as the last boxcar vanished into the darkness, headed for Auschwitz. He wondered why it couldn't have been all those aboard the train, instead of just a small handful. Then, he turned and stared into the darkened woods. A smile appeared on his weary face as he wiped the tears from his cheeks. "But thank you, God, for the 295 who you saved," he whispered to the night. Richard stood there a while longer, then went into the depot to get some much-needed sleep, stopping to take the burning cigarette from the fingers of the sleeping Otto. "Good night, Otto," Richard whispered, then retired to bed.

He awoke before daylight as the first of eleven trains was on its way to Auschwitz, making a short stop at Ostrow. Usually these stops were brief, lasting no longer than ten minutes—time enough to wire ahead to Auschwitz declaring their estimated arrival time. Occasionally, though, a train might be forced to hold in the depot for several hours, due to trains arriving from the eastern front with their cargoes of Russian prisoners. No such delay occurred on this day though, as trains filled with Jews from Warsaw passed through unhindered. Eight empty trains returned to Warsaw, one of which was Colonel Zooke's. Richard watched from the distance as they stopped to hook up the other two cars that had rested through the night. Richard suddenly found himself virtually alone, except for Otto and the other two workers of the depot. They were of no company to him, however, as Otto stayed absorbed in his books and the other two depot workers hated Germans.

The first few days, Richard stayed close by the station, occasionally walking as much as two kilometers down the edge of the tracks. This routine continued for the next two week, and during this time, three more drops of Jews had occurred, totaling a little under 1,000 freed Jews in less than three weeks. The plan was working much better than anyone could've imagined. At first, Richard tried to pass the time reading from Otto's books but quickly grew tired of the effort; many of the books Richard had already read.

Noticing Richard's boredom, Otto brought a thick writing pad and several pencils to the station one afternoon, giving them to Richard with the subtle suggestion that he might draw pictures or write humorous anecdotes, anything to keep him occupied as his constant pacing on the depot porch was driving Otto insane.

Initially, Richard had little to do with the writing instruments, except occasionally to doodle or play games of one-man tic-tac-toe. As the days wore on, however, and finding himself lonelier than ever, his thoughts turned repeatedly to Elisabeth. His physical world, as well, expanded. On occasion, he ventured deep into the forest to discover the abundance of wildlife that made its home in the woods, sitting next to a tree for hours watching and listening to the forest creatures as they roamed free in the war-ravaged countryside. Eventually, the long hours of isolation from the savage world lying beyond the tree line made its mark, so much so that he decided to share it with his beloved Elisabeth, at first recording certain tragedies he'd witnessed since coming to this part of the world. He soon realized these recollections only depressed him that much more. One day, he tore the bitter words up and cast them into a small stream. His mind felt cleansed as he watched the torn papers drift down the swiftly flowing brook.

He began to write anew—this time, love letters to Elisabeth, having no intention of sending them for fear of their interception by the Germans and, thereby, giving away his identity. Some of what he wrote surprised him. His magical descriptions of animals he'd witnessed were exquisite. His imagination flowed as easily as a warm south wind over the Polish hillsides. His love letters soon turned into stories—beautiful stories about the animals of the forest. He gave them names and voices and thoughts. The terrible war and its ungodly cruelty were vaulted away in Richard's mind as he spent his days in the Polish countryside. His world became one of loving and beauty and everything good. Things that could never be real existed in Richard's words, but the words were real and so were Richard's dreams.

June rolled into July and then into August. During this time, the war raged. Hitler ordered his stalemated army to take Stalingrad at all costs and the great siege began. Summer passed into autumn and the releases of Jews continued without any major difficulties. At times, it seemed so simple that entire trainloads of Jews could disappear without attention. It was during this time of late summer and early fall of '42 that most of the German military turned their full attention to the war in Russia. For the first time, concern grew among ranking German officers that defeat by the stubborn Russians was possible. The SS at Auschwitz were fully aware of this possibility, maintaining almost direct contact with the Russian front in the form of prisoners. These Russian thorns just added more hatred to the already maddened SS; they took out their fury on the Russian prisoners who, by now, were arriving by the thousands.

Richard lost virtually all contact with the outside world during his stay at Ostrow, except for the notes with his documentations of Jewish releases given to Colonel Zooke on the average of every four days. Richard's notes amounted to no more than letting the bishop know that everything was working smoothly from his end and that he was well and safe. This was partially true; Richard's health, however, was beginning to deteriorate with the coming of winter. His mild cough inherited in the early summer had been somewhat kept in check with the medication issued by the camp doctor. Now, as the weather grew colder, his cough worsened, and his appetite fell dramatically. Otto went out of his way to bring home-cooked meals to the captain, most of which Otto ended up eating.

Colonel Zooke also took notice of the bishop's failing health and expressed his growing concerns about their future business dealings. He made it known that his selling of Jews was his ace in the hole should the Third Reich fall. The colonel would move to Switzerland and live like a king. Zooke's words and action became more urgent. He pushed for the release of as many Jews as possible without, of course, notice by the SS. He was certain they could double the numbers.

***

Soon it was November and then December, as the four-day releases jumped from 300 to nearly 600, even though by late November and early December many of the Jews would arrive at Ostrow already dead, frozen to death on their journey. Witnessing this added atrocity, Richard no longer paid for the dead arrivals—only the living who were able to make it to the woods. This way, Richard might encourage Colonel Zooke to make better arrangements for the protection of the Jews from the severe cold sweeping Europe. Colonel Zooke, however, only became more caring of those he chose to ride in the last six boxcars. Richard couldn't see that those freed were mostly young men and women, few children, and virtually no old or sick.

The blackness of the Polish nights and the growing weakness in Richard's eyes betrayed him these last weeks at Ostrow. If he'd known what he'd caused by his failure to pay for the dead, he surely would've perished that winter at Ostrow Station.

This was definitely the coldest night of the young winter at Ostrow. The small potbellied stove sitting in the middle of the one-room station pulsated red, filling the aging room with much-needed heat. Otto sat at his desk reading one of his books. Every few minutes, he'd stand and walk to the narrow doorway where Richard lay in his feathered bed. Otto had opened his door wide so that heat from the stove could filter into the small room. He checked the time of night with his pocket watch: 10:10. He stood in Richard's doorway watching the sick bishop tremble beneath his stack of covers. Richard's cough had grown terrible during the last cold spell, and he slept little in the last three days and nights. The bishop hadn't visited his forest or hillsides in over two weeks, grown too weak to make the journey. Yet, somehow, he always met the train every fourth night, forcing his worn body to stand at the edge of the woods to watch as the Jews scurried for their freedom.

Otto shook his head, walked back to his desk, and

sat down. He lit a cigarette and leaned back in his chair, peering into the dark room. The train with the Jews was due at eleven o'clock. As always, Richard had asked Otto to rouse him fifteen minutes before the train was to arrive. Perhaps, tonight, he would let the captain rest.

Time slipped by. A cold north wind gusted against the wooden depot, whistling as the wind seeped through the many cracks and crevices of the weather-beaten boards. A full moon broke above the distant forest that lay across the far side of the tracks. Otto peeked out one of the tiny windowpanes that formed the top portion of the depot door. The tops of the distant evergreens bent violently in the harsh north wind. Otto returned to his desk and smoked one cigarette after another. More time passed. Then, Otto placed his watch back in his pocket and walked slowly to where Richard lay in the tiny room. "Captain, it's getting time for the train."

There was a short pause.

"Thank you, Otto," the weak voice answered.

"Captain, are you well enough to meet the train? It's terribly cold outside."

Another pause.

"Yes, Otto, I'm able."

Otto stood closely as Richard began to stir. Richard coughed heavily as he rolled over on his back and stared at the ceiling. He made his first attempt to sit up, failing miserably. After another coughing gag, he tried again. This time, he was able to sit up on the side of his bed. A faint light shone through the open doorway.

Otto stared at the pathetic-looking figure. "Captain, the Jews who arrive dead in the boxcars look better than you."

Richard lifted his heavy head and tried to focus on Otto's face. Beads of sweat glistened in the faint light as they streamed down Richard's thinning face. Somehow, he managed to get to his feet.

"Captain, let this train pass."

Richard stared at Otto with glazed eyes. "No, my God, no."

Otto stood aside as Richard made his way out of his room. He leaned against the wall to steady himself.

"Here, Captain, put your coat on. It's freezing outside."

Otto helped him don his heavy coat. The sound of a distant whistle passed in a gust of wind. Richard heard its call as he walked to the door. Otto handed him his hat and opened the door.

A gust of cold wind nearly cost Richard his stand, catching himself on the edge of the door. Otto shook his head at the tortured captain. Richard walked out the door, pausing for a moment as he pulled his collar tight around his neck. The wind was a knife, cutting deep into his feverish body. He glimpsed the light of the locomotive as it rounded the distant curve. Richard fought for every foot as he made his way along the edge of the woods. A distant howl of a wolf rode the wind, passing swiftly through the bending evergreens.

The long train came to a stop. Richard waited as he watched Colonel Zooke advance toward him. "So, Priest, you're still able to get out of bed. I'm surprised at your willpower. That God of yours should have made you a horse instead of a priest."

"How many this time?"

"Three hundred and seventy-two of the finest

looking Jews you've ever seen. Much better looking than you, I might add. It's a good thing you're not one of them. You probably wouldn't pay me for you." The colonel laughed. "You got the paper, Priest?"

"You get them unloaded; I have your paper."

Colonel Zooke chuckled as he walked back toward the waiting cars.

Richard propped himself against the tree to watch the unloading. Five minutes and it was over.

The colonel walked back to him. "Thanks, Priest." Colonel Zooke took the paper from Richard, then started back toward the train.

He struggled to make it back. Otto helped him inside the doorway and to the edge of the bed. He trembled as he sat. "Captain, you must get to a doctor."

Richard lifted his head to answer and spied a familiar figure standing in the bedroom doorway. "He won't need a doctor. I'm here to put him out of his misery."

Otto jumped and turned. Colonel Zooke stood in the center of the doorway. He held a large, silver-bladed knife in his right hand. The sound of the locomotive filtered through the depot.

"Your train, Colonel—" Otto stuttered. "You're going to miss it."

The colonel's eyes stayed on Richard. "I got business here tonight," he said. "Priest, it looks like our partnership is about over."

Richard looked at the foggy figure, unable to respond.

"Me and my partners have enough money now and you're about to die," Zooke said. "So, I guess that wraps it up. But hell, you should die happy. Look at all the pigs you saved."

The colonel removed his cap, dropping it to the floor. His eyes seemed to glaze over as he pushed Otto to the side and started toward Richard. Richard could only sit and watch as the scar-faced German neared his bed. The colonel raised the knife above his head, its blade flashing before Richard's aching eyes. He shut his eyes and awaited the blade's thrust.

Wham!

Richard opened his eyes in time to see Colonel Zooke crash to the floor next to his bed.

"You Polish son-of-a-bitch, I'll kill you for that!"

Richard watched as the furious colonel got to his feet. Otto, who'd knocked Colonel Zooke to the floor with an unanticipated right hook, stood in the far corner of the tiny room trembling. Zooke gripped his Luger tightly as he stumbled toward the frightened Pole. The knife, just inches in front of him, caught Richard's eye.

Neither the colonel nor the Pole noticed Richard as he lurched from the bed and retrieved the knife. "Goodbye, you Polish bastard." Colonel Zooke pointed the pistol at Otto's head.

Then, Colonel Zooke began to quiver, his steely-gray eyes dimming. The German folded to the floor. Otto stared at the colonel, then at Richard who stood there looking down at the body, still clutching the bloody knife.

"Are you all right, Captain?" Otto finally said, regaining his composure.

"I killed him. My God, I killed him." Richard dropped the knife to the floor.

"No, you did what had to be done, Bishop Carver."

Richard stared at Otto, blinking. "What did you call

343

me?"

Otto smiled. "I'm Father Paderewski from Krakow. Cardinal Sarkoski sent me here to help if need be. It seems I'm the one who needed your help."

Richard looked confused. His mind was heavily fevered to begin with—and then all this. "I—"

Father Paderewski caught Richard before he fell to the floor.

***

Ten days passed. Near death for most of those days, Father Paderewski performed last rights twice. It became apparent, however, that Bishop Carver had a strong will to live. On the night of the tenth day, Richard regained consciousness. Confused and disoriented by his strange surroundings, he was certain this wasn't Ostrow Station.

A fire burned beautifully in the stone fireplace less than ten feet from where he lay. He turned his head slowly to get a better look at his surroundings. The room was fair sized and cozy looking with its dark wood walls and low-beamed ceiling. A couch sat next to the front wall, beneath a large window covered with chocolate-colored curtains. A spinning wheel sat next to a heavily cushioned chair. An unfinished quilt lay over the back of the chair, affording evidence a lady resided in the home. A narrow doorway led to another room of the house from which emanated a light. As Richard turned back toward the fireplace, it became evident that his bed sat in the middle of the living room, obviously arranged to keep him near the fire. A stone mantle sat above the fireplace; a large portrait centered above the mantle. Richard's eyes were too weak to make out the images themselves. They quickly grew heavy, and within moments, he was asleep again.

Another twenty-four hours passed, and Richard stirred again, this time with added strength. The fire still blazed in the fireplace. He opened his eyes and stared at the flickering flames. Then, the sound of the spinning wheel caught his attention. He turned his head slowly and focused on the cushioned chair and the young lady spinning yarn. Light from the fireplace lit the room. His focus sharpened as he stared at the pretty woman. At first glance, Richard thought it was Elisabeth at the wheel, her long chestnut-colored hair flowing softly over her shoulders. The flames of the fire danced in her eyes like the spirit of her youth. Richard continued to stare at the young woman. His fevered mind saw only Elisabeth at the wheel and not Helena Paderewski, Father Paderewski's only sister.

Helena looked up from her work, staring a moment at the wide-eyed bishop. She smiled as she put her yarn away. Then, she crossed the room to where Richard lay. "How welcome a sight it is to see your handsome eyes, Bishop Carver." She knelt beside the bed and kissed Richard's hand.

His mouth was dry, but he forced the words out anyway. "Where am I?"

Helena smiled and gazed softly at him. Her Polish voice was like music to Richard's ears. "You're safe here. This is the home of my brother, Father Paderewski. You probably know him better as Otto."

Richard's parched lips broadened with a weak smile.

"You're a very sick man, Bishop Carver," she continued. "The doctor says you must have plenty of liquids and lots of rich soup. I've had soup ready every day for ten days now, and tonight you finally get a taste. Oscar .

. . Otto, I mean, said you didn't care for the meals I prepared for you while you were at Ostrow Station."

Richard tried to answer.

"I'm only teasing, Your Reverence, I know you were very sick. I'll be back with your soup and drink."

Helena left the room, and Richard began piecing together the puzzle that last day at Ostrow Station.

Helena's warm tea felt good to Richard's parched throat, and the soup helped soothe his empty stomach. He continued to improve as the days passed. Helena catered to his every need.

Eight days had passed since he'd awoken at the house. Otto, as Richard continued to call him, stopped occasionally to check on Richard and his sister, keeping the firebox well stacked with wood. The fire burned constantly during these bone-chilling days of early January. Richard's cough wasn't any better. It kept him weak. The doctor had informed Helena and Otto of Richard's tuberculosis. As of yet, Richard did not know.

Helena continued to nurse him like a child, uncaring as to what effect the disease might have on her. The days grew into weeks. Otto kept Richard posted on news of the war. The German toll in lives had devastated the Third Reich, and reports indicated over a million Germans had perished since the invasion of Russia. The Soviets retook all of Stalingrad, although not much remained of the city itself. The Russian Army held the Germans in check. This stalemate continued another few months before the Russians pushed the Germans back toward the Polish border, at which time Poland, again, felt the horror of war. In the Pacific conflict, America was still not faring well. The Japanese were well trenched in most of the strategic islands. America was still short on needed war materials, especially naval ships of all kinds. The shipyards back in the States had reached maximum production, but the demand still far outstripped the supply. The German U-boats in the Atlantic continued to play havoc with American and English shipping. It was in this part of the world that Joe was heavily involved.

Richard continued his slow recovery. As he grew stronger, so did Helena's curiosity of the numerous papers Otto had brought with him that first night belonging to Richard. Otto had told Helena he speculated they had something to do with the countryside around Ostrow Station. Helena's curiosity about the papers grew, finally causing her to sneak a look. Her snooping efforts, however, were in vain as Richard had written them in English. She wasn't versed in the English language and neither was Otto.

One afternoon, Helena drew enough courage to ask Richard about the English words. He brushed it off as only silly things he'd written while being bored at Ostrow. This only added fuel to Helena's curiosity. After many days of begging, she persuaded Richard into reading her one of the pages of English words. Under great duress, he agreed to read one page, feeling that he owed the kind girl that much for having nursed him all these weeks. After she heard one of the silly poems, she wouldn't bother him about the others.

Richard sifted through the pages, trying to find one he thought the youthful and beautiful Pole might enjoy. Finally, he found it. His thoughts had been of Elisabeth the day he wrote the poem. For the first time, he'd recite it to someone else besides himself. Richard sat up in his bed. Helena braced his back with heavy pillows.

He took a sip of his tea and then began to read. The firelight flickered, casting a warm glow across the room. When Richard finished, he looked up at the young woman who appeared to be holding her breath.

"That is the most wonderful poem I've ever heard," Helena whispered. Tears rolled down her cheeks.

"You really think so?" Richard said, his voice echoing his disbelief.

"Oh, my dear bishop, God has blessed you with a talent beyond one's greatest dreams. Please read me another," she begged.

She wiped the tears from her cheeks as he sorted through the papers looking for another and then another. Time became of no regard for the two in the warmly lit room. Heavy snow fell through the night as Richard continued to read to the spellbound Polish woman his endless verses of love.

Hours passed. Soon, daylight would break over the Polish land. Richard had fallen asleep, still holding a writing in one hand, drifting off midway through the verse.

Helena took the paper from his hand and slowly guided the exhausted man into the depths of his soft bed, gently covering him. The fire had diminished during the night. Helena rekindled it before going to bed. She looked down at the sleeping bishop. "My heavens, what has God delivered to our people? A man who has saved so many from death and can write like the angels in heaven. The Lord has blessed me with this man's presence. No, he's blessed the world with his presence, as I'm only the first to know of this blessing. My dear bishop, if only you knew how these beautiful poems you've written will affect the hearts of our people. You have put into words what only our hearts have ever been able to feel. Get well quickly, sweet bishop, the world needs you badly. My heart is heavy for the woman to whom you wrote these poems, as her agony must be great to love a man such as you and never be able to have him. Sad, so sad, I will pray for her loneliness as well as yours. Sleep well." She bent over and kissed Richard's forehead. Helena looked at him another moment, wiping the tears from her eyes. Then, she replenished the fire and went to bed.

Chapter Twenty Two

March swiftly moved into April. By now, Richard was more than ready for his travel out of Poland and back to Italy. Otto had kept Richard well informed about the war these last few weeks. The Germans had all but bogged down on the Russian front. The winter of '42 had been devastating for the German Army. When Stalingrad hadn't fallen to the Germans this infuriated Hitler to such a degree that his already unstable reasoning had become further impaired, insisting that his German Army take Russia at all costs. The German generals had suddenly become terrified by the führer's inability to rationalize on the horrible position that the German Army was now put in. It seemed for the first time the German high command officers had serious doubts as to whether they could achieve final victory over the Red Army.

During this same period, the allies were beginning

to muster strength of their own. The winter of '42 had seen the allies sweep across North Africa with forceful authority as freshly made American tanks rolled across the desserts of Tunisia with frightful force, sending the great Rommel on the run. American troops had now become a well-equipped, battle-hardened army.

In the Pacific, things were beginning to look more favorable for the United States and its allies, as freshly made American equipment specifically designed for the amphibious warfare began arriving in great quantities, along with better-trained American troops. Finally, the world was beginning to witness what the sleeping giant of America was capable of when she felt threatened. Only two years before, the world trembled under the advancing Nazis. Now the world watched in awe as the capitalist people from across the sea swarmed from their homeland, bringing with them the greatest army and war machines man had ever seen, along with their unbending will to use them until the threat of oppression was wiped from the earth.

Great flotillas of American ships sailed the oceans of the world, many of which had been built in the Norfolk Shipbuilders International shipyards. Jeff and his ailing father were doing an incredible job manufacturing the great ships. Jeff continued his abuse with alcohol. His guilt and drinking problem wouldn't go away and only worsened with the events that were yet to follow.

With the help of the Polish underground, Father Paderewski had finally been able to arrange Richard's escape from Poland back to Italy. The Germans had searched for Richard for a short time after the murder of Colonel Zooke, never uncovering Richard's true identity.

When the SS approached Goering about the two men who'd posed as his personal representatives at the camp, he flatly denied having any knowledge of the men. Himmler was unable to find evidence that the Field Marshal had had any dealings with the two men.

Richard remained in hiding inside Helena's home until the morning of April 26. The sun awoke early in the Polish spring. The brightness of the day, however, hadn't lifted the spirits of the tiny household. Helena watched with misty eyes as the young Polish driver took Richard's things from his room to the awaiting car.

Richard's heart was also heavy on this departing morning as his admiration for the young Polish girl only added to his dilemma. Richard and Father Paderewski stood next to the car. Henryk, the young Polish driver, finished loading Richard's belongings. Father Paderewski and Richard quickly rehashed the plans for Richard's escape. It was a simple plan that had been worked out to the minute detail. In fact, the Holy Father himself had overlooked the intricacies of the plan, not daring to risk another Cardinal Beroske calamity. Some of the same people Richard had earlier saved from the gas chambers would take an active part in his escape.

Henryk had long finished his loading of Richard's baggage. He sat patiently in the car.

"I guess I'd better go say my farewells to Helena," Richard said, looking at Father Paderewski.

Otto smiled. "Yes, my sister has grown very fond of you."

"You should be proud of her, Otto. She is a sweet and caring person. I would be dead were it not for her."

Having arrived looking very much German in his

striking uniform, Richard now looked as equally Polish, dressed in baggy pants and high-topped shoes. A heavy knitted sweater, a gift from Helena, covered his long-sleeve shirt.

Richard took a deep breath as he started toward her. She sat in her chair knitting a pair of socks for Otto. Helena looked up as Richard neared. Light from the open window afforded more than ample light to see Helena's teary eyes.

"Well, it looks like my time has come to leave." Richard bent on one knee next to her chair. "I'll never forget your kindness. I will return one day after the war to see you."

Helena found a smile, even as her tears fell.

"I have something for you," Richard said. Helena wiped the tears from her cheeks. Richard reached into his shirt pocket and handed her a folded piece of paper. "Please don't look at this until I'm gone."

Helena looked at the paper and then at Richard. She nodded and took the paper from him.

Richard leaned over and gently kissed her on the cheek. "Good-bye, Helena."

She nodded again as Richard turned and walked out the door.

He cried silently as their car left the tiny village of Ostrow. Otto sat quietly beside him. A distant whistle could be heard as another train rounded the curve toward Ostrow Station—as if a final reminder to the American bishop that the war still raged and the atrocities at Auschwitz continued with ever-increasing efficiency.

As the car moved through the Polish countryside, he thought of Helena and the poem he'd given her, entitled "The Beautiful Girl at Ostrow Station"—last poem he would write.

Chapter Twenty-Three

Richard's perilous journey through the war-torn countries of Poland, Czechoslovakia, Austria, and Italy went as planned and without any major hitches, taking eight days to reach Rome and the safety of the Vatican. The long journey had been difficult on Richard though. The long, tedious hours of sleeplessness and lack of appropriate diet weakened his TB-riddled body.

He arrived at the Holy City as he'd left—in almost total secrecy. Only two Italian cardinals that the Holy Father had full trust in knew of the arrival plans of the ailing American bishop. The Holy Father knew the moment Richard entered the guarded gates of Vatican City. The two cardinals, Alfredo of Milan and Giovanni of Naples, escorted Richard to his room and, seeing of the bishop's weakened condition, immediately summoned the Vatican doctor. After a thorough examination, the doctor concluded that what Richard needed most was extended bed rest. So it was ordered, Richard wasn't to leave his bed for several days, having all his meals sent to his room.

During this time alone, Richard's thoughts turned to Elisabeth and certain underlying questions: Was she still in England? If so, had she forgiven him for leaving her, and was she willing to take him back to spend the rest of their lives together? He prayed she would. Oh, how he prayed. Thoughts of her had helped him endure the traumatic days at Auschwitz. He was now ready to leave his tenure as bishop and marry the woman he'd loved for so long. His debt to Cardinal Beroske had been paid. His service to the Jews was as complete as he was capable of performing, even though he still grieved for those he'd failed to save and for those now dying. Yes, he was finally at peace with himself. He'd served his God's wishes to the utmost of his ability and, surely, God expected no more from him now. He no longer felt guilt or remorse about his love for Elisabeth—for having paid a heavy price for this final right to live the rest of his life with the woman he so deeply loved. He prayed for his body to heal so he could be on his way.

His thoughts turned to Lori and Joe as well. He knew the Holy Father had notified them of his safety shortly after his arrival at Father Paderewski's home, but he hadn't heard from either of them as to their well-being. Richard wrote to Lori informing her of his plans to leave the church and marry Elisabeth. It would take several days for the letter to arrive in America. The Holy Father visited Richard in his room his third night back. It was both a jovial and tearful reunion for them both. The pope praised Richard for the great deeds he'd accomplished, especially the confirmed releases of several thousand Jews from Auschwitz. Rabbi Harold Dziobak of Poland asked the Holy Father to thank Bishop Carver personally for the great humanitarian deed he'd done for the Jewish people.

Richard wanted terribly to tell the pontiff of his plans for resignation while they were alone together but couldn't bring himself to spoil the aging pontiff's obvious elation of having him safely back. After all, how long had it been since the holy man had smiled? His reign as pontiff began in war and turmoil and remained so. He was, as well, being openly criticized by certain trusted peers for his handling of the German position. No, Richard couldn't ruin this saintly man's moment of happiness on this night, instead asking only that he be allowed a few weeks leave in order to visit his family in England and America.

The pontiff was more than glad to accept Richard's request. He expressed concern, however, regarding Richard's health. Richard's physical appearance barely resembled the young, dark-haired bishop who'd left the Vatican a mere few months ago. His once-smooth face now was lined with shallow wrinkles and his dark hair was streaked in gray. His eyes had lost some of their sharpness, and his body appeared frail in stature. He was not the same man the pontiff had sent out on the quest for Cardinal Beroske. Without question, the private war Richard had waged against the Germans hadn't been accomplished without serious cost to the American. Before leaving Richard's side that evening, the pontiff granted Richard as much time as he needed away from the church and the Vatican, even though the church sorely needed him. The Vatican had sagged horribly in the diplomatic circles during Richard's prolonged absence. Another week passed. Finally, Richard persuaded the doctor to release him for travel to England. The day of Richard's departure finally arrived. He hadn't sent any advance notices of his upcoming visit to England to either Joe or Elisabeth, not really certain where either would be after such a long absence. He hoped to find one or the other, feeling sure they'd kept in contact with one another. So many troubling questions. Perhaps the most troubling of all was his never-ending guilt about his brother Joe. He knew Joe was also in love with Elisabeth. Joe had made that point very clear to him years ago. Richard had pondered and prayed about this dilemma many times, but in the end, his love for Elisabeth always won out. Perhaps Joe had found someone else after all this time? He could hope. Time would tell.

Richard took a train to Bern, Switzerland where he boarded a Swiss hospital plane to Paris and then on to London. He grew more excited and, at the same time, more nervous as he journeyed across Europe on his final quest for his Elisabeth. Would she still marry him after all this time away? Did she remain in England? Perhaps she'd gone back to America after he'd left her stranded on that barren beach in northern England so many lifetimes ago.

Upon Richard's arrival, he proceeded directly to the field hospital outside of London, where Elisabeth had been stationed when last he'd seen her. She hadn't been there for some time. As he walked toward his waiting cab, idling at the hospital entrance, he wondered what he'd expected. It had been over a year; surely, she wouldn't remain in one place during the entirety of the war. He looked again at the small piece of paper the head nurse had given him— Elisabeth's last known address since leaving the hospital, some six months earlier.

Richard took a seat in the cab. "Do you know Ashley Street . . . on the northern edge of London?"

"Yes, I know the street," the cabbie said.

"Take me to 27 North Ashley Street." Richard folded the small piece of paper, placing it in his coat pocket.

It was mid-afternoon when the cab turned onto Ashley Street. Richard ascertained quickly that this was definitely an American-occupied part of the city. Young American children were scattered up and down the long sidewalks, playing feverishly on the gorgeous May afternoon.

"This is it, ol' chap," the driver said as the cab came to a stop in front of the single-storied frame home.

There was no car in the driveway. Richard quickly scanned the semi-modern home. Open windows in front of the house suggested that, indeed, someone lived there.

"Wait here for me," Richard said, stepping from the cab.

Richard's hopes of seeing Elisabeth faded with the cries of a young infant as he neared the front door. Perhaps the family could tell him where Elisabeth moved. He tapped lightly on the door, not wanting to disturb the crying baby further. He stepped back as the door opened. The woman hesitated at first.

Finally, Elisabeth said, "Richard is that you? Is that really you?"

Richard smiled. "Yes, Elisabeth, it's me."

She looked him up and down, and he remembered how much he'd changed since walking away from her on the beach, what she must think at the sight of him. Her shocked look gave way to a warm smile. "God, I've been so worried about you." She stepped forward, throwing her arms around him and squeezing him tight.

They stood in the doorway embracing one another. Neither could hold back their tears, and once again, their wayward arms held the one they loved.

The cries of the infant interrupted the emotional reunion. Elisabeth backed away, wiping the stinging drops from her flushed cheeks. "Won't you come in?"

Richard removed his hat as he entered the small living room. His casual dress showed no markings of his priesthood, knowing how Elisabeth had always hated the dreaded collar. He studied her, taking her in. She'd weathered the war much better than he had. Her long hair was still soft and wavy, framing her gorgeous face perfectly. Her eyes sparkled in the bright sunlight that passed through the living room window. Her youthful figure was hidden behind the loose-fitting dress and baggy apron that hung from her waist. Once again, the crying infant lying in her crib in the adjoining room interrupted Richard's thoughts.

His attention turned to the open doorway where Agatha had awakened from her midday nap. Then, his eyes shifted slowly back to Elisabeth. "Who is—"

Elisabeth interrupted. "Her name is Agatha, my daughter. Agatha Lori Carver. Joe is her father."

Richard froze, stunned by the announcement. His face went pale, and his legs weakened. Elisabeth rushed to him, taking him by his arm and sitting him on the couch. She, nor anyone else in the family, knew of Richard's grave illness—and would not learn now. Neither did the family know of how Richard contracted his illness, having only been told that he was being held for political reasons somewhere in Poland.

"Are you all, right?" she asked, kneeling in front of him. She took his cold, clammy hand in hers. "Richard, what's wrong with you?"

"Nothing," he finally muttered as he leaned back against the couch. Agatha's cries grew more intense.

"Wait here." Elisabeth squeezed Richard's hand gently. She stood and hurried into the next room. His gaze fixed on the doorway, then Elisabeth and the tiny infant cradled in her arms appeared in the opening. Elisabeth smiled proudly. "This is Agatha." She crossed the room to Richard and sat next to him on the couch.

Richard stared at the squirming child as Elisabeth held her so he could see.

"Let me give her a quick bottle, Richard, and I'll be back." Elisabeth disappeared into the next room, carrying the child with her.

He sat there motionless for the longest time, his thoughts in utter turmoil, totally decimated by the happenings of the last few minutes. He could never have imagined in his wildest dreams such as was taking place. Everything he'd lived for was gone.

Photographs of Joe and Elisabeth sat atop the two end tables next to the couch. He stared at the smiling couple, shaking his head in hopes they would go away. Surely, he was coming down with the fever again, and all of this was simply a horrible dream. With the reappearance of Elisabeth, however, he knew it was no dream. His God had played a cruel hoax upon him, letting him believe during all those months at Ostrow Station that one day he'd reunite with his beloved Elisabeth. Richard's love for Elisabeth had given him the will to endure all the misery and heartache of Auschwitz. It had all been in vain.

Elisabeth sat next to him on the couch. She took his weak hand in hers. The child had quieted and drifted off to sleep in the next room. Elisabeth's smile faded as she said, "Richard, try not to hate me too much for what's happened. I tried so hard to capture you all those years, but your God would have no part of it. That last day on the beach, that was the low point of my life. I laid there crying in the sand, cursing you and that God of yours. And as I lay there, I decided to end it all. As my heart broke, so did my will to live. The dense fog that suddenly engulfed the beach as you left vanished just as quickly. I walked toward the sea, never hesitating as I entered the frigid water. I decided to die that day on the beach. And I was about to succeed when, out of nowhere, a strange man reached for me. He held me over his broad shoulder, carrying me from the sea. I screamed and cursed him for pulling me from my wanted death. He laid my shivering body on the beach. He was wet and strange looking, and at first, I was frightened by his appearance. Then, a warm smile crossed his aging lips as he covered my shivering body with a warm blanket. Where he got it, I never knew. He never spoke; yet his very presence soothed my turbulent soul. He smiled down at me, then turned away and walked down the beach as the strange fog once again rolled in from the sea. He disappeared into the mist, and at that very moment, I believed what you'd told me about the vision you'd seen in the distant fog. I knew your God was God and that, indeed, you were chosen by Him to do great things with your life. I'd simply been a tool He'd used to help fulfill your destiny. Richard, your God never intended for us to remain together. Our short times together were nothing more than a brief appeasement so that you could once again restore your energy for the next task God had planned for you. I don't know this for certain, but I really believe that the whole tragic ordeal with your beloved Cardinal Beroske amounted to nothing more than another steppingstone to accomplish another one of your God's long-range plans yet to unfold."

Richard's mind flashed briefly back to Auschwitz and Ostrow Station. Elisabeth squeezed his hand as she went to her knees in front of him. "My dear, sweet Richard, how foolish I was all those years trying to force you away from your God. At first, it was youth and physical attraction that drew me to you, and then it turned to selfish love. I was so busy trying to steal you away from your God who loves you so that I couldn't see it could never be. As I walked from the beach that day, I suddenly realized that I'd spent my entire life chasing a schoolgirl's dream I could never catch. I knew my great love for you would never wane with this sudden realization, but I also realized that if I were to have any hopes for a life of my own it must be now. I wanted a child so. When Joe returned from sea two weeks later, we were married the following day. As time went by, I finally realized just how much I love Joe . . . as he loves me. Agatha was born nine months later. We've made a good life for ourselves . . . up until four months ago, that is."

The slamming of a car door interrupted Elisabeth's ending. Panic spread across her face. "You must leave quickly . . . it's Joe." She jumped to her feet, pulling Richard from the couch.

"But, Elisabeth, it's only Joe." Richard said, confused by Elisabeth's sudden behavior.

She leaned over in his face; her emerald eyes glistened with fear. "You don't understand, Richard. He found one of your letters. He knows about us."

"But that was before the two of you were married."

The words no sooner escaped Richard's mouth when the front door opened. Elisabeth trembled as Joe entered the room. He was drunk again, as he'd been most of the time since finding Richard's letter to Elisabeth. Richard watched with uncertainty as Joe snatched his officer's cap from his head, slinging it across the room. He knew instantly Joe had been drinking. Joe's body swayed as he peered down at his brother.

Richard smiled, slowly getting to his feet. "Hello, Joe." His smile faded as he stared into the fiery blood-shot eyes of his brother.

"So, little brother, you came back to reclaim what you left behind." Joe looked wildly at the trembling Elisabeth.

"No, Joe that's not true. I'm here—"

"You're here for what, you goddamn Lucifer? A man of God! Shit, you're no more a man of God than those damn Germans I've been killing."

"But Joe . . ." Richard never finished as Joe swung wildly, hitting Richard in the jaw. His weak body crumbled to the floor.

Elisabeth watched in horror as the two brothers glared at one another. "My God, Joe, what the hell are you doing?" she shouted, bending down next to Richard as he lay there wiping the trickle of blood from his swelling lips.

"That's right, Elisabeth. Doctor your lover so he'll once again be able to screw you like he did before. Hell, he might as well screw you; he has me for God knows how long."

"You're drunk and crazy, Joe!" Elisabeth shouted.

"Yes, I'm probably both, but with good cause—my wife sleeping with my brother who's supposedly a Catholic priest. Well, here's what I think of my brother the priest."

Elisabeth wiped Joe's spit from Richard's face.

"Get the hell out of my house, you son of a bitch, before I kill you."

Joe eyes showed he meant what he said. Elisabeth helped Richard to his feet.

"Thank you, Elisabeth." Richard collected his hat

from the coffee table. "I'm sorry for the heartbreak I've caused you and Joe."

Elisabeth wiped away her tears. "You've caused me no heartache, Richard."

"Hell no, you damn harlot. You love sleeping with the bastard."

Elisabeth grabbed Richard's arm as he started toward Joe. "Please leave, Richard."

He looked at her. "Good-bye, Elisabeth."

Joe stepped aside as Richard walked toward the door. He turned, starting to say something, then changed his mind and walked out the door.

"Come back when I've gone to sea, you gutless bastard. Not only are you a fraud, you're also a yellow-bellied coward, hiding behind that cross of yours so you won't have to go to war—you yellow bastard."

The words stung deep into Richard's heart. He approached the waiting cab. Three young boys stopped their sidewalk play to listen as Richard entered the cab, ushered in by the chastisement of the raving naval captain.

Back in London, he got a hotel room for the night. He bought a liter of scotch and proceeded to get very drunk in his room. Three days passed as Richard walked the streets of London during the day and got drunk at night. His already weak body buckled under the added abuse. The traumatic events at Elisabeth's house brought Richard to the breaking point, his mind unable to absorb the added pressure of the Eminence' quantities of alcohol he poured into his body. On the second night, he tried suicide, only to pass out along a deserted alleyway on his way to the Thames River. Guilt riddled his soul, Joe's words pulsating violently in his mind.

The morning of the fourth day, Richard awoke in the open doorway to a deserted building. His head pounded. He tried sitting up, but his body couldn't go anymore. Deciding this was as good a place as any to die, he laid back down and drifted off to sleep.

His eyes ached. He forced them open, gradually focusing on the light from a bedside lamp. He scanned the room, perplexed by his plush surroundings; this was certainly not the place he'd decided to die. Finally, his eyes settled on an elderly man who sat next to a window across the room. He read from a book by the light of a matching lamp. He couldn't tell if it was dark outside as a black cloth covered the window.

Richard's coughing caught the attention of the elderly gentleman. The gray-headed man laid his book down and walked over to Richard's bed. Richard quickly knew who his custodian was as the old man neared. His clerical collar shone clearly in the faint light.

"I see you've arisen from the dead," the smiling priest said in a strong Irish brogue. "Welcome to St. Catherine's, Bishop Carver." Richard's eyes showed his surprise that the priest knew his identity. "Don't be surprised that I know your name, Bishop Carver. The thieves who robbed you had the courtesy to leave your passport in your jacket. It seems you enjoy testing God and His will to let you live. I've found out much about you since you were brought here eight days ago by two American soldiers. You must be a bishop of great importance to have the Holy Father inquire about your well-being, insisting I hold you here until his personal attaché of two reigning cardinals arrive to escort you back to Rome. I assured the Holy Father that there should be no rush in sending the cardinals or worry about your escape. A man as ill as you, my American friend, is damn lucky to be alive. I don't know for what reason you decided to kill yourself, but you came very close to succeeding."

Richard tried to speak but was too weak, quickly falling back asleep. Four more days passed as the Irish priest watched and cared for Richard like an old mother hen. Perhaps the Holy Father had put the fear in him, making Richard his personal responsibility. Whatever the reason, the elderly Irishmen did everything but sleep with the bishop, at times force-feeding him. He did improve with the guarded care. On the fifth day, cardinals Alfredo and Giovanni arrived at St. Catherine's. Their disposition toward him showed their dislike for having made the journey. Although still fragile, Richard made the return trip to the Vatican, but hardly the return he'd thought he'd have made. Instead of coming back happy and asking to resign, he returned decimated, sick, and totally heartbroken. Even now, the occasional thought of suicide flashed through his mind.

His irate doctor, upon seeing what Richard had done to his body while on leave, sentenced him to strict bed rest. He was under the constant care of a male nurse the first two weeks, never allowed to leave his room. As he slowly grew stronger, he felt more and more like a prisoner. The doctor saw this as a good sign and reported to the concerned pontiff every three days.

During this period, the war raged on. Richard, though, had lost total interest in the world happenings and everything else for that matter.

***

He'd just finished his evening meal and was sitting

365

alone in his room, trying to read one of the many books that lined the room's west wall. As always, he showed only meager effort in his toil—not even knowing the name of the book he'd been glaring at the last three days. His male nurse had left for the evening. A knock sounded on his door. "Come in," he shouted out in Italian, thinking it was his pesky doctor making his last call for the day.

Richard never looked as his door opened and closed. "I feel fine, Doc," he mumbled, still glaring at the book's pages.

"I'm certainly glad to hear that, my son," the soft voice of the pontiff said.

Richard turned sharply, surprised by the pontiff's presence. "Your Holiness, I thought you were the doctor." He attempted to rise from his chair.

"Stay where you are, Bishop Carver. A man that looks as terrible as you should stay in bed for a while." The pope took a seat in the chair across from the bed. "The doctor tells me your physical health is gradually improving."

"Yes, Holy Father, I'm getting stronger by the day."

The pontiff nodded. "He also tells me your mental well-being stinks."

Richard was taken aback by the pontiff's frank words. "I'm not certain I agree with his opinion, Your Holiness."

The pontiff leaned over, staring Richard in the eyes. "I agree with the doctor. You're not even close to the same man who left here for a brief vacation. That man showed spirit and a strong will to live, even though he was possibly more ill than you are now."

Richard couldn't counter the pontiff's assessment

even if he wished, knowing the Holy Father spoke the truth.

"Something terrible happened to you after you left here, didn't it, my son? You were found in a deserted alley, having been drunk for who knows how long, near death. No, this isn't the same man that I made bishop. This isn't the man who went on the bold crusade to save Cardinal Beroske and ended up saving thousands of innocent lives instead. No, that man has died somewhere along the way, only his pitiful shell lies before me this night. And what a shame, too. God could have at least taken all of him and not left behind this awful-looking reminder of what the man used to be."

At first, Richard felt a tinge of self-pity upon hearing the pontiff's harsh words, but then he felt a stirring of anger at the pontiff's apparent desecration of what he'd become. Still, he listened to the holy man.

"I've not come here to exorcise you, my son, but from all appearances, perhaps that's what you need. It certainly appears that Lucifer might've entered your body, but I doubt this. I've come to help you. True, I'm not so young anymore, but perhaps my wisdom hasn't faded as fast as my youth."

A smile came upon the pontiff's lips. He sat back in the chair, his sharp eyes settling on Richard's. "Remember when I told you my secret about the vision?"

Richard nodded.

"Since I've told you that great, dark secret," the pontiff continued, "I wish to tell you another." A sparkle appeared in the pontiff's eyes as he told his deep secret, that, until now, he'd shared only with God. "You've been around us Italians long enough now to know that most of us men think we're God's gift to women. Believe it or not, at one time this ugly old man thought the same. My whole tenure in the priesthood started because of a young girl I'd fallen in love with while visiting my aunt one summer in Naples. Oh, how beautiful she was." A glow radiated from the pontiff's face. "The whole summer I courted this Italian goddess. After only a week, I decided to marry her. At the time, she agreed. Well, I left to return to my uncle's house. I worked hard that winter in the grape vineyards, saving my money for my great wedding. I returned to Naples the following summer to marry the girl of my dreams. The following morning, after my arrival in Naples, I went to her family's home. Her mother told me on the front steps that my intended wife had left the week before with a young Sicilian lad. I stood there on that porch and cried like a child. My world had ended, I thought, as I left that house and wandered the streets of Naples for two weeks. I succeed in spending all the money I'd saved the winter before. My marriage money it was supposed to be, but instead it was used to drown my sorrows. All those grapes I harvested in the fields that previous winter, I managed to consume in wine those two weeks in Naples. Finally, I was broke and destitute. I ended up going to a small church outside the city, too embarrassed to return home to my uncles. There, the priest gave me food and put me to work about the small parish. He began to teach me about life in the church. I couldn't understand, at first, how a man like him could be so happy in a place like that. But something happened over a period of time and I forgot about that girl who broke my heart that day. Oh, not all together, I still think about her from time to time. In fact, I saw her some twelve years ago. She came to see me when I was in Venice. Then, I knew the lord had blessed me the day she ran off with that Sicilian. She'd grown ugly and fat. Oh my, she looked terrible."

Richard laughed.

"Do you know if the truth was known, Richard, I would guess that almost all the priests in this city tonight have had similar events in their lives? I know the Italians have." A mischievous smile bent the pontiff's lips. "What I'm telling you, Richard, is that no matter how dedicated a man might be to his work or his God, human factors from time to time hinder these drives and beliefs. Not that God enjoys making us miserable. He does these things to remind us that we're nothing more than his children. Like children, we make mistakes, and we are punished for these mistakes. I feel your illness here might have something to do with one of these mistakes. I've come here to help you during your time of trouble, just like that friendly priest so very long ago when I knew my world had ended." The pontiff leaned over and took Richard's hand in his. "I love you like a son. Please let me help."

Richard looked into the pontiff's kind eyes. Tears welled in his eyes. He fell to his knees in front of the Holy Father, laying his head in the pontiff's lap.

The pontiff cradled Richard's head in his lap. Soon, the pontiff's eyes grew moist. After a long while, Richard began to tell the pontiff of his love affair with Elisabeth. Though hesitant at first, he told all, right up to the last when Joe ran him from his house. Everything that is, except the one thing Richard had buried in the far corners of his mind, his killing of Colonial Zooke. Richard's confession lasted a little over two hours. The pontiff had been a good listener and an excellent comforter to Richard as he told his sorrowful story. When finished, he felt greatly relieved,

lifting the heavy burdens from his weary soul. Within
moments, a faint glimmer returned to Richard's eyes

It was difficult to tell which of the two men felt the
better that night: the pontiff upon seeing his loved friend
once again rejoin the living or Richard who felt tremendous
relief from his heavy guilt. In any case, it seemed to have
helped both. Within two weeks, Richard had recovered well
enough to continue his secretive work he'd abandoned
months ago. He quickly discovered, however, that even
though the eventual outcome of the war was still in serious
doubt the allies appeared to have gained the upper hand.
This scenario was much different from when he'd left his
position to search for Cardinal Beroske.

This was now the first week in December 1943,
American and French armies had landed on the beaches of
Sicily. The US Fifth Army had been put ashore on the
Italian coast. Mussolini was dead, as his own people did
him in, stringing his body up in the middle of a square.
Germany was feeling the daily pounding of American
bombs.

The war in the Pacific, however, hadn't taken such a
noticeable turn in the allies favor. It seemed the Japanese
had turned out to be as much of or, perhaps, a more
formidable foe than the Germans. Their years of
preparation for this war had yielded great dividends in
repelling the fledgling giant of America. Even with the
daily arrivals of superior weapons, the Americans were
virtually stalemated by the fanatical Japanese. The islands
taken by the American marines were paid for at a heavy
price in deaths and wounded. Even though the marines had
taken Guadalcanal in early '43, they remained some three
thousand miles from Tokyo, and many islands of death

remained in between.

Naval victory in the Atlantic also remained in doubt. Even though the Americans were in top gear as far as production of naval and maritime ships, the German U-boats had also begun to peak, their increased numbers neutralizing America's gains in ship production. Virtually the entire Atlantic Ocean from South America to Iceland had become a huge graveyard for allied ships. Joe was in the midst of the heaviest duels, patrolling the waters of the North Sea, off the Northern British Isles.

Richard had heard nothing from Elisabeth since his humiliating departure a few months before. She'd written Lori about the brothers' confrontation, revealing to Lori the love affair between her and Richard. She also told Lori about Joe's finding one of Richard's love letters and the subsequent confrontation between the two brothers.

Lori wasn't surprised by Elisabeth's admission, having long suspecting such a romance. Elisabeth's confession did raise Lori's esteem of Elisabeth, not thinking much of her obvious carryings on with her brother Richard. Over a period, however, Lori came to understand their love affair. Lori only wished that Richard had met Elisabeth before he'd taken his final vows into the church; obviously, that wasn't meant to be.

Chapter Twenty-Four

The weather was cold and overcast when Richard left his office on the night of January 2, 1944. Noticeably tired, he made his way across the open courtyard toward his sleeping quarters. He'd made a remarkable recovery from his lingering illness, gaining some weight back and feeling quite strong again. His once-dormant cough, however, had made a return these last several days, coming with a midwinter blast of cold air. He'd planned to turn in early, after spending a long day in his secluded office, more tired than normal. As he neared his quarters, he glanced at the distant chapel. He considered that time he'd spent in the small chapel since his first arriving those many years ago.

He stopped walking, feeling a sudden urge to go to the chapel. Thoughts of Joe had burdened his mind off and on most of the day. It was a strange and unwanted feeling. He started for the chapel. So many times, over his troubled years at the Vatican, the little chapel had been of great comfort.

He entered the chapel. As usual for this time of evening, it was empty. Richard knelt in his usual place—in the front row, center aisle. He noticed the room felt unusually cold this evening; even on the coldest of Roman nights, the chapel was warm. Perhaps he was coming down with a mild fever. He left his long trench coat on as he knelt to say his prayers, following the same general format in his prayer sayings. Asking God to end the horrid war was always the first and foremost prayer, except for tonight. Not knowing why, himself, thoughts of Joe had started his prayers. He had prayed a lot for Joe these last few weeks, asking God to let his brother forgive him.

Richard was halfway through his prayers when his attention was interrupted by the sound of hurried footsteps. A young priest ran down the small aisle clutching a telegram. "I'm sorry, Your Reverence, but I have an important wireless for you."

Still kneeling in his pew, Richard took the paper

from the winded young priest. "Thank you, Father," he said.

The priest hurried out the chapel. Richard opened the telegram. At first, he felt certain it had to do with the war effort, but as he began to open it, he felt a sudden chill. Not of the weather variety, but an inner chill.

He read the terrible words.

Dear Richard,

I have awful news. On the night of December 31, Joe's ship was struck by a German torpedo and sunk some three hundred miles north of Londonderry, in the North Sea. There are reported survivors, but at this time, the rescue ship isn't certain of their names. Many of the survivors are in bad shape it is reported. Please, Richard, I ask that you come be with me. The ship carrying the survivors is due in Londonderry the night of January 5. I haven't notified Lori about this; I thought maybe you could handle that better than I, the two of you being so close and all. Please come to Londonderry, Richard. I don't know if I'm strong enough to handle the worst if it should come to that.

Love, Elisabeth.

Richard lowered the telegram. His tearful eyes rose, settling on the image of Jesus on the cross above the altar. "Why Lord? What else can my family offer in this terrible war? We build ships that destroy the atheist pigs. Lori works night and day in defense plants, manufacturing bullets with which to shoot the German dogs. Elisabeth labored in the hospital wards, tending the wounded. Joe . . . my God, Joe has been decorated for bravery, killing the dirty bastards that sail the death ships. I know I've done nothing of this magnitude, but, Lord, I've carried your word and your name as proudly as any man, but now this Lord." Richard held the paper up for Christ to see. "Joe is a good man and a God-fearing man. Joe's a new father, God!" Richard stood and shouted, "If you want another sacrificial lamb, take me. I have no one and I'm already sick. Take my life God, not my brother's."

He could hold back his tears no longer. Slowly, he fell back to his knees. The sound of his weeping filled the tiny room with added sorrow. Cardinal Sorento of Florence stood at the back of the chapel, listening to Richard's plea. He wiped the tears from his eyes, turned, and left the tiny chapel.

Richard made his travel arrangements early the next morning, leaving on a night flight to Switzerland. Then, he traveled by Swissair to Paris and then on to London and, finally, to Londonderry.

Chapter Twenty-Five

He arrived on the evening of the fourth, having wired ahead to the American military stationed in Londonderry about his coming arrival and its purpose. The commanding officer of the detachment had a car awaiting Richard's arrival to carry him straight to Joe's command. Elisabeth was there waiting. It was a tearful reunion. Still, she had not heard if Joe was among the twenty survivors, eighteen of whom were critically injured.

Richard and Elisabeth had a quiet dinner together that evening at the base's officers' club. It was a very subdued dinner, as they both seemed consumed by their own thoughts.

Richard finally broke the silence. "Have you heard anything from Lori lately?"

Elisabeth sighed, setting her coffee cup back in the saucer. "I was afraid you would ask that question tonight, Richard. I prayed that you wouldn't."

Concern shown on Richard's face as he placed his elbows on the dinner table. "What is it? What's wrong with Lori?"

"Lori and Jeff are having a rough time of it marriage wise. It seems that Jeff is fighting the same battle with alcohol as Joe. Jeff's father has taken over running the shipbuilding business. Lori said in her last letter that Jeff's father has threatened to have Jeff committed to an institution. God, I hate to tell you the rest of it, Richard. You have enough bad things on your mind now."

"Tell me, Elisabeth. This is my only sister we're talking about here—tell me."

Elisabeth stared at Richard, her emerald eyes glistening with tears. "Lori lost an unborn child a few weeks ago. Jeff pushed her down a flight of stairs, killing the unborn. Lori is doing all right, but she's heartbroken. Jeff has moved out of the house. I hate telling you this added terrible news, Richard—I hate it so."

Richard leaned back in his chair. He dropped his head and prayed to his God. Elisabeth watched in silence as tears fell from Richard's eyes. Finally, Richard wiped the tears from his face, lifted his head, and said, "Thank you for telling me. I'll pray hard for Lori and Joe tonight . . . as well as you. If you're ready, I feel tired now and would like to go to my room and get a little rest."

Elisabeth smiled amidst tears as they got from the

table and returned to their designated quarters, consoling one another along the way and holding hands.

***

Richard was up early the following morning, and the weather was terrible. A frigid wind blew in from the North Sea. He'd taken breakfast at the officer's dining room, after which he found a small, temporary chapel set up on the south end of the base. There were only a handful of men inside the church, a mixture of American and British sailors. No one paid any attention to Richard as he knelt and prayed with the others, attired in civilian clothes. He prayed with all his might that Joe was still alive, and if he wasn't, to give he and Elisabeth the strength to accept Joe's death. He prayed for Lori also and for Jeff, asking God to help them through their terrible times.

Richard hadn't seen anything of Elisabeth during the day. He busied himself wandering around the base, surveying the many ships moored at the massive complex. Elisabeth had been bothered with a terrible cold of late. Richard ordered her to stay inside during the day and get as much rest as possible, promising to inform her as soon as the British destroyer arrived with the American survivors. Richard, too, should have stayed inside and out of the weather, as his cough had gotten worse since his arrival. His mind wasn't on such trivial matters as his health. He paced one end of the naval yard to the other awaiting word of the British destroyer.

It was nearly dark when he entered the American command building. The officer in charge informed him that the British ship carrying the American survivors was due at the west docks around midnight. He assured Richard that he would be notified well in advance of its arrival, giving him a chance to personally meet the arriving ship. Horrible weather over much of the marine area had made the exact time of the ship's arrival uncertain, and another sinking of an American ship only three hours before, no more than ninety nautical miles north of Londonderry Harbor, complicated the matter.

Richard returned to his room without dinner. His body was weary, and his hacking cough had worsened during the day. He no sooner laid down on his bed then he was asleep, only to be awakened a few hours later by the ringing of the bedside phone. Richard answered. A naval captain informed him that the British destroyer with the survivors was due at pier eight at 2:15 a.m. Richard sat on the edge of his bed for a short while, trying to shake the cobwebs from his tired mind. Then, he called Elisabeth in her room to tell her of the news and that he would meet her in front of her quarters at 1:45.

Richard showered and changed into his bishop's garments. This was the first time he'd worn them outside the Vatican walls. He thought this was the proper occasion for such dress if there ever was a proper time. He fitted his black cape across his bending shoulders, knelt by his bed, and made a final prayer to his God for Joe's safe return. His large bishop's ring glistened in the pale light of the room as he opened his door and began the journey to meet Elisabeth.

The wind had waned to some degree but still stung his face as he walked toward the distant barracks. Elisabeth stood out front. She forced a smile as Richard approached. A scarf covered her soft brown hair, her body bundled warmly in a knee-length leather coat. The two walked down the roadway toward the distant piers. Richard knew by earlier observation where pier eight was located.

They walked quietly toward their destination. Elisabeth looked at Richard, then back down at the road. "Do you suppose Joe is dead?"

Richard grimaced as he looked at Elisabeth, staring down at the road. "I don't know, but we'll know that answer quickly enough."

The bright overhead lights running along the edge of the concrete piers afforded plenty of light to study the ships. Dark smoke rose from many of the ships' smokestacks, remaining under power in case of an emergency to leave the harbor within short notice. The cold wind had rekindled its breath as the two neared the edge of pier eight. There was no sign of the British destroyer. Richard glanced at his watch. Only a little after two. They'd arrived early.

Richard looked at Elisabeth who trembled from the bitter cold wind. "Would you mind if I put my arm around you . . . to help you stay warm?"

She looked at Richard, her teeth chattering. "Not at all, my body would more than welcome it."

He put his arm around her shoulders, pulling her trembling body next to his. He'd forgotten how tiny she was in his arms and how wonderful she felt. She placed her arm around his waist, placing her cold hand inside his coat pocket. They stood there in silence staring out over the open harbor and the flashing buoy lights running toward the sea.

Richard stared into the darkness. "Have you been happy with Joe?"

"Yes, I suppose. At least up until the last when his drinking became so terrible. Joe is a good man." Elisabeth looked at Richard with sad eyes as she continued. "Did you know that he has secretly admired you all of his life?"

"Joe has admired me? God, if anybody should be admired, it should be him. Look at all the obstacles he's had to overcome in his life. The stock market crashed, but still he had the courage to get back on his feet and make something of himself."

Elisabeth smiled. "Yes, and who was it that laid the groundwork for that remarkable recovery?"

Richard hesitated. "It was Lori who helped."

"Lori my eye, it was all your doings. Lori told me the whole story."

Richard looked back toward the harbor.

"You see, Richard, that's one thing that you've never been able to understand about yourself. You possess this quality—this magical quality that makes almost everyone you come in contact with either admire you or fall in love with you, as it was with me. You've never acknowledged to yourself that you possess this gift. Perhaps it's this great humility that you have that only adds to your great mystique. God knows I still love you, Richard, but I love Joe also and have for a long time."

He turned slowly. His eyes met hers. Their hearts beat as one as Richard was slowly drawn toward Elisabeth's waiting lips.

Chapter Twenty-Six

The wailing of the ship's whistle broke their momentary trance, their eyes suddenly drawn toward the British destroyer making its way toward pier eight. Within moments, a dozen Red Cross ambulances squealed to a halt next to the bulkhead. Next, an American jeep came to a screeching halt within a few feet of the couple. A naval captain jumped from the jeep and approached Richard and Elisabeth. "Are you Bishop Carver—Joe Carver's brother?"

"Yes, and this is his wife, Elisabeth."

The commander smiled as he tipped his cap. "We've had further word about your brother. He's one of the survivors."

Richard looked quickly at Elisabeth. She grabbed Richard's arm, squeezing tightly. "Thank God," she muttered and leaned her head on Richard's shoulder.

"But I regret to add, Bishop Carver, he's one of the worst wounded. It seems there was a fire as the ship went down and he, being the last off, was burnt severely." The captain paused as he glanced at Elisabeth. "Expect the worst, Bishop," the captain whispered into Richard's ear. Richard stared blankly at the captain, then at Elisabeth who he doubted could have heard the captain's whispered words.

"What's wrong, Richard?" she asked meekly, tears filling her eyes.

"Let's wait and see how he is," Richard whispered, attempting to hide his grief.

They held one another as the vessel made its way to the dock. The ship was well lit. Streams of seawater ran from the upper decks, telling of the anger of the wind-driven sea. The ambulances had lined up beside one another along the edge of the bulkhead; the paramedics stood at the ready, their stretchers and life-support gear close by.

The immensity of twirling red lights from the waiting ambulances flashed haunting shades of red into the faces of the waiting aids. Richard watched in silence as two of the male drivers smoked and told jokes, waiting on the wounded. For a brief horrid moment, Richard had a terrible flashback of the Canada men at Auschwitz. They, too, had told jokes and smoked cigarettes moments before extracting gold teeth from dead men.

Finally, the ship docked.

Richard and Elisabeth silently watched as the unloading of the wounded got under way. One after another, the wounded men were quietly ushered from the ship by the male nurses. Richard had the horrid task of looking at each one, attempting to verify which man was his brother. He grimaced as he viewed the wounded. Many were burnt almost beyond recognition. The morbid line seemed unending. Elisabeth watched from a short distance, and Richard continued his dreaded ordeal. The line of ambulances grew shorter as one victim after another was loaded into the vehicles. A trail of flashing red lights could be seen down the distant roadway. The ambulances moved through the quiet of night toward the awaiting hospital.

Richard watched nervously as the final stretcher-bearers made their way down from the ship, pausing in front of him. He leaned over and peered at the man lying on the cot. A horrid expression swept Richard's face. He glared at Joe's charred face, having seen this sickening picture before while in Baltimore. This, however, was even worse . . . this was Joe, his only brother. Only the bone structure of the face told Richard this was Joe. His hair had been singed from his head. Charred legions crisscrossed his once-handsome face. How could the poor man still be alive?

"This is your brother?" the captain asked.

"Yes, this is Joe."

A young naval lieutenant disembarked from the gang plank, his right arm heavily bandaged. He paused, looking down at Joe. "Is the captain a friend of yours?" he asked Richard.

"He's, my brother."

"Your brother is the bravest man I've ever seen," the lieutenant said. "I served under him."

Richard looked at the wounded officer. "You were on his ship when it went down?"

"Hell yes, I was there all right. We'd just located a German sub. The dirty kraut bastards sank one of our freighters only twenty minutes before. The captain had already ordered depth charges be dropped on the sub, but then we took a torpedo broadside . . . five seconds later, we took another. Goddamn holes the size of houses opened up mid-ship, igniting the ship in flames. Captain Carver ordered abandon ship knowing we were going down fast. We were the last two off the bridge. Most of the other men still alive had already gone over the side by the time me and the captain hit the main deck, just at dusk. A British destroyer sat some five miles off our stern. We knew they'd seen us take a hit and would be steaming toward us. The captain was concerned about the sub still underneath us, fearing she would wait on the British ship to get close and pop her with a couple of her torpedoes. I tried reasoning with the captain, telling him we didn't have time to drop charges on the dirty bastards below us. He wouldn't have any part of that, ordering me overboard. I refused, and the next thing I know, he shoves me over the side of our ship and into the water. I and some of these other lads you've seen leaving here tonight watched in disbelief as this brother of yours made his way to the stern of the ship where depth charges sat in their cradles ready to go over the side. Somehow, the captain was able to jettison a whole damn rack of those depth charges, blowing up the German sub and probably saving that British ship that arrived a short time later. Our ship exploded in flames seconds after the sub blew up. I thought for sure your brother was dead then, but here he is still hanging on, God bless his soul. He'll get a medal for what he did, Preacher. He's the bravest man I've ever seen."

Richard watched as the lieutenant wiped the tears from his eyes, then turned and walked away. The stretcher-bearers hurried Joe to their awaiting ambulance.

Elisabeth, who'd stayed her distance during all this, hurried to Richard's side as Joe's ambulance peeled off into the darkness. "How bad is he, Richard?"

Richard placed his arm around her and said, "Joe's going to die, Elisabeth. He's hurt terribly bad."

The two held one another as the cold north wind howled across the quiet bay. Richard and Elisabeth cried together—not for one another, as had usually been the case, but for Joe, the man who'd also played the game well. Like so many before, he would fold his hand on this frigid January morning. Richard and Elisabeth walked hand in hand back to their quarters.

Chapter Twenty-Seven

Within a few months after the last shot fired in the Great War, stories began to emerge about the miraculous deeds an American bishop had performed for the peoples of

Europe. At first, the majority of these stories came from Poland and from the mouths of such respected men as Bishop Rutgers of Munich, Cardinal Sarkoski of Warsaw, and Rabbi Dziobak of Poland. Yes, even Father Paderewski (Otto) of Ostrow Station. Within a matter of days, Richard emerged as a European hero and a special kind of hero besides. There had been many military heroes during the war, but most had to do with great battles won or the killing of someone important. Yes, Bishop Carver was a special hero. His humanitarian deeds swept the world as swiftly as the first atomic bomb before it.

The news of the American bishop rolled through his own country with raves that approached the bishop's sainthood. Needless to say, Lori and Elisabeth were two of Richard's most ardent fans. Each knew, as perhaps no one else in the world, how deserving this kind man was of such recognition. During the height of this world outpouring, Lori and Elisabeth decided that Lori should give the wanting world Richard's poetry he'd given to Lori the day after Joe's funeral. The press and book publishers fought openly about the rights to such valuable writings. Finally, a large New York publisher bought the rights to the poems, the royalty from which was to be paid to Elisabeth and Agatha, so they might live comfortably for the rest of their lives.

The world welcomed Cardinal Carver's poetry with open arms and pocketbooks. The Catholic Church also rode the wave of the bishop's popularity, elevating the church to heights never before obtained. The pontiff, who had long decided on Richard's elevation to cardinal, was forced to speed up the process due to the enormous outcry of the entire Christian world.

Never in the history of the Catholic Church had such a man as Bishop Carver had such universal appeal, spreading across all denominations. Even the atheistic Russian leaders openly praised the holy man from America and his humane war deeds. So, it was on June 1, 1947, in Saint Peter's Basilica, with utterly every important leader from all regions of the world watching, Richard Carver, the bishop from America, was elevated to the rank of cardinal. The pontiff cried like a young child as his beloved Richard knelt before him, where he was declared cardinal and secretary of state of the Vatican.

He was bestowed with one of the most powerful positions in the church—perhaps only second to the Holy Father. This duty of international ambassador for the church was nothing new for Richard, having been this since his first arrival in the Holy City. The days of secrecy had passed with the calmed winds of war. As Lori and Elisabeth viewed this great honor being bestowed on their Richard, Elisabeth became overcome by emotion and had to be taken from the cathedral before the ceremony's end. On this day, the world witnessed the great man become a cardinal. His picture was spread across every important newspaper of the world the following day after his elevation in the church.

Lori and Elisabeth returned back to the States. It seemed that this final step in Richard's rise in the church had at last ended Elisabeth's quest to one day have Richard to herself. She would never marry again.

The two years following Richard's elevation to cardinal were busy ones for Richard, mostly spent traveling throughout Europe where more honors continued to be bestowed upon the famous cardinal. This one particular week in the spring of '47 was of great importance to Richard when he returned to Auschwitz, fulfilling his promise to Cardinal Beroske that he would one day return with the proper marker for his friend's grave dug that fateful day so very long ago.

Richard stopped a short distance from the spot at which he buried Cardinal Beroske. He took the large bronze cross from one of the Polish priests who'd accompanied him. He turned to the gathering and asked that he be allowed to go alone to the grave, to say his final good-byes to Cardinal Beroske. The gathering stood quietly as Richard walked to the edge of the fence where he'd laid the cardinal to rest, clutching the bronze cross in his hands. Even though there was no visual sign of the grave site remaining, Richard knew exactly the grave's location. He slowly dropped to his knees, gently laying the bronze cross in the exact spot where he'd drawn a cross in the sand years before.

Richard made the sign of the cross and prayed. "I hope to see you in heaven, and I promise you I won't be long." After the ceremony, he wandered about the deserted grounds of Auschwitz, crying unashamedly as he viewed the place where he'd witnessed such horrible things. His eyes still could see the dreaded smoke bellowing from the distant brick chimney and the long, unending lines of Jews awaiting their turns in the gas chambers. Yes, his mind's eye could clearly see these things; his ears, as well, could plainly hear the megaphones shouting the horrible words: *After your showers, you will be assigned to your new workstations.* He stopped momentarily as he was leaving the camp and looked at the distant pines. Bursts of machine-gun fire echoed through the barren yard.

After leaving Auschwitz, he asked that he might visit Ostrow Station. He was driven there along with the rest of his entourage. He requested after his arrival to be allowed to visit the station alone. He walked slowly over the small hill and looked down at the abandoned station. Tall grass had sprung up around the depot, as if nature were trying to hide this blight in history. The train tracks like the station was overrun by the tall grass, making the rails that had carried so many millions to their deaths at Auschwitz barely visible.

Richard gazed toward the distant trees. Once again, his smile blended with his tears. He could see the Jews running for their freedom into the nearby forest. He knelt on the hilltop and prayed. Richard started back to his awaiting caravan, then turned one last time toward the distant track and broad curve where the sound of a train whistle could be heard. After a few moments, he smiled; the ghostly train never rounded the curve. The distant cry of a wolf rode the wind before slowly fading into the distant evergreens.

The famous cardinal would never again visit Ostrow Station, and two years from this very day, the tiny station would be permanently enshrined in honor of the American cardinal and the thousands of Jews who'd run to their freedom from this sacred spot. Richard often thought about Field Marshal Goering and their strange relationship, which was a major factor in the saving of thousands of Jews. Finally, Richard decided it had been the workings of the Almighty and left it at that. Goering survived the war, only to be placed on trial by the allies in Nuremburg. As with so many other top Nazis, he was sentenced to die. An hour before his scheduled execution, he took his own life.

Richard, upon hearing the news, was saddened and prayed for his soul.

Then came the year, 1958 . . . the year that shocked the Catholic Church and the world. Pope Pius XII grew ill and died. He'd been a dear friend and mentor to Richard, who took his death hard. Cardinals from all over the world gathered in the Holy City to elect a new pope. The great cardinals of the church took their assigned seats in the privacy of the Sistine Chapel, where the secret balloting for a new pope had been a tradition for untold centuries. The votes were cast and counted.

A deafening silence filled the room when Cardinal Richard Carver of the United States of America was announced as the victor to become the leader of the Roman Catholic Church. Richard sat stunned, having never imagined the possibility.

Elisabeth's words about Richard's enormous humility had never rung truer as it did at this decisive moment in history. He slowly stood as the eyes of the room fell upon him. Speaking in Italian, Richard addressed the cardinals. "I cannot accept this great honor that you've bestowed upon me. I am not worthy to sit upon the throne of St. Peter." The cardinals looked at one another in disbelief. Could this be? The American cardinal was refusing the highest seat in the land.

Yes, it was true. Richard turned down the papacy that historic day in the chapel. The world was shocked at the cardinal's refusal—all but two souls that is. Elisabeth and Lori knew the reason behind the decision. Many historians would speculate over the years that it had something to do with Elisabeth and her daughter, Agatha. But his love affair with Elisabeth had long been settled between Richard and his God. Richard had stated in his letters to Elisabeth and Lori both that he couldn't be forgiven for killing Colonel Zooke. That one moment inside Ostrow Station had cost the American his seat in the pontifical chair, the chair Pius XII had so hoped he would inherit.

After Richard's refusal of the papacy, he slowly went into seclusion inside the Vatican walls and his health deteriorated shortly after. It seemed to most around him that the famous cardinal had simply decided he'd accomplished the things the Lord had intended for him while on earth.

The world gradually forgot about the one-time great American cardinal as the world was rapidly changing. By the early '60s, Richard's longtime illness affected him constantly. Lori and Elisabeth, along with Lori's children and Agatha, came to visit the cardinal in the spring of '62. They were saddened by Richard's appearance, nothing but a shell of the handsome and powerful man he'd once been. Elisabeth cried in Agatha's lap that night in Rome. It was then that Agatha knew her mother had been secretly in love with this man most all her life. When Elisabeth and the others left that following day for home, they knew they would never see Richard alive again.

One June 29, 1962, Elisabeth answered her door. A young man handed her a telegram and a small package. She was trembling by the time she made it back to the living room. Agatha and Lori had just returned from the grocery store.

"What is it, Momma?" Agatha asked, seeing her mother's condition.

"I don't know yet," Elisabeth said, her voice low

and wavering.

Agatha helped her mother to the couch. Lori sat down beside her.

Lori took the telegram from Elisabeth and opened it.

Elisabeth bowed her head.

"It's from the pope," Lori said, fearing what was coming.

Lori began. "'I'm sorry to send such terrible news. The great and holy cardinal died at 3:40 this morning. He died in peace. I and all the church are deeply grieved by his passing. Cardinal Carver was the most loved man I've ever known, and the entire world will mourn his passing. I pray that your sorrow will be eased by knowing that this divine man has finally joined his father in heaven. His God loves him so. I am sending you a special church edition of his book of poetry that I and the world loves so. May God bless you and your family and give you strength to carry on with life until you are once again with your brother in heaven.'"

Elisabeth and Lori embraced one another, weeping for the man they so dearly loved. Agatha bent on her knees and wept with them. She'd never known her father; her mother's Richard had passed for that man.

With trembling hands, Lori unwrapped the package.

Agatha gazed at the golden-bound book of poetry. "Oh my, what a beautiful book."

Elisabeth wiped the tears from her eyes as she stared at the book, its titled displayed in gold-leaf lettering: *Ostrow Station*. "It's the most gorgeous book I've ever seen."

Richard was laid to rest a few days later, in the tiny

cemetery in Louisiana next to his brother, Joe, and his mother and father. The service ended, and all the world leaders and high-ranking church officials left. Lori and Elisabeth stood next to the freshly turned grave, Agatha a few feet away.

Tearfully, Lori looked at Agatha and sighed. She turned to Elisabeth. "How beautiful a daughter you have in Agatha."

Elisabeth looked for a moment at her daughter, then at Lori. Elisabeth smiled as she said, "Yes, oh yes. But what else could one expect. She was a gift from God."

Epilogue

Time passed as the 1940s became the 1950s. Jeff, denied his war earlier, was released from the asylum in early 1947. When the Korean conflict came about in the early '50s, he was quick to volunteer. Lori wouldn't deny him this time. He was killed in action on July 17, 1952 and awarded the Distinguished Service Cross for bravery.

The tide of war changed rather quickly, starting with Russia's long-awaited offensive against the German invaders on January 15. On June 4, 1944, the American and British armies liberated Rome. On June 6, 1944, D-day arrived with the amphibious landing of British and American troops on French soil. On May 8, 1945, Germany surrendered, and so ended the European war—the most costly and deadly war ever known to mankind.

Far off, in the Pacific, that war, too, was beginning to turn in America's favor. The Marianas were retaken by the Americans in the spring and summer of '44. On October 20 of that year, General MacArthur kept his long-awaited promise to the Philippine people when he'd told them some two years before that one day he would return and liberate them from the Empire of Japan. General MacArthur walked ashore on Leyte Beach of Palo having kept his promise.

On April 12, 1945, President Roosevelt suffered a stroke and died two hours later, while on vacation in Warm Springs, Georgia. By order of newly elected Harry Truman, on August 6, 1945, in the predawn hours of the morning, an American B29 bomber dropped a uranium bomb over the city of Hiroshima, Japan, killing tens of thousands of Japanese. Three days later, an American B29 dropped a similar bomb on the city of Nagasaki, Japan. Within three days, over 100,000 Japanese had been wiped from the face of the earth. Five days after the second atomic bomb was dropped, Hirohito surrendered the Japans.

Finally, and dramatically, the Second World War came to an end. Although the exact figures will never be known, the final casualty figures ended this way: Russian losses were put at 6,100,000 souls, by far the highest of any country; Poland lost 664,000 lives; the Americans, who'd so wanted to stay out of the war, also paid a dear price in lives with 291,000 dead and untold thousands wounded. The enemy also paid dearly: Germany lost 3,500,000 and Japan lost 1,200,000, for a staggering total loss of lives set at 14,595,000 and as many hundreds of thousands who remain unaccounted.

Like all wars, there were no winners, only losers.

The End

Printed in Great Britain
by Amazon